DIRTY GAMES DUET

paige press

DIRTY GAMES DUET

Laurelin Paige

NEW YORK TIMES BESTSELLING AUTHOR
LAURELIN PAIGE

Copyright © 2018 by Laurelin Paige

All rights reserved.

No part of this book may be reproduced in any form or by any electronic or mechanical means, including information storage and retrieval systems, without written permission from the author, except for the use of brief quotations in a book review.

Cover: Laurelin Paige

Editor: Erica Russikoff at Erica Edits, Nancy at Evident Ink

Proofing: Michele Ficht

ISBN: 978-1-957647-27-2

ALSO BY LAURELIN PAIGE

WONDERING WHAT TO READ NEXT? I CAN HELP!

Visit www.laurelinpaige.com for content warnings and a more detailed reading order.

Brutal Billionaires

Brutal Billionaire - a standalone (Holt Sebastian)

Dirty Filthy Billionaire - a novella (Steele Sebastian)

Brutal Secret - a standalone (Reid Sebastian)

Brutal Arrangement - a standalone (Alex Sebastian)

Brutal Bargain - a standalone (Axle Morgan)

Brutal Bastard - a standalone (Hunter Sebastian)

The Dirty Universe

Dirty Duet (Donovan Kincaid)

Dirty Filthy Rich Men | Dirty Filthy Rich Love

Kincaid

Dirty Games Duet (Weston King)

Dirty Sexy Player | Dirty Sexy Games

Dirty Sweet Duet (Dylan Locke)

Sweet Liar | Sweet Fate

(Nate Sinclair) Dirty Filthy Fix (a spinoff novella)

Dirty Wild Trilogy (Cade Warren)

Wild Rebel | Wild War | Wild Heart

Men in Charge
Man in Charge
Man for Me (a spinoff novella)

The Fixed Universe

Fixed Series (Hudson & Alayna)

Fixed on You | Found in You | Forever with You | Hudson | Fixed Forever

Found Duet (Gwen & JC) Free Me | Find Me

(Chandler & Genevieve) Chandler (a spinoff novel)

(Norma & Boyd) Falling Under You (a spinoff novella)

(Nate & Trish) Dirty Filthy Fix (a spinoff novella)

Slay Series (Celia & Edward)

Rivalry | Ruin | Revenge | Rising

(Gwen & JC) The Open Door (a spinoff novella)

(Camilla & Hendrix) Slash (a spinoff novella)

First and Last
First Touch | Last Kiss

Hollywood Standalones

One More Time

Close

Sex Symbol

Star Struck

Dating Season

Spring Fling | Summer Rebound | Fall Hard

Winter Bloom | Spring Fever | Summer Lovin

Also written with Kayti McGee under the name Laurelin McGee

Miss Match | Love Struck | MisTaken | Holiday for Hire

Written with Sierra Simone

Porn Star | Hot Cop

This book may contain subjects that are sensitive to some readers.
Please visit www.laurelinpaige.com/dirty-games for content warnings. May include spoilers.

DIRTY SEXY PLAYER

ONE
WESTON

"NICE ROCK," I said, admiring the diamond ring Donovan placed on the tabletop. I picked it up and examined the stone in the dimly lit lounge of the The Grand Havana Room, the member's-only cigar lounge we often frequented when we were together. The diamond was a big one, in a platinum setting with at least four carats between the large center jewel and the scattering of smaller diamonds surrounding it. A serious engagement ring. I wouldn't expect anything less from one of the world's most successful young billionaires.

I just had no idea Donovan was even dating anyone.

Of course, we weren't as close as we used to be. Physically, anyway. He'd been managing the Tokyo office with Cade since we'd expanded our advertising firm into that market. He rarely made it stateside, and it had been nearly a year since I'd last seen Donovan in person. When he'd shown up tonight unexpectedly asking Nate and me to meet him at the club, we'd guessed he had serious news but that it was about the business.

An engagement ring was a whole new level of serious. No wonder he wanted to do this in person.

"Who's the lucky girl?" I asked, trying not to sound bothered that this was the first I was hearing about her. A glance at Nate said it was the first he was hearing about her too.

"You're asking the wrong question," Donovan said, and bit off the end of his cigar. "The question is who's the lucky *guy*?"

I raised a brow, confused. But not surprised. Donovan was known to speak in riddles. I'd figure out what he was trying to tell me when he was ready to spill. Might as well play along in the meantime.

"Okay." I pinched the ring between two fingers and lifted it toward the nearest light source so I could see the full effect of its sparkle. "Who's the lucky guy?"

He lit the end of his cigar and puffed a couple of times before taking it out and answering. "You."

"Oh, Donovan. You shouldn't have." I clutched my hand to my chest for dramatic effect. "I don't know that we've ever said it, but I love you too. Still, I don't think I'm ready for this." I handed the ring back to him with a shake of my head.

Nate hid his smirk by taking a large swig of his imported beer.

"Very funny." Donovan carefully placed the ring back in its box. "I'm not proposing *to* you, Weston. I'm proposing *for* you."

"You are, are you?" I chuckled at his attempt at a joke. Inside my jacket pocket my phone buzzed with a text. I pulled it out and quickly skimmed the message.

> I need to see you.

Normally I'd be all up for a booty call, but my night belonged to the guys. I deleted the message without reading who it was from, silenced my phone, and put it back in my pocket.

I gave my attention back to Donovan, continuing to play along with his hoax. "Just who exactly are you proposing to *for* me?"

He puffed heavily on his cigar before removing it from his

mouth to speak. "Her name is Elizabeth Dyson. She's the sole inheritor of the Dyson empire. She's twenty-five, classy though spirited, well-bred—definitely a suitable bride. Your union is going to take our business to the next level. Once you marry her, Reach, Inc. will be the biggest advertising company in Europe."

All humor drained from my face. He was serious. Donovan never joked about business. But marriage? "You've got to be kidding me."

"Not even a little bit."

I was beginning to regret not looking at the name before I deleted that text. I'd have loved to have a reason to bail right about then.

But it was Donovan's first night back in town; I really couldn't leave him now. Not to mention, I knew him. Once he got an idea in his head, it was nearly impossible to get it out. My best chance was to listen, find the weakness in his scheme, and then propose an alternate strategy.

If that failed, I'd tell him *fuck, no*, and that would be that.

Hopefully.

Saying *fuck, no* to Donovan Kincaid was often a bit harder in reality than it seemed in theory.

If I was going to stay, I was at least going to need a stiffer drink. I signaled the waiter. "Can you bring me a shot of Fireball?" Nate nudged me. "Two shots of Fireball?"

Then I turned to Donovan. "You'd better explain this from the beginning."

He took a puff of his cigar. "It's a short explanation. Dell Dyson, founder, CEO, and majority shareholder of Dyson Media—basically France's version of Time Warner—died about eight months ago, leaving his daughter the sole inheritor to the bulk of his fortune. However, the will states she can't get her hands on any of it until she's 29—with one exception."

"Ah, I think I'm getting the picture," Nate said, taking a pull on his beer.

My brows remained wrinkled, *my* picture still unclear. "Explain it to me then," I said, turning to Nate. "Because I'm not following."

He set his bottle on the table and tilted his head toward me. "Daddy Dell was a traditionalist. The daughter inherits when she puts a ring on it."

"Oh." Understanding settled in. I screwed my face up in disgust. "That's gross."

"Completely terrible and misogynistic," Donovan agreed, not sounding terribly upset at all. "But there's nothing we can do about the unfortunate setup to her situation, and there is something we can do to get her out of it. Something that works out in our favor. So what we need to do is focus on getting Elizabeth married to our man Weston—"

I started to protest, but Donovan rose a hand to silence me. "*Temporarily* married—a couple of months is all we need for Elizabeth to claim her inheritance of Dyson Media. Once she does, she can push through the merger of Dyson's advertising subsidiary with Reach, and we'll take over as the biggest ad company in the European market."

"Just like that," I said, skeptically.

"Just like that." There was no trace of doubt in Donovan's voice.

"And what makes you think that she'd be interested in this?" I asked. "I mean why would she be interested in giving someone—giving *us*—part of the company? Not why would she be interested in me." I wasn't worried about women being into me. But I certainly wasn't into discussing it with Donovan.

Of course he had an answer for this as well. "I'm in preliminary talks with her already. And she seemed quite interested in the whole arrangement. I didn't specify who her groom would be but told her I had an eligible bachelor. She's thinking about it further. Tomorrow afternoon in the office, all four of us will have a meeting to hammer out the details. I've already cleared your schedule."

It was a good thing the shots arrived then. "You mean I have to have this all thought through and decided by tomorrow afternoon?"

"Oh, you'll agree," Donovan said, confidently.

I threw back the shot. It didn't burn half as much as Donovan's proposal.

I rolled my neck, easing the muscles in my shoulders. "I need a minute to think about this."

"Take two."

I wasn't really considering any of it, but it was an excuse to order another drink and make Donovan pay for it.

I gestured for the waiter to bring two more shots. Then I leaned back against the plush leather upholstery of the bench seat and rubbed my hand across my forehead, pretending to weigh Donovan's offer in my mind.

To be honest, I'd been restless recently. I enjoyed the benefits of my life—my rental apartment in Midtown, my sex life, the view from my office. But my twenty-ninth birthday was looming and that was so close to thirty. A milestone birthday, and what did I have to show for it?

Okay. I was one of five shareholders of Reach, Inc., one of the most successful ad agencies in the world, but everyone knew that was Donovan's brainchild.

What did I have that was purely my own?

A month ago, I'd been so caught up in the desire for clarity that, on a whim, I'd asked a girl to move to New York from LA. It wasn't the first impulsive move I'd ever made, especially not for a girl—a girl I'd been naked with all weekend, no less—but it had been the craziest.

Almost as crazy of an idea as getting married to a stranger in order to improve our business status.

Sabrina, the naked woman, had been a peer that Donovan and I had gone to Harvard with. I'd been fortunate enough to spend a magical reunion weekend with her. There was something about her —a combination of her sexy laugh, serious demeanor, and intelligent brain that struck a chord deep inside me. Our conversation had made me feel warm and interesting and I wanted to capture that. Wanted to make it last.

So much so that right there on the spot, I demanded she take the position of Director of Marketing Strategy. Who cared that there was somebody else who held the position already?

She'd turned me down, wisely, but after she'd left, when the hormones calmed down, I looked into her resume anyway. Turned out she actually deserved the position, and I'd been half-heartedly working on making the transition happen legitimately ever since.

I'd spent good time thinking about making a real go at a relationship with her, too, if I got her to take the job.

I'd even told Donovan about my plans. Had he forgotten?

"But I don't want to get married," I reminded him now. "I want to bring Sabrina Lund to New York City and find out whether or not we fit together."

"Sabrina *Lind*," he corrected, his tone peppered with annoyance.

"Isn't that what I said?" I was starting to feel the alcohol.

"Still bring her here," Nate suggested, always the reasonable one. "She can take the job and settle in. By the time she gets the hang of things around here, you'll be through your annulment and then you're free to date her."

"That could work, I suppose." Still wasn't considering it.

"If *she's* interested, that is," Donovan scowled.

"Why would she not be interested?" I asked.

"She'll be interested," Nate assured me. "But it is hard to move into a new city and get into a new relationship all at once. Better to take it in steps. And meanwhile, you can do this thing for the company."

I could hear the subtext in his words. Subtext that said he thought maybe I owed the company a little more *doing*.

Possibly I was reading too much into it.

I slammed back my next shot and considered what other reason there might be for Nate Sinclair to take Donovan's side. He was usually Switzerland.

"You're just saying all that because you don't want to be the one to get married, aren't you?" I eyed Nate accusingly.

He averted his eyes. "I'm old enough to be her father. It's not really appropriate."

I turned my stare to Donovan. There wasn't a band on *his* finger.

"It wouldn't work," he said flatly, guessing my thoughts. "No one would ever believe I'd get married."

"I can't dispute that." It was hard for me to believe the guy had friends. And I was his *best* friend.

"You are the ideal candidate," Donovan insisted.

"Damn right I'm the ideal candidate." I grinned, giving him my full dimpled smile, because hands down, I was the best looking of all of us. My panty collection proved it. Cade could give me a run for my money with his constant brooding—women seemed to go for that—but he was in Japan. And Dylan Locke's charming British accent only worked on girls outside the UK, and he was never leaving the London office.

So, I wasn't just the ideal candidate—I was the *only* candidate.

But I wasn't doing it. It was crazy. Stupid crazy.

I ran my hand over my face, wondering how much longer I should allow Donovan to think I could be convinced. There was a fine line between hearing him out and becoming roped in.

"Is this Elizabeth person hot?" I asked, my lips numb from the shots.

"Why?" Donovan asked suspiciously.

"If I'm stuck with her I might as well...you know."

"You just said that you couldn't marry her because you've found the love of your life with Sabrina..." I could practically see steam coming from Donovan's ears.

"I didn't say Sabrina was the love of my life. I'm saying she *might* be the love of my life. It's too early to tell."

"Either way," Donovan said, snarling, "it's probably a good idea if you don't sleep with your fiancée."

I exchanged glances with Nate.

Donovan followed my gaze as he tapped the ash of his cigar into a tray. "That didn't sound right, but I stand behind my recommendation."

Again, Nate and I looked to each other. We maybe had less conventional sexual standards than our business partner.

Correction—we *definitely* had less conventional sexual standards. Especially Nate. Which made him a god in my book. But that was beside the point.

The point was that good ideas were for the office. In the bedroom, I preferred my ideas to be bad.

I was just messing with Donovan, anyway. I didn't need this setup to get laid, and I most certainly didn't need this setup to feel like I'd contributed to the company. I'd strung him along far enough.

"Well, Donovan, this is maybe the most strategic and outrageous plan you've ever come up with, also possibly the most brilliant." I patted him on the back. He did deserve credit where credit was due. "But I'm going to have to pass, brother. It's a little too crazy for me."

Donovan sat back and slung out an arm, his elbow resting on the back of the bench. He looked relaxed, far too at ease with my decision, which made *me* uneasy. He was a guy who was used to things happening his way. He didn't like it when his plans were altered. If he wasn't upset now, it meant he had something else up his sleeve.

Which meant I needed to keep my guard up.

Unfortunately, Donovan also had patience. So despite my suspicions, I'd have to wait until he was prepared to move into the next phase of his plan to find out what he was hiding.

I glanced over at Nate who shrugged again before catching the eye of a gentleman at the bar.

"Excuse me," he said, "I know that guy. I need to say hello."

I gave him a wink because there was no telling how Nate knew him—whether it was from his past crazy illegal dealings or from his current wild sexual dealings. Either way, it probably made a good story, and one I'd like to hear.

A good story that I wasn't going to get to hear because I was stuck at the table with Donovan and whatever bullshit scenario he had worked up for me now.

Before he could start in on another one of these brilliant schemes, I started a conversation of my own. "How long are you staying in town, Donovan?"

"Haven't decided yet. A few months. Longer, maybe. Cade's handling Japan for now. Meanwhile, you've been complaining about needing some help up here. So here I am."

"Well." This was awesome. Donovan and I hadn't lived in the same city for years. Our parents owned King-Kincaid Financial, and we'd spent so much time together growing up, we were practically siblings. My only sister was a decade younger, so Donovan had been the one I'd bonded with most. Only four years older than me, he was the one who had mentored me through all my significant firsts. First time drinking, first time smoking, first time sneaking out to meet a girl, first time starting a company.

"Glad to hear it. You should've told me sooner. Are you moving back into—"

"I'll wipe the loan," he said, cutting me off.

And there it was. The bit that would make my jaw drop. The offer that would make me sit up and listen.

"The *entire* loan?" My heart was thumping in my chest now, and I could hear blood gushing in my ears.

"The whole thing. Gone."

Gone. All of it. *Whoosh.* Just like that.

What a fucking relief that would be.

Donovan was the only one who knew that I hadn't put all my own money into the company when we first started up. After nearly draining my inheritance from my grandmother, I'd borrowed the rest of the seed money from him, a sizable amount that I'd slowly been paying him back with the profits earned over our five years in business.

I still owed him a million.

It was quite an amount to just write off, even for him.

The irony of it was that I had more than twenty times that in my trust fund. I could've wiped the loan out myself years ago. If I'd wanted to.

Again, Donovan was the only one who knew why I chose not to borrow from that sizable fund.

And so, since Reach had begun with Donovan and me—and since we had pledged the most start-up money—when he covered my portion, he also got the advantage.

It was one of the reasons why the company always felt like it was more Donovan's than mine.

And it was a reason I often bent to his will, even when I'd rather not.

"Why is this merger so important to you?" I asked, unsure what to make of this offer. It wasn't like Donovan held the loan over me all the time. It wasn't like he wasn't generous. He would give me the shirt off his back if it was the last thing he owned.

But he also knew about integrity, and he understood that I wanted to be a self-made man. And he respected that.

I respected him for getting me.

So if this was that important to him, then I really needed to be listening. Because I would give Donovan the shirt off my back too.

"Number one in Europe, Weston," he said with a gleam in his eye. "We've only been open five years, and it would take a long time to get that title any other way. It's been far more difficult than I'd hoped to crack that market the way we have here."

I always knew the guy was competitive, but this really took the cake.

"And it's just a fake marriage then? Just a sham?"

Dammit. I couldn't believe I was actually considering this.

"A complete farce. You'd start right away, fake a whirlwind romance and engagement. Have the whole thing done in four, five months tops. But the benefits to Reach would last a lifetime. Think of it as your legacy, Weston."

I drummed my fingers on the tabletop. "This is fucking insane."

"You *like* insane," he said, leaning in close, knowing exactly which words would push my buttons.

How did he do this every time? He really was a mastermind. Able to wield the strings of all the puppets, controlling everyone, getting them to do his bidding. Not that I resented him for it. I admired him, truthfully.

And there was that something in my life that was missing.

Not that a fake wedding was going to fix it, but maybe the chance to contribute could make a difference. The chance to leave a legacy.

And to be able to give something back to Donovan after all the things he'd given me—well, that was something I couldn't take lightly.

Plus the end of that loan. To be my own man. Finally.

"Ah, fuck it. I got nothing better to do with my life. Let's be number one in Europe." Actually, that did have a pretty decent ring to it.

The corner of his lip lifted. "You know how to talk dirty to me." He reached into his pocket, where he'd deposited the ring back into its velvet box earlier, and handed it over before taking a long, satisfied sip of his drink.

I dropped it inside my jacket. The small square shape felt like a lead weight against my chest.

I wondered how heavy its contents were going to feel when it was on Elizabeth Dyson's hand.

TWO
ELIZABETH

I DROPPED my sunglasses and my Louis Vuitton purse on the table in the entryway of my mother's condo and headed inside, searching for her. Since it was July and the sun was out, I knew exactly where I'd find her—on the deck outside the living room, sunning.

"Mom," I whined, bursting out onto the balcony. "Did you hear what Darrell's done now?" I dropped the printout from my computer in her lap. Then I headed over to the table where Marie had set out lemonade and poured myself a glass, gulping it down in four huge swallows.

I slammed the glass down on the table and turned back to face my mother. She sat stretched out on her lounge chair, her fingers bright with freshly applied nail polish. Marie was now working on her toes. She ignored the paper in her lap, which made sense—it was written in French and my mother didn't read French very well. Honestly, I'd only printed it up for dramatic effect.

"Good morning to you too, darling," she said, lifting her chin up to present her cheek for a kiss.

"I'm too worked up for pleasantries right now," I said in a huff.

But that wasn't fair to Marie, so I turned to her. "Hello, Marie. The lemonade is perfect today, by the way."

"Thank you," she said, looking up from my mother's left big toe. Or rather, just looking over at *my* feet. "Your shoes are fantastic. Jimmy Choo?"

"Valentino. I bought them to go with this pantsuit. I think they just—" I stopped. Fashion was not what I was here to discuss. And if I got onto the topic of beauty with my mother and her assistant, I was going to be off track all day long.

"That's not important. Darrell—" I threw my hands up in the air. Honestly, my father's nephew was going to be the death of me. I was only twenty-five. I was not ready to be planning my own death.

"Settle yourself down, dear. You're going to break a sweat. Then tell me what it is that Darrell has done to get you in such a tizzy." My mother nodded to the lounge chair next to her.

I was entirely too upset to sit down, but I did try to rein it in a bit.

"He's selling off the children's networks. *The children's networks*," I said again, when neither my mother nor Marie reacted with enough exasperation to satisfy me. "After last quarter's suggestion that they sell off some of the news stations—" It was a sentence I could barely stand to think through to the end. "By the time I get my hands on this company, there's going to be nothing left!"

My mother looked to Marie, who gave an encouraging smile. "Maybe it will just mean less to manage when you take over," the dark-haired assistant, who was more family than staff at this point, suggested.

"Less to manage?" I couldn't believe I was hearing this.

I stomped back over to the lemonade and poured some more, wishing it was laced with vodka. I sipped this time, trying to remember the words of my therapist. *You cannot let your day run you. You run your day. You cannot let your day run you. You run your day.* I repeated the mantra a few more times and then turned back to my audience.

"The company is only as good as the sum of its parts," I explained, as calmly as I could manage. "Dyson Media is everything put together. Darrell wants to slice off bits and pieces, and sell them to the highest bidder so that he can collect money and profit while the company is still his. That means that when I take over, it will be nothing but crumbs. Don't you see? There won't *be* a Dyson Media anymore."

Not to mention that without the company, how on earth would I ever be able to make up for the wrongs of my father? By the time I stood in his place, I wouldn't have any power, any platform. My cousin's pockets would be lined with my legacy, while I was left to clean up the leftover rubbish.

I didn't expect them to truly understand. My mother had never been interested in business, and she'd hired Marie to help her do her makeup and go shopping with her.

Marie *was* really good at shopping, I had to admit. I learned everything I knew about clothing from her, and I was really good with clothing.

But looking good was not going to save the Dyson empire. And neither was waiting four goddamned years to take over. "I have to fix this. I have to do something drastic."

"But what exactly can you do, honey? That lawyer told you that appealing was a lost cause, and Darrell isn't about to let you into the company before he has to. I swear, though," she said, shielding her eyes from the sun as she looked up at me. "If your father weren't already dead, I'd kill him myself for the shit he pulled with the terms of this inheritance. Such an asshole. Treating his only child like this. I can't believe I stayed with him as long as I did."

She'd stayed just ten years. I'd been born after two. She wasn't his first wife, and neither of us were clear on whether he'd even been divorced when she met him. He'd gotten another wife soon after he left Mom, too. But I was the only kid out of all three of his marriages. A daughter. Maybe he would've been more attentive and loving and *there* if I'd been another gender.

I'd never know.

At least he hadn't left us penniless. The divorce had left us with more than enough money. My mother never had to work another day in her life and was still able to live the lifestyle she'd gotten used to. I'd been able to go to the best schools and had the best opportunities. The best toys. The best cars. I never lacked for anything—besides a father.

My bank account meant I could turn a blind eye and let Darrell do whatever the hell he wanted with the company. I could let it go. I didn't need Dyson Media. I didn't need my father's legacy.

But I *did* need it too. For reasons I couldn't explain to anyone but myself.

"You're right. I can't appeal," I said. I'd spoken to a lawyer extensively. Three lawyers, in fact, to make sure I had absolutely no ground on which to fight to get my company earlier than my twenty-ninth birthday. "But there is something else I can do."

"And what's that?"

I watched as she removed the papers I'd left on her lap with the palms of her hands, careful not to touch them with her fingernails, and drop them on the empty lounge chair next to her. She was a nice bronze color already, her skin golden with rich yellow undertones that I lacked.

I took after my father with my fair skin and red hair. She was all Italian and Mediterranean and blond. When I was a kid, and we'd go to the beach, she would soak up every ray while I practically had to wear a full wetsuit just so I wouldn't get burnt.

We were different in so many ways, and I hesitated, wondering how she would react to my decision.

When I didn't respond, she looked up at me expectantly. "Honey?"

"I can get married." It hadn't been the first time we'd discussed it, so it wasn't exactly out of the blue.

"But I thought you said that wouldn't work either. You haven't been dating anyone, and anyone that you brought into this affair would be a stranger. How could you trust them?"

I walked around the table to the chair on the other side and plopped into it, trying to hide from the sun by sitting under the umbrella.

"I still have my concerns," I said hesitantly, "but Donovan Kincaid has approached me with a business transaction that might work."

Honestly, when Donovan had first asked for a meeting, I'd thought perhaps he was working for his father and wanted to sell me on their financial trusts. When he suggested his idea, it was so absurd I nearly walked out of the room.

But there was something about the man that intrigued me. Something about him that *spoke* to me. He was manipulative and scheming and also brilliant. He was passionate about his work and the things that he thought we could accomplish. I was attracted to it—not in a sexual way, though he was an attractive and sexy man. It was more like he reminded me of who I wanted to be.

And perhaps he reminded me of who my father could've been had my father actually been a decent man.

When I left, I'd told him I would think about it, although I hadn't really meant it. But after waking up this morning to the news that Darrell was selling the children's networks, I was actually thinking about it.

"Donovan Kincaid of King-Kincaid Financial?" my mother asked. I supposed my mother *did* pay attention to some business affairs, or at least the lifestyle pages.

"That's his father. Donovan has his own advertising agency,

and he's come up with an agreement where I could marry someone from the firm. It would look genuine, and no one would be the wiser."

"And what would Mr. Kincaid want in return?" she asked, peering at me with that cut-the-bullshit look. She'd been a trophy wife. She knew how these things worked.

Or she thought she did.

The women in our family had come a long way in a generation—I had more than my body to sell. "He wants to merge his company with Dyson's advertising subsidiary. It wouldn't be an outrageous loss. Dyson barely does anything in advertising. Most of their market share and focus is in television. It would be a small price to pay for control of the company."

I hoped, anyway. I really didn't know that much about Dyson's advertising firm.

I really didn't know that much about Dyson Media at all, to be honest.

I didn't know that much about business in general, if I was laying it all out on the table.

Gah! What the hell was I *doing*?

I was being ridiculous, jumping in too fast, dreaming too big. I stood and walked to the edge of the roof and looked out over the street below.

"It's a dumb idea," I said now, all my confidence from earlier suddenly gone. "I have a meeting with Donovan this afternoon. I was going to turn his offer down when we met, but then I saw what Darrell was doing, and...I don't know. I guess I thought I should do something...for some reason."

I heard the scrape of the lounge chair against the deck and knew my mother was coming over to me. A moment later, I felt her hand around my waist.

"You thought you should do something because you knew you could," she said, her warm voice dripping like honey.

I sighed at her.

"Elizabeth, if the company is that important to you, you should take whatever risk you need to in order to get your hands on it. I'm sorry I'm not a better advocate for you. I mean to be. I do. The problem is that you are your father's daughter."

I cringed, hating it when she said that.

"Don't look at me like that. You are. And it's wonderful that you are. Because if you were only *my* daughter you wouldn't be even considering something like this. And I think it's amazing and wonderful that you want to do something so bold and grand. But your father never got things done by doubting himself. He certainly didn't get where he was by dismissing his own ideas as dumb. If this is what it takes to make you happy, I think you should take the chance. And if it's not with Donovan Kincaid, then keep searching."

"You mean it?" I glanced over at her and this time I held her stare, searching for every bit of reassurance. With her encouraging me, the plan didn't seem quite so dumb after all.

"Yeah, I mean it. Go in there confident. Show them you have your father's balls." She pulled me into a tight hug that was quickly followed by an exclamation of, "My nails, my nails!"

I let her go so she could examine her manicure and make sure that it had come out unscathed. Just then, the old grandfather clock chimed the hour from inside the apartment.

"It's one already?" I checked my wristwatch, needing the double verification. "Shit. I have to get going if I'm going to get to Midtown by one-thirty. So much for grabbing lunch first. Thanks, Mom, for the advice and for listening." I bent in and kissed her cheek then walked over to Marie.

"There's chicken sandwiches in the fridge," she said, standing to give me a side hug. "Take one on your way."

"Thanks. I will." I started inside.

"Elizabeth," my mother called after me. She waited until I

turned to give her my full attention. "Are you going to go through with this plan, then?"

I shrugged. "I don't know yet. Maybe. Yes. Probably. I haven't met the groom. I won't agree if the guy's lame. It's a fake marriage, but I *do* have standards. My name is riding on this."

"Maybe you'll get lucky, and he'll be good-looking! Wouldn't it be nice if a woman got to have a trophy spouse for once?"

I laughed, but I wasn't holding my breath. I was taking her advice to heart, though. If Donovan Kincaid's plan was going to be a real option, he couldn't know I didn't know what the hell I was doing. I had to be confident and self-assured, like my father would have been. I had to show the men of Reach that I had balls.

I had to prove I could own that meeting and every man in it.

THREE
WESTON

"WESTON, quit pacing and sit the fuck down," Donovan said—correction, *demanded*—from his seat on the couch at one-thirty the next day. "You're making me dizzy."

It was easy enough for him to sit calmly, enjoying his after-lunch Scotch since he didn't have a hangover and a fifty-pound ring in his breast pocket.

I ran a hand through my hair, ignoring his instructions to move to the couch. "I don't know how you talked me into this. You laced my drink with something?" Drinks. Many drinks. There had been so many drinks.

"You were still rather sober when you agreed, as I recall."

I looked out the window over the city. Our offices occupied the top floors of the King-Kincaid building we rented, and the view was spectacular. We'd designed the space so all of us had floor-to-ceiling windows, and the lounge where we entertained all incoming clients had the best views of all.

Usually, looking out over the small specks on the sidewalks below made me feel powerful and confident, gave me a bit of the backbone that Donovan had naturally. But today I just felt agitated and nervous, like all the people below were priceless pawns in a chess game, and somehow I was going to squish them with my bad behavior.

"Nate really could do this," I said, turning to look at Donovan now. "Twenty years difference... What does that mean these days? It's a fake marriage anyway. Who's going to care?"

"It's important this marriage *looks* like it's real. Those running the business aren't going to want to relinquish power, so they need to be convinced that the two of you are in love if they're not going to contest. Nathan doesn't even give the vibe of a groom."

"And *I* give the vibe of a—?" My sentiment was cut off by the opening of the lounge doors.

Speak of the devil, Nate came bounding in and glanced around the room. "Good, I'm not late."

No, he was late. But so was the Dyson girl.

"I was arguing shades of green with one of the design teams. I swear half the staff we've hired is colorblind."

"You look fantastic. Are you not even a little bit hungover?" I had watched him drink at least as much as I had. How was it even possible?

Nate paused his stride on the way to the mini-bar, his forehead wrinkled in confusion. "Hungover? No." As though the idea were ludicrous. As though he'd never been hungover in his life.

Maybe he hadn't. Now that I thought about it, I'd never been around to see him if he had.

He really was a god.

"Hey, Nate, I was just telling Donovan that we really haven't given as much consideration to your candidacy as bridegroom as we—"

"No," he said with finality.

Donovan shrugged as if to say, *what did you expect?*

"This is bullshit. I shouldn't be the one condemned to—" Once again, I was interrupted by the opening of the lounge doors. This time, Roxie, my amazing and faithful assistant, stood there, gesturing for the woman behind her to come inside.

I moved my gaze to the stranger as she entered the room. She was sharply dressed in heels and a designer pantsuit. The royal blue color showcased her creamy skin and long red hair, which bounced with a natural wave. The tailored pants were business and attitude while the satin cowl neck softened her and gave just a hint of cleavage, so the outfit managed to make her appear both professional and feminine at the same time.

She was a knockout. Put together and made of money. She held her shoulders back and her neck high. She knew how to carry herself.

She was the kind of woman who could carry the world.

"Here you are," Roxie said in her Hungarian accent. "Gentlemen, Elizabeth Dyson here to see you."

Donovan immediately jumped up to greet her. Nate followed suit.

And I forgot words.

What words meant, how to say them, how to translate what they meant when other people said them around me.

The thing was this—I was not particular when it came to which women I took to bed. Tall, short, plump, thin. I liked them blond or brunette. I liked them of all racial and religious varieties. I liked them moody or sporty. I liked cougars. I liked them barely legal. It didn't matter. I liked women. Period.

But I did have a type.

Smart.

That was my weakness. If she had a fantastic body to match, I was a goner. Sabrina Lind, for example. She was that kind of girl. She had everything going on upstairs plus everything going on outside.

And dammit, so did Elizabeth Dyson.

She had yet to open her mouth, and I could tell that she was one of the smartest women I'd ever met. I could spot a hot brain a mile away. I had a sense for it. It was something about the way a woman carried herself. The way she wore her clothes. The way she did her hair, the way she held her lips. A smart woman wore her brain everywhere on her body.

Fuck if Elizabeth Dyson's hot brain wasn't on full display.

"Weston?" The tone in Donovan's voice made it sound like he'd said my name more than once before I heard it.

I shook myself and stepped forward with my hand out in greeting. "Hi, Weston King."

"As Donovan just said," Elizabeth Dyson remarked, her hand closing around mine. Her shake was as firm as her voice, and both were stiff. Neither were as stiff as my cock was threatening to be in my pants if I couldn't keep it down.

I focused just past her, not meeting her gaze, in an attempt to settle myself.

"It's a pleasure to meet you." She included all of us in her appraising look, not lingering on anyone. It was a much-needed reminder that this was an arrangement. There was going to be no flirting, no "player" me, as Donovan had said the night before.

Though, for the life of me, I couldn't quite remember why.

"Let's get started, shall we?" Donovan said, gesturing for all of us to sit down. He dominated most rooms without even trying, and I expected this one to be no different.

Except as we headed toward the couches to take our seats, Elizabeth surprised me.

"Donovan, just a moment," she said, and even though he hadn't been talking, it felt like an interruption. "I'm sure you have things to say, but I have a few things I'd like to say first."

She was still standing, and so the rest of us didn't know what to do—whether we should take a seat, or stand as well. It was common courtesy to wait until the guest took a seat before we did, and here she was still erect.

Shouldn't have thought the word *erect*. It was a bad mistake on my part. I had to think of unsexy things very quickly. *Zombies killing people. Zombies eating their flesh.*

"Go ahead and take a seat," she said, looking mostly at Donovan.

And that's when it was completely clear. She'd taken over. She'd taken *charge*.

She was dominating Donovan.

And something about that was fucking hot. I tried to think unsexy thoughts.

Zombies eating Donovan's flesh.

We sat. Everyone did. Including Elizabeth. Including Donovan.

"Would you care for something to drink?" Nate asked.

"No, thank you. I'd rather just get to the point." She crossed one long leg over the other and set her hands in her lap. Then she leaned back ever so slightly, shifting her gaze from one of us to the next, meeting each of our eyes.

I leaned forward, the anticipation built up so much that I was near the edge of my seat.

"Now. I haven't decided yet if I'd like to take you up on this very interesting offer, but I have considered it very thoroughly. And if I do, there will be even more to take into consideration."

She was a witch. She had to be. Only moments ago, I'd been doubting this arrangement, but now that she was potentially taking it away, I was already starting a mental litany of reasons why she shouldn't.

Which was stupid. I didn't really want to do this. No matter how hot she was topping Donovan.

"I'm guessing that everyone in the room is caught up on the situation I'm in?" she went on.

"Yes, everyone here is aware of the predicament you're in, and of the offer Reach has made you. But don't worry," Donovan continued, predicting her unease. "No one here has said anything to anyone else. And of course, anything that's said in this room will stay in this room."

"That's actually the first thing that we need to discuss," Elizabeth said. "This arrangement would have to be kept fully under wraps. Though it's headquartered in Europe, you all know Dyson Media is a genuine world empire. I hate to bring numbers and figures into it, but it's safe to say that my father's company is well above the net worth of anybody else in this room. Even when we put you all together."

That comment alone should have killed my boner. It was rather emasculating to be reduced to a relative bank account value.

But instead of being turned off by it, I wanted to pull Elizabeth Dyson across my lap and spank that smug grin off her face. Spank her and then...

"That is safe to say," Donovan affirmed regarding our net worths, and he was the one who would know. He had the most money of all of us, and I was certainly no pauper. "And we do recognize what is on the line, Elizabeth," he added. "I promise you that."

"Yes," she said, that sly uptick of a smile bordering on condescending. "I'm sure you do. The point is, so does my cousin. Darrell is currently in charge of the Dyson empire and does not want to give up that position before he has to. He'll do anything he can to prove that any marriage of mine is a false one. If I'm going to get married in an attempt to inherit my company earlier, it has to be a relationship that appears entirely legitimate.

"I can't run away to Vegas. There can't be a small ceremony at City Hall. There would have to be a ring of truth to it, which means there will have to be a wedding of somewhat large proportions. The kind that would be expected of a woman of my wealth and stature. As soon as I announce an engagement, Darrell will likely investigate to make sure I was dating that person beforehand.

Even though he's in Paris, he'll watch over every step of my engagement. I don't assume he'll take anything at face value. To be blunt, my groom will have to be both a convincing choice and invested for the long haul."

"How many months are you talking about here?" I braced myself, afraid that she was going to say that years were required for this game.

"I don't want to be ridiculous, as this *is* a sham relationship. But I do also understand that in order for it to look real, it can't be quite as much of a whirlwind as we'd prefer. So if we announce the engagement fairly soon... perhaps seven months? Give or take."

I almost choked. Seven months? Seven months with my ring on someone else's finger?

I needed a drink.

I stood up and headed over to the bar, pouring myself a gin and tonic. Donovan side-eyed me, but fuck Donovan. It's not like he was the one going through with it; he was just directing the play, as always.

"Seven months does seem fairly reasonable," Donovan traitorously agreed. "A wedding in December and then a month or two to finalize your takeover. And I don't see any reason why annulment couldn't happen soon after."

"I think it would need to be a divorce," Elizabeth said. "Darrell will believe the whole thing was a ruse in the first place. I wouldn't want him to come back in retrospect and re-take over the company. Or try to appeal the decision."

"Divorce?" I directed this at Donovan. I had not intended to have a divorce on my record. I drank my gin and tonic in four gulps and then started to make another one.

"Weston, sit down."

I scowled, cursing under my breath. Donovan was right. This wasn't a good first impression to make, and for some reason I did want to make a good first impression on Elizabeth Dyson.

I abandoned my drink and slunk back over to the sofa to listen to other people plan my future.

"I know a lot of people who could pull off a spectacular wedding in a short amount of time," Nate mused. "With our connections we could book a fantastic hotel with a ballroom—"

"I can handle catering with my restaurant," Donovan offered.

"I'm friends with the Pierce's, Donovan," Nate said. "Mirabelle's has amazing wedding gowns, and I can arrange an appointment. LeeAnn Gregori, the wedding planner, is an acquaintance as well. She can arrange the rest."

Jesus, it was like I wasn't even in the room.

"And you are perfectly okay with a pretend relationship lasting that long? There would have to be dates and public outings. We'd have to be seen together. Is that going to be a problem?" Her eyes darted from one of us to the next.

It occurred to me then that Elizabeth didn't even realize who she was supposed to be addressing, didn't know who was supposed to be her fiancé.

I could still throw Donovan under the bus if I wanted. If this whole arrangement was so easy to take care of—by *them*—then it was only fair that one of them should be the nominee.

But, honestly, that wasn't what I wanted, either. Nate didn't look right next to her, and the thought of Donovan pretending to be her lover made my gut twist in some weird strange way that I couldn't understand. Didn't want to understand.

"Weston?" Donovan asked. "Are those expectations going to be a problem?"

I looked to Elizabeth, watched her features as she realized that I was the suggested candidate and tried to discern if she was disappointed or intrigued.

But her face showed no emotion at all except the lift of one brow.

"Oh," she said as if it should've been obvious. "It's you."

Something in that indifferent stare of hers made me want to eat her up. Tear her apart. Find her heart and see what made it beat faster. I didn't know if it was a sexual attraction or an angry kind of attraction.

At the very least, I needed to stop thinking about zombies while around beautiful women.

But it was more than that; I felt insulted for the second time in as many minutes.

Women didn't ever toss me aside easily. Women didn't look at me with an indifferent stare. And they never made me doubt myself. She should be appraising me with her gaze. At least to flatter me, if nothing else. After all, I was the one doing everyone—including her—a favor.

I had never been as competitive as Donovan about anything. Except for winning the hearts of women, but only because I didn't really have to do very much to try to win them. In Elizabeth Dyson, I was suddenly sensing a challenge, the kind I'd never truly experienced before.

And if she was going to be so stoic about our arrangement, hell yeah, I was into this game. That's why I was called a player, after all.

"I don't see a problem with it," I said, holding her stare.

"Then perhaps this will work out." She pursed her lips and tapped a finger on them as she considered her next move. "I am surprised you didn't choose yourself to be the groom, Donovan."

"We'd never get along," he scoffed. "And who would be the alpha?"

The two of them laughed, and I did too until I realized that the joke was at my expense.

Instead of growling, the instinctive method of showing off my own alpha skills, I took control with more civilized means—steering the conversation another direction. "And what are you planning to do with the company when you take over, Elizabeth, since Darrell's the current CEO?"

"Not as CEO, but as an officer. I'll have to fire Darrell and everyone on the board, since they are all his followers. They were loyal to my father as well. I'll need a fresh start."

"Um." I looked to my fellow businessmen in the room. Was she for real? "You're going to fire everyone who knows what they're doing and then lead the company to greatness with a board full of newbies?" I knew she was young, but this was Business 101.

Her confidence wavered; her forehead knit into little wrinkles of concern. "Oh. Good point. I'll start by hiring just a CEO then, one who can lead them in another direction."

I couldn't believe it. She had no plan. No direction.

I was going to stake our company's future in Europe on this girl? What on earth was Donovan thinking?

I laughed out loud. I couldn't help it—she was insane. "Do you have someone in mind already for this position?" Finding that kind of talent, someone willing to take over a board of disgruntled officers...? That wasn't a role I'd want to play.

"Are you laughing at me?" she bristled.

"I'm just saying the idea needs some work. Where did you go to college anyway?" I was curious now. More than curious. I'd found an opening in which to press my advantage, to show her that I wasn't just an inferior bank account, an interchangeable fake husband. Besides, I would have to know this stuff if we were getting married, right?

"Penn." She threw her shoulders back, announcing her alma mater proudly.

"And they taught you nothing at the University of Pennsylvania?" I was being a dick. Sometimes that happened. People around me learned to live with it.

"I didn't major in business," she said coldly.

"You have your MBA though, right?" Lots of people got their

bachelor's degree in something else before they got a master's in business.

But Elizabeth shook her head.

Jesus. I was afraid to ask, but now I had to know. "What did you major in?"

"Poli-sci," she said timidly.

"You've got to be fucking kidding me, Donovan." How did he find her? A twenty-five-year-old spoiled little brat, planning to take over the Dyson empire with a political science degree? I couldn't have laughed harder.

Turned out there was a good reason dear old dad had been keeping the reins of the company from her. She needed to grow up before she even thought about playing with the big boys.

"I'm sorry, honey, but this is ridiculous," I told her. "We might be able to convince the world, we might be able to convince your cousin. But you will take over that company and it will fall apart in five seconds flat. Is that really what you want to put seven months' worth of fraud into achieving?"

"Weston," Donovan warned.

"I'm sorry, D. I'm just being honest here." What a shame—she would have looked so good in a boardroom, too.

"I'm grateful for your honesty, Weston." Elizabeth shifted to face my partner. "He's right, Donovan. This won't work. I don't need your help after all. I was wrong in thinking that I did." She stood, and smoothly picked up the purse that she'd dropped on the floor beside her, pulling the strap onto her shoulder as she held her hand out to shake Nate's.

"It was nice to meet you, Nathan." She nodded to Donovan, "And good to see you again, Donovan. And you, Mr. King. I'm grateful to have escaped marrying you." She smiled brightly. "Good afternoon."

She spun on her heels and that was that. My engagement over and done with before it began.

Which was a good thing, I reminded myself.

The door had barely shut behind her when Donovan roared in my direction. "*Weston.*"

"I am not wrong here," I protested. Surely they could see that. "Everything that she'd just laid out is—"

"I don't *care*, Weston. She will make this takeover happen with you or without you. With Reach or without Reach. We want to be there when it happens so that we can at least benefit from the fallout. *Fix it.*" He pointed a long, demanding arm toward the door.

I glanced at Nate, who shrugged, but his expression said that he was firmly on Donovan's side on this one. Which made sense. I'd been kind of a prick. I looked around the room, but that was it. It was just us, and I'd been given my marching orders.

Yes, there was nothing left to do but suck this one up and fix it.

FOUR
ELIZABETH

I HURRIED out of the lounge so quickly that I got myself turned around in the offices of Reach, Inc. The open floor space brought lots of outside light in and all the glass front offices looked the same. I passed several people sitting at desks who looked up at me as I walked by, but I was so near to tears that I didn't want any of them to ask if I needed help. I wouldn't have been able to hold it together.

So I threw my shoulders back and put my chin up and walked past, even though that just made me even more lost. Weston's statement, *this is ridiculous*, kept replaying in my mind, but I heard it in my father's voice. *This is ridiculous. You can't do this. Who do you think you are?*

He never said it to my face, my father, but he hadn't needed to. He'd said it by never letting me into his life. He'd said it by giving his company to his nephew instead of his own daughter. He'd said it loudest by thinking that whatever man I married would be more worthy of running his empire than me.

And wasn't he right? Wasn't Weston King right?

I was no one and I didn't know anything. I was just a spoiled girl with a lot of money. I might have a good head on my shoulders, but I didn't know the first thing about business.

I was such a fool to have thought I could walk into that meeting and take control.

I wiped a stray tear from my cheek as I turned down the hall and the elevators came into sight.

Thank God. Escape.

But then I heard the rush-and-click of shoes running toward me across the marble floor. I turned, expecting to see Donovan. He was the one who'd wanted this scheme to work out the most, and he was the one who would care enough to come after me, but instead... Weston?

I sucked in a breath and willed my emotions to hide inside me, in the deep-seated place that I buried most every feeling of mine that mattered. I'd rather it have been Donovan who'd come after me. It would have been easier to remain stoic and confident in front of him, because while he was admittedly good-looking and sexy as hell, he didn't make my knees weak and my palms sweat in the way that Weston did.

Weston, with that killer face and those panty-melting dimples. With that wicked grin and a body that wore a suit better than any other man in the room. When I'd realized he was the one who was volunteering to be my groom, I didn't know if I was overjoyed or in over my head. It had taken everything I had to give him my coolest look while inside I was drowning in butterflies.

To be honest, though I'd decided to approach the meeting with backbone, it was Weston who'd given me the added boost of confidence I'd needed when I'd first walked in the room. His electric blue eyes had sparked energy in me, evoked passion that I knew I owned but hadn't been able to wield until his gaze first crossed mine. He looked at me and made me feel not just like I was beautiful, but that I was worthy of being listened to. He looked at me like I deserved to be there.

How ironic that he was the same man who made me realize that I didn't belong.

Based on everything he'd said, I was pretty sure he hated me even though he was coming down the hallway after me. Even though he was now calling out my name, asking me to wait.

I reached out and hit the button for the elevator anyway.

"Just give me a few minutes," he said, slowing his trot to a walk as he neared. "I know I don't deserve it, but I'm only asking for two minutes. Please."

I scowled, wishing the doors would open. I might have been wrong about the meeting, might have been wrong about what I would do with the company, but I wasn't wrong to try.

And I wasn't going to let him make me feel like it again.

It hurt too much coming from a man I inexplicably wanted to impress.

"I don't need you," I repeated. "I don't need Reach."

"You don't. You definitely don't." His left hand went behind his neck, rubbing the muscles there. "Honestly, we don't really need you either. Which is why there's nothing on the line right now if you'll just come talk to me for a minute. Let me show you something."

He was right again. Reach really didn't need me. Sure, they wanted my advertising company—Darrell's advertising company—but they were doing fine without it. Reach still had massive holdings even without the merger. They would be just fine even if they didn't go after this one market. They didn't need me, and his remark was more than a bruise to my ego.

Because it meant I really wasn't holding any cards.

It was further proof I was clueless and out of my league.

The elevator doors opened with a *ding*. I closed my eyes momentarily and let out a low, quiet breath.

Then I opened them again, and turned to meet Weston's piercing blues.

"I'll give you five minutes," I conceded. Because I was curious. Because I had nothing to lose. Because he was so goddamn cute with that half-smile and that dimple.

"Come this way." His grin had widened, the dimple deepening. He walked backward to make sure I was following him, then, when he was certain, he turned around and retreated into the office space. This time he didn't lead me to the lounge, but toward the opposite corner.

We passed the desk of the woman who had escorted me in—Roxie, she'd said her name when she introduced herself, and then we were inside a corner office that I could only assume was his own. He shut the door behind me and I tensed slightly.

He didn't notice.

How lucky for men to not have the constant worry about being in close rooms with the opposite sex, but I needn't have worried either because the walls to his office were glass and anyone could see in.

But then he moved behind his desk and pushed a button, and suddenly the transparent glass went opaque, and we could no longer see out. And, I assumed, no one could see in.

"Wait a minute," I said hesitantly. "I just met you." Ironic, considering I had been about to marry him.

He raised a brow in question, not understanding my meaning.

Then both brows raised as he got my drift. "Don't worry. The door isn't locked—go ahead and check."

I did so and found he was telling the truth.

I remained by the door and watched him, as next he walked over to the cabinets that ran along the side wall and opened two up. They were the kind that usually hid a TV screen behind them or a safe. When he opened them, I was shocked to discover a dartboard waited behind.

And stapled to the middle of the dartboard was a black-and-white printout of a man's face.

I squinted and took a couple steps forward, examining the face. "Is that... Nash King?"

I didn't know a lot about business, but everyone knew who Nash King and Raymond Kincaid were. Anyone who had any sizable investments had a relationship with Weston and Donovan's fathers in some form or another. Nash was one of the financial kings—har har, the pun—of the United States. He and Kincaid owned so many banks that together they were one of the leading financial institutions of the world.

Why was Weston throwing darts at a picture of his father's face?

I turned to look at my almost-groom. His hands were shoved casually in his pockets and his eyes were cast down, embarrassed.

He shrugged. "It's kind of an old picture now," he said. "I just printed something from the Internet. It would have been even more awesome if I'd brought in an actual portrait, but I'm lazy."

I felt the whisper of a smile on my lips. "Weston King. Do you have daddy issues?" Was *that* what he'd brought me here to show me?

"I didn't say I had daddy issues," he said defensively. Evasively. "But it blows off a lot of steam to throw a dart at people's faces every now and then. I'm not going to say that I have or haven't occasionally placed Donovan's face in that spot, but I *am* telling you that it works. Hold on."

Suddenly, he was in motion. He jiggled the mouse on his computer to wake it up, and then typed something on the keypad. He pushed a few buttons and a moment later, I heard the printer spitting out a piece of paper.

He ran over to it to retrieve the document, and then, snatching up his stapler, he walked back to the dartboard and pinned a new picture up over the one of Nash King.

When he stepped back, we were looking at the famous profile picture of Dell Dyson. It was on his website, on his Wikipedia page, on the book he'd written, on any sort of byline. He'd always thought it made him look powerful, but I only ever saw his arrogance in that expression, in the tilt of his head. I had hoped to see it next as I removed it from the wall of *my* new office, but here it was.

This was what Weston meant to show me.

Oh, boy.

Weston stepped back from the cabinet and held both his hands out to display the dartboard, Vanna White style. "Go ahead."

"No way," I scoffed, but I did spin around, surveying the room for something to throw. "I don't even have any darts."

He was already scurrying back to his desk. "What was I thinking?" A moment later he'd pulled a handful of darts from his top drawer and was handing them over to me.

I laughed, a small chuckle, mostly to myself as I regarded his offering. Talk about ridiculous.

But then, there I was, taking a red dart from his palm and setting up my stance, lining up my aim. It wasn't a fantasy I'd ever had, but the second it showed up before me, I couldn't imagine why I hadn't tried it myself.

I'd never thrown darts before. That was probably reason number one.

I'd taken archery in school, though, and been fairly good at it. Still, nothing, not even that class, had ever made me feel quite as much like I was Robin Hood taking an arrow from Little John as I did right now.

I pulled my body back, rocked forward, let the dart go, and watched it smack right into Dell Dyson's tie. It quivered directly in the middle of his perfect Windsor knot.

Man, did it feel good.

"Wasn't that fantastic?" Weston whispered, as though he knew that admitting it might feel dangerous. "Do another."

This one didn't take any encouraging at all. I grabbed a green one.

I drew back and let it go. It sailed with a whoosh and landed in the corner of the paper, not hitting any of his face or body at all.

"Ah. Shit throw. Try again," Weston encouraged.

I did. Again and again. A yellow dart and blue and another red. Another blue. Each time thinking of a new offense.

This one is for the company that completely blocked women from holding executive positions—including your own daughter.

This one for the seven consecutive years you landed on the worst places to work list for people with families.

This one for the thirty-seven percent difference in pay rates between men and women that exists at Dyson Media.

This one for the summer that you invited me to stay with you in Paris and then left me alone with the nanny, while you entertained at your other houses.

This one for every birthday you forgot.

This one for every Christmas gift that was picked out by your secretary.

And this one for every time that you said you would visit, that you said that you would show up, that you said that you wanted to be there, and you never, ever were.

I was shaking when all the darts were gone.

"Bullseye," Weston said beside me, oblivious to the ragged state of my emotions. "Literally. Bull's-eye, as in, you got that one right in between the eyes."

He went to gather the darts off of the board, and while I was staring at his long, lean backside, perfectly sewn into his tailored suit, I found words spilling out that I never meant to confess. "I thought I had more time," I said quietly.

"Huh?" Weston seemed appropriately confused. "Oh, you can go again after I get them all. I don't own that many." He turned back to pulling out the rest of the darts.

But I didn't mean what he thought I did.

I swallowed and strengthened my voice this time. "I thought I had more time," I said again. "I thought that it would be years before my father died. I traveled after college. I spent time in Europe. I was enjoying my youth. I didn't know he would have a heart attack in the middle of the night. He was only sixty-one and was fairly healthy—or so everyone thought. Nobody expected him to..."

I trailed off, remembering how I'd found out he'd been rushed to the hospital by hearing it on CNN. I'd reached his secretary easily enough, who informed me that I'd been "on the list," but "further down," and she just hadn't gotten to calling me yet.

I was in the air flying to France to be with him when he'd officially died.

I shook off the memories of his death and funeral, a whirlwind of commotion where I'd been made to feel insignificant and inadequate at every turn. The memories were still too fresh and unprocessed, too near the surface to think about without turning into a sobbing mess. Truly, they might always be.

"I was already registered for a master's degree this fall in business at the University of New York. I had planned to learn..." My voice trembled. I swallowed again before going on. "It just took me by surprise."

Weston had gathered all the darts by then, but he stood frozen, listening to me, as though he didn't dare to turn around, as though afraid any movement might break my monologue, and the honest truth was, it might.

I would have never said any of this to Donovan. I would probably never have said any of this to Weston if he were facing me. If those blue eyes were boring into me, I'd have assumed he could already see into my soul.

But while his back was turned, right here in this moment, the truth continued to pour out. And even though he was just a stranger politely listening, it felt good to lay everything out.

So I went on.

"I took poli-sci as my undergrad because it doesn't matter what your bachelor's degree is before you get your MBA, and I thought a background in politics could be helpful. And I *like* politics. But now I'm woefully unprepared, and I'm watching Darrell run, and systematically dismantle, this company. I could let this go. I could take the next four years to become the best business leader possible, to find out everything that I need to know to lead an empire of this extent."

I took a step toward him.

"But if I wait, it would be selfish. It would be because *I* don't feel ready. Because *I'm* scared. Meanwhile, there are hundreds of thousands of other people depending on that company to be their livelihood, and others depending on it to be the place they look to for quality entertainment and programming. If I have a chance to change the lives of the people, the *women* who work for him, if I have a chance to change the lives of the people who watch entertainment put out by Dyson Media, and if that chance makes those lives better... Weston, I feel like I have to take that chance. Whether I'm ready or not."

I turned away with a sigh. I'd said everything, and now I felt dumb. Too dumb to even be able to face his backside.

Behind me, I could hear the rustle and shuffle of movement. He stopped a foot or two behind me, close enough that I could feel the heat radiating off his body, smell his cologne. It made me flushed and dizzy and my heart started to race.

"I could teach you," he said quietly.

"What?" I turned to face him, not understanding what he meant.

"I'll teach you about business while we're together." He tossed the darts back onto his desk and jammed his hands back into his pockets, admittedly a very arresting look. "A tailored, condensed MBA. Everything you need to know to find the right people to run the company. Everything you need to know to make sure you're not being taken advantage of. The Weston King Crash Course in Business."

My skin felt itchy and my insides were fluttering.

Too many times, though, I'd gotten excited by promises from my father, promises he didn't ever keep. I'd listened to my mother ask what the quid pro quo was so many times.

I'd learned from both parents. I'd learned to be circumspect.

I tilted my head, my mouth parted slightly. "And why would you do that, exactly? My advertising company can't possibly be worth that much to you."

Weston threw his head back in a way that said he wasn't really sure why he'd made the offer.

But then he said, "Let's just say I have a soft spot for companies that are vulnerable. And Donovan wants it. And I owe Donovan. We'll leave it at that."

I studied him for another moment. It didn't *feel* like a bad idea, but I also knew that you weren't supposed to use feelings in business—I wasn't completely ignorant in the field. I couldn't see a downside, though, either, anyway I looked at it.

And I really wanted my father's company. The more obstacles I faced—the more everyone else told me that I couldn't—the more I needed to do it, if only to prove I could to myself.

"Okay," I said, such a little word to begin such a big arrangement. But all mighty things started out small. Even the Mississippi River started in some little puddle of bubbling water somewhere.

Weston nodded once, taking it in. Then he drew in a breath, and I could see he was *really* taking it in, maybe even kind of regretting it.

My stomach dropped.

Then his expression changed as he suddenly had an idea. "Let's do this right." He reached into his suit pocket, and I wrinkled my nose as I tried to peer over and see what he was doing. A second later, he pulled out a small box and set it in the palm of his hand.

Immediately, I started giggling.

"Stop giggling," he said, practically laughing himself. "We have to be serious about this. This is a real serious moment between us."

"I can't help it! I'm a giggler."

"First rule of business," he said, "if you want people to take you seriously, you can't giggle."

I sucked in my cheeks, making probably the silliest expression I'd ever made. Weston tamped down his smile as well, though not all the way. I kind of wondered if that half-smile was permanently on his lips, wondered if he even noticed it. It was fitting for the occasion, the tiny upturn of his lips as he opened the black velvet box and pulled out the gorgeous platinum ring with tiny diamonds surrounding a large one that had to be at least four carats.

I could almost believe he meant this. Could almost believe he was enjoying it.

"Give me your hand," he said, taking it before I'd actually given it to him. Goosebumps sprouted up my arm at his touch, or maybe just because I was so thrilled that this was finally happening, I was *that* much closer to my dream.

Yeah, definitely that.

He slipped the ring over my knuckle to put it into place. It fit perfectly, which made me certain that Donovan had had a hand in it.

"Elizabeth Dyson, will you do me the honor," he said in a very warm tone, as he dropped to a knee, "of becoming my bride."

Part of me wondered if he should've added the word *fake* in there, because that's what this was. It was fake; it wasn't real. Even though this moment was beginning to feel very, very real.

But on the other hand, it *would* be a real wedding. We would have real marriage certificates. It would really be on file in the state of New York, and when we got divorced, that would really be on our record, too. We would have to file taxes together.

There wasn't really anything fake about this fake wedding at all.

So maybe how he'd asked was appropriate indeed. And there was only one appropriate answer for him.

"Yes, Weston King, I will."

FIVE
WESTON

ELIZABETH CRANED her neck to look past me out the car window.

"This is where you like to hang out?" she asked when she saw where the car had stopped. "There's a line a mile long."

It had been two days since we'd decided to get engaged, and we were putting the scheme into action. She'd taken the ring off her finger for now, figuring it best to wait to announce the engagement until after we'd had a few public sightings. This would be our first, but so far, she'd complained from the minute she'd picked me up, and if she kept it up, I was going to have to...

Well, I wasn't sure what I was going to have to do, but I knew what I wanted to do. Especially with her wearing that black and white striped sundress with the kind of skirt that bounced up just the way I liked—it was simple and elegant and not at all what most women her age would wear on a date that involved a nightclub, but somehow, with those strappy high designer fuck-me shoes, she pulled it off.

Problem was, it also made me want to do just that—strap her high on my waist and fuck her.

But I wanted to do that with most girls I spent any time with. Elizabeth Dyson might be my favorite brand of sexy, but she wasn't special. I could fuck her once or twice, but eventually I'd get bored with her, like I always did, and then I'd still be stuck with her through our arrangement. It would feel like a real relationship, and I had zero interest in that.

Besides, I was about ninety-nine point nine percent sure that Elizabeth was not the type to fuck around for fun.

That point one percent of doubt was what my cock kept twitching about.

"The line wouldn't have formed yet if we had come straight here instead of going to dinner first," I said, with an edge of complaint of my own. "I never take my dates to dinner."

"That's exactly why we had to go. I'm not supposed to be like all your other girls. I'm the woman you're going to choose to marry." It wasn't the first time she'd explained this tonight, and it showed in her tone.

"Right, right." Except if I ever *did* get married, I was still sure I'd never let the woman drag me to the French froufrou place Elizabeth had insisted on going.

Thank God that part of the night was behind us. Now we were on to the fun. Since she'd said that we would need to be seen out on the town, and since she didn't have any regular haunts, I'd recommended the place *I* frequented.

That meant The Sky Launch.

"Anyway, don't worry," I assured her as I pulled her out of the backseat, feeling oddly comforted by the contact of her hand. "The line isn't for us."

It was a Friday night so the club was busy, even though it wasn't yet ten o'clock. I was known here, so I pulled her to the front desk where the bouncer let us in with a nod. We were halfway up the entrance ramp when Gwen, one of the managers, approached and gave me a hug.

I felt Elizabeth stiffen at my side, and so, simply to rile her up more, I kissed Gwen on the cheek, something I didn't normally do because she was happily married with children.

Sometimes I'm a dick just because it's fun.

"It's been a few weeks since you've been here," Gwen said, prying.

"I've been...preoccupied," I said, making it sound like the things that had kept me busy had been sexy things.

They hadn't been. Not recently. The office really had grown too big to manage with just Nate and me. But it wasn't cool to admit to being a workaholic. Plus, I liked the way it made Elizabeth silently fret.

As though prompted by my thoughts, the woman at my side cleared her throat.

"Gwen, I'd like you to meet my girlfriend, Elizabeth Dyson."

Gwen's brow arched in surprise. "Did you say...*girlfriend*?"

I had almost tripped over the word myself. I wasn't sure I'd ever actually used the word in reference to anyone connected to me in the whole time I'd been alive.

"I did. I did say girlfriend." I was saying it again, just to get used to the sound. *Girlfriend*. It wasn't that terrifying, really. Girl. Friend. Nothing to it.

"This must be serious then." Gwen turned to Elizabeth and shook her hand, then held it with both of hers. "I've known Weston for quite some time now, and he's yet to have introduced me to anyone as his *girlfriend*. It's a real pleasure to meet you."

Elizabeth's eyes wandered over to the wedding ring on Gwen's finger and I saw her expression relax just a bit.

There went that fun.

"It's been a whirlwind of a romance," Elizabeth said, and I had to look down at my shoes so that no one saw how utterly disgusted I was with her phrasing. *Whirlwind of a romance* didn't sound convincing; it sounded like a bad Hallmark movie.

I needed to remember to tell her that later.

"I'm delighted to finally meet some of Weston's...friends?" Elizabeth said *friends* with a bit of a question in her tone, as though she wasn't sure how to refer to Gwen.

"Gwen is one of the managers here at The Sky Launch," I said, taking pity on my *girlfriend*—the more I thought the word, the easier it came out. "She knows how to take care of us. Is my regular spot available?"

"Of course," Gwen assured me. "I had a bubble room saved the minute you called and said you were coming. Right this way."

We followed Gwen across the dance floor and up the stairs to the second floor of the nightclub, and though I held Elizabeth's hand in mine as we walked across the dance floor, I made sure to keep my eyes on Gwen's behind.

I was a player; it was to be expected, and I liked the way it made Elizabeth bristle and fume. Plus, it was important she knew early on that although she was marrying me, my eyes could still wander.

It *was* a fake marriage. I still got to look.

In fact, I still got to fool around—discreetly, of course.

On the second floor, Gwen handed us off to the waitress who showed us to our bubble room, one of several that overlooked the dance floor below. These rooms were the highlight of The Sky Launch, the reason that I loved this club so much. The tables were enclosed in a private setting, but the wall around them was glass so that you could see out and everyone could see in.

It combined the perks of VIP with all the exhibitionism I could want.

"This is interesting," Elizabeth said with what sounded like disdain in her tone, once she was seated at the table and the waitress had left.

I unbuttoned my sports jacket and threw her a glare. I couldn't imagine the places that she hung out.

Actually, I could. Boring places. Coffee places. Places that only served wine. Places that required you to wear a tux.

Places I sincerely hoped I wouldn't be forced to frequent as part of this charade.

"If you hate it so much, make sure we're seen here tonight, and we don't have to come back again." I picked up my drink menu even though I knew what I was going to get, just so I didn't have to look at her for a minute. Looking at her confused me too much.

It was hard to correlate that rockin' body with the things that came out of her mouth.

"I didn't say that it was terrible. I said it was interesting. I haven't been here long enough to find out if it's terrible." She looked out at the dance floor beneath us, gazing at the sea of sweaty bodies pulsing to the steady beat. "I like that you can have a conversation in here. While the music's going. That's nice."

The hint couldn't have been stronger. I set my menu down and gave her my attention. "Let me guess, you have something you want to talk about."

"There *is* something I think that we should go over. I hadn't thought that we needed to talk about it as soon as tonight, but I realize now that we do." She was talking fast and not looking at me, and I could sense she was maybe nervous, which intrigued me to no end.

"Go on."

"You *do* know you can't see other women while we're engaged, right?" She looked up at me now and met my eyes. Her irises were startlingly blue, almost as startlingly blue as my balls were going to be from what she just said.

Except that she was wrong.

So I corrected her. "You mean no one can *find out* that I'm sleeping with anyone." She couldn't actually be suggesting I wouldn't sleep with anybody. For seven months? I couldn't remember the last time I went seven days. It wasn't going to happen.

She sighed, a great big heavy sigh that brought her whole upper body to rest on the table between us, drawing my eyes to the way her breasts peeked over the neckline of her dress. "No, Weston. I mean, you can't sleep with anyone. Even discreetly. It's too big of a risk."

I laughed. Then I started scanning the ceiling for hidden cameras. "Is there a film crew in here somewhere? Because there's no way you're serious."

"I knew this wasn't going to work. You can't keep it in your pants for even a minute, can you?" She picked up her phone and started to text somebody. "There's just too much on the line for me here. Donovan should've been the one to volunteer; he would have been able to go seven months."

"Are you texting *Donovan*?" I wasn't sure if it bothered me more that she was texting Donovan while she was on a date with me, or that she'd suggested Donovan had the strength to do *anything* longer than I did.

Either way, I was bothered. A lot.

"Stop," I said. "Don't text him. There's no need. I just didn't know. We hadn't discussed it yet. That's all." I ran a hand down my thigh back and forth, back and forth. Fuck, was I really, actually, agreeing to discuss this?

"I already texted him," she said smugly, setting the phone down. "It's too late."

I rolled my eyes. "We don't need his input. Let's discuss this, just you and me."

"It's just you and me right now. Go for it." Her tone wasn't angry or unreasonable. She was simply meeting the obstacle head-on.

Which was admirable.

I owed it to her to be admirable as well.

I stretched my neck, trying to get rid of the kink that had suddenly shown up, and thought quickly. "You know," I said, leaning forward. "A lot of guys get married, and it doesn't mean they stop fooling around."

God, that sounded terrible. I didn't know if I'd ever get married for real, but if I did, I didn't want to be the kind of guy who fooled around on his woman.

But I wasn't getting married for real. So it was okay to play an asshole in *this* marriage. Hell, maybe it could even give us fuel for our divorce.

I was about to suggest that, but she spoke before I could.

"I'm sure that's acceptable among *some people*." She sneered as she emphasized 'some people.' I didn't know who some people were, but if some people were the kind that fooled around on their fiancées she'd had every right to sneer. "But I can't be engaged to that. I wouldn't tolerate it. Weston King would bring his girlfriend to this club, so we're here. Elizabeth Dyson wouldn't stand for a fiancé fucking around behind her back—"

"This wouldn't exactly be behind your back." Maybe it wasn't the right time for a joke.

"And she *definitely* wouldn't stand for it in front of her face."

I wracked my brain trying to figure out where all of this was coming from. Certainly the evening hadn't gone that badly. Had it? "Is this about the hostess at the restaurant?"

"I came out of the bathroom, and she was at our table giving you her phone number." She'd lowered her voice as if even letting me know that a girl had been flirting with me might be telling too many people.

I knew it!

I took a breath so I wouldn't get too eager in my explanation. "First of all, she was not giving me her number." I'd known Lexie from somewhere or other and she'd come over to show me pics of her new clit piercing. Elizabeth must have seen me take Lexie's cell phone and assumed we were exchanging numbers.

Now that I thought about it, the real explanation didn't sound any better.

"It doesn't matter what *really* happened," Elizabeth said now, her volume rising. "It matters what it *looked* like. And it looked like she was trying to hook up with you while you were on a date with me."

Her nostrils flared, and angry splotches of red appeared on the creamy skin below her collarbone.

She was cute like that, all flustered and worked up. I could imagine that blush creeping up her neck and flooding her face when she was lost in a fit of passion. Part of me wanted to see her like that. All frantic and unnerved because she was squirming underneath me...

Whoa. Hold on there.

We had to change the topic. "Fine. We'll be monogamous. Or not sexual. Whatever. I was just throwing the idea out there. We were talking about making it look real and everything." Good God, I hoped she knew what she was asking of me.

The doors opened to the room, and I realized we didn't have the privacy setting on. It was the waitress coming to take our drink order. I chose the house gin specialty, a martini made with house-infused spirits and a Meyer lemon-rosemary simple syrup. Elizabeth ordered—surprise, surprise—a glass of Merlot. The waitress left and Elizabeth's phone shook with the vibration of an incoming text.

She picked it up and I tried not to look like I cared about what it said, but I wasn't fooling anyone.

"Donovan says there's already a pool going to see how long you can make it." She typed something in response and threw her phone into her purse.

I wrinkled my brows. "A pool? Betting how long I can go

without sex? That's ludicrous." Though it wasn't really that ludicrous because I was already having withdrawals and I hadn't even gone without sex yet.

I was also more than a little annoyed with Donovan for turning my sacrifice into office amusement. "Who's in on this pool? What did you respond with?"

"I put in a wager for two weeks."

I laughed, a real, hearty, from-the-belly laugh. That was not at all what I had expected her to say. "That doesn't serve you well if I fail within two weeks. You need me to stay celibate for seven months."

"I do need you to stay celibate for seven months, but at least I get *something* if you fail as soon as I think you're going to fail at this rate." She was annoyed.

"At this rate? I've been a perfect gentleman all evening. What makes you so certain I'm going to fail?"

"You can't even keep your eyes off the waitress."

I'd been checking out the waitress? It was so natural I hadn't noticed it. I couldn't even remember what she'd been wearing, or whether her hair had been long or short.

Honestly, the only woman I'd been thinking about all evening was the one sitting across from me, the one in the dress with the tight top that molded against her full, round breasts. The one with the mouth that curved naturally down into a kissable pout. The one whose hair lay in perfect cascades down her shoulders.

"Well, fuck you all. I can make it the whole goddamn seven months. You'll see."

And of course, that's what Donovan had meant to do by having a pool in the first place. He knew it would just get me all up in arms. Get me all pissed and want to prove everyone wrong. He wasn't even here, and he still knew just what to say to push my buttons.

I could never decide if he was an outrageous asshole or a giant I could never measure up to. Maybe he was both combined—an outrageously giant asshole.

"Then it's settled?" she asked, with that snotty look on her face and just the smallest touch of doubt. The littlest hint of vulnerability.

It was that hint that made her so soft when she was trying to be so hard. That hint that made me want to reach across the table and touch her, even just take her hand in mine.

But I didn't.

I had to remember that she was also the woman putting a chastity belt on my lower regions for more than half of the year. Just thinking about it made my balls ache.

"It's settled." Thank fucking God for porn and my left hand.

"Then I'll cancel my wager."

"You aren't doing me any favors," I said, maybe a bit too harshly. "But thank you."

We were silent then, the conversation killed by abstinence. Sure there were still things to say, things to work out, but I wasn't in the mood to get into wedding details and I sure as hell wasn't getting into business now. The Sky Launch was sacred. This was not a place for business.

Elizabeth took the silence as something else. "I'm sorry, Weston. I really am. I imagine that a healthy sex life is important to—"

"Don't apologize." I didn't want to hear Elizabeth Dyson discussing my overactive dick. I couldn't control my hard-on already.

We fell back into the quiet. The waitress came in, left our drinks on the table along with the tab.

A romper. Long auburn hair.

That's what the waitress was wearing, that's what she looked like. I made sure to notice this time. Truth is, there was a time I would have noticed earlier.

Hell, maybe it was time for a cleanse. I had been bored lately. Maybe a sex break would solve that. Not that I wanted to find out, but since I didn't really have a choice...

The waitress left, and I hit the privacy button out of habit. Elizabeth and I sipped our drinks silently. She looked out again over the dance floor, then studied the buttons along the length of the table that operated the glass window. She pushed the one that turned the glass opaque.

"Clear it," I ordered.

She looked up at me, startled. Then she pushed the button to make the glass clear again. "You have lots of glass in your office too. You like being seen?"

If she thought I was a dirty oversexed player before, she couldn't handle all the things I was really into.

Of course, that made me all the more eager to tell her. Something about her prissiness made the idea of shocking her a turn-on.

"Yeah. I do."

She pursed her lips, considering. She peeked out the window again, this time looking out to the other bubble rooms. Most held parties of people gathered around the circular bench enjoying their dinners and their drinks in a place where they could talk. A couple, though, were opaque.

She turned her gaze back to me. "What exactly do you do with girls when you bring them here?"

God, I felt like I was on Secret Confessions. "Do you really want to know?"

She took a swallow of her wine and licked the little drop of Merlot that lingered on her lip. "I wouldn't have asked if I didn't want to know. I'm supposed to be one of those girls. Remember?"

Of course, she could never really be one of those girls. One of *those* girls would've had her panties off already. That was too crass to tell her outright.

But there was a whole Internet that could tell her for me. "Pull up YouTube. Search my name and The Sky Launch."

She hesitated a moment before she pulled her phone back out of her purse. Then she swiped the screen, entered her password, and searched as I'd told her to. I didn't look to see what she was watching—I kept my gaze only on her face as she played first one video, then the next. Then a third.

I watched her eyes widen. I watched her pupils dilate. I watched her lips part and her breathing get heavy. I could only imagine what she was seeing.

Random footage from people on the dance floor taking film with their phones of the most eligible bachelor in New York caught once again at his favorite nightclub with the flavor of the week. I'd watched plenty of those videos. I'd whacked off to a few of them. They didn't usually show very much of me, but they often showcased a topless girl, sometimes more than one. Always in a bubble room. There was no mistaking what was going on in here.

The window was always clear.

And I always made them come.

Elizabeth's face was red by the time she put her phone back in her purse, the same red color that I'd imagined earlier.

I really needed to stop imagining that.

"Wow." She swallowed and I watched her throat as it delicately bobbed. "People really do watch you up here."

I almost laughed. *That* was her takeaway? "Yes, people really do watch."

"And you...like that." I couldn't tell if there was judgment in her voice or not. But of course she was judging me.

"Hey, before you get all high and mighty—"

"I'm not." She said it so emphatically that I stopped speaking. "I'm not," she said again. "I'm just saying that—if that's what you like, and if that's what you bring girls here to do...and if I am supposed to be your girlfriend, and if we're supposed to make it convincing..."

She paused and took a deep breath, and I thought I knew where she was going, but that really couldn't be where she was going, could it?

"Then we have to make it believable, too."

My dick perked up. She'd said exactly the words I'd hoped against hope to hear come out of her mouth.

Well, how about that? Elizabeth Dyson might be a fun girl after all.

SIX
ELIZABETH

HOLY SHIT, I was in over my head.

How on earth had I not seen it coming?

It wasn't like I hadn't prepared for our date. I'd researched Weston the minute I'd left the Reach offices and learned the essentials. Turned out the man used those panty-melting dimples to get women. A lot of women. But I could have guessed that just from the short time I'd spent in his presence. Sex emanated from him like cologne. As though he'd put it on with his aftershave and pomade.

So I'd chosen the restaurant, I'd chosen my clothing, I'd provided the driver—all of it so that I would feel that I had some sort of an ounce of control on my first outing with this stranger. The stranger I was about to pledge myself to in legal matrimony. I'd thought maybe that would put me on some sort of an even playing field.

But it had only taken a few hours to realize that nothing could put me on an even playing field with Weston King.

What I'd failed to realize was that it wasn't Weston I needed to compete with—it was his women.

And they were at every turn. Beautiful, strong, smart women. Women he knew, yes, but the ones he didn't know seemed to notice him and swarmed as though they were bees, and he was the hive.

He was just as attentive. Whatever it was they said or did, or however it was they smiled or walked, they knew how to catch his eye, because he checked out every damn one of them. Or it felt like he did.

And here was I next to them, plain and insecure, a little bit awkward and a whole lot inexperienced. And somehow, I was supposed to capture him the same way all these women before me had. Keep his eyes on me and off of them for the duration of our time together.

I'd only had three steady boyfriends. My mother was the one who knew how to handle men like Weston. She was the one who knew how to flirt and flaunt. She was the one who knew how to be sexy and desired. Who knew how to be confident in her skin, to bring men to their knees.

She was the one who men stared at in the way that Weston was staring at me now.

And he was only staring at me because he thought I was one of those girls, because I'd just suggested that maybe I should pretend to be one.

He did realize I'd meant pretend, didn't he?

"I'm not suggesting that we actually *do* anything," I clarified. "But we need to make it seem like we're doing the same things you do with other girls up here. Stage it."

"Right." He grinned.

And I had to hold back a shiver. That dimple was pure sin. It was distracting and unnerving and just plain rude. I was trying to be practical and salvage this whole sham while he acted like he was looking forward to this. I wasn't even sure what *this* was yet. There were several variations of sex shows in those videos I'd watched. I was bendy enough. Years of ballet gave me experience in physical performance. The trick was figuring out which position was the easiest to fake.

I looked around our set, weighing our options. "If I stand on the bench with my hands on the window with you behind me..."

"Come over here," he ordered as though I hadn't even spoken.

My heart skipped a beat at the subtle edge to his command. "Why?"

"If we're going to make this believable, you're going to have to be closer. Come over here and sit on my lap. Straddle me."

Now my pulse raced inside my chest. Of all the positions we had as options, straddling his lap was definitely the most intimate.

I scooted tentatively around the bench and then turned so I was on my knees facing out the window. I paused when I was next to him, not quite sure how to do the next part. I'd never done this before. Never straddled a guy. Not to trick people into thinking I was fooling around, certainly. Not even because I was actually fooling around.

I took a deep breath, gathering my nerves, but before I'd gotten it together, he grabbed my elbow and tugged me so that I fell across his lap.

Well, hello.

"There you are," he said.

His body was warm, and I instantly had the urge to curl into him. I fought against it, sitting back on his thighs, away from his pelvis so that it wouldn't be too weird. Too intimate. Still, we were close, our faces only inches from each other. I could smell his cologne and his shampoo and the faint scent of sweat underneath—a scent that was pure Weston. And, shit, he was even more gorgeous close-up. His skin, flawless. His eyes, deep pools of blue.

I swallowed, suddenly nervous.

Weston seemed to sense my anxiety because next thing I knew he was reassuring me. "I'm keeping my hands on the bench next to me. Okay? You can lean on my shoulders to give yourself some balance, if you want. And then anything that happens here? It's all up to you. You run the show."

I ran my tongue across my lips in a circle and nodded. "Okay." My voice sounded unusually high and shaky, and my palms felt sweaty as I settled them on his shoulders to balance myself. I shifted my hips, trying to get comfortable.

And accidentally slid forward, my pelvis hitting his.

Whoops.

My cheeks went red as Weston let out a low chuckle. I was sitting on his lap. With nothing between my crotch and his except a pair of panties and his pants. And whatever he had on underneath his pants.

And now I was thinking about what he had on underneath his pants.

I looked at the windows past him, trying to distract myself. Lights flashed and swirled around the dance floor in time to the beat, the only part of the music which made it into the sanctuary of the bubble room. I could tell it was crowded, but I couldn't make out faces the way they could probably make out ours. "I don't know if anyone's looking," I said.

"Don't worry about them. Just focus on what you're doing."

Easy for him to say. He wasn't facing them. He was only looking at me.

Nope. I couldn't think about that either. Just had to focus on the task at hand.

I closed my eyes. "So just pretend that I... That we are... That under my dress..." I couldn't even say it.

Weston leaned forward and murmured near my ear. "Yes, pretend that under your dress you are not wearing any panties. I have my dick out. I'm working you, and you are showing me exactly how you like it. Now go."

Just like that, my panties were damp.

I didn't know if he was saying those things to loosen me up or to get a rise out of me, either was possible.

Whatever his intent, it did the trick. He set the scene. I felt my face flush like the women in the videos as I imagined him rubbing his crown against my slit before nudging his tip inside and then burying himself to the hilt.

I opened my mouth in a silent gasp, acting out how I was sure it would feel. *Good. It would feel so good.*

This was so...weird. So hot and sexy and arousing and weird.

I wondered if he was feeling it too, feeling turned on, or if it was just me. It wasn't like I could ask though, and knowing probably wouldn't help my performance anyway.

So I concentrated on me. Focused on the task.

"Do I move or something?" I bucked my hips forward and felt the friction against my crotch as it rubbed the fly of his pants.

Mmm.

"Yeah," he said breathlessly. "That's good. That motion. Just like that."

"Okay. Okay." I rocked against him again, and again, my hips tilting back and forth, my clit brushing against his fly. Every time, stroking and kindling a fire in a fireplace I hadn't had cleaned for some time. I spread my thighs a little wider and braced my knees against the bench so I could swing my pelvis all the way forward, in and out, in and...

Oh.

I froze. "Is that—?" But I didn't have to ask. There was most definitely a fat, thick ridge pressed against the crotch panel of my panties. I guess that answered the question of whether he was feeling it too.

My eyes flew open. "Oh my God!"

"Look," he said, ready to defend himself. "There's an extremely attractive woman sitting on my lap. I cannot help what happens to my cock. It has a mind of its own."

A really *big* mind of its own.

"Just pretend it's not there," he said at the same time I said, "I'm pretending it's not there."

Like hell I could pretend it wasn't there. I wasn't even sure I wanted to.

Our eyes met momentarily. His were lit up and crazed, mirrors to how I felt inside.

I rocked forward again, without even thinking that I wanted to, and I had to bite my lip because it felt so incredible rubbing my pussy along the outline of his cock.

"That's great," he hissed. "Pretend it's not there just like that, and you're great."

That was exactly what I planned to do. Glad we were on the same page.

Though *plan* wasn't quite the right word for what was going on with me at the moment. My body was just moving on its own, rocking steadily, trying to ease the ache between my legs, trying to rub against the firm thickness anchored beneath me.

But nothing was enough.

I twisted and circled my hips. I writhed. I let go of his shoulder and grabbed my breast with one hand, brushing across my nipple with my thumb. Everything I did only made the buzz louder, the hum in my veins more intense.

I'd forgotten about the glass windows and the crowds below. The performance was no longer for anyone but me. The end goal wasn't about looking like one of Weston's girls—it was about *becoming* one of them.

But I was aimless and an amateur, and I needed help.

"Tell me what you're doing to me," I begged. "Tell me what you would be doing to me right now."

"I'm so deep inside you," he said without any hesitation. "I'm balls deep, my dick is touching the very end of you." His hips bucked up, and I wondered if he knew he was even doing it. "I have my hand under your skirt and I'm rubbing your clit in tight circles, and it's driving you insane. You're so wet that my thumb keeps sliding off your nub." His voice was strained as he talked, and I could hear his fingernails digging into the bench on either side of us, clawing into the upholstery.

God I wanted him to touch me. If he touched me I'd explode. I was already so close.

"Then I grab your ass to pull you closer, so I can fuck you even deeper, and you tilt your hips up slightly. I tell you to touch yourself because you're on the edge and I want you to come for me. I want you to come when I tell you. Come all over my goddamn cock until you're shuddering and writhing and gasping for air. Do it, Elizabeth. Come all over me. Do it now."

I closed my eyes, but all I could see was light behind my lids, bright starbursts sprayed across the darkness. My hand fell back to his shoulder in an attempt to steady myself as a torpedo-strength orgasm ripped through me, splitting my insides, leaving me shaking and trembling and moaning out in ecstasy.

I threw my head back and called his name once before falling forward, limp and spent.

What the fuck just happened?

I hadn't even caught my breath yet when I flung my head up again, shock and horror surely written all over my face. Fortunately I found only another full-dimple smile on his.

"I didn't mean to do that," I said.

"It's okay. Really. You were great."

I scrambled up to my feet and smoothed my dress down as if I could hide my entire being with the movement. I couldn't help it. My eyes wandered down to his pants that were still straining at the zipper. His eyes followed mine to the wet spot that now darkened the material. A wet spot I had clearly left behind.

If it were possible to die from humiliation, I would have right about now.

"You know what? That's hot." The rasp in Weston's voice suggested that he wouldn't mind if I got more of him wet.

And even having just finished coming down from the best orgasm of my life, there was a part of me that wouldn't mind getting more of him wet myself.

I met his eyes. There was no way he wasn't thinking the same thing I was thinking. We were already here. We were already about to be engaged. We were obviously into each other.

"It wouldn't be a good idea," I said, yet for the life of me I couldn't think of any reason why it wouldn't. Sure, I'd never fooled around with a man just for the fun of it, but that didn't mean I couldn't start now. The words were already out of my mouth though, so now all I could do was wait and see how he reacted.

"Right," he agreed. "It would be a terrible idea."

"Because it would just complicate things," I said.

"Exactly. We're stuck together for the better part of a year. If we crossed this line now, we couldn't go back. And that would be a long time to have to be around each other afterward. As you said, it would complicate things."

"Right. Glad you see it the way I do." I swallowed, grateful that my voice hadn't caught. I understood what he was saying, but it sounded a lot like an excuse. A nice way of saying I'm not really *that* interested.

My throat suddenly felt tight and my eyes began to sting. This was the downside of being one of Weston's girls, I realized. Any night of fun would end in being casually dismissed.

How did his usual dates handle it so gracefully?

Probably they knew it was always coming, which I should've known too, but where rejection was concerned, I was already a bruise that refused to heal. I'd been overlooked too much of my life by the only man who'd ever really been important to me. My father had wounded me, and any other rejection felt like fingers pressing against purple and black skin, and I recoiled from the pain.

Also, I was a little bit angry at Weston now that I thought about it. How was this behavior supposed to sell me as a businesswoman? It had been my idea to give the performance, but Weston had been the one to say I needed to do a better job of selling myself as a smart, competent woman, one worthy of running the Dyson empire. How could he let me do *this* with him? Slutting it up only justified my father's points. And now I was going to be all over the Internet, and the headlines weren't going to convince anyone of anything except that Weston King gave good orgasms.

I had to keep my head in the game. The *long* game. Proving our relationship would be pointless if I didn't prove myself first.

Which was why I couldn't have sex with Weston. *That* was the reason.

It was also why nothing like this could ever happen again. Not even for the show. It shouldn't need to now anyway. If we were truly dating, we might have engaged in the same behavior he had with women of the past in our earlier days, but as I'd told him, *I* was supposed to be different. I was the girl he married—not the girl he fucked in a bubble room then never called again.

It was time for me to take charge.

I lifted my chin and cleared my throat. "Hopefully that display was convincing. Because we're not doing that again. We'll come back to The Sky Launch every Friday night, since it's your hangout. We'll let ourselves be seen here, but when we get to this room we'll turn the privacy windows on." I stared at him head-on to make sure he understood what I was saying. "Once we are engaged, the world doesn't need to know what we are doing in here anyway."

"Uh, okay," he said, obviously caught off guard. He shifted in his seat, reminding me he was still...uncomfortable. "You just want to come have drinks every week?"

"You can use that time to teach me the business like you promised," I said coldly. I didn't give him a chance to disagree. "I'm going to go to the restroom now and clean up. That will give you some time to take care of your little...problem."

I turned before he could say anything and headed for the exit, but I heard him call after me, "It's not little!"

I could tell it wasn't, just from the shape I'd rubbed against. Weston was packing, there was no doubt about that.

But I wasn't in the mood to give him any less rejection than what I'd felt. I swiveled my head in his direction, tossing my hair over my shoulder. "I guess I'll never know, will I?"

With those parting words, I left the bubble room.

SEVEN
WESTON

"YOU GOING to tell me what you're moping about today?"

I glanced up at Donovan who was flipping through LeeAnn Gregori's portfolio while we waited for Elizabeth to arrive for our meeting with the famed wedding planner.

What the hell did he mean by moping? I glanced down at my body language— my arms folded, my shoulders hunched.

My frown deepened.

I was irritated, that's what I was. And I had been for the last several weeks, the source of my irritation none other than my bride-to-be. For the last month we'd played the fake courting game, going to lunch at least once a week, where we usually ended up bickering about restaurants or menu items, and attending the symphony where I always fell asleep before intermission.

Then every Friday night we'd returned to The Sky Launch where she'd sat so perfectly innocent beside me, asking questions about mergers and stock options while her lids fluttered as she thought. And each time I was forced to give her knowledgeable answers when all I could think about was pulling her back onto my lap. Making her hips grind against my dick the way they had that first night, when she was putting on a show. I wanted to make her grind against my dick for real.

I hadn't changed my mind about what I'd said—fucking was a bad idea. It would make things messy, and I didn't do messy. She'd already proven that she couldn't mix sex with business by how she'd acted immediately after. One orgasm and she'd turned cold and snide, shoving her nose up as though what we'd done was dirty or beneath her. Imagine how she would have reacted if I'd treated her to a night at the Weston Inn. Dirt and filth were the house specialty—money back guaranteed.

But it didn't change the fact that I was still attracted to her, that I still thought about her pouty lips and perky round breasts, that I could still remember the scent of her arousal drifting in the air as she pressed her pussy against my straining cock. Fuck, if I didn't hear those breathy little moans in my sleep, and the way her face twisted in pleasure as she called out my name haunted me when I sat at my desk trying to concentrate on marketing conversion rates. My hand was getting such a workout from the memories that I wouldn't be surprised if I got carpal tunnel before our marriage was through.

None of this was anything I was going to admit to Donovan, though, because that asshole was the reason I was in this shitty situation in the first place. I was starting to believe my misery was his form of entertainment, and I wasn't giving him anything I didn't have to.

"I'm not moping." Shit, even I could hear the scowl in my tone.

"Good. Brooding looks much better on me than it does on you." Donovan shut the portfolio and crossed one leg over the other at the knee.

I clenched my fist, but took a breath so I wouldn't be tempted to punch him.

"She's late," I said, when I was calm. We'd been waiting in the lounge for ten minutes, but Donovan knew I was speaking about

Elizabeth and not LeeAnn Gregori, though technically she was late as well.

"She's probably in traffic. It's rush hour in New York City. No one's on time."

That was Donovan, always making excuses for her. "You really should've been the one to marry her," I grumbled, the thought making my stomach turn in weird strange ways.

He shook his head and opened his mouth, but before he could give me his usual spiel, I added, "People would have bought it."

"I was about to say that I don't really care for the girl."

My jaw dropped, and I stammered wordlessly for several seconds. "What?" I finally managed. "What does that have to do with anything?" As if *I* cared for the girl.

He narrowed his eyes in my direction. "Do you really want me to prove that *you* like her more than *I* do?"

I hesitated. Because...could he? Prove it?

Of course he couldn't prove it. He was bluffing, as always. I *didn't* like her better. I barely liked her at all.

But Donovan was good with his propaganda. So it was best not to let him speak, best to drop it.

Except I didn't want him thinking I actually *liked* Elizabeth.

Which made it a good time to tell him my other news.

I sat forward and rested my elbows on my thighs. "I officially offered the marketing job to Sabrina Lind today," I announced.

His chin tilted up ever so slightly. "Oh?"

"I should have done it a long time ago. Robbie will be leaving for London in three weeks, and we need the spot filled. I've just been busy, I guess." Busy playing boyfriend to Elizabeth. Spending all my time focused on her had made it difficult to remember why I'd wanted Sabrina to transfer to New York so badly in the first place.

"What did she say?" Donovan asked, seeming only slightly

interested. It was a rather important position in the firm, though, so he was surely cataloguing it somewhere in his brain.

"She said yes. We have to work out the transfer package and help her find a place to live. She'll be here in a month."

"I'll take care of it," he said quickly. Then he changed the subject abruptly. "I have news as well."

"Oh?" I tilted my head back toward him.

"I've decided I'm staying. Cade has a handle on the Tokyo office. New York City seems to need me. I'll stay and take on operations."

That was so Donovan. Making all the decisions for the firm without asking anyone else's opinion. Not that I wasn't glad to have him here. The work had grown to be too much for Nate and me, and I really didn't give a fuck about operations. Just, it would be nice to have a say in things every once in awhile.

I pretended it didn't bother me. "Great. Glad you decided to stay."

Before anything else could be said about it, the doors opened to the waiting room. We both looked up expectantly, hoping to see Elizabeth, but in walked a middle-aged woman with blond hair streaked with gray, skin freckled from too much sun, and the purplest eyeshadow I'd ever seen on someone not in drag. She was dressed in business casual, which still meant lots of bling, and platform heels covered in rhinestones. Apparently this was LeeAnn Gregori.

"Gentlemen!" she exclaimed, and then her brows furrowed. "I'm sorry," she looked down at the tablet she was carrying. "I had noted that I was meeting with a bride and groom. Not a groom and groom."

"The bride's not here yet," I said as quickly as I could. Not that there was anything wrong with a groom and groom getting married, but there was no way anyone was groom and grooming me with Donovan. I had my manhood to defend.

"I see. Well, in that case," she took a step forward, her hand out, "I'm LeeAnn."

"I'm Donovan Kincaid," he said, rushing in before I could introduce myself. "This is Weston King, the groom. Elizabeth Dyson is the bride. She's running late. Also, as we mentioned on the phone with you, this wedding is on a very tight deadline. We are looking at a December date, but it will be a very large affair. Money is not an issue; we're quite prepared to pay whatever is needed. Tell us what we can do in that amount of time."

"Yes, yes, we can do something spectacular in that amount of time... Tell me again what your relationship is to this wedding, Mr. Kincaid?"

I bit back a smile. It was always a highlight of my day to watch Donovan get questioned on his authority. It actually brightened my mood quite a bit.

Just then, Elizabeth burst in. She was out of breath and her face was flushed from rushing. My cock jumped in my pants, remembering that she'd looked that way when she'd come on my lap, tempting me into another fantasy of putting that look on her face in other ways.

"Hello, I'm sorry I'm so late. I'm Elizabeth Dyson." She held her hand out to LeeAnn. "You must be the wedding planner. I've heard so much about you. You're quite famous among my mother's friends."

"A pleasure to meet you, Ms. Dyson. I'm honored to work with someone so notable as well. We were just discussing what Mr. Kincaid's involvement was in your wedding to Mr. King?" LeeAnn shifted her eyes from Elizabeth to me.

Elizabeth slipped in between me and Donovan, looping an arm around me as she placed a hand on my partner's arm. "Oh, Donovan is my life coach. I don't do anything without his say-so. I invited him here to advise us. I hope that's not going to be a problem?"

I couldn't decide if I was impressed at how easily Elizabeth could act on her feet, or if I was annoyed at how eagerly she covered for Donovan.

And why *was* Donovan here anyway? Didn't he think we could handle this on our own? Or did he just insist on having his fingers in every pie?

Though I had to admit, it was really nice to have somebody else handle all the big details of a wedding I didn't give a shit about. Almost as nice as watching his face as it registered with him that he'd just been demoted from Fortune 500 company owner to life coach.

"Not a problem at all," LeeAnn said congenially. "If everyone is here, let's sit down and start planning, shall we?"

We sat down and LeeAnn filled out a few initial details about us in her tablet. Then we jumped right into making arrangements.

Immediately, we hit a snag.

"I do not think we should have the engagement party at The Sky Launch," Elizabeth said patronizingly.

"What's wrong with The Sky Launch? It's our place, honey." I made my voice sticky sweet, playing the part of fiancé. "We're there every week, after all."

Her eyes narrowed. "It's *your* place. How many other women have you taken there? Need I remind you of all the videos on YouTube? Half our guests will be attending and remembering their own trysts with you!"

I rolled my eyes and looked to Donovan, then to LeeAnn. "It's not like I'm actually inviting ex-girlfriends to the engagement party." Well, I'd slept with so many women, it was kind of impossible not to invite a few. Or, okay, a lot. "There won't be *that* many of them," I amended.

"I would tend to agree with Elizabeth on this one," LeeAnn, the traitor, began, "but unfortunately on such short notice, there aren't many other available places that will hold four hundred to five hundred guests. Unless you want to book the Marriott, I could maybe get—"

"Ew, no. Not the Marriott." It was Elizabeth's turn to look to Donovan.

"Considering the circumstances, Elizabeth," his subtext was clear—fake arranged marriage was the circumstance, "I think The Sky Launch is a perfect venue for the engagement party."

"Fine," she huffed. "But I want to be in charge of the music."

LeeAnn interjected before I had a chance to give my opinion on the matter. "I think that's a fair compromise. Moving on."

And so it went. We argued about everything. Every venue, every arrangement. Everything from catering to clothing to wedding-day events to photographers to whether or not we would be throwing a joint engagement shower (I put my foot down with an emphatic no). There was absolutely nothing we could agree on, which was insane because none of it even mattered. I swore half the time it felt like she was arguing just for the sake of arguing. I knew I certainly was.

There was one thing I did feel strongly about, though. "I don't want my parents involved," I said.

"Do they...do they know about me?" Elizabeth asked, and I realized I hadn't informed her yet that I wasn't planning to tell them anything other than that I was getting married.

"Of course, sweetheart," I said, careful of my audience. "They're excited to meet you. I haven't told them *everything* about us. Don't worry about that." I winked and met her eyes to make sure she understood what I was saying.

She nodded once, but her brow furrowed. "And you don't want them involved."

"That's correct."

She continued staring at me, her mouth open in that cute little annoying way that said she wanted to say something, and so help me if she did, I wasn't sure what I was going to do.

"No parents. Got it." LeeAnn entered the information in her tablet.

"No, my mom will be involved," Elizabeth clarified. She opened her mouth to say more, then shut it. Then opened it again. Then shut it.

Good girl, I thought. Leave it alone.

But then she turned abruptly to me. "You really need to include your parents, Weston," she said, her lips set in a smug line that made me want to draw her across my lap and spank it off of her.

"No, actually, I don't."

"Why?" She stared at me, her blue eyes looking inside me as though she could see through my walls. As though she thought I would divulge my reasons to her here, of all places.

"It's none of—" *your business*, I started to say, but Donovan cleared his throat and I caught myself in time. "Our life is none of their business," I said, instead.

"It's their *son's wedding*. And what about your sister?"

Shit. I hadn't thought about Noelle. "We can involve my sister somehow. What can an eighteen-year-old girl do as part of the wedding?" I directed this last part to LeeAnn.

"She could greet people as they arrive, and since you've decided against a receiving line, you'll want to have a guest book. She could manage that."

"Great. Have her do that," I said.

"Awesome. Stick a teenager behind a table all night when she'd rather be mingling and dancing," Elizabeth muttered.

I glared, but otherwise ignored her. "As for my parents, they don't need to be seated at any special time, they don't need to have any special recognition, and they certainly don't need to pay for anything. And that's final." I looked over at Donovan, because he was the one person in the room who would understand.

But he didn't say anything to either back me or refute me.

"Okay, then. You heard him. He doesn't want his parents," Elizabeth said in obvious disagreement. She leaned toward our planner. "Make sure that if anyone asks, it's clear that was Weston's decision, and not mine."

God. Sometimes she was a real bitch.

A gorgeous bitch that made my pants feel too tight every time I looked at her too long, or thought about her just right, but a bitch all the same.

"At the wedding itself," the gorgeous bitch continued, "We should probably have a large family picture taken, with all the extended family. I have a cousin that would really like to be in that portrait." She looked at Donovan and me to see if we understood, and we did. She wanted to make sure that her cousin Darrell was invited to be in that photograph. That he was part of one piece of the wedding, so he would feel like the whole thing was real.

"Good idea, Elizabeth," Donovan said, and she beamed.

"We'll send him an invitation to the engagement party too, though I'm sure he won't tear himself away from work to attend." Again she sounded bitter, and this time, when the bitterness wasn't directed at me, I felt a tinge of sympathy for her. That she had to play this charade in the first place, for a piece-of-shit asshole who didn't give a damn about her personally.

Not that I was about to let her know.

"And your bridal parties? Do you have ideas of who you'd like to have in your line?" LeeAnn went on, marking each of our requests in her tablet.

"There are several people I could choose. I have some good friends from college..." Eliza-bitch chewed on her lip as she considered.

Donovan shook his head. "Make it simple. One attendant each. Don't you think?"

"Yeah, one attendant is good," I agreed. The simpler the better. Having fittings and rehearsals for something that wasn't going to last was a waste of time, not only for us, but for these friends of ours as well.

"You're right," Elizabeth said. "I'll pick my friend Melissa from college."

"If we're going with old friends, I guess that's you, Donovan," I said.

LeeAnn looked confused. "I thought you said he was your life coach?"

"Donovan is my life coach. He's Weston's best friend. He's a lot of things to a lot of different people," Elizabeth explained.

"I see," LeeAnn said, though it didn't really look like she did see.

Donovan side-eyed me. "Do you really think that I would be the best choice for planning your bachelor party? And writing the speech about true love to toast you with at your reception?"

I rubbed two fingers along my forehead. A bachelor party from Donovan actually might be fun. It would be all cigars and Scotch, but I would probably regret everything that happened afterwards. And weren't those the best kinds of nights? But any speech he wrote on true love would be so depressing half the audience would grow suicidal.

"Brett Larrabee," Donovan and I said in unison. Brett was a roommate from college, a guy I still kept up with pretty well. He was extroverted, charismatic, a good speaker, the life of most parties, and a decent friend. Most of all, he wouldn't mind being the best man for a night, even if he found out later on that the whole thing was a farce.

"I'll give him a call," I said.

"Great," LeeAnn said, relieved that at least one item had been ticked off without a fight. She had to be wondering why on Earth we were marrying at all. "We have that settled."

We managed to continue without any brawling through the

next few items, but then we got to the details of the actual ceremony and hit a doozy of a bump.

"I hate traditional vows," Elizabeth said, her jaw tight. "I do not want to read traditional vows at our wedding."

"LeeAnn just gave us seventeen different options. We don't have to use any of the ones that say 'obey and honor.' We can use one of the more modern ones. But we definitely don't need to write our own!"

Because of course she wanted us to write our own vows. For our not-real wedding. For our not-real relationship. Was the girl insane?

"It's not just that they are old-fashioned and outdated. Yes, some of them are more modern," Elizabeth flipped through the booklet of vows LeeAnn had given us to look through, "but they're just so standard. So conformist. So trite and overdone."

Fake wedding. I said it really loudly in my head, zooming it toward her, hoping that she would hear me. *Fake wedding, Elizabeth. Overdone is okay for a fake wedding.*

But apparently she didn't hear my thoughts, because she continued to speak her side. "I really think we should write our own."

I was going to murder her. I'd actually tried to get along with her for the most part. It had been hard, especially with how close she was sitting next to me. Every time she moved, her scent would drift toward me—a combination of tropical body wash and expensive perfume, a smell so purely *her* that it made me want to bury my head in her neck and breathe her in until I was high. And every time her skin brushed against mine, my dick perked up. And every time she argued, I wanted to choke her or fuck her or both.

God, I was so fucking horny and blue balled.

And I was not going to sit there and listen to her try to twist me around her pretty little finger one more goddamned minute.

"Excuse me, LeeAnn. Donovan, may I please speak to my

lovely fiancée alone for just a moment?" *So that I can wring her lovely neck.*

"Of course. Donovan, why don't you come in the other room. I can show you those examples I have of invitation vellum." She stood and he followed, giving us a warning glance before he disappeared behind the closed doors.

As soon as we were alone, Elizabeth turned to me. "It's my wedding."

"It's a *fake* wedding."

"Nobody else knows that. I'm going to be judged on this. Everyone will look at me and say, 'Elizabeth Dyson, boring, unoriginal.' I need to have original vows."

"Then we will pick the most original pre-written vows there are. But we are not writing our own. I refuse."

She drew her lips into a tight line and folded her arms across her chest, the action showcasing her tits, not that I noticed. "Why don't you want your parents involved?"

"Maybe I don't think it's fair to bring them out just so you can play fantasy wedding." Ouch. I went there.

But she didn't flinch. "That's not why. You have another reason."

"And I'm not telling you what it is."

She took a deep breath in, her breasts heaving and expanding. "Fine. I'll drop it."

"We're still not writing our own vows."

I swear she growled. My dick jumped at the sound. "This is stupid. You can't write your own vows because you can't think of something nice and genuine to say about me?"

Honestly, I could think of *a lot* of nice and genuine things to say about her. Things a man who had no real interest in a woman probably shouldn't say to that woman. Things that a woman like her might be scandalized by hearing. "No. I can't."

"You're an asshole." But she'd taken a step closer to me.

"You're a bitch." I noticed our bodies were only inches apart now, her mouth was tilted up towards mine, her eyes pinned on my lips.

And suddenly all I could think about was kissing her. I couldn't give a fuck about vows or parents or secrets or anything but finding out what her lips tasted like, what they felt like against mine. If they stayed pressed shut until I worked them open or if they eagerly parted for my tongue.

I bent closer, leaned toward her—

And suddenly the doors burst open again.

"We found your invitation material," LeeAnn said with a boastful grin. "You'll be quite pleased, it matches everything else you selected. Have you sorted out the vows?"

Elizabeth jumped back the minute we were interrupted, putting as much space between me and her as she could in as little time as she had.

"It's settled," she said, before I could even remember what the disagreement had been. "We'll do pre-written vows. A version of the traditional. Minus the honor and obey."

LeeAnn raised a brow. "Oh. So the groom won this round."

"Yeah." I glanced over at Elizabeth but she wasn't looking at me. "I guess I did."

Why then, did it feel like I'd lost?

EIGHT
ELIZABETH

"OH NO, oh no! What did you do?" Weston's anguished voice came from behind me.

It was the night of our engagement party, and we'd been bickering for weeks. Since the meeting with our wedding planner, to be precise, and *bickering* was maybe too light a word. Outright arguing might have been more like it. The only time we hadn't been arguing was that strange moment when I thought he was going to kiss me, when everything calmed down except the beat of my pulse and the flutter in my tummy, and the noise between us finally hushed.

But the moment had passed, our lips never met, and the calm turned out to be only the eye in a hurricane of constant tension.

I expected tonight to be more of the same. Luckily, I'd arrived at The Sky Launch first, having only managed to do that by telling him our meeting time was a full hour later than it was. I turned from the florist, prepared for another battle but when I caught sight of him, I nearly lost all the air in my lungs.

I'd seen pictures of him in a tux before. My Internet search had turned up quite a few of him in various versions of Armani and

Tom Ford. I couldn't say that I hadn't lingered over one or two of them. The man did photograph so well.

Turned out pictures didn't tell half the story.

His jacket was custom-fit, tightening in at his hips, making the broad stretch of his shoulders accentuate his muscles. He spun, surveying the nightclub, and I caught sight of his backside, which was equally stunning. His jacket was tailored in just the right spots and hit perfectly below his ass, hinting at the treasure underneath. He was breathtaking. When most men wore tuxedos, they blended in. Weston King wore one, and all heads turned.

Fortunately he didn't see me gawking, because he was too busy gaping at the dance floor.

I strode over to him. "Exactly what is it that I did?" Because there was no doubt in my mind it was me he was yelling at.

"The music. The jazz? The flowers. This isn't a nightclub anymore. It's like a banquet before a symphony." He turned to face me at the end of his sentence, and I didn't miss the slight look of shock when he saw me.

I stood up taller. I'd chosen a rather conservative gown for the evening—a white halter top dress that went all the way to my feet. But it was a mermaid shape that hugged every curve of my breasts and my hips. I'd watched every last gram of carbohydrates I'd put in my mouth for a week to make sure it fit me like a glove.

I knew I looked good, with my hair off my neck and my shoulders bare, but I hadn't gone extravagant. I'd left that for my mother, who would most likely be wearing glitter, decked out from head to toe. LeeAnn Gregori would be her only competition for bling queen.

But Weston looked at me like I was wearing the most beautiful gown at Bergman's—or like I was wearing nothing at all—and it made my stomach do a slow roll.

Then he shook it off. "What did you do to *my* Sky Launch?" he demanded again, even more enraged than he was a second before.

"It's an engagement party! We're not here for dancing. We're here for mingling and meeting our guests. And you said I could be in charge of the music."

"I wasn't expecting it to sound like Muzak. Plus I see we're only serving champagne? At this rate, everybody's going to be asleep."

I crossed my arms over my chest, shifting my weight to one hip. "Well then, good. Then maybe they won't realize the set for all those video files of you fucking random girls was up in those bubble rooms."

"Darlings, darlings," LeeAnn said, showing up out of what felt like nowhere. "I know that all this wedding stuff can be so tense, but you lovebirds really should kiss and make up before your guests get here, which will be any moment now. Smile. Enjoy yourselves! This is your night!"

Before either of us could react to her, she was off to attend to some other aspect of the party.

Weston opened his mouth, probably to say something else smart, when Gwen strolled up to us.

"Hello, you two," she said, a gift bag tucked under her arm. She hugged first Weston, then me, then stepped back to admire us both. "You look beautiful tonight, Elizabeth. That dress is absolutely gorgeous! You've really found yourself quite a catch, Weston."

His cheek muscle twitched, but then he gave his dazzling dimpled grin. "Didn't I?" He said it so smoothly that even I almost believed him. "I already know she's going to be the most beautiful woman in the room, and I haven't even seen any of the other guests yet."

Goddamn, he was a charmer. And if he kept looking at me the way he was now? At least people would believe he was smitten with me. I'd just have to ignore the dampness in my panties.

"He's good," Gwen said to me.

I bit back a laugh. "You have no idea."

"I hope you aren't nervous about anything," Gwen said, now in business mode. "We have everything under control. The food, of course the alcohol, the music. And I have a gift here. It's from all of us. Our manager, Alayna, wanted to wish you well in person, but she's still at home on maternity leave with the twins. I'll just set this on the gift table. Have a great night!"

She took off in the direction of the bar, which was where the gifts were being collected, and I swiveled to thank Weston for his believable performance, but when I met his gaze again his smile had disappeared, and he was back to the frown that I'd seen going on four weeks straight.

"Congratulations on one person fooled," he said, beating me to the punch. "Now, just four hundred more to go."

Yes. Four hundred more to go.

I took a deep breath, rubbed my lips together to make sure that I still had gloss on them, and turned in time to see that our first guests had been led into the club.

Fortunately it was just my mother, dressed in a bright purple gown with a slit up to her thigh and rhinestones embroidered over the net mesh that—barely—covered the skin between her breasts.

I tried not to roll my eyes. "Where's Marie?" I asked, searching over her shoulder as I hugged her.

"Parking the car. You look beautiful, baby. Everything going okay?"

Thank God. Someone I could bitch to.

I started to answer her, but just as I opened my mouth she noticed my groom-to-be.

"Weston! You're adorable." Her voice was sticky sweet, her pose suggestive with her hips sticking out.

I recognized that tone of voice. I recognized that pose.

"Mother! You're hitting on him?"

She shrugged. "You didn't tell me how good-looking he was. I'm Angela." Weston took her hand but somehow she turned the handshake into a hug—classic move of my mother's.

"He's my *fiancé*," I snarled.

She looked back at me, her eyes fluttering. "*Fake* fiancé."

"The fiancé part is very real. I *am* marrying him." I stuck my hand out with the engagement ring and wiggled it. "We are getting married, and this is my engagement party to prove it." I didn't know why it bothered me so much to see her flirting with him. It wasn't the first time my mother had flirted with a man in front of me, nor the first time my mother had flirted with one of my boyfriends. Not that Weston was my boyfriend or that our relationship was even real, but still.

My mother stepped away from the hug, but her arm remained around Weston. Her eyes grazed his backside. "The marriage will end soon enough," she said with a smile.

Weston latched his arm through hers. "It's nice to meet you, Mom."

My mother faked a shiver. "Ooo, I love the way that sounds when you say it."

"You two are the worst." I slapped Weston's arm with the back of my hand. "Keep it in your pants—both of you—during this party. And Mom, I know you can't help yourself, but please try not to be such a MILF for the next few hours, okay?"

Then with the brightest smile I'd ever put on my lips, I swiveled toward the door, ready for yet another performance at The Sky Launch. Hopefully this one would fall under the genre of art film rather than porno.

For the next while, I discovered it wasn't too hard to feign enthusiasm for my betrothed. Most of the initial guests were people that I knew quite well—my friends, my bridesmaid, people I'd gone to high school with. Even though I had to pretend that I was madly in love with Weston, their energy and excitement was easy to act off of, and both of us could make it a game. There were too many people to spend much quality time with any one person, but good conversations were had and it was entertaining to try to embarrass

Weston in front of his work associates. Of course the payback was him trying to embarrass me in front of my friends.

Despite the underlying current of friction between me and my betrothed, the party was going quite well.

Until his parents arrived.

I'd wanted to meet them, especially since finding out Weston wasn't letting them in on the truth behind our relationship. I'd tried more than once to ask why he wouldn't be honest with them, but each time he'd been just as elusive as he'd been in front of our wedding planner. His secrecy only made me more intrigued.

"Weston!" his mother exclaimed. "And you must be Elizabeth!"

I put my hand out to shake hers.

She frowned and pulled me into a hug. "We're going to be family. No handshakes for us."

Her voice was sweet, her perfume light and lavender. She was pretty, but her makeup was age-appropriate—*mother* appropriate—her clothes as well—a long mauve gown with a beaded jacket. Her hair was coiffed perfectly, and her French manicured nails were filed to a reasonable length. Her blond hair and blue eyes matched her son's, and even though I was sure she had a dye job—it was unlikely she'd reached her age without any gray hairs—it still looked natural. Unlike my mother, whose platinum locks definitely came from a bottle.

She seemed warm, put together, and genuine. For some reason, maybe because of Weston's insistence to not include her in the wedding, I'd expected she'd be terrible.

It was nice to be surprised. "It's wonderful to finally meet you, Mrs. King."

"It's Maggie, please." She even had a nice laugh. A polite one that didn't sound gregarious or overbearing.

Maggie turned to hug her son, who let her begrudgingly, so I swiveled toward Nash King. While I could see that Weston took mostly after his mother, there were some characteristics that he shared with his father. The dimple, for instance. Both of them had that crazy dimple. He also wore a tuxedo well. Not Weston Kingwell, but better than most.

"Dad, this is Elizabeth, obviously," Weston said without a lot of emotion, and it was Nash's turn to pull me into his arms and embrace me in a welcome hug.

"I'm delighted to meet you. Weston hasn't told us much about you, but from what we've heard, you seem like the right person for him. We've always wanted more children. And I look forward to having another daughter. I hope you'll call me Dad."

My gut dropped. I hadn't considered what it would mean to play this charade for Weston's parents. What fooling them would feel like. It was one thing to fool acquaintances and associates. Quite another to be welcomed into his family. To be invited to call his father my own.

I hadn't been prepared for that.

My throat was suddenly tight, and I was grateful that Weston was there to interrupt so I didn't have to say anything.

He slipped his hand around my waist, his touch sending an unexpected shock through my body, and pulled me to him. Putting on the act. "Don't get all clingy on day one, Dad. She's mine, not yours."

Somehow, despite the dizzying effect of his proximity, his words didn't make me feel any better. Because I *wasn't* his. And that was sort of the whole problem.

Nash put his hands in his tux pockets, looking so much like his son in the manner if not in his physical characteristics. "We'd just be happy if you shared her a little, son. Bring her by for dinner sometime."

"We'd love to!" I answered, caught up in the need to feel at ease about the situation with them in whatever way possible.

However, my fiancé responded at the same time. "We'll pass."

"Weston," I chided, sure that he was kidding. But one look at his tense jaw and stiff shoulders said that he was absolutely serious. "Surely we can make time for one meal..."

"Please do!" Maggie's smile had slipped, her eyes bright with hope.

"We can't," her son insisted, ending the conversation.

I bit back the desire to argue further, though inside, a funnel cloud of rage was stirring. "I'm sorry," I said, trying to smooth things over with the Kings. "We're just so busy between now and the wedding. I'm sure Weston has a better memory for our calendar than I do."

"It's not a calendar issue," Weston said.

My face went hot. "I'm so sorry..." I trailed off, not knowing how else to make excuses for my groom-to-be.

"Don't worry about it, honey," Maggie said, clearly hurt. "We aren't new to his life. We were hoping you'd make things better, but I see that's not how things are going to be."

Make things better? What things? How could Weston have a bad relationship with these people who obviously cared very much about him?

Whatever the problems were between them, Weston seemed to think we'd engaged enough for the evening. "Thanks for coming, Mom and Dad. We have to see to our other guests." With his hand still at my waist, he steered me away from them and into the crowd.

"What the hell was that?" I hissed so only he could hear.

"I don't know what you're talking about."

"You know exactly what I'm talking about. Your parents were nice and warm and caring." I was so frustrated and worked up that I was having trouble getting words out. "And you were so...mean! You should be respectful. A fiancé of mine would be respectful."

How could he be like that? Did he have parental baggage of some kind? Did his dad work too hard? Not pay enough attention to him? His dad was *here*. Whatever he thought his folks had done, he couldn't possibly understand what real parental baggage was.

Weston stopped and turned to look at me, his eyes harder than I'd ever seen them. "You know what? You don't know the first thing about it. I give respect to those who deserve it. I've known them my whole life. You've known them for five minutes. Grow up."

I felt like I'd been slapped. My eyes stung and my face burned, and the worst part was that I'd deserved it. Everything he'd said was true. I was in the dark on this subject, but only because Weston had left me there.

Maybe that's what hurt most—that he didn't *want* to let me in.

And wasn't that a dick move to keep it from me and then get angry when I didn't understand? He knew how important this union was, what the stakes were. How believable was it for a bride to not know much about the relationship of her husband-to-be and his own parents?

"You're right," I said, thrusting my chin forward. "I don't know the first thing about it. Because you've been too much of an asshole to *tell me*."

His eyes sparked and he began to say something in response, probably the kind of thing that shouldn't be said in the middle of our engagement party, but before he got the words out, someone nearby sang out our names. "Weston, Elizabeth. The stars of the show."

We turned to see Donovan with a woman I didn't know.

Without missing a beat, Weston slipped his arm in mine and directed us toward them, likely eager to escape the heated conversation. A smart decision, while admittedly unfulfilling.

Once again, I put on my smile.

"Elizabeth, you know Donovan," Weston said, sarcastically. "And this is Sabrina Lind, our new Director of Marketing Strategy."

"Delightful to meet you. It's so fascinating to see how my love —" as I spoke, Weston glanced covertly around us, and when he seemed to be satisfied with what he saw, he cut me off.

"No one's watching. And Sabrina knows."

"Oh thank God." I dropped Weston's arm with a huge sigh of relief. "If I have to gush about him a minute longer I might have to throw up."

Donovan flashed a sly grin in my direction. "Elizabeth, I think you and I might get along better than I once thought."

Even among people who were part of the farce, the tension between Weston and me felt thick and taut, and I desperately needed a reprieve.

I cozied up beside Donovan, hoping he might be a balm. "I told you, Kincaid, this deal was really better suited for you and me. I can't believe you turned down the offer."

Not that I really wanted to marry the man. He was too ambitious for my taste. Even for a fictional marriage.

I shared a smile with Donovan then turned my eyes to Sabrina. She was pretty. Prettier than pretty—she was probably the most attractive woman in the room with her dark hair and dark eyes and legs that went for miles. And she had a respectable position at Reach. All that beauty plus brains too. Good for her.

Good for *Donovan*.

"You were up for the nomination of groom?" she asked cautiously.

"No one would ever believe I'd get married," Donovan said dismissively. "Besides, Weston looks much better on Elizabeth's arm."

I didn't miss Weston shooting daggers in Donovan's direction.

And I absolutely didn't miss Weston saying, "Sabrina, you're absolutely stunning."

She thanked him, and I felt my insides ruffle. "She is gorgeous, Kincaid," I said, subtly reminding Weston that this woman belonged to someone else. "You make quite an attractive couple."

"We're not a couple," Sabrina said at the same time that Weston said, "They're not a couple."

And then I realized.

My insides sank like an elevator with the cable cut, but somehow I managed to keep my voice from shaking as I asked Donovan, "You're here alone?"

"I'm not," he said.

But he wasn't here with Sabrina. And Sabrina knew about our sham, which meant...

"Sabrina is from Weston's stable," Donovan said, and now my suspicions were confirmed.

"You are a fucking asshole." Weston scowled.

"Ah." Jealousy spiked through my veins with the sharp sting of everclear in the punch at prom. "Recent?"

"The most recent, I believe," Donovan said, trying to be helpful, or stir the shit—the latter was more likely. "Last girl he spent any significant time with before you, anyway."

Sabrina's face went red, a mixture of anger and embarrassment, if I had to guess. It was the color that I felt, even though I was pretty confident I'd managed to keep it from showing on my skin.

And who else knew about her? Was I the laughingstock of the town right now? Letting my groom parade his ex-girlfriend under my nose.

The way they kept exchanging glances, I couldn't actually be sure she was an ex.

"Huh. I might want in on that pool after all," I said, spitefully. "What were the terms?"

Weston ran a hand through his hair, which made him look ridiculously sexy. "For fuck's sake, I'm not going to fuck around."

I wanted to trust him, but the compliment he'd given her, the fact she worked in his office, the way they kept looking at each other... The scale was tilting against him.

I winked at Donovan. "We'll talk later."

"Fuck off," Weston muttered in Donovan's direction. He scanned the room again. "People are watching us. Better play cozy."

He took my hand without looking at me, and the lie of his fingers in mine burned my skin. Because he'd probably rather be holding hers.

"Is it you who wants to fuck around?" he asked suddenly. "Is that why you keep bringing up concerns about me?"

I rolled my eyes, hoping to hide my stupid confusing emotions. "It was just a joke. You're so sensitive about everything I say."

"Everything you say is a criticism."

"Everything you do is stupid." Good one, Elizabeth.

He swung his head toward me. "Anyone told you lately you're a bitch?"

God I wanted to claw his eyes out, stomp on his feet, and then grab him by the lapels and kiss him hard.

What the fuck was wrong with me?

"Not since the last time you told me, which was, I think, oh, twenty minutes ago."

From a few feet away, I heard an older gentleman exclaim, "There's the happy couple!"

"That's us," I said with a big grin, looking over to see who was calling us. "Mr. Jennings!" The loan officer from my mother's bank. If he pinched my cheeks like he usually did, I was going to have to dig my fingernails into Weston's arm so that I didn't reflexively punch him.

At least I wouldn't have to worry about Weston checking out his cleavage.

After visiting with Mr. Jennings, Weston and I did another round of the room to make sure we'd seen everyone, which proved to be a true test of our acting skills. By then, I was tired and miserable, my feet and my spirit hurt. The contention between Weston and me was worse than ever, but I didn't have any energy left to give to our arguing.

Finally, after what seemed like decades, it was time for us to wrap things up and make our formal speech. I'd volunteered to be the one who spoke, not trusting that Weston's remarks would be either on point or appropriate.

I took my place at the microphone and welcomed all our guests once again. "It's so lovely to have all of you here to celebrate Weston and me, and our future together. There isn't anything we'd like more than to share our happiness with those that we hold most dear, and that's all of you." Even though I could only name a third of the people in the room. "Please make sure to finish off the hors d'oeuvres and the champagne; there's plenty to go around and we're not taking any home with us."

There was the expected round of applause and cheering.

And then it happened. The thing I should have been prepared for. Why hadn't I been prepared? Someone—was that Nate Sinclair?—heckled us to kiss.

Then it was several people heckling for us to kiss. "Kiss her," came from Weston's assistant, Roxie, clear as day.

And my bridesmaid, Melissa, "We want to see you kiss!"

Soon it was the whole dance floor cheering in unison, "Kiss, kiss, kiss, kiss."

Weston, better at improv than I—or at least this kind of improv—already had his hand at the small of my back, drawing me to him, away from the microphones. "I guess we better give them what they want."

Hell, it was only a kiss. With someone I was truly beginning to think I might hate. Why did I suddenly feel so nervous? So terrified? So absolutely weak in the knees?

"We should have practiced this," I whispered. My belly fluttered as I met his blue, blue eyes.

He dimpled, leaning closer. "Just let me lead, for once."

I parted my lips, my tongue running nervously around them before his mouth brushed softly against mine, testing me. Tasting me. Then, when I tilted my chin up for more, his lips pressed firmly and eagerly, sending heat through my body like a fever, unraveling the knots of tension in my shoulders and back and winding a different kind of tension in the pit of my belly.

I threw my arms around his neck, without even thinking as I did. Thank God he was holding me, because I wouldn't have been able to keep standing on my own, the way that his kiss spread through my body. I could feel it everywhere. In my toes. My knees. In my belly button. I felt it at the bottom of my spine and behind my eyelids, which were closed, and underneath my toes. I felt it in my mouth. In the places where his tongue searched and explored, and I for sure felt it in the deepest core of me, spiking arousal that I hadn't felt in—well, maybe ever.

It was just a kiss and I felt like he was undressing me. Just a kiss, and I felt like he was discovering things about me that I didn't even know about myself. Just a kiss, and I never wanted him to stop kissing me.

Then the kiss was over, and I was out of breath and dazed, confused by the applause.

"You okay?" Weston asked, quietly. Smugly.

I was still clutching him, and I let go quickly, then pretended that I'd done it just to straighten my dress. "I'm fine."

I spun toward our audience and smiled once again. They clapped some more, and as soon as possible, I made an excuse and escaped to the restroom.

Alone outside the ladies' room, I put a hand to my chest and attempted to get control of my breathing. I was a wreck from that crazy, incredible moment. From the dizzying lust that Weston sent spiraling in me with just a simple kiss. And also from the herd of other emotions taking residence inside. Hurt by the secrets Weston had chosen to keep from me. Anger because they threatened my whole end goal. Shame for what these lies did to his family. The sharp prongs of jealousy for a woman I'd just met because she probably knew more about the man I was going to marry than I did. Confusion because all of these feelings wrapped around a guy who wasn't supposed to be anything but a stepping stone to what was next. Inferior because...well, I didn't even know how to pinpoint the source of that particular feeling.

And then that kiss...

SHAKING MY HEAD, I slipped into the restroom to fix my lipstick and freshen up. In front of the mirror I reminded myself that tonight wasn't about Weston. It was about me. It was about me moving in the right direction, toward the target—Dyson Media. The party had gone practically flawlessly, in that regard. We'd sold ourselves as a couple, and I needed to feel good about that.

I did feel good about it. Really good.

Feeling confident after my mental pep talk, I came back out of the restroom to find someone else in the hall. Someone whom I'd invited, but hadn't expected to show up.

"Darrell," I exclaimed. My heart rate sped up again, and this time it wasn't because of Weston or because of kisses that had knocked the wind out of me, but because the person who could ruin my whole scheme was standing in front of me. "I didn't know you were coming. I'm so glad to see you." I stepped forward to give him a kiss on the cheek.

He took it brusquely, then looked me over. "I wouldn't have missed this for the world." He straightened his tie and brushed a wisp of orange hair out of his face.

"Did you just get here? I should introduce you to Weston." I was talking too fast, eager to make sure he saw everything he needed to validate my betrothal as real.

He shook his head. "No need. I've been here for a bit. Saw that speech and kiss of yours." He paused, studying me. "That's some act you have going on there."

"Act? I don't know what you're talking about." How could he know? *How could he know?* We'd been careful in our setup, spending time together, being seen. We'd been attached to each other all night. Our chemistry was good.

"You and the King boy. You think I'm going to buy that you're suddenly engaged to such a perfect candidate for husband? Of course I was going to come and check this whole thing out. The relationship screams sham, and I intend to prove it. It shouldn't be too hard. You're not capable of pulling off a scheme like this."

"That's ridiculous," I said, breathlessly. "We're in love." It sounded so weak, so trite.

"Right," Darrell sneered. "Love. I bet you think that YouTube footage proves it too."

He'd seen the video. My face went red with shame. Well, wasn't that what I'd wanted?

But then it hadn't been what I'd wanted, and by then it had been too late.

Darrell snickered. "That video does prove one thing: how slutty you are. Your mother spread her legs for money too, and how did that work out? She didn't end up with anything except a measly trust fund. And that's what I'll make sure you get too because you're *not* getting your hands on my company."

And the feeling that I'd had, the feeling that, just maybe, Weston and I could survive this crazy scheme after all, it left with a whoosh.

As I watched Darrell stalk back down the hall, unable to think of a parting shot to offer, I realized he was right about one thing—I had no idea in hell what I was doing.

NINE
WESTON

THAT KISS.

God, that kiss.

It was Monday, two days after the engagement party and all I could think about was that goddamned kiss. My balls ached from it. My stomach twisted inside from it. It kept me up nights, kept me distracted through work all morning, made my dick sore from all the jerking off I'd done in the shower, and *still* it wouldn't leave my mind.

And it was stupid, because I really was starting to think I might hate the girl—the girl being my fiancée, of course.

By the end of Monday I'd thought about her so much—thought about wringing her neck while I led the weekly executive meeting, thought about scratching her up while I walked Sabrina through her new duties, thought about spanking her ass while Donovan gave me the rundown on the latest financial goals—that I'd even put Elizabeth's picture on my dartboard and thrown darts at her. Then I'd felt so guilty about marring her gorgeous face, I'd immediately printed another and slapped it over the autographed copy of

Watchmen that I had in a frame on my shelf. A guy should have a pic of his bride-to-be on his desk, right?

So now I had to hate her and stare at her and fight my dick for having a mind of its own for the better part of the afternoon.

She was driving me insane.

I had to remember why I was in this predicament in the first place, why I was still participating in this stupid farce. There were a million and one reasons why I should just quit the whole thing and walk away.

But there were also reasons why I shouldn't. Good reasons.

I'd told Elizabeth I would help her, for one. And I'd told Donovan. And also because of the money. Mostly, of course, it was the money. I didn't know why I listed that last.

And to remind myself further, I decided to make a phone call that I normally made monthly but had neglected the last couple of months in all the Eliza-bitch hubbub. I sat back in my chair and dialed the number that I knew by heart.

When the female voice answered, an easy smile spread over my lips. "Hello, Mrs. Clemmons, it's me. Weston."

"Weston, it's so good to hear from you. It seems like it's been ages. How are you? And you know I told you to call me Nicole." She was always cheery, no matter what time of day I caught her, no matter what the circumstances were in her life. But there was no way I was ever calling her Nicole. I'd known her and her husband since I was five years old. Remembered climbing onto her lap at company picnics. Her twins were the age of Noelle, my little sister.

"I'm good, I'm good. How are you, though? Did you get my latest check?" I hated always bringing it back to the money, but it was the reason I was calling. The reason I always called.

"Yes. Thank you. I did. I can't tell you enough how much I appreciate it."

I ran a hand through my hair. "Good. I'm glad. I wish I could do more. And how are the twins?"

"Well, some days are better than others. Eva is trying a job outside the home now with this great program that works with autistic kids. Zach, though..." She trailed off, and I understood. Zach would probably never be able to work in the traditional sense. His outbursts and tantrums hadn't been managed, and his speaking skills were still at an elementary school level.

"I understand. You're still getting good home help though, right? Because if you're not, I will—"

She cut me off. "Our help is fine. The money you send is perfect. It covers everything we need. It really is more than enough, Weston."

"Good." I sounded like a broken record, I'd said that over and over again. *Good. Good.* What else was there to say?

A beat went by.

Then I asked the question I hated asking the most. "And how's Daniel?"

She sighed, but when she spoke she sounded bright. "He only has thirteen more months on his sentence. And the lawyer says he might be able to get parole soon. So we're looking forward to that."

My door opened, and I looked up with a scowl. I'd had it closed for a reason. Nate walked in, and he didn't know anything about this phone call, which meant I needed to wrap it up. "Well, that's great. I hope that goes well. Just let me know if you need anything on that front. I'm happy to help out."

"I will."

"Great, then. I'll be talking to you later. Have a great night." With my vocabulary of adjectives reduced to the word *great*, I got off the line so fast I barely heard her say goodbye. Which made me feel guilty—more guilty than I already felt—but I wasn't about to entertain questions from Nathan, and if I'd stayed on the phone with her much longer I was certain to face interrogation.

As it was, Nate was eying me. He'd slumped in the seat opposite my desk, an ankle crossed over the other leg at the knee, and laced his hands behind his head. I waited a few nervous seconds while he stared at me then remembered that I had a bone to pick with him.

"You're the one who started the kiss chant at the party on Saturday night, aren't you." I didn't put a question into my accusation.

His grin gave him away. "And that was some solid entertainment. Thank you, Weston."

"You're a giant fuckwaffle."

"Damn," Nate said in awe. "Fuckwaffle is usually reserved for people who really offend you. I'm surprised. If the tables had been turned, you would have been catcalling *me* to kiss Elizabeth."

I frowned for a number of reasons, not the least of which was that the tables never would have been turned, because Nate had absolutely refused to put himself in this position. Also, the idea of him kissing Elizabeth made me want to vomit and punch him all at once.

But he was right—under different circumstances, I would have been the guy in the crowd stirring the shit.

Just.

That kiss.

"It wasn't cool," I said. "You know the circumstances. A lot is riding on this, and it was bullshit to put us on the spot like that. This isn't a fucking game."

Nate barely blinked. "You're in a foul mood. What broomstick is up your ass?"

The broomstick of a very feisty red-headed witch, that was what.

I stood up from my seat, walked over to my printer to get the Opportunity Analysis I'd printed earlier, and forced myself to pull my shit together. There was an opportunity here, somewhere, I had to remember that. Had to hold onto it. With that in mind, I took a deep breath that did nothing to calm me down, walked back over to my desk, and threw the document down without sitting myself. "I'm under a lot of pressure, okay?"

"Or, rather, you're *filled* with a lot of pressure. You need to get laid."

I leaned a palm on the desk and glared at him. "What makes you think that I haven't?" Fuck him for even thinking he knew anything about it. Even if he was right, he was only guessing. "I know you guys have a pool and everything, but how are you going to know if you win?"

"Oh, we'll know," Nate said, laughing. "But seriously, what's your damage?"

I rolled my eyes and sat back down in my chair. "Your vernacular is dating you." Sometimes it was hard to remember that Nate was fourteen years older than me. He was just so cool most of the time. Then he went and said something like that, something that came right out of the eighties.

But while he was here, and since he was so cool, I actually would be dumb not to take him up on some advice.

I placed my other palm on the desk so I was leaning evenly on both hands. "You want to know what my deal is? Here's my deal. I'm engaged to a woman I don't like. Can't even be in the same room with her without getting into an argument. And what's more, I'm stuck with her for the next several months. But the worst part, the abso-fucking-lutely worst part, is that despite how much I can barely stand her, and how much she's taking up all my time with this wedding planning and this fiancé shit, and how much she's messing with my head, and getting into my business, I still want to rip off her clothes and give her the best orgasms of her life. Like how can she be so insanely attractive and a total bitch all at once? I can't even figure it out."

Nate nodded, taking everything in. "That doesn't really sound like a bad problem to have."

"What the fuck are you talking about? It's the worst problem of my life!" Okay, I'd lived a privileged life. "Even with the help of porn, I have blue balls every single minute of the day. How the hell am I supposed to get her out of my head?"

Nate put his hands out in the air like the answer was obvious. "Simple. You fuck her and get it over with."

I threw my head back. "Did you miss the part where I said I hate her?"

"So hate-fuck her. Your cock will be happy."

I shook my head. Nate obviously didn't understand, which was weird, because he was a god with these things. Didn't he have the answer to every sexual problem? "I can't fuck her."

"Why?"

"Because—" I trailed off, not quite remembering why I couldn't, besides my personal feelings toward her. "Because Donovan said I couldn't."

Nate laughed. "Oh, well then. If Daddy said you can't."

"Shut up." But now I was really wondering... Why couldn't I fuck her?

Oh yeah. The part that came after. "Because I still have to be engaged to her for several months. See the problem?"

Nate raised an eyebrow. "Have you *never* seen a girl again after you slept with her?"

"Of course I have." I couldn't think of a single one that I'd seen on purpose, but whatever. Then I straightened and pointed at him excitedly. "Sabrina! I've seen Sabrina! I even *work* with her."

"So what's the problem? And you're so confused about why you'd want to give a qualified woman *that you slept with* a job, that you've decided you must want to have some sort of relationship with her in the future. Have you ever banged a woman and not been weird about it after? Do you not know how to do casual sex?"

"Never mind," I growled. "Forget I brought it up. What did you come in here for, anyway?"

"There's a showing tonight at a gallery I used to deal with.

Want to come? I know women are off-limits to touch, but you could always...watch."

Shit. Watching Nate in action was a dream come true.

Strangely, I wasn't as disappointed as I thought I might be to have to turn him down. "Wish I could, man." I checked the clock on my computer. I had to get going. "But Elizabeth wants to have dinner to discuss our current living arrangements."

Nate's eyes rolled. "Sounds like a fun time. Sad I'll miss it."

"You should take Donovan. Or—better yet—Sabrina, who I am *not* confused about, asswipe. She's new here. Someone should entertain her." She'd only been in town a week, and I knew I should feel guilty for throwing her into the city without being available to guide her around.

"I can't ask either of them," Nate said as we stood up together. "They're having dinner."

"Ah," I said, only half listening. We headed out of my office where I paused to hit the lights and lock the door behind me. "Wait. They're having dinner *together*?"

"It seems so."

"Huh." I took off toward the elevators, wondering if I should be jealous. Though Nate couldn't understand, Sabrina was the girl I was planning to actually have a relationship with later, after all. Probably. Maybe.

But of course I shouldn't be jealous. Donovan knew my plans, and he'd known Sabrina from Harvard as well. He was likely being a good friend to both of us by taking her out when I couldn't.

Besides, I couldn't really muster up any animosity toward Donovan. I was too plagued with animosity toward Elizabeth. Just like how I couldn't muster lustful thoughts for Sabrina lately because I was too consumed by lust for my fiancée.

I'd let Elizabeth think otherwise at the engagement party, of course. Just to piss her off. Sometimes it was too easy.

Unfortunately, where Elizabeth Dyson was concerned, I was beginning to find that I was even easier.

"NOPE. NO WAY. NOT HAPPENING." I was trying to make it clear that there was no way in hell I was moving out of my apartment.

Elizabeth's eyelid twitched. "It's only for the rest of our engagement. I'm not asking you to give it up permanently."

"I don't care. I'm not moving my stuff. I'm not living in your West Side overpriced snobby-ass apartment. I'm not doing it."

"What do you have against the West Side?" she hissed in a quieter voice as a waiter walked by, in case somebody might overhear us.

"Well, for one thing, it's twice as far from the office as my place. That's a lot of time I would waste every morning on unnecessary travel. You don't work, so you don't understand. That's not something you have to worry about."

"But that's not the Upper West Side's fault. And don't say that I don't work with that snide tone of yours." The corners of her mouth turned down like she was offended, hurt even. "It's not like I do nothing with my days. I'm studying. Working on all the information you give me to learn."

"And you can learn just as easily in my place." Not that I wanted a woman living in my apartment either. Though the idea of having her there, in my space, somehow didn't bother me as much as I thought it might. She'd take the extra bedroom, of course, but just having her close by...

"Your place is probably a pigsty." She raised her voice just enough, causing a nearby patron to look over at us.

"No, it's not." For the record, it's really not. Totally not a pigsty. I just didn't spend the money on those fancy maids like Miss

Moneybags did. I cleaned the old-fashioned way—with my own two hands. When I got around to it, that was.

"I don't know why you thought we would ever agree on any of this." I took a swig of my beer. "We couldn't even agree on what appetizers to order."

She shook her head and chewed her lip. I'd watched many other women do that in my day—come on, it was one of the sexiest things women could do. But the way Elizabeth chewed on her lip was unique. She pulled her bottom lip to the side so it puckered out, like a sideways fish-face. It was actually kind of funny-looking, and not exactly attractive, and yet whenever she did it, my dick leapt like a dog at a bone. I wanted to bite her lip for her. Wanted to tug her into my lap and gnaw on her like a puppy.

She was a witch, I tell you. A witch.

"I was afraid of this, so I came prepared. We're going to have to make a schedule, and that's all there is to it." She reached into her purse and pulled out a notepad and a pen. It was somehow charming that she had both in this day and age of electronics. She'd clearly carried them since way before we started our lessons at The Sky Launch, and I knew it, but I never failed to be charmed by it.

"What do you mean when you say schedule?" I asked suspiciously, rubbing the back of my neck with my hand. I didn't like schedules. I barely liked the schedule that I kept for myself.

"Look," she said, meeting my eyes, and I had to take a moment to catch my breath. Every time I met her startling blues, I found they had that effect on me. "Darrell was very serious when he told me that he's going to do everything he can to rip us apart. We *have* to make it look like we're a real couple. In real life, a modern couple would be living together in some shape or form at this point in time in their engagement. If we're not going to agree to live in one place, we've got to be sharing both of our apartments. Going back and forth. You know, make it look like we're spending time together. Like we're..."

"Like we're fucking each other on a regular basis," I said and immediately regretted it. Just letting my mind go there for even half a second gave me a semi.

"Yes, that."

I was beginning to see her plan. "So you're saying we need to start sleeping at each other's houses. All right. I got it now." I thought about it for a minute. That couldn't be so bad, could it? Move a few essentials over to her place, make sure to only be there on the weekends so the travel wasn't too far to work. Have her near me so much more of the time than I already do... Have that much more temptation...

Yeah, what could go wrong?

"Fine. I want to be at my place as much as possible during the week. I'll clear out the guest room for you and give you a key. I'm guessing you'll do the same for me?"

"I'll email you a schedule then. Don't bring over too much at once or it will look obvious." She jotted down the notes that I'd given her. I watched her pretty cursive handwriting. *His place on weekdays. Exchange keys. Clear out guestroom. Hire him a maid.*

"Hey, you don't need to be hiring me—"

"If I have to live there, there *is* going to be a maid."

I leaned forward. "The thing is, sweetheart, you don't have to live there. So there will not be a maid." I held her stare, but I realized now that she was bent forward too, and that it would only take just a little bit more movement on either of our parts for our lips to meet, and suddenly all I was thinking about was that damn fucking kiss again.

Shit, she was in my head. She was under my skin. She was about to be in my apartment. The one place she wasn't was in my pants, and I was beginning to really wish otherwise.

The stare-off was some sort of game of chicken, and I should have been the one to lose because of the way she was making me feel—all twisted inside—but somehow she was the one who backed down.

"Fine." She crossed *hire him a maid* off her notepad.

When she looked up again, she didn't look quite at me, but straight past. Her eyes narrowed and then widened in surprise.

"Clarence?" she asked after a minute.

I frowned in confusion and then followed her gaze to find she was looking at some guy behind me.

She stood up out of her chair and said it again. "Clarence. It *is* you!"

One of the guys at the next table got up and came over to us. "Elizabeth Dyson. How are you? You look great."

He hugged her and my entire body went stiff. Who was this freaking dude? My eyes darted from him to her with eager curiosity. The funny thing was, the Clarence dude looked familiar, but I couldn't quite place him.

Their embrace ended, and he stood back, but not back far enough for my taste. Only far enough so that he could look her over again. Slowly, this time.

I recognized that look. The one that was already eating her up, undressing her with his eyes, mentally dragging her off to the bedroom—

I stood up so quickly that my chair shook and almost toppled over. "Hi," I said, my hand outstretched so he was forced to shake it, making him move away from Elizabeth. "I'm Weston. Have we met?"

The Clarence guy looked quizzically at Elizabeth—my fiancée—then back to me. "I don't think so. Clarence Sheridan." He shook my hand, but there still wasn't enough distance between him and my girl for my comfort.

My *fake* girl, I reminded myself, but my inner caveman didn't hear any distinction.

When I was done shaking Clarence's hand, I put my arm

around Elizabeth, drawing her next to me. She gasped quietly as I did, but her body was pliable, and she melted into the curve of my arm easily enough.

"Sheridan," I asked. "Any relation to Theodore?" I'd gone to school with a Theodore. That was who this guy looked like.

"He's my older brother. How do you know him?" he asked, almost suspiciously.

"We went to Harvard together. Small world." I turned to Elizabeth. "Honey, have you told me about Clarence? I don't remember you mentioning him. At all." God, I was such a dick.

"It was so long ago, Weston. Clarence and I went to high school together. We haven't seen each other in years." She looked flustered.

Suddenly, all I could think about was whether or not she'd fucked him.

"You're going to invite him, aren't you, honey?" I poured on the honey, extra thick, and pulled her closer to me, possessively. "To the *wedding*?" Yeah, I emphasized the word *wedding*. Because she was mine, not his.

Well, she wasn't his.

Her cheeks burned.

"Wedding?" Clarence said, catching on. "You two are getting married. That's great! Congratulations."

"Yes! Married. That's right," she said, as though she'd just remembered, and by God I wanted to spank her so she'd never forget again. Or kiss her. Or both.

"Yes, of course. If you want to come to my wedding, that is," she stammered. She'd totally fucked him.

Did she want to fuck him again?

My ribs ached with the question.

"I wouldn't miss your wedding for the world," the douchebag said. Douchebag was a more fitting name than Clarence, I'd decided.

"Oh," Elizabeth sounded surprised. And a little disappointed. "I guess I should get your current address." She looked toward the table. Then at me, her eyes blinking as if she'd forgotten I was there. "Sweetheart, can you hand me my purse so I can get Clarence's phone number?"

No fucking way I was letting her get his number. I pulled out my phone from my pocket, sure to keep my other arm still around Elizabeth. "Here. You can put your digits in here." I handed my cell over.

While Douchebag was putting his numbers in, Elizabeth jabbed me with her elbow and sent darts at me with her eyes.

She could send darts all she wanted. I was the one who fucking taught her how to shoot darts in the first place. And no fiancée of mine was going to have some other dude's number in her phone. Not some dude that she used to fuck, anyway.

When the asshole was done, he handed the phone back to me, and I put it in my pocket. "Got it. We'll send you an invite. It will be great to have you there. Now if you'll excuse us, our food is getting cold."

Elizabeth jabbed me again. I'd have a bruise in my side from all her jabbing, but it would be worth it.

"Of course. Sorry to interrupt. But when I saw Elizabeth, I had to come over and say hi. Hey, I texted myself, so I've got your number now, too." Douchebag grinned at me, smug. Then again at her—but if I were giving an objective, very non-gay evaluation, I'd have to say he did not have a smile anywhere near as stirring as mine. He leaned in to hug her again or kiss her cheek or something intimate, which was awkward since I was still holding on to her tightly, but somehow they managed a half-embrace thing, and then he went on his way. Finally. Thank God.

As soon as he was seated again, only a table away from us, Elizabeth turned to me with her full wrath. Some dark little part of me was starting to really enjoy her anger. It was the only time she ever let herself get passionate, since our night in the bubble room.

"What the fuck was that?" she hissed.

"I was just playing the part," I said. "And be careful, he's not very far away. We need to *keep* playing the part, don't you think?"

I pulled her seat out for her, and this time when I sat down, I scooted close to her and dropped my arm along the back of her chair. Then, not feeling it was enough, I let my hand slide down to her shoulder.

"What are you doing?" she asked. As if it wasn't obvious.

"I already told you. Playing the part. He's going to keep looking at you. Ex-boyfriends tend to look at their ex-girlfriends a lot." I snuck a glance at Douchebag myself, and sure enough, he was peeking over at us.

"How do you even know he's my ex?"

"Oh, it's quite clear. And if you don't want him to know what's up—"

"Do you really think it matters if an ex is in the know? It seems you don't, since Sabrina is in on it."

Sabrina? Sabrina only knew because I hadn't wanted her to have a wrong idea when she'd taken the job. And because Donovan had told her.

But for some reason I didn't want to explain that to Elizabeth. Maybe because I liked the way she was so worked up about Sabrina. Because it was kind of cute. Kind of sweet. Kind of gave me an upper hand. Made me a little less upset about Douchebag.

"Sabrina is another story," I said, brushing her off. My fingers grazed against the bare skin at her neck, and maybe it was accidental the first time, but her flesh felt so warm and silky, I couldn't stop my fingers from running back and forth, over and over again.

She swallowed, her eyes down, but I didn't have to wonder if she was reacting to my touch, because goosebumps sprouted down her arms.

Still, her next words came out cold and tight. "If you get to make decisions about the people close to you who know the truth, then I get to make the same decisions about the people close to me." She turned her eyes up at me, shocking my fingers still with her piercing stare. "And that means ex-boyfriends. That means Clarence. If I want Clarence to know that this isn't real, that's my call. Not yours."

We didn't say anything more, just ate in silence.

But I kept my arm where it was, kept my fingers rubbing her skin, her satiny-smooth skin, and I was left again to wonder which version of Elizabeth was real—the one who snapped at me and wanted to reserve Douchebag for when we were over?

Or the one who shivered, leaned in close, and reacted like crazy to my touch?

TEN
ELIZABETH

"DON'T THROW AWAY the pad thai," Weston said from behind me.

I peered over my shoulder at him, surprised I hadn't heard him come in, before going back to the takeout. I opened the container and sniffed at the ingredients, making a face at the awful stench before throwing it in the trash. "It's three days old," I told him.

I walked over to the sink and washed my hands, noting the time on the microwave clock. It was 9:00 p.m., and Weston was coming home late for the second night in a row.

He squeezed by me to open the refrigerator door, and I tried to ignore his eyes on me in my short nightgown. We'd been living together for a month, and goosebumps still sprouted on my skin whenever his gaze traveled down my body.

"You threw out the Chinese too?" he asked, obviously irritated.

"It was even older." I flicked the water droplets off my fingers into the sink, then grabbed the washrag to scrub at the stain that I'd just spotted on the counter.

"Jesus, there's nothing in here but your stuff. Yogurt, fruit.

Hummus. What am I supposed to eat?" I heard the clank of a beer bottle, then the shutting of the door.

I glanced behind me to find him leaning against the refrigerator. His suit jacket was off, his sleeves rolled up, his tie loose, and his hair scruffy like he'd run his hand through it several times. Or like *someone* had run a hand through it. Was he late because he'd been messing around?

I cared because I didn't want him jeopardizing our plans, of course.

I wished that was the only reason I cared.

"You have a box of shrimp Cup of Noodles from Amazon that came today. I left it in the coat closet. Just heat up some water and you can have that." So juvenile. It was true what they said about bachelors—they were just overgrown boys.

"You opened my mail?" Again, he wasn't happy.

"I thought it was mine. I didn't realize until I opened it."

"Why would it be something for you? This is my house."

"And I live here during the weekdays. It's easier to have mail sent here." Sometimes it was hard to believe that he had an MBA.

"Did you even check who it was addressed to?" He brushed past me to toss the bottle cap into the sink, sending tingles down my spine from the contact.

"I guess I didn't," I said, grabbing the bottle cap out of the sink and tossing it into the trash can. Where it belonged. "Is it really that big of a deal that I opened your mail? Are you expecting something you don't want me to know about?"

"I don't know. Maybe. Don't you think you're taking this couple thing a little too far?" He mumbled the last part, but I still heard him.

I threw the washrag into the sink and nudged him out of the way so I could open the dishwasher and load the few dishes—*his* dishes—that were still sitting there from breakfast.

"I suppose I kind of am. Since I'm the one cleaning up after you like a wife." I shook my head, cursing that I was once again doing housework because of him. "You need a maid, Weston. You live like a pig." I honestly didn't know why he didn't have one. Who had a penthouse in Manhattan and didn't have a housekeeper come in at least once a week? I thought the whole cleaning profession thrived on serving his particular demographic—single, rich, male.

"Maybe I don't like spending money on things I can get someone to do for me for free." His tone of voice, matched with that half-smile of his, made the statement sound dirty.

My knees swayed and my pulse ticked up. He was standing too close, and I was intoxicated, as always, by his swagger.

Intoxicated and disgusted.

"You're so full of yourself," I said, walking into the main room. I needed distance. More distance than I could find in his two-bedroom apartment, but I'd take what I could get. I discovered he'd left his shoes, briefcase, and jacket in a pile on the floor. I picked them all up and carried them to his bedroom door and left them there, then walked to his bookcase and found a glass that had been neglected there since who knew when. I picked it up, intending to take it back to the dishwasher, except I noticed the shelf was filthy.

"When was the last time you took a duster to any of this?" I brushed a layer of dust off with my hand.

"Are you a germaphobe or something? Are you seeing someone for that?"

Ignoring him, I pulled some of his books from the bookshelf. "Your comics are covered with the stuff. Doesn't this bother you?"

"They're not comics. They're graphic novels. Don't touch them." He ran over to me to grab the comics—er, graphic novels—out of my hand, and replaced them on the shelf. With his sleeve, he wiped the shelf clean.

I shook my head again. "A maid, Weston. Hire one or I'll hire one for you."

"A little dust never killed anyone. And I'm not getting a maid. I'll clean it when my schedule eases up, okay?"

Right, he didn't have time because he was too busy working. He was working *a lot* lately. He claimed they had a lot of big accounts, but the other thing that I knew he'd been spending time on was training his new hire—Sabrina.

I tried not to let it bother me, tried not to imagine him with her all day, late into the evenings, having dinner together. Sharing a drink. Sharing more than a drink.

"You don't have to tell me again," I said, insolently. "You have to work. I've heard it before." I cringed internally. I could hear what I was saying and how I was saying it. I sounded like a nag. Shit, maybe I really *was* taking the couple thing too far.

But it was a compulsion—the nagging, the wondering. The needing to know. The harder I tried to stop, the more I couldn't stop. Even now I didn't want to ask, and yet here I was asking anyway, "With Sabrina?"

He leaned against the arm of the sofa and crossed his legs at the ankle. "That was last night. Tonight we were pitching to a big client. Phoenix Technology. We sealed the deal, if you were interested."

"Congratulations. Glad to hear all your *hard work* pays off." I tugged at the hem of my nightgown, rolling it around my finger absentmindedly.

"Thank you." He took another pull of his beer. "I'm still not getting a maid."

"Of course you're not. Because you're cheap." I crossed to load the glass in the dishwasher.

As I put the gel pack in and started the cycle, I watched him from behind the kitchen counter. He made me so confused and riled up every time I was with him. Every interaction felt unsatisfying, even if I'd won the argument. I still wanted to poke more, wanted *him* to give me more; though, if he asked me, I couldn't tell him what.

I poked at him now. "Maybe I should let you fuck a maid. At least we could have a clean apartment."

"*Let* me? Look, I don't know where you got the idea that you're the boss of my dick, but you are absolutely not. My abstinence is a fucking favor, not an obligation."

"Really? How about *my* abstinence?" I challenged. "Is that a requirement to this deal?"

His brows rose. "You're the one who said we needed to be chaste, babe. If you're getting your pipes cleaned, then you sure as hell better let me off the chain."

I rolled my eyes. Nothing was getting cleaned around here that I wasn't cleaning myself, especially my pipes. "I'm not the one who is going to fuck this up, Weston. But if you're fucking this up, then I don't want to be held on a leash, either."

"Meaning?"

I bunched my hands into fists and rested them on my hips. "Meaning—give me Clarence Sheridan's phone number." I didn't even really want to call him. I'd barely thought about him since we'd bumped into him that night at dinner a month ago. He was an ex from high school. My first real boyfriend, yes. The guy who'd taken my virginity, but we'd broken up seven years ago now. Seeing him again had knocked the wind out of me because it had been so long, not because I still felt anything for him.

But I'd use any weapon in my war against Weston King. If he got to have an ex to fire me up with, I got to have one too.

His lips settled into a flat line, his face going hard. "My phone's dead. I'll give it to you later."

"Figures," I mumbled. Either it was to piss me off or it was because he really thought I wanted to hook up with Clarence.

And if Weston thought I wanted to hook up with my ex, wasn't it logical to assume that it was because *he* wanted to hook up with *his*?

Or because he already had.

I came around the kitchen island and crossed my arms over my chest. Unless we had a date to be seen together at some event, this was usually the time of night that I slunk off to my bedroom. It was where I should be headed now, but the tension between us was particularly taut, and I felt especially unsettled with our evening's conversation.

He stared at me, drinking his beer, and I swore he could see into me, could see how crazy he made me. He stared as if he knew I needed something, and he was just waiting to hear me say it. He kept staring until I began to shift my weight uncomfortably from foot to foot.

"Go ahead. Ask what you want to ask," he said, finally.

Do you want me? echoed through my mind. It hadn't been what I was thinking, but now that I had, I couldn't stop. My arousal hummed up a pitch. My nipples furled into tight beads.

I leaned forward slightly at my torso, wishing, wondering—if I asked him that, what would he say? Would I be satisfied with his answer or would it feel like another rejection?

I didn't dare take the risk.

"What happened at the meeting with Sabrina?" I asked instead, hating myself as I did.

"What happened with Sabrina?" he asked with a sharp mocking tone, as if to say, *how dare you even ask* but also *I'm so glad that you did.* "Let me tell you."

I didn't want him to, not really. How could I enjoy this, hearing about the woman I was in a silent competition with? How could I not? I had this sick compulsion to know everything about what they'd done together, to somehow make her pleasure mine.

He set his finished beer down on the coffee table and took a step toward me. "She came into my office after everyone else was gone, when it was dark, so we were alone. She had that look on her face, you know what look I'm talking about. The look that said she was thinking about my cock. Remembering the way that I'd been with her. Remembering how good I'd been to her. She was biting her lip, kind of like you're biting your lip now."

I let go of my lip, and felt my face redden, having been completely unaware that I'd been biting it in the first place.

"She was probably remembering that ride in the taxi. We'd gone to dinner and she wasn't wearing any panties so I put my fingers up her skirt, played with her. Stroked her until her clit was nice and plump and she was writhing in the seat. I could tell she was about to explode. The way she kept gasping, moaning, and begging, calling my name. But I wouldn't let her come. Not during the car ride. We got to my apartment, somehow made it across the lobby and into the elevator. When the doors closed. I lifted her up against the wall, and put my mouth to her pussy. It only took a couple strokes of my tongue before she was coming all over my face. The look on her face said that's what she was thinking about as she came over to my desk and leaned over with those nice tits of hers showing."

I was breathing so hard, enraptured with his sexy, dirty story. A story that I shouldn't want to hear at all, and I *didn't*, yet I couldn't stop listening, needing to hear every detail of his past, and of what happened next. Even though I knew when I thought about it later, it was going to hurt like hell. But right now all I could feel was the buzz between my legs, my panties going damp, the thrum of my want pulsing through my veins.

"She looked up at me with those big doe eyes," Weston continued, taking another step toward me. "Fluttered those eyelashes, licked her luscious lips. And said, 'Weston, can you please help me go over this report one more time before you present it to Phoenix tomorrow?'"

I swallowed as an odd form of betrayal started to rise up inside me, double-crossed by both Weston and my own body, which leaned forward and heated with his coarse words.

Weston let out a laugh. "You should see your face."

"Fuck you."

"I know, right? It was a good time we had back there in May, Sabrina and I. I'm hard just recalling it." He rubbed at the crotch of his pants, and I could see that he was at least semi-aroused.

The want that was simmering inside, just barely staying tethered, pulled and strained, screaming to be released. I took a shaky breath. I could feel his eyes on me, could feel them watching my throat and my mouth and the movement of my eyes.

He took another step toward me, and I wanted to walk away and toward him all at once. "You want to help me with this, Elizabeth?" And I couldn't tell anymore if he was taunting me or inviting me. Couldn't remember if I should be offended either way.

An alarm bell rang in my head, a warning that this was wrong for some reason or every reason or maybe there was no reason at all, but I was scared, and so I repeated what I'd said before. "Fuck you. I'm going to bed."

I managed to restrain myself so that I walked rather than ran to my bedroom and quietly shut the door behind me.

Forty-five minutes later I was still tossing and turning, still twisted inside from my interaction with Weston. I couldn't stop thinking about him. About Sabrina and him, and me and him, and his cock, the way he rubbed at his pants, the way it felt underneath me all those weeks and weeks ago now at The Sky Launch. He was such a player that even when he wasn't playing with other women, he was playing with me. Even if he didn't mean to, even if he didn't know he was doing it, I felt like I was always part of his game, always being shuffled around, never knowing which side of the deck I was on.

The apartment was quiet and I was sure he'd gone to bed too, but I needed to get out of my room. Just needed to be free for a moment, escape from the oppression of that closed door, anything to free myself from my thoughts. I opened the door and slipped into the darkness, quietly heading into the living room and then stopped short when I realized that I wasn't alone.

Weston was still out there, sitting on his modern armchair by the windows that ran floor-to-ceiling like they did in his office, like they did in the bubble room. He hadn't seen me, because he was facing out, looking into the city night. The lights were off, but the moonlight was streaming in, and I could see him clearly, could see the bottle of lube on the table next to him.

And, in his hand, was his fully erect cock.

His pants were open just enough so that he could hold it, and he was stroking himself, not too slow, not too fast. Just fast enough that he could enjoy it. And I could tell that he was enjoying it because his face screwed up into an expression of tension and release, tension and release, with each stroke. I could hear it, too. Hear the sound of his hand moving quickly over the thick shaft. The sound as the lube spread up and down underneath the palm of his hand. I could hear him grunt. The fall between the fast breaths while he worked to bring himself to climax.

I was fascinated and mortified. I couldn't look away. I didn't want to look away. I wanted to watch him, wanted to imagine that it was my hand rubbing along with his, my hand brushing across the top of his crown and down the other side of his shaft, up again and across the top and down and faster, faster, and faster. I wanted it to be my mouth. I wanted it to be my body. I wanted to be riding him. Wanted him to make those moans and grunts. While my thighs slapped against his.

I could imagine it so clearly that I felt my pussy clench on the verge of an orgasm. What would he do if I joined him now? He couldn't turn me away, could he?

I took a hesitant step forward.

Just then, his breathing changed, his body stiffened. His hand froze and he shook as liquid squirted from the top of his dick all over his hand and glistened in the moonlight. A long guttural low sound escaped from his throat, accompanying his release. A sound that ended in a single word. A name. "Sabrina."

I turned around and ran back to my room and closed the door. I crawled under the covers and pulled them up high, pulled my knees up to my chest, pressed my legs together, hoping it would calm the buzz between my thighs. I could put my hand between them and rub it away, like I had so many times thinking about him in the last several months. It would ease the ache between my legs.

But nothing I could do would rub away the ache in my heart.

ELEVEN
WESTON

I WOKE up the next morning with a hangover of shame and regret.

I'd been so angry, so irritated, so annoyed.

The worst part was that I hadn't just been upset with Elizabeth—I'd also been upset with myself. Because as every terrible thing had come out of her mouth, with every word she'd said, all I could think about was her pretty lips and her curved hips and wonder what the feel of her skin was like at the base of her spine. Wonder what sounds she'd make if she was under me.

Of all the women I could fantasize about, why did it have to be her that turned me on? It was bad enough to be celibate, bad enough to have to go months without getting my dick wet. But then for her to be the object of my horny daydreams, with her gorgeous face and her curvy body and her tight ass—even her arrogant personality showed up in my fantasies, as she argued with me and tried to boss me around while I made her come over and over again around my cock.

Whatever I'd done to piss off the universe, karma was a cruel bitch.

So when I'd finally found myself alone, I couldn't take it anymore. All that stress and tension between us left me wound tight and needing a release in the worst way. In hindsight, I should have gone to my room to, uh, work out my frustration, but I was tired and lazy and still adjusting to living with another person. Maybe part of me even liked the idea of whacking it while she was next door sleeping. It felt defiant and provocative.

And, damn, was it a turn-on to feel like I was provoking Elizabeth.

I was already thinking about her, imagining what it would be like to sink between her creamy thighs and slip inside her, wondering if she was as hot and fiery inside as she was outside when I looked up and caught movement in the glass in front of me.

When I realized it was her reflection in the window, that she was watching me, I almost came right then.

I'd thought I was an expert in what's-hot-to-spank-to. Nothing I'd ever thought up was as erotic as that moment. Not even close.

I'd quickened my strokes, and I could feel her shock across the room. I could feel her fascination. I could feel her want, her desire, just as heavy and untamed as my own.

But she hadn't been willing to reveal herself or join in like I prayed she would while I focused on her image in the glass.

And that drove me fucking mad. Lunatic mad.

It wasn't like *I* could make the next move. I couldn't invite her to come sit on my lap without coming off as a perverted bastard. It had to be her. My cock was in my hand, but the cards were definitely in hers.

So as erotic as it was having her watch, as mind-blowing as it felt knowing that the woman I was thinking of was turned on at the sight of me hard and exposed, I was too pissed to give her any hint that she was the reason I was out there furiously beating off.

And, instead, I was an asshole. An asshole that refused to say *her* name—the name that had burst like fireworks in my head while

I'd stroked myself, up and down—and instead chose to say *another* name. The one that I knew would make her turn around and walk away.

Afterward, sitting in the dark with my Elizabeth-inspired orgasm fading into memory, I'd felt like shit.

I'd wanted to run after her to tell her I was sorry for the lie, and for all the rest too—for the fighting and the pushing. I'd wanted to tell her how crazy she made me, and how crazy she was for pursuing this dream of hers, but also how fucking much I admired her for not giving up and for actively trying to be a better person than the person her father had been. Wanted to tell her how inspiring it was to know someone with integrity these days, especially in this fast-paced, rat race business world where it seemed like no one had integrity.

But I didn't.

Instead I'd tucked myself away and went to bed like the good fiancé she wanted me to be.

I hadn't expected that I would still feel so shitty in the morning. It wasn't the first or fiftieth time I'd woken regretful after having been a jerk since the beginning of our courtship. It wasn't the first morning after I'd jerked off to her, even, but it was the first morning I'd woken up and truly wished things were different between us.

Most days, we hit the building's gym together first thing, and not because I tried to go at the same time she did on purpose. It just worked out that way. Today, however, I couldn't stand to see her. If I did, the guilt would double and the knot in my stomach would tighten with the terribleness of the lie I'd told, mixed with the weight of the want I had for her.

So I skipped my workout and waited until I heard her leave the apartment before making my way out to the front room. I made my breakfast quietly and alone, drank my coffee, staring out the window at the street below, hating how silent the apartment was without her. Hating how used to her movements and noises I'd gotten in the last several weeks. She'd left a coffee mug and a spoon in the sink. Normally I'd leave those, but today I washed them out and put them away. Then I unloaded the dishwasher, thinking it might help unload some of the regret weighing on my spine.

All it did was make me late enough to still be there when she walked in after her workout. So much for slipping out without seeing her.

I picked up my briefcase and brushed past her heading toward the door. "Slept in," I said gruffly. "Running late." I couldn't even bring myself to talk in full sentences to her.

Her voice came casually from behind me. "I need a copy of your health records. Can you get that for me?"

The request was out of the blue and her tone flippant. As though she hadn't seen something so intimate the night before, as though she hadn't participated by staying in the room to watch.

I turned my body toward her and tried not to stare at the vee of her sports bra's neckline. "I don't see why you would need that."

She wiped at the sweat on her forehead with her towel then draped it around her neck. "I need to know if you're clean. A woman would want to know this about the man she was marrying."

The tension that had stretched taut between us the night before pulled tighter, as though any moment it would snap.

Shit. She was pissed.

Well, so was I. "Did you forget we are not actually sleeping together?" It hurt in my gut to say it. More than it likely hurt her to hear.

"I don't want any STDs biting me in the ass later. If someone else found out you had something and leaked it to the media and then Darrell found out, I'd be screwed." A single rivulet of sweat drew down her gorgeous neck and over her collarbone. "Besides, I should have some insurance that you aren't fucking around."

I took a step toward her, my empty hand opening and closing reflexively at my side. I wasn't sure if I wanted to wring her throat or swipe the drop of sweat off of it with my thumb and suck it off. Or watch her suck it off. "No one's finding out anything, because I'm fucking clean."

She didn't budge. "Then it will say so in your medical records."

Goddamn, I wanted to bend her over. Wanted to pull down those tight Lycra yoga pants and show her all the things that she'd likely imagined while she watched me last night.

It was because of what she'd seen last night that she was demanding this now. It was because of what I'd said. I was sure of it. I considered confronting her. She couldn't deny it—I'd seen her, and God, it would be so vindicating to hear from her own lips how much she'd liked it. I'd make her admit how chickenshit she'd been not to have joined me.

But I was chickenshit too.

And stubborn.

"I'm not getting you my medical files, sweetheart," I said, staring at her one last long second. I straightened my tie, opened the door and, with more strength than I knew I had, walked out.

I HADN'T FORGOTTEN about her at the office. How could I? She was foremost on my mind as I tried to dig myself through the hectic morning.

But when Nate suggested the plan for the evening, I decided to pretend everything was cool at home and I texted Elizabeth, hoping that *she'd* forgotten our latest fight.

> The office is going to Red Farm to celebrate landing Phoenix. Significant others invited. Meet at eight.

I was slammed on all sides with the new contract. Things were coming at me nonstop, but she responded immediately, so I was still holding the phone when the text came in.

> No.

Goddammit. I really didn't have time for this. I shot her a quick text back.

> Everyone's going. You need to go.

Wasn't that what our whole scam was supposed to be about anyway? Being seen together?

I dropped my phone on my desk and tried to catch up on the emails I was frantically sorting through. The phone buzzed less than five minutes later.

> Are you going to get me what I asked for?

Obviously she hadn't forgotten anything.

> I'm not getting you shit.

> I'm not going anywhere

I stood up from my desk quickly, wanting to flip it. Or kick something. Or at least throw some darts, but I didn't have time for that because we had an emergency morning meeting to celebrate landing such a big account and to announce it to the staff. I gathered my things and went downstairs to the conference room.

Thankfully Nate was making the announcement to the team, so I didn't have to be friendly and boisterous. While he did his stuff, I tried once again to get Elizabeth to come with us.

> It's going to seem weird if my fiancée isn't at the celebration, don't you think?

I made sure my phone was on silent so as not to interrupt the meeting, then stared at it, waiting for her reply. Seconds ticked by feeling like hours, but she replied not too much later.

> At this short notice, I don't give a fuck. I'm not at your beck and call.

I bit back the urge to curse loudly and stuffed my phone in my suit pocket, noticing Sabrina eyeing me from the seat at my side. I sat back in my chair wondering if she'd seen the conversation on my phone.

Probably not.

She was likely only looking at me because we'd had a Thing once. And we still might when this farce was over. If I was smart, I'd focus all my fantasies on her now, for real. She didn't drive me mad like Elizabeth did. Didn't make me want to rip my hair out. Didn't make my eye twitch.

Didn't consume my thoughts and make me want to tear off all her clothes and then mark up her creamy white skin before telling her all the ways that she made me think the world was a better place because she was in it.

Yeah. Focusing on Sabrina definitely didn't make me want to do that.

I kept thinking about the two of them through the rest of the meeting, about Elizabeth and Sabrina. Or rather, I kept thinking about Elizabeth, and wondering how I could force my thoughts to the beautiful brunette sitting next to me instead. Even when I tried to muster up memories from the weekend we'd spent together naked, it all turned into Elizabeth.

What kinds of sounds would Elizabeth have made if I'd fucked her against the wall like that? What expression would she have made? How would she have felt around my cock when her pussy tightened and came?

I couldn't take it anymore. I had to get her out of my head.

And the only way I knew to get a woman out of my head was to get another woman in it.

When the meeting was over, Sabrina stood quickly, eager to get back to her work.

I called after her, feeling guilty as her name crossed my lips. She was my subordinate, someone I worked with on a daily basis, and after what I'd done last night, saying her name at the worst time, for the worst reason? I'd poisoned it.

And here I was using it again for my own selfish reasons. I was such a fuckwad. But I was also unrepentant.

She turned back to me, tugging on her hair. "Yeah?"

I didn't know what I was doing.

But I gave her my widest smile and winged it. "I wanted to let you know that Phoenix was particularly impressed with our marketing objectives. It was one of the main reasons we landed the account." All of that had been true, and it was a good idea as her boss to praise her for it. If I were more focused on my job, I would've done that earlier.

Maybe.

"I inherited a very qualified and talented team," she said, modest as always.

I shifted my weight on my hip. "You did. I know you did. Tom Burns also let me know a few things."

"Like what?"

I looked up and saw Donovan watching us. There was nothing that I'd said that was inappropriate, but with the thoughts I'd been having about her—or rather the thoughts I *hadn't* been having about her but had been *pretending* to have about her—plus the tension I was having at home, it was seeming more and more like maybe doing something reckless was my only way out of the spell Elizabeth had over me.

And Donovan never approved of recklessness.

"We should talk about it privately," I said to her. God, I was such a dick. Was I really doing this? "Meet you upstairs in my office in fifteen?"

She blinked a couple of times, and I wondered if she understood what I was getting at. "Sure. I'll be there in fifteen."

By the time I got up to my office, I was having second thoughts about using Sabrina as a source of distraction. It was wrong on so many levels.

I needed to confront my real problem, head-on.

I took a deep breath and tried once more to reason with my fiancée about the evening's plans.

> It's Friday. We were going to The Sky Launch anyway. Just go to Red Farm instead.

I sat in my chair and rocked onto its back wheels while I waited for her reply. When it came, I almost fell over.

> We don't usually go to the club until later, and I already told you I didn't want to go out tonight because I have to pack and get up early for my trip with Mom. Did you forget?

Trip? What trip?

I picked up my office phone and called my assistant, Roxie, too lazy to walk out and talk to her in person.

"Do you know anything about Elizabeth going on a trip?" I could hear how terse I sounded.

Roxie's throaty Hungarian accent sounded both through the receiver and from outside my office. "It's her mother's birthday. She going on a spa trip in Connecticut with her for the week. It's been on your calendar for weeks. Did you forget?" Her echo of Elizabeth's words just riled me up more.

"I didn't forget, thank you," I snapped. I'd totally forgotten. "I just didn't know it was this week." I hung up before she could say anything else.

I bounced my foot rapidly up and down. Elizabeth still had to eat. I sent another message.

> We'll be home early enough. Just go to the fucking dinner.

> I'll be home early enough because I'm not fucking going.

I could feel my face getting hot with anger as I read her reply. I was still staring at it when a second message came in on its tail.

> And send me Clarence's phone number. Now that your phone isn't dead.

I didn't even realize how pissed I was until the growl came out of my throat. I was so angry. So frustrated.

So hard.

As angry as we'd been with each other, it was probably good that we weren't going to see each other tonight. Even better that we weren't going to see each other for an entire week. I would get my apartment to myself, wouldn't even have to stay at her place.

But... I *wanted* to see her.

I wanted to stay at her place. I wanted to fucking be in her arms. I wanted to be in her bed, wanted to be inside her—and since I still couldn't stand her, the whole idea had me in turmoil.

I ran my hand through my hair. Both of my hands through my hair. One after another, willing myself to settle down, but I heard Roxie's voice outside the office.

"Go on in. He's in a mood though. I warn you."

"I heard that," I yelled.

"You were meant to," she called back.

Then there was Sabrina standing in my doorway, her hands tugging at her hair like they often did, a gesture I'd found adorable when I'd first met her a decade ago.

And now?

She was striking, she really was. A natural beauty. She'd grown up to be even more sophisticated and beguiling, more sure of herself. She was serious and put together. She wasn't feisty or passionate. She wasn't late for everything.

Why did I have to remind myself that these were good things?

"Hey, what's up?" she asked tentatively. "Is there a problem?"

"Not exactly." I dropped my phone on my desk. But it sat there, staring, mocking, Elizabeth's texts shouting in my head at the mere sight of it.

I opened my desk drawer and threw my phone inside, as though that would silence the buzz buzz of my thoughts.

It was weak, but the only idea I had at the moment.

I turned my attention back to Sabrina.

"Have a seat," I said, and the world did seem a little less noisy now that my cell phone was tucked away.

She walked farther into the room somewhat cautiously, and slunk down in the chair facing me. "I'm here."

"You're here." I didn't even remember how to do this. Didn't remember how to talk to a woman.

What the hell had happened to me?

I shook my head and attempted a smile. "Anyway. As I was saying downstairs, Tom Burns spoke to me yesterday, and he had some interesting things to say about you."

"Really? Like what?" She blinked rapidly, seeming nervous.

Women were nervous when they were into a guy, right? Shit, I needed to be closer, needed to get the barriers out from between us.

I stood up and circled around so I was right in front of her, then leaned back, half sitting on the desk behind me.

As soon as I sat, she bolted to a standing position, startling me.

"Whoa," I said. "You okay?"

"Yep. Just edgy today." She tugged on her hair. "Go on. Tom said...?"

"That you stayed as late as anyone else, and that you provided some of the last minute additions to the project, such as the global message component. That was one of the selling points in the strategy."

"Really?" Her eyes were level with mine now, her focus completely on me. She was into this, then, if I was reading this right.

And I wasn't. Yet.

"Yes. Really." I kept on with my praise. I wasn't a quitter. "I wanted you to know your commitment to your team didn't go unnoticed. Everyone seems to be responding really well to you. The staff likes you. Your team likes you, and I'm really glad you came." I *was* glad she'd come. She'd done great things for the company, made my job easier. She was probably better at the work than I was.

And I was glad for other reasons. Surely.

She was still playing with her hair so I reached out and took it from her and tugged it myself, making a play of sorts.

Had coming on to a woman always felt this unnatural?

"Thank you. I appreciate that." Her cheeks grew pink. "Was that everything?"

I nodded, keeping my eyes on hers. "Yeah, that's everything." I chuckled at myself. What else was I supposed to say? No, that's not everything, I was hoping we could meet at a hotel later so I can remember why I like you better than the woman I'm marrying.

That wasn't smooth at all. Three months out of the game, and I'd forgotten all my moves.

"Okay, then. Thank you again." She started to leave, then hesitated. "Oh, and congratulations on the account."

She definitely wanted me. All I had to do was want her back.

Or at least try to.

"Congratulations to both of us." I put my hand up in the air to give her a high five, and when her palm met mine, I left my hand there, let it linger, and when she started to pull away, I laced my fingers through hers.

Yeah, this was how to do it. It was coming back to me now. It didn't have to be tawdry.

"You're coming tonight, aren't you?" I asked, my confidence rising incrementally along with my self-loathing.

Out of the corner of my eye, Donovan appeared in the open door frame.

Sabrina glanced over and noticed him too, but instead of pulling back, she entwined her fingers around mine. "Uh, yeah. Of course."

"Good. I'll save you a seat." We held hands, stretching our arms until she was too far away to touch, and then we let go. I watched after her, though, my heart beating hollow in my chest, my stomach feeling empty.

I sighed again and turned to my partner. "Kincaid. Whatcha got for me? Budgets for the toothpaste campaigns, I'm hoping."

He closed the door.

Which was immediately a bad sign. There was no need to have the door closed to discuss toothpaste campaigns.

"What the goddamn hell are you doing?" he hissed.

Of course. I should have seen this coming a mile away. "Oh, Christ. You're really going to be like this, aren't you?"

He paced toward me, his face looking as enraged as I'd felt all morning. "Our reputation is on the line. Our company is on the line. Elizabeth's company is on the line."

I stood up from the desk to answer him. "I know what's on the line. Trust me."

"Trust you? I walked in on you with your hands all over Sabrina," Donovan said, disgusted. "Your door was wide open. The glass is clear. Anyone could have seen you."

I circled behind my desk, putting a barrier between us so that I didn't kill him. "Because there are so many spies in our office just dying to call up Elizabeth's cousin and tell him about some harmless office flirtation? I bet he chases his own secretary's skirt. Have you seen the guy?"

Donovan's eyes narrowed to thin slits. "You're lucky it was just me," he said in a tone so quiet and controlled, it made my scalp prickle.

"*So* lucky. To think, I might've missed out on you telling me what was what and putting me in my place. Like always. Thank you. I appreciate it. Now if you don't have anything *business* related—"

He cut me off. "This isn't one of your games, Weston. You can't charm your way through this like you do everything else."

God, he sounded like my father. Not because my father had ever said words like that, but because Donovan thought he had the right to say things like that.

And he didn't. No right at all.

I leaned my palms onto the desk and bent toward him. "If you didn't think I was capable of it, then you shouldn't have insisted I be the one to do the damn job. It isn't like I wanted it." I held his intense stare for several long seconds, neither of us backing down.

Finally, I spoke again. "Look. I'll be where I'm supposed to be. I'll go through with the wedding. I'll wear the ring. I'll continue playing house—playing the part like I have been, which has been an Academy Award-winning performance. But like hell do you get to keep popping in like you're directing this show. You were the casting agent, Donovan, that's all. Now step aside, and enjoy it when you get to put Reach's name on Dyson's advertising subsidiary, because that's where you get to take *your* credit. The rest of your role is done."

We stared at each other for a few more seconds, and I had a feeling he wanted to say something else, but by God, no way was I letting him have the last word. "Now, do I need to call security?" I said, acting like the total asshole that I was. "Because this is my office."

He straightened to his full height. "Technically, it's *not* your office, is it?" And he turned and left, shutting the door behind him.

Fuck him.

Fuck him for having the last word and fuck him for bringing up the money I owed him, for reminding me that I didn't have a proper stake in the company yet.

But also, *thank* Donovan. Because he reminded me why I was doing all of this. Why I was suffering day in and day out with a woman who made me question everything that I wanted and desired.

But seriously, fuck them both. Both Donovan and Elizabeth.

And if this was really how it was going to be—Donovan barking orders, Elizabeth not playing her part to the limit, not being as committed as I had been—then I was done playing by the rules. Tonight I would go to Red Farm without my fiancée, and if I flirted with Sabrina, so be it. If I had fun with Sabrina, then good for me. If anyone else was put off by it, well, maybe they shouldn't have treated me like this when all I was doing was my best.

I opened the top desk of my drawer and grabbed my phone. There was one more text I needed to send if I was going to feel completely liberated enough to do what I wanted this evening. I searched and found Clarence Sheridan's number and sent it to my wife-to-be.

I might be a dick, but fair was fair.

TWELVE
ELIZABETH

"I'M PLANNING on getting a restorative herbal massage," my mother said as I dropped a sleep mask into my suitcase. I shifted the cradle of the landline receiver so I could hold it with my chin and rifle through my dresser drawer at the same time. "Or should I get the chakra balancing massage instead?"

"What does it say the difference is?" I grabbed a handful of panties from the drawer and dropped them in the suitcase, then shuffled toward my closet for some yoga pants. To be honest, I wasn't really paying attention to the types of services she was telling me about. She would change her mind by the time we got there.

The spa was in a resort in Connecticut—only a couple of hours away, but the driver was arriving early in the morning and I wanted to be packed tonight. I'd already spent an hour on the task, which was too long. We planned to spend most of the weeklong trip wrapped in seaweed and on massage tables, so it shouldn't have been that big of a burden to pack a bag. Problem was, I was too distracted by thoughts of Weston.

Naked thoughts of Weston.

Thoughts of Weston doing the things I saw him doing last night in the dark.

"I don't know, one's Thai style, the other one's Swedish with a focus on chakras. Oh!" my mother suddenly exclaimed. "We could do the massage for two!"

I closed my eyes and pinched the bridge of my nose. "Those are for couples, Mom. They're romantic and sexy-like."

"I'm sure they wouldn't mind if we did it together. There's a discount if you do it together." With the money my mother got from her divorce, she didn't need to worry about bargains. But she remembered where she came from, and she could never turn down a buy-one-get-one-free special.

"Sorry, Mom. I just don't want to see you naked." But there was that guy I *did* want to see naked.

And now I was thinking about him again. Or still. Missing his presence, trying not to notice what time it was or that he was likely out with his friends, eating dinner now. Trying not to wonder if he would show up at my house at all tonight, considering I was leaving in the morning. Our last texts had escalated in tone and tension; I had no idea whether he even wanted to be in the same room with me at the moment.

I didn't want to be in the same room with him.

But I did.

No, I didn't.

"What's Weston going to do while you're gone?" my mother asked, as though she could read my mind.

"I don't know. And I don't care." With five pairs of yoga pants and four long-sleeved T-shirts, I returned back to my suitcase and dropped them inside. "Don't you remember what it's like to live with a man, Mom? Because it's really terrible, and I'm glad I'm getting a break."

She laughed. "Of course I remember, honey. Why do you think

I'm divorced? But aren't you worried that this particular man might muck up your deal while you're out of town?"

I'd been conflicted about this. He'd promised me over and over again that he was faithful to our commitment, that he wasn't going to do anything to mess up my chance at getting Dyson Media, but did I trust him?

Part of me did, actually. A deep-rooted part of me trusted him when he said he would keep it in his pants. It was my head that thought otherwise, the reasonable part of me that knew what men were like and what temptation could do to a man. That was the part of me that said perhaps he was fooling around, or *would* fool around, given the opportunity.

Luckily, I had someone who had my back. "Donovan will look after him," I told my mother. "He knows how to keep Weston in line."

A muffled ringing sounded from somewhere in my bedroom—my cell phone.

"What's that? Do you need to go?"

"I won't know until I find my cell phone and check the caller ID," I said, annoyed. I had stuck my cell somewhere when I was bitter with Weston, but where?

Oh, yes. Under my pillow.

The name on the screen said, Kincaid, D. "Mom, I gotta go." I clicked off the home phone before she had a chance to say goodbye, and clicked on my cell. "What's up, Donovan?"

"What are you doing? And why aren't you here?" He was serious, straight to the point like always, but this time there was also a note of something I'd never heard in Donovan. Panic?

"I'm at home, and I'm talking to you. I am not where you are because I don't know where you are." Then I realized he was probably out with everyone else at the company, celebrating their new account. "Oh, I mean I'm not there because I don't want to be."

"You *do* want to be. Get down here. Now."

I turned to look at myself in the dresser mirror, see if my makeup had still held up from my earlier outing to the library. It had, but it didn't matter because I wasn't going anywhere. I wasn't jumping because Reach said so.

"What's the point? Why do you want me there so badly?"

"Elizabeth, I should think you would trust me enough to not have to go into a lengthy explanation. Let me just tell you this—Sabrina is here."

At the mention of her name, my stomach curdled. I had nothing against her personally; she was a nice woman. Probably. But I knew what kind of thoughts Weston had about her, and that made her dangerous.

But she was also an employee for the company, so of course she would be at the celebration dinner with the rest of the staff and higher-ups.

"Sabrina works with Weston every day," I said, not quite so sure of myself.

"Tonight, though, they aren't working."

If Donovan hadn't convinced me I should be there, the text message that waited for me when I hung up did. It had been sent earlier in the day, but I was only just seeing it now—Clarence Sheridan's contact info, forwarded from Weston.

Sure, I'd asked him to send it, but I'd asked more than once, and he'd been pissy about it. Was it reaching to think he might've sent it to relieve his guilt about whatever he was planning to do with Sabrina?

I wasn't certain, but I was damn sure going to find out.

I changed quickly into a dressy jumpsuit and heels. Instead of taking the time to wait for my driver, I went to the front desk of the apartment building and got the doorman to hail a cab. Twenty minutes after my phone call with Donovan, I was on my way to Red Farm.

It was easy to find the group I was looking for when I arrived at the restaurant. They took up most of the main room, the company staff spread out along two long tables. I spotted Weston, Nate, and Donovan immediately at the far end and headed over to them. The food had already arrived; dumplings were in the middle of the table being shared family-style. As if by fate, there was one empty seat waiting next to Donovan. Weston sat across from him, Sabrina at his side.

And Weston's hand was on her thigh.

"Elizabeth!" Weston jumped up, eyes wide, voice pitched high. "What are you doing here?" It almost sounded like he was glad I'd come, but the sting of seeing his hand on the other woman's thigh was fresh. Had he known I'd seen it? It was probable he didn't. It was possible he did.

It was possible *everyone* knew.

And that thought pissed the hell out of me.

He bent to kiss me, but just before his mouth met mine, I moved away. His lips landed on my cheek. It was only for show anyway, not like we were kissing for the fun of it.

"My *fiancé* had a celebration. Thought I should be here," I said, answering his question with the subtlest emphasis on the reminder of who he was to me. Real or not.

"I'll move so you two can sit together," Nate offered.

I waved him off. That would be the mature thing to do, but I was in battle mode. All of the people at this end of the table were in the know, and the rest of the employees didn't seem to be paying any attention to what happened down here. If my fiancé could flirt with somebody else, so could I. Weston King wasn't the only player in the world.

"Don't be silly. I don't need to sit by him. I'd much rather sit by Donovan." I slipped in next to the man, who eyed me curiously. "Now. Next time the waitress comes by, I'm going to need a drink."

Probably a double to give me enough nerve to go through with this. I put my arm around Donovan's back and ruffled the hair at the base of his neck. "So. I'm here!"

I kept my eyes pinned on Weston's, eager to see his reaction to my flirtation. He seemed annoyed, but not as annoyed as I would have preferred. It didn't help that Donovan's response was to bend forward to take a bite of his dumpling, acting as if I wasn't even there.

And it most definitely didn't help when Weston, sure I was watching, returned his hand to Sabrina's knee. Thank God, he at least was subtle enough so that only Donovan and I could see.

"You said you weren't coming," he muttered accusingly.

"I hadn't planned to. But." I turned and looked at Donovan again, slipped my eyes up and down him longingly. Or I hoped it looked longing. "Donovan called and told me I needed to be here."

Weston sneered. "Wasn't that thoughtful of him?" Then the asshole scooted his chair closer to the woman beside him. "Sabrina, have you tasted the seared pork and shrimp dumplings yet?"

"No. Where are they?" She fluttered her eyes, all doe-like and naïve.

He lifted his chopsticks with a bite of dumpling on them. "Have some of mine." Then the asshole fed dumplings to his little girlfriend in front of me. She even had the nerve to groan.

I could happily have murdered them both for this rude display.

Not to be outdone— "Donovan, the pan-fried lamb—" I started for the dumpling on his plate, but before I could feed him anything, he picked it up and dumped it on my plate. "You can have it."

Obviously, he was not playing along. I consciously smoothed out my frown and smiled at him. "Guess that's better than swapping germs."

"Elizabeth's a germophobe," Weston said snidely.

"I am not." I grabbed the chopsticks next to me and attempted to pick up the dumpling, remembering too late that I'd never been very good with the things. "Just because I'm concerned about the diseases that come into my house doesn't qualify me as a germophobe." I chased the dumpling around my plate, growing more and more frustrated with each failed attempt to capture my food.

"She's asked for a report of clean health."

"I think that's reasonable." I'd only asked for his medical records because I knew it would rile him up. Because *I'd* felt riled. It was payback.

Finally, I snagged a piece of pastry and lifted it toward my mouth, but just as it reached my lips, it fell to the plate. "Goddammit."

"Guys," Nate sounded like he was trying not to laugh while hushing us. "Lovers' spats are fun and all..."

Weston apparently didn't get the hint. "Why do you even care when there's no way I'm sharing anything I've got with you anyway?"

It shouldn't burn like it did to hear him say that—twice in one day, no less—but it did. Especially in front of Sabrina, for some reason.

Well, fuck him.

I reached over and stole the unused fork from his setting. "Big words, King. Just remember the thing you want out of this relationship isn't as replaceable as the thing I want."

I stabbed the pan-fried lamb and put it in my mouth, and it tasted fucking delicious. Like redemption. It melted on my tongue.

Melted like the conversation had melted into a tense silence.

"Speaking of replacements..." Nate said breaking the hush. "Did I ever tell you guys about the time I needed this original painting by this Brazilian artist, Luiz Hugo Sousa?"

Weston, who'd been staring at me, moved his eyes eagerly to Nate's. "This sounds like the beginning of a good story."

"The problem was, the girl who had possession of it didn't want to sell. Fortunately, I was fucking her at the time. It wasn't even particularly valuable, but my boss wanted it, and that made it powerful. I needed it more than I wanted her, and that's saying a lot considering her oral skills."

I needed Dyson Media more than I wanted Weston. That was the lesson here. Silently, I thanked Nate for the reminder. *Eyes on the ball, Elizabeth.*

"Skipping past the details: I got bombed on Jäger one night and decided to paint a replacement."

Weston and Sabrina laughed, and so did a couple of other staff members who were now gathering around for Nate's telling of the story.

"This is what made you stop doing Jäger?" someone asked.

"Oh, that came years and many adventures later. Long story short, there's a reason I don't paint for a living. I took the original and left a real Ecce Homo in its place. You should have seen this mess. Turns out I might have had a career as a ninja warrior, though, because the escape route I had to take to get out of her apartment that night was insane. If I hadn't been drunk enough to feel invincible, I never would have tried it. I still have the scar on my upper arm from the barbed wire." He started to pull down his shirt at the neck, searching for the mark. "It's partly covered by the tattoo."

"What did she do when she woke up and saw it?" Weston asked.

"Left me about a hundred messages threatening my life and manhood, until I tossed the burner and picked up a new phone. And then what *could* she do? She couldn't display mine, obviously, but once her friends had seen the real thing, it wasn't like she could hang any copy. It would have been glaringly obvious. Guess she has a white space on her wall now."

"Is there a moral to the story?" Donovan asked, unamused.

"I suppose if you need a moral, Kincaid, it's that there's never a replacement for the real thing." Nate looked at his partner hard. Real hard.

I glanced over at Weston, willing him to hear the point. But, surprise, surprise, he'd tuned us out and was whispering something in Sabrina's ear.

"I'm not sure the person who needed to hear you got the message," I said to Nate.

He looked from me to Donovan to Weston to Sabrina and back to me again. "There's more than one person at this table tonight who needs to hear it."

More people crowded around us from the other tables, the staff becoming looser from drinks and more jovial as the evening passed. The mood had lightened considerably since I had arrived. Weston got up from the table without a word, heading to the restroom, most likely. Someone took his seat, and another round of dumplings were set on the table.

Some nice guy from creative tried to get to know me by asking all about the wedding. It might have done my ego some good if I'd thought he was flirting, but I had a feeling he was gay.

And even if he was flirting, he wasn't nearly charming enough to make up for the stab to my heart when, five minutes after Weston left the group, Sabrina nonchalantly left the table and followed after him.

THIRTEEN
WESTON

I'D GONE to the restaurant that night with every intention of flirting with Sabrina, and maybe making out with her in the back of a cab. I needed the reminder of what it felt like to have other lips on mine, needed to remember what it was like to kiss another woman, a woman who wasn't Elizabeth. And maybe, with luck, I could get her out of my head.

I had zero intention of inviting Sabrina to meet me in the back of the restaurant for a buddy bang.

But when Elizabeth showed up, everything changed.

Before she came, I had my hand on Sabrina's leg. The warmth of her, the soft silky tenderness of her skin that was supposed to get my cock going, only had me wondering what Elizabeth's skin would feel like in comparison. Were her luscious thighs as soft to the touch? Would goosebumps prickle along her skin if I rubbed my thumb on her like this?

Even with a gorgeous woman beside me, with her attention completely on me, all I could think about was pale complexion, red hair, blue eyes.

And then the woman I was dreaming of was standing in front

of me, dressed in a pale gray jumpsuit with lace over the arms and décolletage. She was more covered than Sabrina was, but my cock was more interested than it had been all evening.

I'd been grateful at first—she'd shown up! She'd come to Red Farm, even after all that fighting back and forth over text, she'd come out for me.

And my gut twisted with guilt and turmoil over the way I'd been flirting, but I thought maybe all could be forgiven, that the whole day would be turned around, and we could forget everything going on between us if Elizabeth would just sit by me.

I stood up to kiss her, and I don't ever usually do that. Even for show, not since the engagement party. But it felt natural and right, and I wanted to.

And then she turned her head.

And I realized she wasn't here to make amends at all.

Especially when she started flirting with Donovan. She couldn't keep her hands off of him. What—had Clarence been busy for the night? She had to come and parade her disinterest in me *in front* of me? Every time she touched my friend, every time she glanced at him, it felt like a chess move, like she was taking out one of my pawns.

But I knew how to counterattack.

She ruffled his hair, and my hand scooted higher on Sabrina's leg. She'd sharpen her gaze on him. I'd offer a forkful of food to Sabrina. It was intense and it was tedious. I was annoyed, but more than a little turned on.

But it wasn't a game with casualties until she brought up how easily I could be replaced.

For weeks, I'd been teaching her how to be a better businesswoman, been bending to her rules, living in the same house, keeping it in my pants, been stifling my irrational planet-sized desire for her, been doing all of this so that she could get her hands on her company—and I could be replaced?

So I didn't know if it was to hurt her or to get over her or because *I* was hurt—probably a combination of all three, and I was too fired up to narrow down the specific motivations—but I leaned down and invited Sabrina to meet me in the back of the restaurant.

I could replace Elizabeth, too.

Five minutes later, I was slipping into the cubby by the kitchen, a cutout in the wall covered by a decorative curtain, trying my hardest to turn my thoughts to the woman meeting me and away from the woman waiting back at the table.

Soon, I saw Sabrina walking past. I pulled her into the cubby with me, pushed her against the narrow wall, and pressed my lips against hers, kissing her aggressively, asking for permission with my tongue—permission to let me use her, use her to help me forget about that other woman, the woman I really wanted to be kissing.

Sabrina, sweet Sabrina, opened her mouth, her tongue meeting mine. She was familiar and safe. She was easy because I didn't have to work for her. I didn't have to second-guess what she wanted or what I wanted, for that matter.

But I did need to be sure she knew what I was after.

I broke the kiss and leaned my forehead against hers. "I'm going to be completely honest, Sabrina—this is a booty call and nothing else. You have every right to slap me and walk back out there. But I hope you don't. I'm sensing you need a release right now too."

Was it weird that I hoped that she *did* slap me? Hoped that she kneed me in the nuts and told me I was a pig before walking away, never looking back?

She opened her mouth to respond, but before she could there was a rustling outside the closet. Someone walking too closely past, and I leaned even farther away from her than I already was so I could peek out of the curtain.

Donovan. Fucking Donovan. Checking up on me again.

"What is it?" Sabrina asked.

I shook my head. I couldn't tell her that another one of the execs in the office knew that she was back here in the closet with me—how embarrassing for her.

And suddenly it hit me—how embarrassing for *me*.

What was I doing? I wasn't into this buddy bang. The only reason I was semi-hard was because Elizabeth had shown up. I was a fucking shitshow, and honestly, because Donovan was out there playing boss—playing *father* again—it made me wish so goddamned hard that I could go through with this, but I just couldn't. It was wrong on so many levels. Even if I could get my dick into it, my head was yards away.

"I can't do this," I said.

Sabrina's head snapped up. "I was just going to say the same thing."

I let go of her, and ran my hand through my hair instead. "I'm sorry." Then I registered what she'd said. "You were?" That was a surprise. I thought she'd been into me.

"Yeah. It's not..."

My mind filled in the blanks, while she tried to look for the right words. *It's not appropriate. It's sleazy. I can tell you're not feeling it.*

Eventually she said, "The timing."

"The timing," I agreed. Fucking timing. Before Elizabeth and after Elizabeth. Was my life reduced to those two time periods forever?

"I'll go out first," she said.

I waited much longer than I needed to after she left. Three minutes, four. Seven minutes. I didn't know what I was waiting for—to figure it all out, for my temper to settle down. Something.

When I finally got myself together and walked back to the table, Donovan, Sabrina, and Elizabeth were all gone.

I slumped down in the seat next to Nate. "Where did Elizabeth go?" I asked, wishing I didn't need to know. Stealing a swig of his beer because I did.

Nate shrugged. "She left when Donovan left."

I tensed. I'd been in a closet with another woman, and I had no right to ask, but I couldn't help myself. "Did she leave *with* Donovan?"

My partner eyed me strangely. "If you think that Donovan would go home with Elizabeth, you're more fucked up over this girl than I thought."

That wasn't exactly an answer. "So...she didn't?"

He scrubbed a hand over his face. "They left the restaurant at the same time. When I glanced out the window, Donovan was putting Elizabeth in a cab."

"Good." I was more relieved than I deserved to be. More relieved than I wanted to let on. "I mean, good someone made sure she got home okay."

He swiped his beer out of my hand and glared. "You know that I know about this kind of shit, right?"

Oh, right! Nate, the god of everything.

I leaned forward, eagerly, ready to learn. "Yeah, yeah, man. Do you know something now?"

"I do. I do." He bent in toward me, as though about to share his best-kept secret. "D is not into your girl." He paused for effect. "And your girl is into *you*."

I let that sink in.

"You do know who your girl is, don't you?" he asked when I didn't say anything.

"Elizabeth?"

"Phew. You aren't as stupid as I thought you might be after tonight's bullshit. Now, what are you going to do with this information? Hint: the answer shouldn't include being in a closet with your ex."

I stared at him. "Nate, you don't know what you're saying. She can't stand me."

"I think you're wrong."

There *was* tension between us—sexual tension. There had been from day one. But Elizabeth had made it clear that there could be nothing between us. Because she was focused on her end goal. Because she wasn't interested in a player like me. Because she would want a guy she could be proud of.

"I don't think—"

"Weston, get the fuck out of here and find out."

I started to argue yet again and then remembered—Nate was my hero. Why the hell would I question his advice?

FOURTEEN

ELIZABETH

I SHUT the door of my West Side apartment behind me and headed straight for my room. Friday nights the schedule put us at my place, but I didn't have any idea if Weston would show up.

If I were placing bets? My wager would be no.

Even though I was alone, I slammed things around as though people could hear me. Slammed the door to my closet open, slammed my dresser drawer. I changed quickly into my nightgown, even though I knew I wouldn't fall asleep anytime soon. My insides were a storm of emotions—fury, jealousy, want.

God, how I wanted Weston.

That's what it all came down to. How much I wanted him to be here, rubbing his hand on *my* thigh, to be leaning into *my* ear, beckoning *me* to some secret rendezvous. How much I wanted his secret nighttime fantasies to be about *me*.

Another door slam.

But this time it wasn't me. I stomped out of my bedroom knowing it was him, yet still knocked utterly out of breath when I saw him there, his brow furrowed, his hair a mess from dragging his hand through it so many times.

He was magnificent. A goddamned hottie. A sight so pretty he almost hurt the eyes.

He dumped his keys in the bowl by the front door, his eyes on mine. Sparks shot between us. We were both wrapped up in an electrical storm, and I could feel him pulling me toward him, despite everything that happened this evening. I wanted him; I hated him.

I wanted him.

"That was fast," I said, snidely, remembering who he'd disappeared with when I'd last seen him. "I guess your reputation isn't based on your lasting power."

"I didn't fuck Sabrina," he said, toeing off his shoes, gaze pinned to me. "Ask me why."

I took a hopeful step forward. "Why not?"

He tugged his cowl-neck sweater over his head and tossed it on the floor behind him, leaving his chest bare. Goosebumps sprouted down my arms and legs. "Because she wasn't the one I wanted to fuck."

My stomach flipped. My thighs started shaking.

"So, if we're in a fight," he continued, "let's hurry up and get it over with so we can get on to what's next."

It only took two steps before I crashed against him. His lips were firm and demanding, taking my mouth roughly, exploring every part of it. He kissed the way he fought—mean and hot, bordering on explosive. I wondered if he could make me come with just a kiss. The question was enough to make me realize I wanted his lips other places. On my breasts. Between my thighs.

Without any warning, he spun me around, shifting me so that I was face up against the wall. He pressed up roughly against my backside and lifted the hem of my nightgown so his hands could palm my ass.

"You've fucking teased me for so long, Elizabeth. Do you feel that?" He rubbed his erection in between my ass cheeks. "Do you feel how much I want you?"

Yes, I felt him.

But I was desperate to be sure. "Is it... Is it for me?"

"All for you, baby. Only you." He nipped at my neck, his hands moving upward to cup my breasts underneath my nightgown. "Three long months of watching you prance around left me with a hard-on that doesn't ever ease up." He rocked his dick against me so I could feel every bit of his painful erection. "Tell me you've wanted this too."

"I've wanted you," I confessed breathily. "From the moment you got down on your knees for my fake proposal. I wanted you then, and every day since."

He hissed as if that admission was painful. "Too long," he said. "Too long."

He drew one hand down over the flat of my stomach and slid beneath the waistband of my panties. "A landing strip," he sighed as his touch brushed over the thin column of hair above my folds. "It's been killing me, not knowing."

My knees buckled at the thought of him imagining this. Imagining it in such detail that he'd needed to know if I trimmed, if I waxed. If I was au natural.

He caught me with his arm around my waist while the other went deeper, slipping easily to find the sensitive bundle of nerves awaiting him. Swiftly, expertly, he began rubbing me toward ecstasy. Staccato gasps escaped from my lips.

"You like that? Does it feel good?" He rubbed his cock again between my ass cheeks while he massaged my clit, first slow in one direction, then quick in another. "You don't deserve this, because you've teased me for so long. You don't deserve this, but I'm going to let you come because I'm a nice guy. Tell me I'm a nice guy to let you come."

The tension was already building, I was already nearing the edge.

But even in the throes of passion, I did not surrender. "No."

"You don't want to come?" His fingers kept swirling across my clit, making me dizzy.

"You're not a nice guy. You're an asshole."

Immediately, Weston took his hands off me and stepped back. I whirled around, my palms flattening back against the wall, and faced him down. He hadn't gone too far, and was rubbing at the bulge in his pants. But I worried now that he was going to give up, abandon me.

"You said you were going to fuck me." Was it a challenge? An accusation? I was too strung out on the memory of his fingers down my panties to tell, and so desperate for them to return.

He nodded. "Oh, I am. Take this off." He stepped forward and grabbed my nightie, pulling it over my head and tossing it to the ground before stepping back again to admire me.

"Jesus, you're so fucking gorgeous," he said more to himself than to me, stroking up and down over his imprisoned cock.

And then I was tired of looking. I'd been watching him, been looking for too long—*months* too long. I wanted to be touching.

I closed the distance between us and grabbed for his belt. He laughed, rough and cruel, his hands coming down flat across my back and smoothing all the way down to my ass cheeks.

"Eager to find something there?" he asked, his teeth grazing along my neck.

I was too focused on my task to answer. I had the buckle undone and now was working on his zipper.

"Didn't get enough from your peep show last night?"

I froze, my hand now on the shape of his cock outside his boxer briefs. He'd seen me?

"I saw your reflection in the window. Watched you watching me as I stroked myself." He pushed my panties down my butt cheeks so he could press his fingers between my thighs, and into the slick wetness along my crotch. "I was so pissed you didn't come and join me. I had to say someone else's name, just to punish you, even though the whole time I was thinking about you."

He'd seen me. And he'd lied.

I felt relieved and murderous all at once. Relieved and off-the-charts aroused.

"I told you you aren't a nice guy." I reached inside his boxer briefs and wrapped my fingers around the silky smooth skin of his hard erection, fulfilling my own fantasy from the night before. My blood shot hot down to my pussy.

"You're right. I'm not nice." He stuck a long finger inside me from behind, and I moaned. "I'm still going to let you come. Because I want to see you fall apart."

His words made me shiver and this time when he stroked inside me, his thumb brushed against my clit. And another shaky moan escaped my lips.

His cock jerked in my hand.

"You like making me feel good," I said, moving my hand up and down the length of him.

"I like torturing you," he corrected. He backed us up and spun me around until I was facing the kitchen island. He pressed his hand down on my upper back so that I would bend over it.

"Spread your legs," he said as he knelt down behind me. I spread my legs and stretched my arms across the island.

Weston pulled my panties the rest of the way off my legs. Then he grabbed my ankles and ran his hands up my calves, then moved them inside my knees and up my inner thighs until they were right where I wanted them. And then it wasn't his hands, but his mouth. His tongue. I jumped at the first warm swipe of his rough tongue across my slit.

He followed with a quick swat of his hand on the outside of my thigh.

"Oh," I squealed, then glared at him over my shoulder.

He dimpled at me. "Don't move, or I'll smack you again." He kept his eyes on mine as he lowered his head back to my pussy, his hand rubbing away the sting where he'd slapped me.

The thing was, the sting of the smack felt good, especially with the added rub afterwards. And the way his tongue moved along me combined with the lingering hurt to give me pleasure I didn't know I needed—so maybe I did a little more writhing on purpose.

"You liked that." He smacked me again on the other cheek, rubbing it away immediately, and I hummed as he did. He echoed my moan against my pussy and my knees nearly went out from underneath me. It was a good thing I was holding onto the island. Especially when the tip of his tongue reached out to my brush my clit with feather-like strokes.

I swear I started to purr.

He anchored his hands on my hips, his fingers digging into my flesh as his tongue made its way from my clit down to my hole in long luscious strokes. And then, just when I didn't think I could take it anymore, he pushed his tongue *inside* me, as far as his fingers had been. He was fast and strong, licking against my G spot, tongue-fucking me until I began to see spots in front of my eyes. He let go of my side and began to rub my clit with the pad of his thumb. I bucked my hips against the island, trying to get away from him, trying to get closer. Trying to get away. I couldn't tell what I wanted except that he was completely in control of giving it to me, and that scared the shit out of me.

He hooked his arms around me at my hips, though, so that I couldn't move and dove even deeper with his tongue, and that was when I finally reached the top. Unable to escape, having to stay there through the torment, having to give into his wicked attack.

"Holy shit," my teeth were chattering. "Holy shit, holy shit. I'm going to come." And I wasn't just saying it, I was actually doing it. My whole body was trembling and shaking, my legs and my arms and my knees and my insides as I groaned out a guttural sound I'd never made before.

Weston kept licking me until I was done. Until he'd coaxed the very last bit of my climax from my body, and I felt good everywhere.

When I was completely spent, he stood and pulled me to him, my back to his front. He still had his pants mostly on, but the warmth of his chest against my back sent shivers down my body. I could feel his cock again at the crack of my ass, but this time it was bare and begging for a warm place to nest.

"I need to be inside you," he said at my ear. I turned my face and his mouth was waiting to devour mine. I kissed him, kissed the taste of myself off of him until it mingled with whatever taste had been in my mouth before, until I couldn't distinguish what was him and what was me.

When he broke away, I was breathless.

"I need to be inside you," he said again.

"Yes," I said, because I needed that too, and because it was all I could say. "Yes."

"Should I stop for a condom?" he asked.

I didn't want to stop for anything. "Do you usually suit up?"

"Every time. Every single time." He rubbed the head of his dick up and down across my slit, so close to where I needed him. It was distracting. But I still heard what he said—heard what he *meant.*

That this was the first time he'd ever suggested not using a condom with a woman.

If he'd worn one with everyone else, there was no need for him to wear one with me. I had an implant. I couldn't get pregnant. Because of that stubborn streak I had, though, my first impulse was to say no, to tell him to go grab one.

But a bigger part of me embraced that desire I had to be different from everyone else, from every other woman he'd been with. Because I was so desperate to stand out from his crowd of women. To be the one unlike the others in his eyes.

"You're my fiancé. And I'm on birth control. I think at this point in a relationship we would not be using a condom."

It seemed to be exactly what he wanted to hear, and next thing I knew he was bending just a little bit, and I could feel his cock at my entrance. Then the tip was inside me, and then all of him was thrusting forward, in, and up.

We both grunted as he fed himself in completely.

"Holy shit, Elizabeth. You feel even better than I imagined." He bent his mouth to kiss me again, his hands gripping my breasts like handholds while he bucked into me over and over and over again. Each stroke came fast and deep, stretching and filling me.

I turned my mouth away from him to catch a breath, and he sucked down my neck, murmuring as he did. "So tight. So fucking hot."

Then he got bossy. "Touch yourself. You need to come again."

It felt so good, just having his cock rub inside me, and I was already so drained from the first orgasm. "I can't."

"You have to. I have to make you come again. Touch yourself, or I'm going to stop."

As if he didn't trust me, he took one of his hands off my breasts and used it to direct my hand down to my clit. Then he helped me touch myself, two fingers from him, two fingers from me, rubbing together in my juices, swirling around my sensitive bud. His other hand tweaked at my nipple, pulling it and tugging at it, sending sharp twinges of pleasure-pain down to my pussy. Then there was the *slap slap slap* from the top of his thighs against the bottom of my ass, and the clink of his belt as it rattled with each thrust. I couldn't come again. But it was all so fucking hot, so goddamn sexy.

And I *was* coming again. Tightening around his cock, pulsing, and keening.

"Just like that," he coaxed. "Fall apart, just like that."

This time when I finished, he turned me toward him and lifted me up so that my legs wrapped around his waist.

"Take me to bed," I said, half begging.

He nodded once. "Whose bed do you want to go to?"

"Yours."

It wasn't just that it was closer, but also, in the midst of all the hormonal fireworks, I was able to rationalize that it would be the bed I could leave when I needed to. And I'd have to leave it eventually.

But I wasn't thinking about that now. Now, I wasn't thinking at all.

Weston's room felt like miles away as he carried me with his cock between us, rubbing against my sensitive clit. Even just after my orgasm, I wanted him back inside me. I knew it was another form of torture, and while it was torturing him as well, it had to be pleasing him more to know what it was doing to me.

We kissed as we walked, little mewling sounds escaping from the back of my throat, sounds of need. Sounds of begging. I begged for mercy. Mercy that I didn't deserve, mercy I prayed he'd give me.

Once in his room, he tossed me onto the mattress and turned on the bedside lamp so I could see him, so he could see me. The bed frame in his room was high off the ground, and after he finished undressing, when he tugged my thighs to bring me to the edge of the bed, we were nearly lined up. I only had to lift my hips slightly to be able to reach him.

I bucked up before he even asked, impatient, greedy.

He chuckled, his dimples mocking me. "More?" he taunted, grazing his fingers across my wet slit. "You already need more?"

I propped myself up on my elbows and stared at him, my eyes saying what my voice was unwilling to. *Please, please. More, more.*

He rubbed the head of his cock against my entrance, teasing me by sticking it just barely inside before pulling out. I lurched forward, trying to get what I craved.

"You can't have it until you ask. Until you tell me what you want. Until you tell me *I'm* what you want." With his hand, he continued to rub up and down my slit, making wide circles around my electric bundle of nerves.

Goddammit, he was going to make me do it. Why was I so stubborn?

"Give it to me," I uttered. Would that be enough? I put my hand down to where I wanted him, landing on the spot he was purposefully avoiding, but he quickly swatted me away.

"Not good enough. Tell me it's me. Tell me it's my cock you want." He pushed just the tip in again, circling his hips so that I could feel him everywhere around the mouth of my entrance. I gasped, and he pulled out again.

"Fuck," I cried at his absence, my resolve crumbling in the face of my need. "It's you. Your fucking cock, Weston. Goddamn fucking asshole. Your fucking cock is what I want. Now get it in me."

With a satisfied grunt, he wrapped his arms around my thighs and thrust in hard, deep. He drove into me over and over and over again, showing me how magnificent his body was, how much he wanted me, needed me. I was mesmerized in the moment and swept away with waves of pleasure at once, swept away in watching him, in knowing how much he enjoyed being watched.

He lifted me higher, and my breasts began to bounce uncontrollably with his thrusts. I had the self-conscious urge to cover them up until I realized that Weston's gaze was trained on them, his eyelids half-closed like he was drugged from the erotic sight.

And he had other plans for my hands.

"Play with yourself," he gritted out, directing me to move my fingers to my pussy. "You need to come before I do."

I was already close to the brink; it wouldn't take long. I moved my hand down and only a couple of brushes of my two fingers—up and down, up and down—and then I was exploding, the tightening in my pelvis and my thighs transforming into strong bursts of cold-hot pleasure soaring down my legs into my toes, through my belly and torso, escaping up my throat in a hoarse, raspy cry of murmured curses and words that meant nothing mixed with words that meant everything—Weston's name and God's.

Weston sweetly coaxed me through my total abandonment. "You're so gorgeous when you come apart. So beautiful, baby. Let go. Just like that. You turn me on so much. Just like that." His fingers were digging into my thighs. And he was lifting up my legs higher until his body stuttered, his pelvis stilling against mine, as his face twisted into a new expression of anguish and delight. His orgasm was accompanied with a long wrenching groan that made me shake, its sound so erotic and primal.

Then he was finished.

He collapsed onto the bed beside me. We laid there for several minutes, me half off the bed, both of us on top of the bedspread. Though my body was finally still, my thoughts were now racing, circling so fast I couldn't keep any one thread in view. So I focused on my lungs and air and the in and the out of breathing.

After a few silent minutes, when my heart rate was beginning to settle, he sat, and I sat up with him. Then he stood, and I followed suit, awkward, not knowing how I was supposed to act. He pulled down the bedspread and the sheet, and I turned to leave. What else was there to do? He hadn't said a word to me, and I hadn't said a word to him. I'd never done this before. Never done casual sex. How did it work?

Running away was the easiest solution.

But before I could get too far, he wrapped his arm around my waist and tugged me back. "Where do you think you're going?"

I shrugged, unable to look at his eyes. His beautiful eyes that could always see right into me. "To my room?"

He pulled me closer until I was flush against him, his body warming mine, which was cooling with the sweat that had glistened all over me from our fucking. He kissed the top of my head, wrapping both arms around me now. "But if you go to your room, then I can't fuck you when I wake up in the middle of the night."

I relaxed, leaning into him. Then he wanted me again, as much as I wanted him. I cautiously lifted my gaze to his. "I don't know how to do this," I confessed.

He raised a brow, questioning.

"I've only ever slept with guys who were my boyfriend."

His mouth curled up ever so slightly, and he rubbed his thumb along my bottom lip. "And what would you do with your boyfriend, after you had amazing mind-blowing sex?"

Well, I'd never had amazing mind-blowing sex before. Just regular sex. But I let my mind wander back to those occasions, trying to remember the usual pattern after making love. "I guess...whoever would usually just hold me."

Weston let go of me.

I thought for a moment I'd scared him off, but he climbed in the bed and scooted over enough so that there was room for me. Then he reached his arm out inviting me into it. "Come on then. If that's what your boyfriend would do, I imagine that's what your fiancé would do, too."

My breath caught somewhere in my chest, trapped under the sudden expansion of my heart. I managed a quiet, "Okay." Then I turned off the bedside lamp, crawled into his arms, laid my head on his chest, let him wrap himself around me, and fell quickly asleep.

HE WOKE me in the early hours, climbing on top of me in the dark and easily slipping his cock into my entrance, as though he'd already memorized the way. We spoke no words, the only sounds the quiet gasps and moans of pleasure as he moved inside me, less furious, but still driven. I traced my fingers along his chest and shoulders, admiring every part of his solid form above me. Wanting him even as I had him. Wanting more of him. Wanting all of him.

After we'd both come, he drifted quickly back to sleep, spooning me from behind. I reached out and set the alarm on his bedside table, then lay awake for quite some time listening to the gentle even pattern of his breaths, wondering what all this would mean for us *after*. Wondering what would change.

Realizing nothing would change.

We'd had sex. That was all. But we were still two people tied to each other only through a business arrangement, nothing else, and even though his body felt good inside mine, even though he turned me on, even though he pushed all my buttons in the best ways—and the worst ways—we had no commitment to each other. Not really. And Weston was definitely not the kind of guy who was interested in more than a tumble or two. I wasn't naïve. I couldn't be stupid about him because he'd stuck his dick in me. I'd learned about men like him from my mother.

I'd learned about men like him from my father.

I barely slept after that.

When the alarm went off in the morning, I quickly turned it off, hoping not to wake him, and started to slip out of bed.

But Weston snagged my wrist and tugged me back down.

"Where do you think you're going?" he asked like he had last night, his voice rougher with sleep this time.

"I have to take a shower and get ready. My mom's driver will be here in an hour."

He lifted his head from the bed, his brows knit in confusion. "Driver? Are you going somewhere?"

I sighed in exasperation. No, nothing had changed. "My mother's birthday trip. You never listen to me."

He laid his head back down on the pillow. "I remember, I remember. I just forgot." He stroked his fingers along the length of my arm, up and down. "When will you be back? Friday?"

I nodded, trying to ignore how much I loved the feel of his fingers on my skin, how this simple touch could make my insides twist and my pussy slick.

"Let's have dinner then. Friday night." He sat up, simultaneously pulling me to him and kissed me. Briefly, but sweetly. "Okay?"

"Okay. Friday." That meant I had one week to get my head together. One week to try to forget how incredible our night had been.

But how did you forget a night that was unforgettable?

FIFTEEN
WESTON

WHEN I WOKE up later that morning, I could still smell her in my bed.

I could smell her in my room. My room that wasn't even my room—a guest room in her apartment that felt lonely and bare without her. It was an excuse to go to my own place for the weekend, a chance I didn't get often these days.

But without her, it would feel just as empty.

It was fucked up. *I* was fucked up. I'd slept with her, we'd done the deed, we had the sex. She was supposed to be out of my system by now. This wasn't how things were supposed to go.

I went down to the gym in her apartment building and did twice my usual number of everything—twice the arm workout, twice the back workout, double the time on the treadmill. When I headed back up to the apartment, her fancy maid had come in and changed the sheets, made the bed, and sprayed some kind of scented spray around. It no longer smelled like Elizabeth, which made it better. And worse.

Maybe it would just take a couple days to get her worked through my bloodstream. It had been so long since I'd had good sex

—sex at all, even—that maybe my body needed time to metabolize the endorphins. I gathered my stuff from her place and went home to bury myself in work for the rest of the weekend. There, I put my own glasses in the sink, and tried not to notice how quiet it was.

Monday morning wasn't any better. She was still in my head, but in new ways. In the past, everything had been my imagination, which had been frustrating because all I could do was fantasize about what it would feel like to touch her skin and hear her moan and see her face when she completely let go.

Finally, I'd gotten to enjoy it all, and that was exhilarating. But I felt like a man who'd been to the moon, and was now trying to readjust to life on Earth. It was satisfying and unsatisfying all at once. I found myself equally happy and confused. Jubilant and aching. Longing for what, I couldn't even begin to know.

It wasn't until I was in the elevator headed up to the offices at Reach, and other people were filing in, that I realized I had another dilemma that I hadn't considered yet.

And she was now standing next to me riding up to my floor.

"Morning," Sabrina said, her eyes shifting, looking everywhere but at me.

Now this was awkward.

She was probably embarrassed because of what happened in the closet on Friday night. She'd said it was okay, but it had to be embarrassing, to be standing next to me today. To still have to work with me when I'd rejected her.

And I hadn't only rejected her, I'd gone and slept with another woman the same night. An incredible, sexy, amazing, outspoken woman.

Was this something I needed to tell Sabrina about?

Considering how I'd told her I wasn't going to sleep with Elizabeth, and that I'd suggested we could get together when this whole charade was over—yeah, I probably needed to tell her.

Others got off the elevator on lower floors, and soon we were the only two people left. My gaze focused on the dial as we climbed closer to our destination, wondering if I should do this now or later.

Finally, I burst out, "We need to talk."

She side-eyed me. "If this is about Friday..." She gathered her thoughts and started again. "If this is about the restaurant, I don't think there's anything else that needs to be said."

Damn, I'd really stung her hard.

I had to sting her again. It sucked, but it had to be done. "This isn't about the restaurant."

"Oh." She rubbed her hands on her skirt. "Okay."

We arrived on our floor, and I stepped out of the elevator with her, assuming she would follow me to my office. But she lingered behind me.

"Right now good? If you're free..."

Sabrina's shoulders slumped. I would have to try to be gentle with her, as she was obviously upset already. "I'm free. I'll just drop off my bag and be there in a few."

I headed to my office, checked in with Roxie, put my briefcase down, unbuttoned my suit jacket, and got settled in at my desk. It was about ten minutes later when Sabrina arrived.

"He more relaxed than he was the other day, but something has him on edge. Good luck."

"I still hear you," I called out to my assistant, while simultaneously admiring how she'd correctly assessed my mood, and in such little time.

I stood up from my desk and walked toward her as Sabrina came in, so that I could close the door. The door was for Donovan—because he'd screamed at me about leaving it open while I'd been with her on Friday. But I was aware that Sabrina might think it was for other reasons, so I made sure to keep the windows clear. I invited her to take a seat and then returned to sit behind my desk.

She sat down and crossed one leg over the other and seemed to be as nervous about this conversation as I was. And no wonder. She was probably expecting that I would give her some consolation, a bunch of reasons why I hadn't been into her, and she'd have to relive the awkward moment all over again.

She hadn't realized yet that it was much, much worse.

She sighed.

I inhaled. "Friday night, after you left the restaurant..." I trailed off, not sure quite how to finish that sentence.

God, I didn't know how to fix this.

My silence seemed to urge words out of Sabrina. "Things change, you know, Weston. Things don't always happen the way we plan and—"

"I slept with Elizabeth," I blurted out. Ripping off the Band-Aid. That was the best way to do it.

She sat stunned. "Uh, what?"

I straightened my shoulders and met her eyes. "I slept with Elizabeth. I didn't mean to. I don't know where things are headed in the future, but I thought you deserved the truth."

"I see."

I studied her face, seeking a change in expression, finding none. It wasn't quite the reaction I'd expected. It was too calm. Too controlled.

"Are you upset?"

"No! Not in the least."

Huh.

Shouldn't she be at least a *little* disappointed that I hadn't held out for her? Or perhaps she was just very good at hiding her emotions.

She went on. "We didn't have an arrangement between us. I didn't expect anything from you."

Man, Sabrina was really letting me off the hook here, and I was grateful.

I grabbed the stapler from the corner of my desk, needing something for my hands to do. "I know, but we were in a closet together.

And I know I was acting weird that night, but it wasn't you." I pushed the stapler down several times, wasting a bunch of staples. "It was because I was all wrapped up with her, and this bullshit that's going on between her and me."

I searched for the right words to untangle the mess I'd made. Of my desk. Of the situation. Of my life.

Sabrina narrowed her gaze, watching me closely as I returned the stapler to its original position. "So you and Elizabeth...?"

It was obvious she was asking if we were a thing now.

"No. God, no." I'd answered too quickly. I needed to think about it. I picked up my pen and started flipping it back and forth between my fingers. "I mean." *Were* we a thing? We were engaged. We had an arrangement. "I don't know. It's complicated. Anyway."

Complicated. That was too simple of a word. It was more than complicated, actually. It was knotty. It was convoluted. It was all I could think about.

Sabrina sat back in her chair and folded her arms across her chest. "What does this mean for the pool? I had good money on you holding out."

"You placed a bet too?"

She shrugged, then grinned. "I'm joking. Any bet I would have placed seemed to be against my better interest."

I dropped the pen and put both palms flat on the desk. "But you're really okay with this situation?"

She smiled again. "I am." Her smile faded, and I tensed. "Actually, I slept with someone this weekend too."

I sat up straighter. This was...unexpected.

She paused to take a breath. "I slept with Donovan."

The air suddenly felt thick between us, my eyes squinting at her, my blood feeling hot, and not in the sexy way.

"Uh. Say something?" she prodded.

"I'm trying to decide if I'm jealous or if this relieves me of my guilt." I was also trying to decide if sleeping with a girl I was still entangled with made Donovan a giant douchecanoe. Well, more giant than I already gave him credit for.

She reached across the desk and playfully punched my lower arm. "It relieves you of your guilt. Jerk."

I nodded. "Donovan, huh?" I inhaled, trying to calm whatever fury was stirring inside me and nodded again. "I have to admit—I didn't see that coming."

But I hadn't seen much of anything besides Elizabeth in the last several weeks. Correction, last several months. Time was flying by, and I was spending all of it with the woman I was soon going to marry.

So I couldn't really say if Donovan was being a bad friend or a good friend. Was he looking after Sabrina? Helping her feel more at home in the city, less lonely, less rejected? Was he really interested in her? Or was he being a fucking prick, telling me I couldn't have her, and then banging her to prove it?

Whatever it was, I was cool with it on Sabrina's end. She was content with her one-night stand, which she insisted it was, as we talked more. And she couldn't know about all the layers of baggage between me and Donovan.

So, good for her. And maybe even good for them.

Definitely good for me and Sabrina. It felt like whatever we'd had was resolved and done. It was probably the most grown-up way I'd ever ended a relationship in my life, much more mature than the dodge-and-delete method I'd perfected over the years.

If only dealing with the other woman in my life could be as easy.

THE REST of the week sauntered by in a state of unease. Each minute ticked by slowly; each hour seemed agonizingly long. Before I'd slept with Elizabeth, she'd been a distraction at work, creeping into my thoughts while I tried to concentrate on what I needed to at the office. I'd often been consumed with my anger, my irritation, and my desire.

After I'd slept with her?

I was twice as consumed. Twice as agonized. Each night now, I tossed and turned, unable to sleep, even after jerking off. It was like before I'd been so horny and filled with lust, and now I was in need of something else. Something that no amount of alcohol or work or time in the gym or staring at my graphic novels could fill or replace. I just wanted to talk to her, to fight with her.

I missed her.

Jesus, I'd never missed a woman in my life. What the hell had she done to me?

By Friday I was so wrapped up in this new amazing-terrible-wonderful-irritating emotion inside of me that I was anxious for her to return that night. Nervous to see her again, but anxious for it nonetheless.

In desperation, I stormed into Nate's office over lunch.

"You said it would make it better," I said accusingly as I walked in.

He cocked his head at me, setting his deli sandwich onto his desk, which was set at standing position. He gestured at the chairs stationed by the windows, indicating that I should take a seat. I strolled over and sat down in one of them, my foot bouncing as I unbuttoned my suit jacket.

He strolled over and sat down in the seat opposite of me. "I take it you and Elizabeth..." He let the silence fill in the blank.

"I thought you could tell. You said you'd be able to tell." I was feeling grumpy, grumpy at Nate specifically since he was the one who'd suggested that sleeping with Elizabeth was the right thing to do, and though I didn't regret it, it really hadn't seemed to fix anything.

"Oh, I can tell. You've been much happier." He reconsidered.

"Or, you were earlier in the week. Now it seems you've gotten yourself riled up again. Want to tell me what's going on?"

I bent over and leaned my elbows on my knees, noticing they were both bouncing now, and tried to put this problem into words. "Well, we did it, like you said we should. It was supposed to get her out of my system. It was supposed to get me over her. But it hasn't changed anything. I'm still just as fucked up about this. She's been out of town all week long, and I'm still thinking about her. She's everywhere. I can't get her out of my damn head."

"Uh-huh."

"I'm miserable." I shook my head. "Except at the same time, I'm not, because I keep remembering that night and all the…things…and the…ways…" I could dish about sex as well as the next guy, but it didn't seem appropriate to dish about Elizabeth. "And remembering it makes me feel all weird and…good. And shit."

Nate nodded. "Right."

"I know what I have to do, though," I said, the idea coming to me suddenly.

"Of course you do. What is it?" Nate asked patiently, and it didn't escape me that this felt an awful lot like the therapy sessions I'd tried a couple of times a few years back when I'd first realized my father was an asshat. Minus the rage and the overpriced bill.

And I'd just had a bigger breakthrough in Nate's office than anything I could have discovered from that stuffy psychiatrist.

"I have to have sex with her again." I jumped up and started pacing the room. This was brilliant, and obviously the right answer. We had to continue to be together through the engagement anyway, and of course, this had been why I had been worked up all week. Because I didn't know how to deal with the after-things, with women I wouldn't bang again after we'd had sex once.

So the solution here was to just keep doing it. That hadn't really occurred to me as an option for some reason.

Perhaps because living together and sleeping together with the same woman—a woman who was wearing a ring that I put on her finger—felt an awful lot like a real relationship, the kind I'd always managed to avoid.

"All right," Nate laughed harder than I thought he needed to. "How does Elizabeth feel about this? Do you think she's open to continuing?"

I shrugged, not really seeing why she *wouldn't* be open to it. It had been pretty damn good sex. "I haven't talked to her since."

Nate's jaw went slack, his eyes wide. "You haven't talked to her since you slept with her? Not at *all*? Not even a text message?"

My pacing slowed and I began to feel a new sense of dread. Shit. Had I fucked this up already?

"Look, I don't usually talk to the girls afterwards. They are usually texting *me*." Which begged the question—why *hadn't* she texted me? Had it not been as good for her as I'd thought? Had I done something wrong? Did she...regret it somehow?

Nate frowned and shook his head. "I don't know, man. Women really like to be reassured after that kind of thing. Especially if you want to have another shot with them."

I sank back down in the seat across from him. "Shit, Nate." I ran a hand through my hair. "Is it too late now? She comes back tonight. We're supposed to have dinner. What do I do?"

Nate nodded, thinking. "Your best plan is to make it seem like the space was part of your strategy. And then reassure her. *Reassure her, Weston*," he repeated. "Make sure she knows she's special to you."

It was my turn to frown. Special to me? I didn't like that. To be certain, I'd never wanted to continue sleeping with a woman like I wanted to continue sleeping with her, so that made her special in a way. But I didn't want to give her the wrong idea or anything.

This was still a business arrangement.

Nate seemed to sense my train of thought. "You don't have to tell her you're in love with her. Just let her know that you had a good time with her. That you're not just using her for her body. Are you using her for her body?"

In the week that she had been gone, I had thought about Elizabeth's body a whole hell of a lot. The things I wanted to do to it, the things I'd already done to it, the things I wanted her body to do to mine. But I'd also thought about conversations I wanted to have with her. Things I wished I'd said, things I was sure she'd argue with, but I'd made up counterarguments, and then made up fascinating ways to make up after we argued about it.

"No. I can honestly say I'm not just using her for her body." Why did that feel like such a gut-wrenching admission?

"I know," Nate said, again. The therapist who saw all. "Just making sure *you* knew. Now make sure *she* knows."

I left Nate's office and immediately started composing a text message as I walked back to my own corner of the floor, worried I was already too late.

> Still on for dinner tonight? We could meet at Gaston's at seven.

Nervous, I hit SEND, regretting it immediately. Elizabeth liked making decisions. I should have given her the choice of restaurant.

I stopped in the middle of the hall, halfway between Nate's office and mine, and sent another message.

> Or we can go somewhere else. Tell me where and I'll make the reservation.

I sent it, shaking my head at myself for not taking care of this earlier in the week. Donovan owned Gaston's—I could always get in there last minute. Finding reservations last minute elsewhere was going to be tough. There were only a few strings I could pull through some clients. Some other strings I could pull if I called my father.

I didn't want to call my father.

But she responded before I had to get too worked up about other options.

> Gaston's is fine. I'll see you then.

Immediately I felt better.

Except then another text came through.

> Could you give me Elizabeth's number?

Clarence Sheridan.

Why the fuck did he want her number? Was he still into her? If I gave it to him, would he call her? Would they get back together?

"You're setting a great example for the staff," Donovan said sarcastically, startling my gaze up from my screen. "Maybe if you were more focused on your work than your phone, we'd actually get some stuff done around here."

It was a typical snide Donovan remark, one that I would usually let roll off my back, but I was stressed about this latest text, and he'd pushed me to my limit. He'd been playing me like I was his puppet, telling me what to do and when to do it, telling me who I could sleep with and who I couldn't, treating me like I was a pawn on his chessboard. That was annoying enough, but to get razzed about it too was pushing me over the edge.

On top of that, he still hadn't told me about sleeping with Sabrina, and that pushed a bunch of emotional buttons that I had yet to face. Not the least of which was— why hadn't he confided in me about it? Why did I have to find out about it from her?

I'd been so irked by his lack of disclosure, I'd purposefully not told him about sleeping with Elizabeth.

And I was still irked. More than irked.

So instead of shrugging off his asshole comment like I normally would, I looked him right in the eye. "So, you and Sabrina, huh? Maybe it's *your* distraction that's compromising office production."

I left him in the hall before he could reply, knowing Donovan hated it when he didn't get the last word.

Back in my office, I made a decision. I'd waited too long to take control of my own life. I'd let others run the show while I'd sat back playing whatever cards I was dealt.

Well, no more.

It was time for me to be the dealer.

Starting with Elizabeth.

I would take Nate's advice—make a plan, find the words, let her know that I wanted things to go on.

And I dealt with Clarence's text the same way I dealt with all annoying messages that came in on my phone, usually from *my* ex-lovers, not someone else's—I deleted it and never thought about it again.

SIXTEEN
ELIZABETH

I RETURNED TO MANHATTAN, feeling cool and calm and confident. Relaxed. A week without Weston had cleared my head. I was a new woman, pampered and refreshed.

At least, that's what I'd told myself throughout the entire car ride home.

All of it was bullshit. It was evident even in the way that I had dressed for tonight's dinner with Weston. My dress was a load of mixed messages. I'd intended to wear something smart and modest. Instead, here I was in a low-cut black sexy mid-length. It cinched in my waist and hugged my hips, creating a perfect hourglass. While it didn't scream seductress, it was definitely one of the more provocative outfits I owned.

Maybe I just wanted to remind Weston what he'd had. What he couldn't have again. That's what I said to my reflection in the mirror by the coat check at Gaston's as I double-checked my appearance.

I turned to the host, already fifteen minutes late. "Are you ready to be seated, Ms. Dyson?" he asked. "Mr. King is waiting for you."

I wasn't ready. I would never be ready. "Yes, please."

He took me inside the restaurant, toward the tables near the windows. Gaston's was fine dining, and the view was spectacular, since the restaurant was located at the top of the building on Fifty-Ninth Street, just across from Central Park, which was framed by the city itself. It was a romantic spot, and as we approached the table, Weston stood for me, handsome in his business suit, his dimpled grin greeting me.

Butterflies took off in my stomach at the sight of that smile; it wasn't a reaction I could control. So I smiled back. As the host pulled out my chair, Weston leaned forward and kissed me.

"Now that's a way to say hello," the host teased.

"I haven't seen my fiancée in a week," Weston said, his eyes never leaving me. "I've missed her."

The butterflies turned into an avalanche of snow at his words. His endearment wasn't just intoxicating, it didn't just make me feel fluttery inside—it made me feel overwhelmed, like I was being crushed with the weight of something bigger than I could handle.

Was it even real? Had he really missed me? Or was this part of the show we were putting on?

I was trembling as I took my seat, grateful there was already wine on the table. Weston reached to pour me a glass before the host could offer, so with no other task to complete, the man left, and we were alone.

I smoothed my napkin on my lap and grabbed a hunk of bread, eager to keep my hands busy as Weston finished filling my glass.

"How was Connecticut?" he asked, setting the bottle down as I took a sip of my wine. It was white and crisp, like the autumn air had been outside.

But here inside, the air was warm, and the chardonnay felt good going down. "It was relaxing. We did a lot of relaxing." And a lot of thinking. A lot of thinking about Weston and his lips and his tongue and his body. His body inside mine.

"I didn't reach out, because I thought you might want space."

"I still had to share the suite with my mother. And she's messier than you. Though we had housekeeping every day, so that made it bearable."

"That's not what I meant by needing space."

I swallowed and glanced up at him. "You mean because we had sex." I'd wondered if my phone wasn't getting texts initially when I hadn't heard from him, but then I'd gotten one from Marie asking about my mother, and another from a college friend.

I shook my head. I couldn't feel that bad about his silence, because I didn't try to reach out to Weston either. Then I recited the words I'd said over and over and over again to myself this last week. "Nothing's changed."

At the same time, he said, "Everything's changed."

We stared at each other, both of us caught off guard by the other's answer. *Everything's changed.* My heart began to race for no reason except for those two words.

Weston looked almost hurt by what I'd said. "What do you mean nothing's changed?" he asked, his brows furrowed.

I looked around to make sure that we were in a private enough section that no one could hear us. We were. "Because nothing has. We're still just pretending for the sake of our respective businesses. We're still only in a *fake* relationship. You still don't want to live in my apartment all the time. You're still insistent that you want to split our time between the two places. You still won't get a damn maid."

I looked at him as though I had proven my point, which I felt I had, and yet I went on. "You still have yet to tell me what's going on with your family."

He waved his hand, stopping me from going on. "My family has nothing to do with anything. They are not a part of this. And it's irritating that you keep bringing it up."

"And *I'm* still going to be irritated every time you mention Sabrina's name."

He glared at me. "I was a dick about that, and I admitted it. But she works with me. I'm going to mention her name—"

"Look, we're still fighting, even." Nothing had changed.

"This isn't fighting," he said.

"What is this, then?"

"Foreplay?" He grinned, his eyes gleaming mischievously.

"It's bickering, like we always bicker," I said, trying to ignore the images that last comment brought up and how they made my legs shake. "How can you say things are different?"

"Yes, yes. All that. Still the same." I was suddenly moving closer to him and realized he was pulling me nearer with his foot wrapped around the leg of my chair. He didn't stop until we were side by side instead of angled toward each other, until we were looking out the window into the quiet darkness that was Central Park.

He put his arm on the back of my chair, his mouth near my ear. "But now," he said, his breath tickling my neck, sending electric shocks through my veins. "We can fuck."

I was suddenly hot everywhere, and it wasn't from the wine. My cheeks felt red and flushed. I turned my face toward him and our mouths were so close we could kiss.

"You want to...? Again...?" I tightened my glutes and thighs as I asked, as though that could hold the want and desire inside me, as though that could keep my panties from getting wet. I'd tried so hard in the week I'd been away from him not to imagine another night of passion. Tried not to relive the one night we'd had.

But every time the lights had gone out and my eyes had closed, he was all I could see, and I swear I had his touch memorized. Goose pimples would sprout up just by thinking of him. By remembering his mouth on my collarbone, his lips along my shoulders, on my breasts. It was absolute torture to share a room with my mother.

All my masturbation had to be done in the shower, and with the insane amount of lust that was inspired by my daydreams of Weston, I'd found myself making excuses to take more than one a day.

But in no time during any of that fantasizing had I ever thought he would want to do it again. He was a player. Weren't those guys only into one-time-per-woman deals?

I felt his fingers on my shoulder now, on the opposite side from where my head was turned. Felt his touch grazing down my bare arm. He looked me directly in my eyes.

"Do you *not* want to do it again?" he asked, curiously, as though he hadn't even considered that was a possibility.

"I didn't think *you* would want to do it again," I informed him honestly.

"Oh, I want to do it again, Elizabeth. I really, really want to do it again. It's all I can think about."

My breath caught, and I pulled my head back, studying his face to be sure he was telling the truth. Everything in his expression said he was sincere. "I didn't know."

He moved in closer, his lips brushing against mine. "I'm sorry I didn't make it clear. I should have texted you. I should've called."

I really hadn't expected that from him, but now that he'd suggested it, I wanted to know more. "What would you have said?"

He brushed his nose against my skin down to my earlobe and said in a hushed voice. "I would've told you how much I thought about you all week. How blue my balls were over you." His hand was on my knee, moving higher onto my bare thigh. "I would've told you how I couldn't stop thinking about touching you. I would've told you how hard you make me. I'm hard right now. I need to know if you're wet."

I was, and his hand was sliding higher on the inside of my thigh, about to find out the answer for himself. It was so fucking hot and so amazing and I wanted him to keep going, wanted his fingers to touch me and find out...but—

"Wait. Stop." I recognized the feeling of panic before I could even understand the reasons why.

Fortunately, Weston was a decent man and he pulled away, immediately taking his hand off of me, and setting it back in his own lap. He left his other hand on the chair behind me, but he gave me space. Too much space. I missed how close he had been just a moment before.

But now the waiter was here asking if we were ready to order, and I couldn't even think—I was still wanting Weston's hands on me and wishing he was inside me—I couldn't be bothered with the daily soup and fish specials.

"We're going to need a moment," Weston said, reading me. "In fact, I'll signal you when we're ready."

The waiter nodded and shuffled off to his other tables. There was a beat of silence, and I took a swallow of wine, trying to figure out what I was going to say to Weston to get him to touch me again. Also, how not to panic this time when he did.

How was I going to explain to him what was going on inside my head when I couldn't even explain it to myself?

Thankfully, he asked the right questions, the kinds of questions that helped me think, helped me sort myself out.

"Can I ask why? No judgment. Are you not into me? Or is it that we're in public? Because it's okay if you're not into that like I am. Just because it turns me on, doesn't mean it has to turn you on."

I swiveled my face toward him. "That's just it. It *does* turn me on. A lot. I think I kind of made fun of you at first when I realized that was something you're into, and then I realized that it was really awesome."

He nodded. "Really awesome." He paused, and his face changed. "Then it's me. You don't want me touching you."

"Weston, I can't... I don't even know how to put into words how much I want you to touch me." I looked down at my hands, too embarrassed to face him for this. "This doesn't make any sense to you, I'm sure. I wish I knew how to explain. See, it's one thing if Darrell thinks all I'm good for is spreading my legs. If he thinks I'm slutty it doesn't matter. And it really doesn't matter if most of the Internet thinks I'm slutty, either, though. I mean it kind of does. Since I'm trying to build a reputation of being a classy woman and everything. One step at a time, I guess."

I snuck a glance up at him and saw he was listening to me carefully. "I know the Internet isn't here right now, that it's just me and you. And that's the problem, because I really do care what *you* think of me. It really matters to me that you respect me and that you think that I'm capable of being this thing that I'm trying to be."

Out of the blue, tears stung my eyes, and my throat got tight.

"You're the one who's been teaching me and building me up for this, and if you don't think I'm a classy person, if you only think that I'm worthy of spreading my legs, then—"

He cut me off. "I respect the fuck out of you." His hand was back on my knee, but comforting this time, not attempting to make a move. "Are you saying you're worried that having sex with me takes that away? That if I find out you're into kinky things, I'll think you're less brainy?"

It *was* what I was saying, but I couldn't trust my voice. So I just stared at my hands, twisting them around each other.

"Did you know the minute I saw you, I couldn't breathe? I lost all ability to speak. I didn't even know words anymore. It wasn't even because you looked amazing, which you did, by the way. It was because I could tell you were the smartest person in the room. Do you know how hot that was? I am *so* attracted to you, Elizabeth. I have been from the minute you walked into that Reach lounge, because I could tell you were a woman who knew what she was after, a confident woman, a smart woman. And the way you could just bulldoze Donovan? That took some serious skill. I have mad respect for you. I spent that entire meeting hiding my boner."

Air stuttered into my lungs. I burned with the relief of it.

"And every time you speak, every time you argue with me—I wouldn't put up a fight if I didn't enjoy hearing what you had to say." He leaned in close again, his lips brushing my neck. "The only reason I want to touch you right now so fucking bad is because I respect you."

Under the table, I took his hand and guided it up under my dress toward the damp spot on the crotch of my panties. I let go of his hand once he was where I wanted him, and grabbed on tight to the chair edge while he slipped his fingers inside my panties to find my clit under the hood of skin where it was hiding, plump and aroused from his words.

I could feel him smile at my ear. "So wet. You want this so bad." He massaged expertly in fine circles, small and then wide, clockwise then counter. "You're so disciplined and strong, your eyes on the goal. Not even giving in to your own pleasure when you think it might take you away from what you want in the end. If you had any idea how much this stuff fucking turns me on, Lizzie... I wish I had half your ambition. Your drive." I opened my legs wider, making it easier for him to dip his fingers down my slit and back up. "I wish I had your brain. You're the total package—sex and smarts all in one. The sexiest thing I've ever had underneath me. The sexiest thing I've ever had in my bed, in my mouth, around my cock."

I focused on the cars driving through the park, the dots of light beneath us as my orgasm built. Each compliment, each line of praise was as much of a turn-on, as arousing as what he was doing with his hands, and it wasn't long before I was exploding, right there in the restaurant, coming from just his whispered words in my ear and his thumb on my clit. I tried to swallow my gasps, tried not to make a single noise. Weston took his free hand and covered my mouth to help stifle the sound, and I turned my face toward his, locked my eyes on his baby-blue gaze, and for the first time in my twenty-five years—as I was climaxing in a French restaurant owned by Donovan Kincaid—it occurred to me that maybe men didn't just hurt women after all.

"Can we go home now? I'm not really in the mood to eat anything," I said, when I'd come down, desperate for another orgasm with him inside me.

"The only thing I'm hungry for is you."

And for the second Friday in a row, we skipped The Sky Launch and stayed in.

SEVENTEEN
WESTON

"YOU GREW UP OUT HERE, not in the city." Elizabeth made it sound more like a statement than a question as I pulled into the driveway at my parent's house in Larchmont, probably because I'd told her this already.

"Yep." It was Thursday, nearly a week after she'd come back from her spa vacation, and we were taking another trip, this time together and just for a day. I'd borrowed one of Donovan's cars to make the ninety-minute drive out here to the suburbs. It seemed stupid to use Elizabeth's driver to come to my childhood home, and even more stupid to take a train, especially if we planned to lug a bunch of crap back with us.

"And your dad did that commute every day of your life?" she asked as I put the Tesla into park in the circle drive.

"Ten-hour workdays, five days a week. He had a driver so he worked in the car both to and from. He still does it. Mom says his days are shorter now." I turned off the car and looked over at my fiancée. "Mom wanted the house. It was the price she had to pay. At least that's what she always said to me."

For all her talk of sacrifice, I'd learned it had a limit.

But we hadn't come out here to get worked up about the past.

"Let's do this," I said to myself more than to Elizabeth, then opened the door of the car and ran around to her side to open hers. Together, we walked up to the front of the Georgian-style house. I pulled out my spare key—it was strange that I had one, and not strange, too. After all, I'd grown up in this house. And yet now it felt like it belonged to somebody else, like I was an intruder sneaking up on it.

With sweaty hands, I entered my code into the security pad, praying it still worked, and when the light went green, I put my key in the door, and we slipped inside.

Once we were both in the house, I took Elizabeth's coat, then peeled off my own and hung them both in the hall closet. I couldn't shake how nervous and uncomfortable I felt being here. Being here with *her*. There were so many ghosts from the past, memories of a lifetime spent in these rooms. Thankfully, we didn't need to take a tour of the grounds and visit them. It was a straight shot to where I was headed today—through the gallery, past the living room, into the library.

I grabbed Elizabeth's hand and started tugging her in the direction I wanted to go, when Linda, our housekeeper and my former nanny, appeared in the archway coming from the dining room.

"Weston," she greeted me affectionately, her Swedish accent still lingering after all these years. I let go of Elizabeth's hand so she could hug me. "What are you doing here? It's been so long. You nearly gave me a heart attack. I heard someone walking through the house. I thought we had a prowler."

I kissed her on the cheek. "Just me. I didn't tell anyone I was coming. It was last minute. Needed to grab some things from the library." I turned toward Elizabeth. "Linda, this is my—" I paused. I'd introduced her as my fiancée to everyone in town, including my parents, but in some ways I was closer to Linda than I was to them. It felt weird to tell this lie to the woman who had gotten me through both AP European history and my first wet dream.

My former caretaker finished the sentence for me. "I've heard much about your fiancée, Elizabeth. I'm right to assume that you're her?"

"That's me," Elizabeth said, smiling nervously. She held her hand out to shake, but Linda drew her in for a hug that Elizabeth did well in tolerating.

"I'm so glad to meet you. A little heartbroken that it hasn't happened sooner." Linda glared at me in the way she always had when I was younger, the glare she used when she wanted me to know she was disappointed in me without actually saying the words.

"Well, you've met her now. You can stop with the guilt trips." I snagged Elizabeth's hand again and started toward the library. We were already going to be here all day, and I didn't want to risk staying any later than we had to. "I don't mean to cut this short, but we have, you know..."

"Always busy, that one," Linda said, sticking her tongue out. "Go on into your library, and I'll bring you some coffee and cookies."

"Thank you, Linda. You're the best." I turned forward, pulling Elizabeth closer to me as we headed to the library.

"She seems nice. Pretty, too," she said, looking back to where Linda had just disappeared into the kitchen.

"Oh, you can't even imagine how many times I spanked off to her when I was growing up." Confessions of a former horny teenager.

And then we were in the library, the reason for our trip to Larchmont and my day off from Reach.

"This is it," I announced.

It wasn't that the library was so spectacular. It was that all my books from school were still here, including all my textbooks, complete with the notes I'd taken in business school. That wasn't the kind of thing that you could just buy on Amazon and have shipped to you. I'd tried to keep her out of this piece of my life, but so much of the stuff I wanted to teach Elizabeth was here on these shelves.

And the more time I spent with her, the weirder she found that separation, so this seemed like a good idea.

My parents had always believed that sharing was what you did with books. And I did rightfully own a lot of the ones that were here already, so it wasn't like I was doing something wrong by showing up and grabbing what I wanted. But I had purposefully not announced my intentions, afraid my mother would have skipped her weekly bridge game, or worse—that she would've told my father, and he would be here when we arrived.

No, this was perfect. A quiet house, with no one but me and Elizabeth and Linda.

"This is really nice," she said, trailing her fingers along the spines of books that lined the bookshelves as she walked along them. "My father had a library like this in his château in France. He never let me touch those, though."

She drew a book out of the section dedicated to Peter Drucker and flipped through the pages. "And you're serious that I can take whatever I want? Your parents won't miss them?"

"My father will only be pissed if you take any of his Steve Berry's or Dan Brown's. Other than that, he won't even notice." I headed toward the wall that I knew contained my textbooks from college and started pulling the books I wanted to take. *Business Ethics: Concepts and Cases, Consumer Behavior, Anatomy of a Ponzi Scheme.* I laughed to myself, finding the last one on the shelf.

My father could've written that book.

I flipped open my old earmarked copy of *Business Law* and sunk down in the oversized leather armchair while Elizabeth collected books she was interested in. Thirty minutes went by, then forty, and soon I found I was not reading at all, but staring out the window at the bay in the backyard. It was a beautiful house to grow up in, a beautiful life that I had taken for granted.

It was the kind of place I liked taking girls home to, to impress them, the kind of place that Elizabeth was already accustomed to. The kind of place where she deserved to live. I felt an ache between my ribs because I couldn't give it to her, which was dumb, because I wasn't trying to give her any life at all.

And even if I were, I hated the kind of sacrifices this house had required. Yes, my mother loved her maid and her groundskeepers and her water view—at the cost of only seeing her husband two days a week. At the cost of everything he did during his time away from this house.

Reach would one day be that successful, as big as King-Kincaid had been for my father and Donovan's father. I believed it, not just because I believed in myself and our company, but because Donovan had the skill of not letting anything go any way except exactly how he'd planned. And he planned for us to be successful. So it would happen.

But even when it did, I didn't want to only come home to see Elizabeth on the weekend, only see our children from the doorway of the bedroom while they slept in their beds every night.

Why this fantasy had Elizabeth's name in it, I had no idea. Except that she was the one currently wearing my ring and playing my bride-to-be.

Anyway, I guessed I'd rather live in the city. I could raise kids in the city, as tricky as that was. Donovan had grown up that way, and he'd turned out...well, he'd turned out.

And I was a long way away from having kids, so all of this was ridiculous overthinking, inspired by being in my childhood home with someone who had me talking about weddings all the time.

There was a bustle in the house all of a sudden, voices coming from the vicinity of the kitchen. Linda had already brought us the coffee and snacks, and a glance at the clock on the wall said it was about time for my mother to be home.

Elizabeth heard it too, and looked over at me expectantly.

"I'll go tell my mother we're here," I said, getting up before she could offer to join me.

I left the room, closing the library doors behind me, afraid that whatever conversation I had with my mother might escalate quickly, and I didn't want to disturb Elizabeth and her studying.

As I'd suspected, I found my mom in the kitchen, filling up a glass with ice water from the dispenser in the refrigerator. She looked over her shoulder at me, then back to the task at hand.

"Linda said you were here," she said crisply, obviously upset. "If you'd told me you were coming I would have had lunch prepared."

"Lunch wasn't necessary, Mom. We didn't come for food. We came for books." I stuck my hands in my jean pockets, avoiding the temptation to reach out to her physically.

She turned around toward me and took a swallow of her water, then put it down on the counter between us. I'd left that barrier on purpose.

"Books. You came for books?" It seemed like she was sorting through a lot of thoughts in her head, a lot more than she was speaking out loud.

"I'm helping Elizabeth brush up on her business skills, and there's a lot of textbooks I left here."

She nodded. "Your father's not going to be happy he missed you. Are you coming home for Thanksgiving at least?"

I hadn't spent a holiday in this house for more than three years. It was amazing that she kept asking. Amazing how I still got choked up when I told her, "No."

"Your father won't be happy about that either," she said sharply.

I looked out the window and caught a heron flying, tracked its flight with my gaze. It was easier than watching her when I said, "Yep. I'm sure he'll be disappointed."

I knew she wanted me to offer her more, but I didn't have more to give her. It was hard enough being on her turf. Couldn't she see that?

When I turned my head back to her, she was patting the kitchen counter with her hand soundlessly. Our eyes met, and hers were brimming with tears.

Jesus. Not today, Mom. Please.

But I didn't say it. I didn't say anything. I let her talk instead. Let her say the things pressing against her heart, pushing those tears to the surface.

"I understand why you're upset, Weston. I do. I didn't for a long time, but I do now. I just don't understand why you're so upset with *me*."

"I'm almost *more* upset with you than with him," I said, exasperated. She *didn't* understand. She didn't understand at all.

"Why? What did I ever do except—"

I lurched forward and placed my hands on the counter. "You encouraged him, Mom. You *begged* him to do the wrong thing. You could have convinced him—"

"I couldn't live without him! We would've lost everything. Our house. Your trust fund. The company, Weston. Everything. Don't you get it?"

The sacrifice was too great to pay. That's what she was saying.

Too great for *her* to pay, anyway. She didn't care that someone else had to pay it for her.

Well, I did.

"I came for the books, Mom," I said, pushing off the counter, stepping away. "I didn't come for this conversation."

I headed back into the library and shut the doors behind me when I was inside. Then I locked them, afraid my mother would come in after us. I didn't need any more of her tears and her heartache. Her excuses.

Elizabeth looked up from her book, but the look I gave her said I wasn't in the mood to talk, and she went right back to reading.

My mother did try the door handles, but she didn't knock when she was unable to open them. Ten minutes later, though, a text came across my phone from my sister, Noelle.

> Mom says you're not coming home for Thanksgiving.

> I'm spending it with Elizabeth's family

It was manipulative of my mother to get my little sister involved.

> I was really hoping to meet her!

> You'll meet her at the wedding.

I felt bad about not telling Noelle the truth about my arrangement with Elizabeth. I knew I'd tell her eventually, maybe even at the wedding if I got a moment alone with her. If not, sometime later. There was a decade between us, but I liked the kid. And if she told my parents, I guess I'd have to live with that. It didn't really matter if they knew.

"You're texting Sabrina, aren't you?" Elizabeth said from where she was curled up on the couch.

I let my gaze shift over to her, a grin playing on my lips. I hadn't told her about the shift in my relationship with Sabrina to just friends yet. It was too fun to let her stew with jealousy.

"It was my sister," I said.

"Oh. I was sure it was Sabrina because of the way your face got all broody. She's usually the one who has you riled up."

No, it was usually Elizabeth who had me riled up, and she

knew it. She was taunting me. Even after a week of sex every night, it still seemed poking and prodding was our foreplay.

I didn't mind at all.

But we were still in this house and my head was still in the other room with my mother, and I needed to untangle the knots in my psyche before I could play naughty with her.

"I have a business ethics question to pose to you," I said, suddenly wanting to tackle this from another angle.

"Should companies have a no-fraternization rule amongst managers and their employees?"

She stretched her legs out on the ground in front of her. "I do think that would be a good policy. I'm surprised Reach doesn't have such a rule in place."

I laughed. "Donovan and I are co-CEOs and all three vice presidents are dirty, filthy men. The only one of them who might have suggested a no-fraternization policy just banged my next-in-command." Maybe I wasn't too interested in keeping the information to myself after all.

Elizabeth's brows rose in shock as she figured out who I must be talking about. "Donovan slept with Sabrina? That's surprising." She twisted her lip in that awkward cute way she often did. "Were you jealous?"

"As far as I know, it was only a one-night thing. Don't get too excited." She'd kicked her shoes off earlier, and her toenails, crimson from her trip to the spa the week before, tempted me. I reached down and grabbed one of her feet and set it in my lap, massaging her sole. "Anyway, that wasn't the ethics question I wanted to pose."

"You can ask me anything as long as you're doing that," she said, sinking into my massage. She closed the book she'd been reading and tossed it aside. "Hit me."

"So let's say you're a major shareholder of Dyson Media, and you also participate on the Board of Directors. And then the board votes for you to take a role as an officer. You're responsible for maintaining the best interest of the corporation. Not only are you actively involved in the day-to-day operations, but you also report to the shareholders."

"Once I inherit, I'll hold seventy-five percent of the ownership. The majority of the shareholders will be *me*."

"Right, but even if you are the majority, you're still responsible to everyone."

"I know, I know," she said defensively. "Do you think I don't listen to anything you say in these little lessons of yours the last few months? Sure doesn't seem like *Darrell* acts like he's responsible to one-hundred percent of the owners. But go on."

"There's a company scandal. Something that goes deep on many levels. It's maybe not illegal, but definitely unethical." I tried to be vague in the scenario. I didn't want her to assume I had any reason for being specific.

She ticked her head to the side. "Do I know about the scandalous behavior as it's going on? Or only after it's discovered?"

"You know from the very beginning," I said moving on to her other foot.

"Well, that doesn't sound like me. I would've nipped it in the bud as soon as I knew about this terrible behavior." She moaned at the end of her sentence as I found a particularly sensitive spot on her foot, and my dick went semi-hard.

And that was the problem with this proposed situation—Elizabeth never would be involved with a scandal like this to begin with.

"But just say you were. For whatever reason, you were convinced it was the right way to go, and then it becomes not the right way to go. Someone's going to have to take the fall for it, because the news gets out and everyone knows Dyson Media is involved with this really terrible scandal."

"So is that the question? If I take the fall for it?" She stared up at me with her big beautiful eyes blinking, so brilliant she could see to the end of my scenario.

"Yeah. That's the question. Do you take the fall or do you let someone within the company take the fall?" My heart started pounding in my chest, my hands felt sweaty as they rubbed the inside sole of Elizabeth's foot. It was a stupid, silly example of a question, and I was placing all this weight on it. I was desperate for Elizabeth's answer to give me some sort of absolution, and I didn't even need absolution. I felt good in my decision. Felt good in my stance.

I did want to hear *her* stance, though.

She tilted her head again, her eyes lifting upward and to the left as she considered. "I suppose I'd have to let somebody in the company take the fall for me. Which is terrible. And I feel godawful about saying that." She wrapped her hands around her belly as though it gave her an ache.

I stared at her hard. "Why?" Did my voice tremble when I asked? "Why would you let someone else take the fall?" That didn't seem like her character at all.

"I'd want to do the right thing. And the problem is the right thing would've been to never be involved in the scandal in the first place. But as an officer and a board member, you told me that my main responsibility is to protect the best interests of the shareholders. *All* of the shareholders. I would imagine that if a major officer went down in a big scandal, that wouldn't be good for the best interests of the shareholders. So wouldn't the right thing, wouldn't the most ethical thing, be to uphold my responsibility to the people counting on me? Protecting the shareholders would protect the integrity of the company, which would protect the majority of the employees. It's the best answer for everyone."

It was the right answer. It was the answer that would keep Dyson Media afloat if it was ever embroiled in the kind of scandal we were talking about. The answer that a wise, business-minded person would give.

But it was also the wrong answer.

Because I wanted her to say something else, wanted her to change the decisions of other people with what she'd said.

It was stupid, but it made me upset, made me mad all over again at my mom and my dad and all the other people who did stupid things.

I pushed her feet off of my lap, and then pulled her roughly onto it instead.

I brushed her hair to the side, kissing along her neck, biting her fair skin, until it turned red and angry.

"Did I say the wrong thing?" she asked in between gasps.

"Nope," I said shortly.

"But you're upset."

"Yep. I'm upset. And now I'm going to fuck you." I quickly unbuttoned her blouse and pulled down the cup of her bra, so I could get her nipple in my mouth, so I could tug it between my teeth until she whined.

"But you *are* upset?" she asked again, even as she rubbed her trouser-clad pussy against the rock hard bulge in my jeans. "At *me*?"

"Not at you." I sucked on her nipple some more and then took over pinching it with my fingers between my thumb and forefinger. "And at you, too, maybe. It doesn't matter. We're going to fuck it out and everything's going to be fine."

I tangled my other hand in the back of her hair and yanked her head back so I could lick along her neck up to her mouth. Then I kissed her wildly, aggressively, as though I could wipe out everything she'd said with my tongue, and replace it with my own saliva.

We moved fast, and urgently, and she didn't ask again about my mood or where it came from or who it was pointed at; she just seemed to understand that she could fix it and was intent on fixing it fast. We only undressed as much as needed to fit ourselves together, moving as quickly as possible. While I worked on getting my cock out of my jeans, she stood up right there on the chair, placing a leg on either side of me as she pushed her trousers all the way down below her knees until they bunched at her ankles.

Then she sat down on me, taking my cock inside her expertly after only—what had it been? A week plus the one night before she went on her trip. She knew how to line me up, knew how to swallow me in, and she was still so new at this—new at me. Damn, she was a quick learner. Sharp and astute and fun to challenge.

Even more fun to let her ride.

When she was seated on top of me, and I was so deep, so snug in her tight pussy, I wondered for half a second if I should wait for her to stretch and get used to me before plowing into her the way I needed to.

But before I could make up my mind, she took over, bouncing on me exactly the right way, up and down, fast, hard, fucking herself with my cock like she needed it as much as I did. Like it hurt her as much as it hurt me not to be completely inside her over and over and over again.

And when she began to wear out, and her rhythm slowed, I put my hands on her hips and did the lifting for her, forcing her up and down, up and down, up and down, making her take all of me, take all of this rage and anger and betrayal.

She came without me once even touching her clit, just from the position, just from her body rubbing against my pelvis in the right way. And when she threw her head back and cried out my name, I lifted my hips up and bucked into her from below, thrusting wildly as though I were driving away the nightmare that had become my life in the last seven years. Chasing it chasing it chasing it away until finally my own orgasm came and there was light and bliss and warmth and a life that was almost in my grasp if I could just hold onto it somehow, somehow.

And then it was over. Gone.

I wrapped my arms tightly around Elizabeth, pulling her to my chest, kissing her forehead and her face, any part of her my lips could reach, my eyes still half blind from the spots my climax had spattered in front of them. I didn't feel angry anymore, or upset, or even disappointed.

I just wanted to go home. To my *real* home, in the city. The place I'd built for myself with my own sweat and hard work and —*yes, Mom*—sacrifice.

So we gathered up our stack of books, loaded up the car, and Elizabeth and I headed back toward my apartment in Manhattan. And, for the first time since we'd started the schedule of living together, I was really glad I had someone to go home with me.

EIGHTEEN
ELIZABETH

I COULD FEEL the blood run to my face as I read the Google alert that had come through on my email. The headline had to be wrong. I clicked through to scan the entire article, my jaw dropping with each new word.

"What's wrong?" Weston asked from the seat next to me in the back of the car. It was Sunday, and we were driving to get Weston fitted for his tux. I didn't need to go along with him, but there was a fundraiser ballet afterward that we planned to attend together—part of playing the role of couple, of course—and it was just easier if we went to the fitting together first.

Or maybe that was an excuse.

I also found that I liked being near him a lot lately. And not just because of the sex.

Right now I was especially glad he was around, because I couldn't deal with the shock of this article on my own.

I looked up from my phone and over at him, shaking my head. So many thoughts were rushing through my mind, and I couldn't figure out which one to hold onto. I searched his face, as if he could read my mind and find the thoughts that needed to be spoken, bring them to my lips.

He studied me right back, then realizing the source of my anguish was my phone, took it from me and quickly read the article on the screen. The statement said that Dyson Media was selling off the advertising portion of the company, the very subsidiary that I intended to let Reach buy at a very reasonable cost after I got my hands on my inheritance.

When he was done reading, he frowned, but he didn't seem quite as upset as I would be in his shoes.

"I won't let him go through with it," I promised aimlessly. "I'll find a way to stop Darrell from selling." *I'll find a way to make this —us—worth it for you.*

I didn't know how, but I had to.

"I'm not worried about that part," Weston said. "What worries me is him trying to start a sale at *this* point in time, only a month away from our wedding—" He broke off as he handed the phone back to me.

"It's as though he isn't factoring me in at all. Does that mean that he's so confident he can prove we're a fraud that he doesn't think I'll actually get my hands on the company? Or is this a head game, and he's trying to freak me out? Because it's working." I twisted the ring on my fourth finger, wondering how long it would be there if this deal went through.

In the few short months I'd worn it, I'd become accustomed to it and often found myself playing with it, especially when I was nervous or worried.

Like now.

Weston glanced down at me, noticed me fidgeting and pulled his own phone from inside his suit jacket, scrolled through to find the contact he wanted, and put it on speaker. As the phone rang, he said, "I'm sure it will be fine, but D will know what to do. He probably has—"

He was cut off by Donovan's voice coming clear and loud from the phone. "I already know, and I'm on it."

"What does 'on it' mean?" I asked, sitting forward so he could hear me.

"Oh, you're there too?" He sounded irritated, snappier than usual, which only made my anxiety worse. If Donovan was in a bad mood about the situation, surely there really was something to worry about.

"We're both here," Weston said. "I have you on speaker. Tell us what you're doing."

"Donovan, if I'd thought for even one second that Darrell would try to sell the advertising portion of Dyson Media, I would never have offered that as a bargaining chip. Darrell barely blinks at the advertising company. I didn't even think he knew it existed from as much attention as he normally gives it." I couldn't explain my guilt. My cousin's actions weren't my own, but I did feel responsible for the predicament we were in now.

"Of course you wouldn't," Donovan said, possibly trying to be reassuring. "And I approached *you* with the idea, not the other way around. But there's no way the sale can go through before your wedding. At which time your lawyers will step in and halt all major deals from proceeding. I've already sent your team to work on the matter."

I could practically hear the quotations around the word *your*.

"Meanwhile, I'll need to send someone over to France to make sure your cousin isn't trying to overhaul things at the firm in preparation for the sale. I'll reach out as a potential competing buyer, and slow things down that way."

"He won't sell to you," I said. "He knows Weston is one of the owners of Reach."

"And I'm sure all of this is just a scare tactic because of that. I don't need him to actually sell to me anyway. I just need to be a speed bump. I imagine I have a contact or two that can help with this."

Weston gave a shrug of his shoulders that said the plan was better than anything else we had.

And truthfully, it *was* a pretty good plan. I probably didn't need to worry about it, and everything would go exactly as Donovan said.

But it did scare me that Darrell had made this move. It meant he either felt threatened, or he knew somehow. Knew that I was using this small piece of Dyson Media as the ace in my hand. And the only reason he would know that would be if someone had talked.

But that was impossible. Wasn't it?

"I'll need to get some papers signed by you for the lawyers," Donovan said. "Where can I find you today?"

"We'll be at Colletti's Tuxedos in about two minutes," Weston said. "And our afternoon is already booked."

"Then I better hurry and get the papers together so I can meet you there." Donovan hung up without even saying goodbye.

Weston pocketed his phone and shifted to look at me. "He's calling your bluff. He doesn't know anything. He's guessing that I would want that company. If anything, this means he believes in our marriage, and he knows that when we get married and you take over the company, I would want to take the ad company and give it to Reach."

I nodded. It made sense, what he was saying. More sense than Darrell having a mole inside Reach.

"Okay. Maybe that's right. But why would he do this now, if the sale can't possibly go through before our wedding date?"

"He might not think you pay enough attention. He might hope you're too busy with the wedding and the honeymoon to even notice the sale go through. And," Weston said, his eyes sparking a little, "he might've even tried to get the sale to go through earlier and been delayed. For this reason or that."

I relaxed just slightly, and noticed the whole side of my body was touching his when I did. He put his arm around me and brought me in closer. "Thanks for talking me down."

I felt so secure in his arms. He smelled so good, and his body was so warm. I wanted to take his strength and believe in it, but I reminded myself for the hundredth time that it wouldn't last. "I'm just so afraid he's going to find out this is a fake wedding, a fake marriage—"

"Hey," Weston pushed me away just enough so that he could meet my eyes. "You need to stop calling this a fake wedding. This is a real wedding. I am *really* getting married to you, Lizzie. You are really going to be my bride. In one month, you are going to be Mrs. King."

I took a deep breath in, and thought about that for a moment. I was *really* getting married to the man whose arms were holding me. I was going to stand up in front of all our friends, family, and business associates in a white dress and walk down the aisle toward *him*. Toward Weston.

And when everything was over, when the marriage had been dissolved and the final papers signed, that memory would still be real.

I realized my heart was pounding, racing faster than it usually did.

"You're going to be Mrs. King," he repeated as the car pulled over to the curb in front of Colletti's Tuxedos. "Which means you need to start acting like a queen."

I shivered a little at the thought of ruling by his side.

Married.

I was getting married.

We checked in at the counter for Weston's appointment, then he perused accessories on the wall while I watched a handful of men parading around in matching tuxes nearby. A few women were with them, critiquing the fits of their suits, laughing and having a good time. One of them was obviously the bride, deciding how she wanted her party to look, giving her attention to every detail of what would be the best day of her life. Certainly the most expensive. She went up to the one that had to be the groom and brushed lint from his shoulder before kissing him on the lips. "You look so sexy, baby," she said, flirting.

Was that the role I was supposed to play here today?

When her fiancé left for the fitting room with the tailor, she went back to giggling with her girlfriends and scrolling through her phone.

Perhaps that was how a normal bride acted, but it wasn't how this bride was going to act. It wasn't how Mrs. King would act.

It wasn't how this *queen* would act.

When Weston's tailor called him forward, I stood up and followed. Weston glanced over his shoulder at me and cocked his head, slightly confused.

"I'm just playing my part," I said.

That seemed to mollify him, and we walked into his assigned fitting room together.

The tailor didn't seem bothered at all by my presence and pointed to a chair where I could sit while Weston went into the dressing room to get into the tuxedo. It was his second appointment. The first time he'd come in on his own to be measured for the initial suit. This time, the outfit was being fitted to his body in particular. It was all about adjustments and hemming. He'd said it wouldn't take too long, but I'd never been to a tux or suit fitting, so I didn't know exactly what to expect.

I *had* expected that Weston would be drop-dead sexy when he walked out of the dressing room—I just didn't expect to actually drop dead from his sexiness.

The tuxedo he'd worn the night of the engagement party had

been a traditional fit, and he looked suave and hot, but this one was an ultraslim fit with a vest, and it hugged every part of his body, as though it had been molded to him.

I trailed my teeth along my lower lip, trying to manage the breath that was desperately trying to escape my body at the sight of him.

One thing was for sure, I couldn't sit through this. I had to stand, stand and watch while the tailor did his work. The gentleman who was working with Weston—Colletti himself, I soon learned—frowned at the sight of Weston. I couldn't understand that—what was there to frown at? But I stepped closer, trying to see the same flaws in the fit as he did.

The man bent down to kneel at Weston's feet and tugged first at the pant leg. "These are the shoes you'll wear?" he asked.

"Yes," I answered before Weston could answer. Colletti glanced at me. I nodded. "He needs to wear suspenders to keep the pants in the right place."

Weston growled. "I hate suspenders. I'll be fine without suspenders."

I looked from Weston to Colletti. Colletti shrugged. "If you want the classic flare to last through the whole event, you wear the suspenders."

I could see what Colletti was saying now, about where the pant hit on the shoes. Without a belt to keep them properly at Weston's waist, and everyone knew you didn't wear a belt with tuxedo pants, the pants drooped and the leg fell too far onto the shoe. "He'll wear the suspenders."

Weston moved his eyes toward mine, and I could see the challenge behind them, but there was something else too. Admiration? Respect, maybe.

He didn't argue, which was good, since I was the one picking up the tab for this whole wedding thing. Was this what it was like to act like a queen?

It sure did feel pretty good.

Colletti went on to examine the jacket sleeves that were slightly too long—the shirt didn't show a half inch beyond the cuff. He made some markings, then turned Weston around to look at his back. He pulled me over for this.

"The shoulders fit good, see? And through here." Colletti gestured at the middle of Weston's torso. Then he tugged at the bottom of the jacket. "But this—this length was okay twenty years ago. Today we tend to keep it shorter, just below the behind." He lifted the back of the jacket for a second so he could figure out where to adjust it higher, and there was Weston's perfect ass, molded into the slim tuxedo pants.

Damn, those pants fit well.

"So what you want to do about the length?"

"Shorter," I answered, feeling like a billionaire asking for the clerk to bring the skimpiest dress out for his secretary. But, seriously. It was a shame to cover up so much of that backside.

When I circled back around to face Weston, the gleam in his eyes said he didn't only find this highly entertaining. He also found it kind of arousing.

I glanced down at the front of his jacket where the break—which was perfectly split, according to Colletti—displayed a slight bulge.

"Don't give it any attention," Weston said quietly while Colletti fussed at the back of his collar. "That's certainly not going to help."

It didn't help the dampness of my panties, that was for sure.

Colletti finished up his measurements, wrote out a receipt, and handed it to me. "Okay. Final adjustments will be ready in three weeks. Make an appointment for pickup at the front desk." He shuffled out of the room.

"I guess you're allowed to change now," I said, suddenly aware that we were alone.

"Yep." Apparently also aware of our aloneness, Weston

grabbed me at my elbow and escorted me into the dressing room with him.

"I said *you* could get dressed now." I meant to sound authoritative, but my voice came out flustered and breathy. My heart was racing, and I could hardly pretend I didn't know what he was after.

"But you've been so helpful with the rest of this fitting. Surely you're not going to abandon me now." He clicked the door shut behind me and began working on undoing his pants. I was already excited, already ready for whatever he wanted. Even though we were in public, even though this was inappropriate.

Especially because we were in public. *Especially* because it wasn't appropriate.

When his cock was out—fully hard, his tip dripping—he pushed me to my knees. "How about you measure that?"

I glanced at the dressing room door. From a standing position, the two feet that it rose off the floor didn't seem so revealing. Down here was a whole other story.

"If anyone walked into the fitting room and saw me on my knees, they'd know exactly what I was doing."

It was kind of hot.

"Then you better hurry and get measuring," Weston said, rubbing his crown along my mouth, painting my lips with his pre-cum.

I hesitated only half a second before circling my fingers around the base of his cock and slipping my mouth around his hot, soft, tight skin. Because that's what I wanted to do.

And even queens bowed down to their kings.

We were quiet and fast, Weston whispering instructions and praise, one hand wrapped in my hair, the other braced on the dressing room door. I sucked him all the way in until he hit the back of my throat before drawing back, bobbing at a rapid speed while I massaged his balls, and when I looked up at him, he was watching us in the mirror, his expression fascinated and hypnotized, and so turned on.

I was going to get off to that sight for years to come.

It was only a few minutes later that I ducked out of the dressing room so that Weston could finish changing. Luckily no one else had come in and caught us.

Well, almost no one.

Donovan was waiting for me in the fitting area where Colletti had made the adjustments to the tuxedo.

I had no idea how long he'd been waiting there, or if he'd paid any attention to what was going on in the dressing room though, so I acted like he knew nothing, brushing my likely messy hair behind my ear as I crossed over to him.

"You have those papers?" I asked, loudly enough so that Weston could hear that we were no longer alone.

"I do. Why don't we take these outside, so we have some place to lay these all out."

I followed Donovan out into the main part of the store to a display counter that showcased cufflinks. He spread some papers across the glass and handed me a pen. I quickly found the places to initial and scratch my signature, then handed him the pen back after he gathered the papers together.

"Thank you for this," I said. "Thank you for always being on the ball. I really am sorry that this—"

He cut me off. "How did it fit?"

He had to mean the suit, not the cock. It wasn't some terrible, dirty, sexual reference, but my cheeks went red anyway, and I stammered, "What?"

"How did Weston's tux fit?" he asked, his voice cold, his eyes hard.

It hadn't been what he'd said the first time, though. And it seemed that even though he'd corrected himself, there was something hidden or manipulative in the way he was looking at me. This was the Donovan Kincaid people whispered about. The ruthless emperor of the New York business world.

I didn't know what to do except answer. "It looks good."

He smiled tightly. "Weston does always wear a tuxedo well."

"Yes. He does."

He opened his jacket and put his pen in the inside pocket, then turned his gaze back to me, his expression serious. "It's not for keeps, you know." There was no question in his statement. It was very definitive, very final, and very confusing, because I wasn't sure what he meant about keeping anything.

Did he mean the tux? I'd paid for it, but of course I would give it to Weston. Why would I have any use for a tux? A tux that fit Weston so perfectly.

And then it clicked, and I knew what he'd meant. I knew because I was so like Donovan in so many ways, and because Weston fit me in so many ways. I realized he was talking about *him*.

Donovan was talking about Weston.

Telling me that I couldn't keep Weston.

My chest pinched like I was wearing a corset and somebody had tightened the straps much, much too tight. Which was crazy because I hadn't even considered keeping Weston, but for someone to say that I couldn't, for Donovan to say that I couldn't...

"I don't gather that it's really any of your business," I managed to say. Not at all queenly. More like a woman who had been gaslit and underestimated and harassed and was still trying to find her confidence in this man's world.

"Oh, my dear, but it *is* my business. This whole arrangement has been my business. And the arrangement we made was that you would have Weston temporarily. I'm sure you know by now that he's expecting to end up with Sabrina. She's rather suited to him, isn't she?"

My cheeks went redder, this time from rage. "That seems odd when you're the one currently banging her."

He didn't bat an eye. "I'm just doing a friend a favor, keeping her entertained until Weston's not so tied up."

My backbone crumpled, the little that I had anyway. Had Weston asked Donovan to be with Sabrina? Was he planning on being with her when our divorce was final?

It wasn't like I could ask him. He wouldn't even tell me about his family. Why would I expect him to tell me about his love life? The only arrangement we had was to wed and divorce. We had no arrangement that we would mean anything to each other in between.

I felt my eyes get watery, and I blinked extra hard, trying to make the tears go away.

Weston came out of the fitting room then, chipper and upbeat, likely from his recent orgasm. I, on the other hand, was a smashed bug on the bottom of Donovan's shoe.

"Did you get everything you needed, D? Damn, whatever you said has Elizabeth all worked up again." His tone was concerned and compassionate, and I had to swallow and look at my shoes.

"I'm okay," I lied. "Really. Donovan was just reminding me of Reach's commitment to our agreement, and it made me a bit emotional." I was stupid for defending someone who'd just made me feel like shit, but it wasn't fair to be angry at him. He'd only spoken the truth. The truth I'd reminded myself of so many times before. It just hurt to hear it spoken out loud.

And wasn't it the job of a good businesswoman—and a good queen—to act in the best interests of her company? Not herself.

"Good," Weston said, putting an arm around me and rubbing his hand up and down along my skin. "We are committed. All of us."

Right. Committed right up until we said I do. The marriage *was* real—but the feelings were not.

NINETEEN
WESTON

"DID YOU GET IN OKAY?" I asked, stretching out on my bed, fully clothed. Elizabeth had only been gone half a day and I already missed her—missed her in my bones, and in my blood. And not even the kind of missing her that meant I wanted to jerk off, though I'd probably end up doing that too.

"Yeah, I did." She sounded so far away, but she *was* far away. Utah might as well have been a million miles from here. She'd gone early for Thanksgiving, and I was set to meet her in two days, on Wednesday night.

Two days and it felt like a lifetime.

But even though she was physically far away, I couldn't help the feeling she was far away in other ways too. She had been for a couple of weeks now, or maybe it was me who was feeling closer to her than I should.

Ever since the day at my parents' when I'd realized that she was a form of home to me, I'd started to cling to her, started to think of her in a new light. I started to think of her as more of an anchor than an obstacle, and instead of counting the days toward our wedding with anticipation, excited for the day when I would finally be rid of her, I hated the fact that our moment at the altar was just another step toward our demise.

Was this what love felt like?

And if so, how could I get her to look at me, to feel for me the way I was feeling for her?

There had been moments before when I was certain she did, but lately I wasn't so sure.

"Is the rest of your family there yet?" It was small talk, but I didn't want to let her go just yet.

"The house is too small to hold everyone. They'll come for dinner on Thursday. Right now it's just me and Nana and my great-grandmother." She paused, seeming to stifle a yawn. "What did you do tonight?"

"I worked. Then had dinner with Dylan—he's in town from the UK visiting his son. We went to Gaston's with Sabrina and her sister." I'd gotten tipsy and spent half the conversation debating with Dylan about whether love was real.

Me—arguing for the side of love.

It was Elizabeth's fault. And if I was under her spell, I didn't ever want it to be broken.

"Oh," Elizabeth said, her voice suddenly tighter. "That sounds fun. Hey, I've been thinking. There really isn't any reason for you to come and join me here. It's already awkward pretending we're a real item to Nana, and you're not even here yet. It's not like there's going to be anyone who sees us together in Utah. The whole point is to be seen, right?"

The buzz I'd felt from the wine suddenly wore off and soberness hit me like a brick wall. I moved the phone to my other ear and ran my hand through my hair, thinking fast. I needed to see her. Needed to be with her.

"But... There are still people who could see me here. And it would look wrong if I was here for the holiday without you. No, it's better if I'm where you are. What if Darrell tracked our flights?

Hired a PI? Let's just stick to the plan. It keeps our asses covered." Which *was* true, I just didn't mention that I wanted to spend the week with her. Wanted to sit at a table over a meal where we expressed our gratitude and, at least in my heart, know that I was grateful for meeting her.

"I guess I'll see you Wednesday then." She sounded resigned. Maybe she was just tired from her flight. "Call me when—"

"Are you done with me already?" God, I was so desperate. I'd never been desperate. This was a new one for me.

"I was. Do you have more to discuss?"

"Well, we've never had phone sex."

She laughed lightly, and just the sound of her giggle got me semi-hard. "Weston, I can't. Not here. Nana's just in the other room."

"Where's your sense of adventure?"

"I guess I left it in New York," she said with finality. "Good night. I'll talk to you Wednesday."

She hung up, and I tossed my phone to the bed, giving up on jerking off. It wasn't an orgasm that I wanted. It wasn't a business arrangement I wanted. I just wanted her.

IT WAS early evening and the sun was just setting when I arrived in Salt Lake City. I picked up my rental car and followed the directions to Elizabeth's grandmother's place in Bountiful, amazed at how little traffic there was on the short drive. The airport was only twenty minutes from her house. Elizabeth and I were staying in a hotel, but we'd agreed to meet here, where she'd been staying the last couple of days, so she wouldn't have to take a taxi.

I pulled into the long driveway of the single-family house around six-thirty p.m. It was simple and small—white siding, no front porch, probably no more than two bedrooms if I guessed from the outside. My father would refer to it as a shack. I knew that Angela, Elizabeth's mother, hadn't come from money, but I still double-checked the address to be sure I was in the right place before knocking on the door.

A blonde-and-gray-haired woman who looked very much like Elizabeth's mother greeted me, an exuberant smile on her face. "You must be Weston. Come in, come in."

I set my bag down, and Elizabeth suddenly appeared behind her.

My chest got warm and tingly just at the sight of her. It was weird, because usually my emotions for women originated much lower. And when she slipped into my arms and kissed me hello, the tingly feeling expanded through my limbs into my fingers and my toes, and all I wanted to say when she stopped kissing me was, "I'm home."

But I got ahold of myself somehow and said the more appropriate thing. "I'm here."

She formally introduced me to the woman who answered the door, Nana, Angela's mother. She was in her mid-seventies, spry for her age—spry for a woman twenty years younger, even—but though she looked like her daughter in her features, she dressed much more plainly, wearing no makeup, her hair just towel-dried instead of the perfect grooming her daughter preferred.

Next, Elizabeth showed me in and introduced me to a woman sitting in a recliner in the living room. Grandmama, Nana's mother, had turned ninety-five this year, Elizabeth boasted proudly. She had white frizzy hair, what was left of it, anyway. There were several spots where her scalp could be seen, patches of dry skin showing through which matched the red, angry splotches that dotted her arms. Psoriasis, most likely. Or just age. She was stout, not one of those frail old women that comes to mind when someone says 'geriatric.' And her face was radiant, her eyes bright, her cheeks rosy, as she stood to greet me.

"No, no, please," I said, trying to stop her from getting up. "I can come over there. No need to stand."

"Oh, we're about ready to have supper anyway. It's time for me to get on my feet." Her voice was cheery, her whole persona delightful.

"Then at least let me help you stand up." I moved toward the chair, but she stopped me again.

"It's actually easier if I do it myself," she said, and I suddenly began to rethink the notion that Elizabeth got her gumption from her father. "See, I rock back and then rock forward, and the chair just sort of lifts me up." She demonstrated the motion as she spoke.

I exchanged a glance with Elizabeth, who was grinning just as widely as her grandmama. When she'd made it to her feet, Elizabeth was there with her arm offered. "I'll help you to the table, but then Weston and I are headed to our hotel."

"You aren't staying for supper?" She looked to Nana as if asking permission. "I'm sure there's plenty to go around."

"I did make enough for everyone," Nana confirmed.

"I'm sure after the long flight and everything..." Elizabeth began.

"We'd love to stay," I finished for her. Because there was nothing in the world I would rather do than stay and soak up the warmth of these happy people, so honest and real. So different from my own family.

There was a dining room, but supper was served in the kitchen around a small table that barely fit four chairs, and we had to pull the table out from the wall to accommodate all of us. The meal was simple—soup and homemade bread and canned pears that I learned came from a tree in the backyard. There was prayer before we ate. It wasn't scripted, and we didn't hold hands —just a short, simple grace, words of gratitude and a request for blessings.

Grandmama's words came quickly to her tongue, and I could

tell her mind was still sharp as she made these personal requests to a God she sincerely believed in.

When she finished, and the food began to be distributed around the table, Elizabeth looked over at me covertly and mouthed the word *sorry*. As though I would've been bothered by a prayer when it had been my favorite thing about the day so far, especially the part where Grandmama had thanked God for her great-granddaughter's visit and the man she'd chosen to share her life with. Even if it was a lie, God knew, it was the intention of this woman that meant so much. It made my throat tight and dry.

It was funny how these women were so surprising when I thought I knew all about them. I'd already learned so much about this branch of the family—about all of Elizabeth's family—in the months we'd been together. She wasn't guarded about the people around her the way I was. It shamed me when I thought about it, how she could be so transparent and giving when I was closed off and embarrassed.

She didn't seem to be worried that I would associate her with her family members, that I would blame her for anything they had done or who they were, whereas I was scared to death she would discover things in my family's past, and would never again look at me the way I sometimes caught her looking at me now.

The way I wanted her to look at me all the time.

During dinner, I got Nana and Grandmama's version of the family history. Grandmama had lived in the tiny white house since she'd gotten married in the forties, had raised all seven of her children here, somehow stuffing most of them into two rooms in the basement. Nana, her middle child, had three children of her own, two who lived in Utah still, and her baby, Angela, who had run away from home at an early age to explore the world. She'd met Dell Dyson and found the world was more interesting with dollars in her bank account. Nana had spent a lot of time in New York with Angela and Elizabeth in place of a nanny before she grew too old to need one. Then, when her father got sick, she moved in to take care of her parents."

"So she's the black sheep," I said, after Grandmama added that Elizabeth's mother's line was one of the few that no longer practiced the Mormon religion.

"She's not a black sheep," Nana said, offended. "She's welcome here anytime. She just prefers I come visit *her*. She likes her fancy things. Even tried to buy us a fancier house time and time again, but we're happy with what we have. Doesn't stop her from sending us all sorts of New Age technology, though I do admit to enjoying my TVR."

Elizabeth tried to hide her giggle. "It's DVR, Nana. It's part of your cable subscription." She turned to me to explain. "I helped them get it figured out last time I was here."

"Angela is so kind with her money. She sends it all the time. But we have no need for anything," Grandmama said, her finger pointing at the table as though she really wanted me to hear that point. "Besides occasional repairs to the house, we just put the rest in savings. It can pay for my medical bills when I need it down the road."

"I don't think that's coming anytime soon," Nana said. "Your mother lived to be one hundred and five."

Grandmama sighed as if that was the last thing she wanted to be reminded of. "Well. We'll see."

When dinner was over, Nana started to gather the empty plates and stack them in a pile until Elizabeth stopped her. "We'll get that. Go watch your shows with Grandmama."

I stepped into line, gathering items and carrying them to the sink alongside her. We put leftovers in Tupperware and made room in a fridge already crowded with pre-Thanksgiving cooking, and soon we were side by side at the sink, loading it to wash the dishes by hand.

"I don't hear you bothering *them* about hiring a maid," I teased.

Elizabeth narrowed her eyes at me, but she had a smile playing on her lips. "They don't want a maid. They don't even want a dishwasher." She handed me a sudsy plate to rinse off and put in the dish rack.

"Why do we need a dishwasher?" Nana asked coming in behind us. "What would we do with our days if we didn't at least clean up after ourselves?"

"But at least you *do* clean up after yourselves. This one," Elizabeth gestured to me, "does not. He needs a maid so I don't have to be the one who does it."

Nana put a hand on my shoulder, warm and friendly, as though she'd already welcomed me into her life. "This one works hard all day. He's earning the money. He doesn't need to clean up after himself."

I could practically hear Elizabeth choke on her shock.

"Yeah," I teased. "I'm earning all the money."

"Oh, you do not," she said, but Nana had already walked away. Elizabeth flicked at me with her fingers, spattering water on my shirt and face. I flicked water at her right back, and then we were both laughing, and I vowed right then I would never, ever get a maid if it meant that I could do dishes with Elizabeth Dyson forever.

AFTER DINNER, we stayed to watch TV for a bit with the older women. "Their shows" turned out to be murder mysteries on PBS, British detectives from the 1920s era. There was lots of talking and everyone was glued to the screen. I mostly nodded and kept my arm around Elizabeth, and tried not to stare at her profile and how her skin glowed from the light shining off the TV screen.

"We'll have twenty-eight here for dinner tomorrow," Grandmama said with a sigh when the show was over. "Better get to bed. We're going to have to get up early to start the turkey."

"Twenty-eight," I gasped. "Where are you going to fit them all?" There was only the TV room and a large master bedroom upstairs plus the living room, dining room, and kitchen.

"It's tight, but we've done it," Nana said. "You'll just have to see how it works out tomorrow. We'll be stuffed in more ways than one."

Everyone laughed and it was our cue to leave for the night. "I'll just run out to the camper and get my suitcase. But I can be back here as early as you need me to help cook, Nana."

"You stayed in a camper?" I supposed that made sense. There was only one bedroom in the basement now, the big dorm room having been turned into a playroom for the grandkids when they visited.

"Yeah, it's in back."

"Then why don't we just stay there?" I'd thought the whole reason she and I weren't staying here was because it would be awkward having sex in the same house with her grandmothers. Because we both knew we couldn't sleep in the same room and keep our hands off each other. But an unattached room next door? That sounded like it would work just fine.

"There's no room service in the camper," Elizabeth said. "And no plumbing, so we have to use the bathroom in here."

"I don't need room service, Princess."

She rolled her eyes and huffed. "Obviously I don't either. Since I've been staying there myself for two days." She wandered into the living room where I'd left my bag and hoisted it onto her shoulder. "If we're going to stay, then you'd better go take your turn with the toilet."

I chuckled to myself and did as she'd told me as she let Nana know about the new arrangements, then I took my bag from her, and she led the way to the backyard.

If Elizabeth's room service remark had been meant to warn me about the state of the camper, I didn't pick up on it. It was old, beat up, well used. It was definitely from Grandmama's era, and as we climbed inside the rickety thing, I almost wondered if it would fall apart on us. Inside, there was a dining table surrounded by two benches; a kitchen, which consisted of a sink, counter, and range top that looked a hundred years old; and a bedroom in the back with a mattress that took up the total width of the trailer. A long, thick cord ran underneath the door behind us and led to a space heater on the floor in front of the bed.

"I'm guessing this is what they call vintage," I said, setting my bag down. It was cute despite the weathering with it's wood-paneled walls and the benches wrapped in teal pleather—the kind easily wiped down and probably highly toxic.

"Vintage is one way to put it," Elizabeth said, walking over to the space heater and turning it on. She sat on the bed and began pulling off her shoes. "*Well-loved* is another. My mother bought her a new one about twenty years ago when Papa was still alive, and they turned around and gave it to my uncle. They said this one was still good. They didn't need a new one."

"I suppose it still does what it's supposed to." I followed her into the bedroom, eager to touch her now that we were alone.

Eager just to be with her.

"Nowadays it's just used as an extra room when family visits, but it's here at least as long as Grandmama is alive. My great-grandfather inherited it from someone before they got married. It was pretty much all he had to his name when they wed. He'd grown up a poor farmboy. He was super smart though so he was able to become a schoolteacher. And she was..."

I sat on the bed beside Elizabeth, tilting my body toward her. "She was—what?"

She let out a sigh. "She had money. Her dad was a lawyer. She married down, so to say."

Like how Elizabeth was marrying down by marrying me.

Sweat suddenly gathered at the back of my neck. "And then what?"

She waited a beat before breaking into a smile. "And they lived happily ever after." She laid back on the bed, her body turned toward me.

I followed suit, stretching out and facing her.

"They didn't have much money," she went on. "They took their honeymoon in this camper. They raised seven kids in that tiny house. They grew a lot of their own food, relied on goods they canned themselves, had a newspaper route for extra money, and camped for every vacation they took, but they were super fucking happy."

Her expression was soft as she talked about these people she was so fond of.

And I was anything but soft.

When I reached for her, it wasn't out of anger or lust or a need to satisfy something within myself. I simply reached for her, and she reached for me, lips meeting gently, kissing without frenzy, without bruising intentions.

We undressed each other slowly, and it felt like I was discovering her body for the first time, feasting on something new. I spent time on every inch of her skin, licking and sucking, learning her landscape like it was a place I'd never been. I was grateful for every part of her that she let me see, thankful for her trust and the honor, and I showed her in every way I knew. I made up ways just for her, watching her closely to gauge what she liked. What she loved.

So many times I'd prided myself on giving a woman pleasure, but it had always been for my own satisfaction. So I could take the glory. So I could bask in the title of best lover. But with every kiss, with every graze of her skin, tonight I truly wanted *her* to feel good. Wanted her to know how beautiful she was, how fucking incredible.

I wanted to please her.

I wanted to love her.

And when we were completely naked, shivering from the way that we moved across each other, I slid inside her, thrust deep, deeper, deeper still, my eyes locked on hers, wanting nothing but to give her everything I felt inside. Wanting to give her this crazy, insane, turbulent feeling racing through my blood, skittering across my nerves. The same thrill that I felt when I got a beautiful woman in my bed, that high that always disappeared when the orgasms died down, but which with Elizabeth, lingered and grew and exploded, even when our clothes were on, our bodies not quite touching. I wanted to share that with her. Wanted to ask her with each thrust, *do you feel this, do you feel this, do you feel this?* And not mean my cock, but that crazy fucking shit going on inside me. That bizarre, wonderful magic love stuff circulating through my veins.

Do you feel this? Do you feel it, too?

I held her close against me when we were finished, our bodies sticking to each other as our sweat dried. I thought of her great-grandfather in this camper almost eighty years ago, how he held the woman he'd loved in his arms, how it was all he'd had and it had been enough.

And I got it. Because this could be enough for me too.

All that was left was for me to find out if Elizabeth felt the same.

TWENTY
ELIZABETH

I SLIPPED OUT of the camper early Thanksgiving morning while the sky was still dark and frost still tipped the grass in the backyard, not because I was worried about Nana getting the cooking underway without me, but because I was worried that if I stayed too long in the paradise of Weston's arms, I wouldn't be able to leave.

In the two-plus weeks since Donovan had reminded me of the business arrangement—of Weston's loyalties—I'd tried to stay true to myself and my own goals. Tried to remember first and foremost that this charade was just that—a charade. I hadn't stopped sleeping with Weston because I only had so much self-restraint, but also because it was easier than a complicated discussion of why we *shouldn't* keep sleeping together. And the *why* was that I was falling for him. And I was worried about my heart.

How embarrassing that confession would be.

And it wasn't like I needed another man to reject me in my life.

But every day in his presence, and his arms, and his bed made the next day harder to get through without wanting more, more, more. Without dreaming that there wasn't an expiration date on us, without fantasizing that the inheritance of Dyson Media wasn't the cherry on top of my nuptials, rather than the whole reason for them.

And last night had been especially hard.

Whereas our usual tense and fraught living situation led to rough, wild sex, this time it felt as though he were making love to me. As though he were giving himself to me in ways he never had.

I'd been right there with him too, receiving all he had to offer, letting him take from me too, pretending I wasn't a wreck over it.

God, I'd gotten so good at pretending.

But there were only nine more days until our official wedding date, and then we were flying to a remote island where we could ignore each other for the two weeks of our honeymoon and begin the process of moving on. I just had to be strong, had to keep my head clear. Remember that this was all a game and play it like I had nothing to lose.

Nana was already up when I got inside the house, thankfully. She set me right to work peeling potatoes and it was a much-needed distraction. Cooking overtook the morning and by the time Weston awoke and joined us, my aunt Becky had arrived, instrumental Christmas music was playing in the background, and there was enough hubbub to keep me from having to deal with him one on one.

Dinner preparations took the rest of the day and early afternoon. Weston jumped in, helping as soon as he got himself showered and dressed by setting up extra tables, bringing up the dining table leaves from the basement, pulling the metal folding chairs out of the carport. By the time we were finished, there was a large round table set up in the master bedroom for the kids, a long banquet set up in the living room, and the dining room was stretched to max capacity.

At two o'clock more family began arriving. Aunt Nora brought the pumpkin pies that everybody hated but no one would admit,

Aunt Debbie brought the pecan pies that everybody fought over. A can of olives was set out for early nibbles on the dining room table. The younger cousins quickly discovered them and walked around with black fingertips until Aunt Becky admonished them and swapped out for a fresh can that she supervised until dinner was served. Finally, each table was loaded with portions of all the sides. Green bean casserole, stuffing, mashed potatoes and gravy, rolls, glazed carrots, yams. And in the middle of each table sat a plate of turkey, already carved and dished up from the birds in the kitchen.

Everyone gathered in the living room for prayer, which was given by Nana's younger brother. Then the room burst into a fit of joyful noise as everyone dispersed to their designated seats, ready to enjoy the amazing feast.

Weston and I were seated at the long table in the living room with most of the spillover adults, as I liked to call them. The oldest adults were the ones who got to sit in the dining room with Grandmama; those included Nana and her siblings. With most of the people around us being our age, the conversation was lively. Weston had plenty of opportunities to show off his business knowledge as the men began discussing their recent investments, and the latest trends in stocks. With his connections to King-Kincaid, they were quite eager to hear his opinion.

"I'm not really one to give advice on investments," he said. He placed his hand over mine on the table. "But I do recommend investing in Dyson Media. I hear it's about to go through some management changes that are going to be quite excellent for the company."

I smiled tightly around my mashed potatoes, trying not to blush. The majority of women in my mother's family were homemakers. It felt odd for me to discuss business.

"We'll invest," my cousin's wife, Sheila, said. "I'm looking forward to you taking over. You're going to be amazing. Go women!" She gave me a wink and I winked back.

"Unless she has a baby," her husband Jeff said.

My body tensed, my chewing paused, and Weston's hand suddenly felt stiff over mine. This was not a conversation we'd prepared for.

"Women can't have babies and jobs these days?" Sheila's tone seemed to indicate this was a discussion that had been had before in her household.

Jeff didn't seem fazed. "Every family needs to make the decision that's right for them. What decision have you made? Will you quit working when you have children?"

I coughed, choking on my turkey. Weston handed me my water goblet, and I gulped half of it down.

"Uh, we haven't talked about it," he said while rubbing my back.

"You're getting married and you haven't talked about it?" Katie, another cousin, asked, her expression aghast.

"No, we've talked about it," I said, trying to recover. What kind of engaged couple hadn't discussed children? "Weston meant we haven't *decided*. Haven't decided when we're having them. Not if I'm quitting. I'm not quitting."

"Right. That's what I meant," he said, and from the way he looked at me, I could almost believe he was imagining the same thing I was—beautiful, blue-eyed babies with red hair and deep dimples. Smart and playful and independent.

But of course he wasn't imagining that. I wasn't even sure Weston liked kids.

I wasn't even sure Weston liked me, most days.

"Will you be joining in at Dyson Media?" Jeff asked Weston, changing the subject. I'd never been so grateful to my cousin in my life.

"I'll be staying with Reach. It keeps my hands busy," Weston said. "Of course, any time Elizabeth needs my advice, I'm happy to give her my input."

"Oh, that's right," Jeff said. "You have your advertising business. Wasn't there some sort of a scandal a few years back with King-Kincaid? Some banking thing? I hope that didn't affect your own business."

Scandal? I raised a brow and looked at Weston.

He shook his head definitively. "There were rumors when the house financing bubble burst. Nothing really stuck. It was before my business got started, but luckily I had no problems."

Weston moved his attention back to eating, and while he'd brushed off the comment, I noticed his body had stiffened, and I suddenly wondered if there was something there, something I had missed, something I hadn't thought to look at.

Then someone was asking me to pass the mashed potatoes and someone else began a story, and I forgot all about it again.

AFTER DINNER, Weston and the men got the tables torn down and put away within ten minutes then chilled out while the women cleared dishes and washed them in the kitchen. I ignored the sexist division of tasks that resulted in more work for the women. Everyone seemed happy, and that was what mattered, I supposed.

When the last plate was dried and put away, I went to the door of the living room and waited for my uncle John to finish his story. As I waited, I watched my cousin's baby playing, recalling the earlier dinner conversation. Was this something I wanted?

She had a toy car she was trying to roll back and forth but kept getting frustrated when it didn't roll smoothly over the shag carpet. She started to fuss, her cry escalating in the crowded room.

Her father was already soothing a toddler on his lap, and her mother was in the kitchen whipping cream, so I stepped forward to soothe her when Weston, whose back was to me, beat me to it. He slipped from the couch to the floor, then laid down and showed her how she could roll the car on him, allowing her to make a racetrack of his torso and legs.

She squealed, delighted, and he was sexier than I'd ever seen him.

But it wasn't just sex appeal. Yes, the feelings I had watching him with this baby were primal and base. Some sort of innate need to produce offspring was set off at the sight of him, the same feelings I'd had at the question of us having kids.

But there was heart appeal, too. Like, this was the kind of guy I wanted to be a parent with. The kind of guy who would wear a suit all week, do the dishes with me at night, fuck my brains out in the bedroom, then lay down on the floor and play with his child. The kind of guy who could be in it all the way. Not just for me, but for everything that came with.

I could picture Weston as that guy. I could picture it so well that I had to swallow twice before asking the room who was ready for pie.

After everyone was full of dessert, the games began. Some went to the back room to watch football on the big TV; the youngest kids went downstairs to play their own board games. A group of adults sat around the dining room table and began a vicious game of Uno. Aunt Becky won several rounds, as always, but the trickiest hands, the most draw-fours and surprise reverse cards were placed by Grandmama.

Weston played a good hand, too, and I hated myself for being impressed with how savagely he played against me even while he played footsie under the table. It was the same game we always played—the push and pull. The I hate you/I want you. The poke and prod.

It was getting harder and harder for me to play this game.

At eight o'clock, when families started to clean up and announce they were going home, I let out a deep sigh of relief.

Not much for goodbyes, I busied myself with cleaning up while various cousins made their farewells. I tied up the bag of trash from the kitchen and pulled it out of the trash can. I'd just started to open the door to take it to the backyard when all of a sudden Weston was at my side.

"Let me help you with that," he said.

He was the one I needed to be away from the most. Reluctantly, I said, "You can grab the recycling," and nodded to the blue can next to the trash.

He collected and tied that bag, and a minute later we were heading out together into the chilly, crisp night air toward the large cans that were in the back of the carport outside.

"That baby Nicola," Weston said, as we walked. "She is just the cutest. I could gobble her up. She's so happy!"

"She does seem to love everyone." I was glad that I was ahead of him, and he couldn't see my frown. Even though I'd loved watching him play with her, it irritated me to hear him talk about her, for some reason.

Maybe I was just irritated with him in general.

"And, man. Aunt Becky," he went on, and I had to bite my tongue because that struck a nerve too. "She's a killer at Uno. Grandmama needs to watch her back with that one. Though, really, Grandmama can probably handle herself. Hey, do think we should invite cousin Jeff to the wedding? And his wife seemed super cool too. Maybe we could go in with them on a gift for—"

I dropped the trash bag in the outside garbage can with a grunt and cut him off at the same time. "Stop it."

He looked at me curiously, cautiously, as though he wasn't sure if I meant the talking or the recycling.

I grabbed the recycling bag out of his hand and put it where it belonged, then turned to face him. "Stop it," I said again, more harshly. "They're not your family. We are not going in on gifts for anybody together. He's not *your* cousin Jeff. She's not *your* aunt

Becky. And it's not *your* grandmama, either. They're *my* family. Mine. Not yours."

He stood there with his mouth open for several seconds. Then I thought I caught a flash of pain behind his eyes, but it was dark and the carport light cast shadows across his face, so I couldn't be sure. It was enough, though, to cause a sharp stab of doubt.

"You're right," he said softly, sincerely. "I got too into the role and crossed a line. Sorry about that."

He turned to go back toward the house, his shoulders low.

"Weston—?" I called after him, suddenly worried I'd been wrong about everything. That he'd felt it too—that strange, real connection between us, pulling us to be something more than just an arrangement—and I'd just fucked it all up by not giving those feelings a chance.

But when he stopped and swung his head back at me, he was smiling. "Everyone's leaving," he said, as though I hadn't just snapped at him. "That means all the leftover pie is ours. We got to beat your grandmas to it, though, so come on."

So it was like he'd said—he'd gotten into the role. With the estrangement between him and his own family, it was probably natural that he soaked up the warmth of one that was so ready to give it.

Regardless, it was still true that he'd crossed a line.

And so had I, by imagining a life with him. I needed to stop with the daydreaming and wishful thinking. Needed to harden myself. Needed to learn how to ignore these feelings before they got out of hand.

For all my father's flaws, I couldn't forget the most valuable lesson he'd taught me—there was no room for emotion in business.

TWENTY-ONE
WESTON

"ARE YOU NERVOUS?" Nate asked from behind me.

I met his eyes in the mirror, then moved my focus back to my own image as I finished knotting my tie. Elizabeth had chosen a standard tie rather than a bow in a deep midnight blue that matched my pocket square. It was a perfect color for December. Moody and wintry, and it brought out the blue in my eyes.

Brought out the blue in my mood.

"Why would I be nervous? It's not as if this wedding means anything to me."

"Yeah, but the girl means something to you."

I glanced at his reflection once again, frowning. I knew Nate was the one to talk to about sex and women and good times, but I wasn't so sure he was the one to confide in when it came to heartache. And though I'd never felt this feeling before, that was the best description I had for it—heartache—the pain, tightness, and anguish in the general vicinity of my heart.

It had been there ever since that day in Utah when Elizabeth had reminded me so bluntly that her family was not mine—that *she* was not mine. She would never be mine. And there was no longer any reason to ask how she felt about me because she had made it plain and clear then.

After the trip and in the week that we'd been home, I'd barely seen her. Between preparing for the wedding and getting things wrapped up at the office before I left for our honeymoon, there was just no time. And that was a good thing. Because these days when I saw her, I didn't want to fight and I didn't want to just fuck, and yet those were the only two things I was allowed to have.

Thankfully Nate was the only one who knew she'd become such a weakness of mine.

"I do like her," I admitted, turning to him. "I'll be disappointed when she goes. But it's the circle of life, right?"

He chuckled. "That's the spirit. By my watch you have thirty minutes. Do you need anything?"

"I could use a drink." And another week before this was over. Another month. Another lifetime.

Nate slapped me on the back. "Save it for after the ceremony. Then you can have all the drinks you want." He headed for the door of the dressing room. "Speaking of drinks, I have a date waiting for me in the bar. I've got to get down there to her. Oh, your mother was saying she wanted to see you. Should I send her to your dressing room?"

"God, no. She can see me after. When I have that drink in hand."

He laughed again, but then grew serious. "It's worth the pain," he said. "Trust me."

"My mother isn't worth any amount of pain," I said, wishing he would just go and give me the alone time I needed before going through with this.

"I'm not talking about your mother, Weston."

"Yeah. I think I knew that."

He laughed as he left, and I was alone, which I had wanted. I could finally take a moment to consider whether it really was worth the pain. It wasn't like I'd never been sorry to lose a girl before. When I was a teenager, it seemed I'd been sorry to lose *every* girl. Every one of them, back then, I'd wanted to keep forever. Wanted to love forever. Was devastated when they stepped out of my car, snuck out of my room.

It was nothing more than my desire to have something of my very own. Eventually I learned that if I didn't get attached, I didn't experience the stab of pain that accompanied their departure.

At least once this particular heartache was done, I'd have Reach. Debt-free, something that belonged to me.

So Nate was right—the pain would be worth it. Eventually.

Still wishing I could have a shot of hard liquor instead, I walked over to the fridge to get a water bottle when there was a knock on the door. I'd already seen everyone I was expecting to see for the afternoon.

Which meant...fuck. It was probably Mom.

I girded myself for an encounter with her that I absolutely wasn't in the mood to have when I already had so much emotional baggage to deal with.

But when I opened the door, it wasn't my mother standing there.

"Kelly?" She was the last person on earth I expected to see. A senator's daughter I'd spent some time with about three years ago in Colorado. Mostly naked time. She must've made it onto the guest list somehow.

"Callie," she corrected, seeming mildly irritated. And deservedly so considering all that we'd done. It was a slap in the face that I didn't get her name right. This was why I didn't do reunions.

"Callie. I'm sorry. I have a lot on my mind today." I opened the door farther. "Come in. I'm glad to see you. Come in."

She hesitated a moment, seeming to consider, then with a deep breath she crossed the threshold into the dressing room, and I shut the door behind her.

I didn't remember much about Callie, but I tried to recall what I could. I'd met her on the slopes of Aspen and the week that we'd spent together had been a combination of daredevil skiing and acrobatic sex. She was attractive, more petite than Elizabeth, more athletic. Her eyes were a soft brown and her hair a light chocolate. She was one of those natural kinds of girls, the kind that didn't wear makeup and liked adventure. She'd been a fun time that I hadn't thought about in, well, years.

But here she was, standing in front of me, clutching the strap of her purse like she was nervous or excited to see me.

Either was possible.

I was suddenly nervous as well, awkward. I hated confrontations with women from my past. At least I had an excuse now for why there would be no further confrontations—a.k.a. I was getting married in less than an hour. It almost seemed fitting to see her, out of the blue as it was, since it was the last day of my bachelorhood and all.

Or temporarily, anyway.

"I really didn't want to bother you today," she said before I could ask her why she was here.

"No. No bother. I'm ready to go and just twiddling my thumbs. Are you here for the ceremony?" Now that I looked her over, she wasn't at all dressed for a wedding. She wore leggings and a cotton dress over it. A scarf was wrapped around her neck and she still had her coat on and open, as though she'd come directly to my room, not bothering to stop at the coat check or find a seat first.

"No. I'm. Well," she chuckled. "I wasn't invited. Which is fine. I didn't come for the wedding, is what I mean. Congratulations and all. I just came today because I knew I could find you here."

She was definitely nervous.

Which definitely made me more nervous.

"Look, Weston, I know this is a terrible time to talk to you, so I thought I could just see you and make an arrangement to meet with you again some other time—a more appropriate time. I tried texting you a few times this summer, but you never responded, so I wasn't sure if it was still your number. And then I tried calling your office, but your assistant is really good, actually. She doesn't let anyone through to you without a specific agenda, and I wasn't going to share my reasons for talking to you with her. I didn't think it was a good idea just to show up at your place of business either. I imagined it would be the same scenario. Not that this is any better." She seemed to rethink her actions then shook her head. "Anyway I'm here now because I didn't know how to find you without getting lawyers involved and that was definitely not the way I wanted to go—"

The hair on the back of my neck stood up. "Callie. Why would you need to get lawyers involved?"

She took another deep breath. "I'm doing this wrong. I don't want to do this on your wedding day. I promise. Just tell me when I can meet you again, and I'll leave."

But I knew it in my gut, the way she was acting. I felt an innate sense of psychic dread. The kind that made my skin prickle and the air hum.

"I think you need to tell me what you have to say *because* I'm getting married today, Callie." I said her name like it was a weapon. The only one I had.

She paused a moment. Then dug into her purse and pulled out a photograph and handed it to me.

My hand was shaking as I took it from her, because I already knew what I would see. Blue eyes, deep dimples, hair darker than mine, but the features could've been a twin for any picture in my baby book.

My voice was scratchy when I spoke, my eyes never looking away from the little boy in the image. "What's his name?"

"Sebastian," she said, equally choked up.

And then it hit me, full force, like a basketball thrown while I wasn't looking and landing squarely in my gut—*I had a son.*

I staggered back to the armchair and sat down, one hand over my mouth as I studied the toddler, memorizing every detail of him. His smile, his chubby cheeks, his squishy hands. The adorable overalls he wore. The shoes on his feet that looked too small to be real.

I had a son.

I already knew he was mine—it was evident just from looking at him. Anyone would be able to see it. There wouldn't need to be a paternity test with the proof he wore on his little face. And Callie had money—as much as I did, if not more—so her reasons for being here weren't likely monetary.

There was no reason to doubt her, but plenty of reason to ask, "Why are you just telling me about him now?"

"I made a bad decision. I should've told you sooner."

I tore my eyes from the picture and looked at her, anger quickly filling me. This—this tiny *person* had been brought into the world without any thought at all of me, and she'd summed it up in the same words she might use to describe ordering a second dessert.

"You made a *bad decision*? What the hell is that supposed to mean?"

She took a step closer. "Look. I really didn't want to talk about this today. There's not enough time to go through everything—"

"Try," I demanded.

She searched the room as if searching for her answers, then resolutely sunk into the chair opposite me. "I didn't know if I *wanted* to tell you. That's the honest truth, and it's terrible. Go ahead and hate me for it, but I didn't know you. I didn't know what kind of a father you would be. We only spent five days together."

"You didn't know me so you decided that I didn't get a chance to prove myself? That's not the way that paternity works. That's not fair. That's not even legal." My voice was too loud, and I knew it.

"I know. Don't you think I know that? But you have a reputation of being a ladies' man and that's not the kind of person who usually wants to be a father."

"I didn't even get a chance to decide that." A bit quieter now but still just as intense. Just as pissed off.

"You didn't. I made a bad decision. I said that. But I was trying to do what was best for our son."

The phrase *our son* froze me, and I couldn't speak for several moments because I couldn't deny that I didn't know what kind of decisions I would make if I was making them for *our son*.

"This is probably more information than you want to know," she continued, "but my dad was never really around. He was a full-time senator—a career politician, and we don't get along. I thought that maybe instead of a sometimes father, Sebastian would be happier without one at all. That it would be less disappointing for him than the way I felt, always watching my father leave. Recently I've reconsidered and decided I should have given you the chance to be a different dad than my dad was to me. Because I haven't changed my mind about that, Weston. I can't have an unreliable father in his life. I can't let him be hurt like that. I won't let you do that to him."

I tilted my chin up, ready to argue because of her tone, but how could I argue with those words?

She knew I couldn't, and she went on. "I screwed up by not telling you about him before now but—here he is. He turned two in October. He's never had a dad. Here's your chance. If you want to be a father and actually be in his life, I welcome you."

The same sort of deep and long emotions I felt for Elizabeth stirred in me at Callie's words. Her invitation was long overdue, and I was pissed and hurt, and both were emotions I didn't have time to deal with at the moment—she was right about that.

On top of that there was recognition in her words. I understood what she meant about not wanting a sometimes dad. My father had probably been in my life more than hers, and I already knew, having never really thought about what kind of parent I wanted to be, that I wanted to be a better dad than him.

"I have to get married," I said to Callie, not trying to dismiss her, but cognizant of the other woman—the one who was waiting for me to say 'I do.'

Her birthright was the one I was here for.

"I know," Callie said. "That's why I'd wanted to wait. Please, let's talk more. Be angry at me. Be pissed. But, please, don't make any rash decisions about this. Let's talk first before you decide whether or not you're going to claim Sebastian. Because if you can't really be there, really commit to being in his life, then I don't think you should be there at all."

She didn't have a legal right to make that plea. Though, with the strings her father could pull in his office, it wasn't a battle I would ever want to take up.

And she was right, if I did want to be this little boy's dad— Sebastian's dad—*my* little boy's dad, it had to be all or nothing.

If I made this decision, it wouldn't be for sometimes. It would be forever.

I thought as quickly as I could with my head buzzing like it was. "I don't leave for my honeymoon until Monday. Can I see you tomorrow?"

We exchanged information, made a plan to meet, and then I escorted the woman who had changed my entire life out the door.

When I was alone again I only had five minutes left before I was due to line up for the ceremony. Five minutes to get my thoughts together after this bombshell that Callie had laid on me. It wasn't enough time.

And yet I already knew what I wanted to do.

I felt it in my bones. In the way my heart sang at the memory of those tiny dimples, perfect replicas of my own. In the way this was finally something of my own, something I could do right—of course I would be there for Sebastian. Even if it changed everything. Even if I wasn't ready to be a father. I was ready to try.

I wanted to try.

And he wasn't the only one I wanted to try with. If I was making long plans now, laying out a future, I couldn't pretend anymore that this day-to-day shit was gonna work. I had to set anchors, had to plant roots. And maybe Elizabeth really didn't want to be mine, but before I let her walk away, I had to try one more time to fight for her for real, fight like it mattered, starting today.

Because if I was going to give my child a home, I wanted it to be perfect. And for me, perfect was the home I already had.

TWENTY-TWO
ELIZABETH

I TILTED my face up as Marie put the finishing touches of gloss along my lips.

"And Nana is already seated?" I asked my mother, who was fussing with the bow at my back.

"Yes," she said, losing patience with me. "I already told you Nana is seated. Along with Aunt Becky. And Grandmama already called and wished you a happy day."

"What about Weston's parents?"

"You know this would be easier if you would stop talking." Marie gave me a stern look.

I let my expression deliver my apology and parted my lips exactly the way she'd asked so she could finish her application. "All done," she said after a minute. She dropped the gloss into her makeup bag and stood back, wiping her hands on a paper towel.

"Oh, Elizabeth, you look gorgeous," Melissa, my maid of honor, exclaimed. She looked beautiful herself, in a midnight blue gown, simple and classic, exactly the style I preferred. Mirabelle had been a genius at finding the particular details she'd noticed I liked.

And all for a wedding that didn't even count.

My mother came around from behind me and stepped back with Marie and Melissa to take me in. Tears sprang to her eyes. "Baby, you are stunning. Absolutely stunning." She took my hand and pulled me over to the mirror so I could see for myself.

My breath caught when I saw myself in the high-necked ivory Vera Wang gown. It was simple, with a halter bodice and an elongated silhouette. I'd elected for no train and no veil, the one unique detail the T-strap razor-back which I turned to admire now.

I really did look stunning. Like a bride. Like a *queen*. A lump gathered at the back of my throat, and I had to swallow hard past it.

"It's too bad..." I trailed off remembering that Melissa didn't know the truth and just squeezed my mother's hand instead.

"Yes," my mother said, before Melissa could ask. "It's too bad your father couldn't have been here. He would've been really proud of you."

My mother's cover-up only made the knot in my stomach tighten more, but I appreciated her effort.

There was a knock on the door, and Melissa opened it to find LeeAnn Gregori. "Places," she said. "It's almost showtime."

Funny how she'd chosen exactly the right word—showtime.

I hugged Marie and my mother, and they went off to take their seats. Then Melissa embraced me and slipped into the hall to line up, not as worried about being seen since she wasn't the bride. I stayed behind the door, waiting and wishing for something impossible.

The next knock, I assumed, was my cue, but when I opened it, Donovan was standing there.

"Just came to check in."

I sighed, not really interested in seeing him. After he'd warned me off at the tux shop, Donovan had ended up going to France himself to work on halting the sale of Dyson Media's advertising subsidiary and prepare for the upcoming merger with Reach. I hadn't seen him since then, and I was grateful for what he'd done, apparently having slowed Darrell's plans down. But it didn't override my irritation that he'd said the things he'd said to me before he'd left.

"I'm good," I said. "It's about time for me to go, so..."

"I know. I just caught you. There's something else I wanted to tell you," he added, as though he was unsure how to say it.

I looked up, my curiosity piqued. "Yes?"

"I came here today with Sabrina."

My eyes rolled, and if I didn't need it I would have thrown my bouquet at him. "More entertaining for a friend?"

"No," he said. "I'm keeping her for myself."

Keeping her for himself? As though she were property. As though she were an object passed between friends.

But nevermind that chauvinistic choice of words that Donovan had used—did that mean Sabrina wasn't Weston's?

I didn't have to speak the question out loud, it was written all over my face, and Donovan answered it unprompted.

"I led you to believe that Weston was planning to end up with Sabrina," he said, seeming uncomfortable with his admission. "And that may have been more of what my plans had been than his. I thought you should know that."

"Oh," I said digesting this information. That was quite a lot to take in and I only had a couple of minutes now until I was set to meet my groom face to face and exchange wedding vows. "It would've been nice to have known this, I don't know, before today."

Before I'd written off any possibility of exploring the feelings Weston had sparked in me.

"I'm sure it would have been. The main message isn't any different, Elizabeth. I would still give the same warning, if you'd like to hear it. Weston has never settled down with a woman for more than two weeks. I appreciate that you've felt a connection between the two of you, but I don't recommend you put any faith in that lasting. If you do, it'll only get messy. There's already a pool set up on how soon the divorce will go through. That's advice given as a business partner who doesn't like messes. But it's also given as a friend."

"A friend?" I scoffed. "A friend would have told me the whole truth sooner and let me decide how to think and feel for myself. You just assumed you knew what was best for me." *Just like my father*, I mentally added.

I took a slow breath through gritted teeth and let it out before speaking again. "I appreciate what you've done for me and Dyson Media, Donovan. But if you don't mind, I think maybe you aren't qualified to step in as Weston's protector anymore." I stepped closer and put my hand on his arm. "That's *my* advice, as a friend."

For a moment he looked like he might argue, but then he simply said, "Advice taken."

LeeAnn peeked in then and gave the signal.

"Walk me out?" I asked Donovan, and with a nod, he led me to the foyer outside the Onyx Ball where the opening strains of "Appalachia Waltz" could be heard, my chosen processional just beginning to play. He left me standing behind my maid of honor where she waited, still hidden from view. And after she took her trip down the aisle, it was my turn.

No going back now, even if I wanted to. My future was waiting.

With my shoulders thrown back and my head held high, I stepped into the doorway of the ballroom, and the entire audience stood to face me.

It was nerve-racking, and threw me for a moment to see an entire room standing at my presence, to have so many people looking toward me. It was a feeling I had intended to embrace, as I wanted to be the officer of a company that was so much larger than this simple ballroom could hold.

It was more intimidating than I had counted on.

But even with all eyes on me and the wave of anxiety that produced, the thing that made my knees buckle and the breath stutter from me so that I had to try to catch it in large gulps was the sight of Weston standing at the end of the aisle, waiting for me.

And everyone else in the room disappeared.

What had felt like an overwhelming number of footsteps between us became simple and easy, like crossing a well-worn path, one I could travel blindfolded. I set him as an anchor and he reeled me in, and there was no way I was imagining the look on his face as I neared him. As though he'd never seen anyone more beautiful, as though he'd never wanted to look at anyone but me.

As if I were his queen.

When I finally slipped into place next to him he took my hand in his, and I could feel that he was trembling, or maybe it was me. I was glad that it wasn't a time for us to speak, because there weren't words that I could say in that moment. Nothing seemed to sum up the feeling in my chest. And whatever wisdom there was in remembering that all of this was a performance, that every bit of this was going to have an end, I couldn't listen to any of that right now.

There was just this. Now. Our hands joined together.

Whatever happened after didn't matter.

The officiant welcomed everyone, the words he said already a blur even as they came out of his mouth, my head whirring too much to focus on any one particular phrase or sentiment. He did a reading, something we'd chosen early in the planning process, and then his speech began where he talked about the definition of marriage, where he imagined the life that we were creating together, and the future that we could bring to the earth as Mr. and Mrs. King.

I let his speech go by, background noise to the pressure of Weston's palm against mine. The way the warmth from his body traveled into mine was biology, I supposed, but right then it was mysterious and magical.

For the rest of my life, if this was all I had to hold onto, just this, this moment and this connection—this connection that Donovan said not to make too much of—it would be enough. This magical, fascinating spark that ebbed and flowed and never broke. I couldn't buy that anywhere. I couldn't barter it from anyone else. How lucky that I'd managed to discover it and grow it with this man whom I never would have met if it weren't for my father and his old-fashioned notions.

Maybe there was something wondrous about that too. How things came around. How karma turned the tables.

Then it was time for us to speak, for us to say our vows.

The officiant instructed us to turn to each other and Weston took both of my hands in his, and I realized I'd been wrong about needing something special and original because even hearing the traditional vows I'd settled for come from Weston's lips today, spoken while he looked at me the way he was looking at me, was going to be incredible.

Even if he didn't mean them, there was enough to build a fantasy around.

But when he started speaking, I didn't recognize the words that came from his lips.

"I didn't know what I was getting into when I met you, Elizabeth," he said, and my heart started hammering so hard against my rib cage that I was sure that he and every person in the room could hear it. "I had no idea that my house would be cleaner or that I would be late to every event that we attended together. I certainly didn't have any idea that you would change me so much. Not just me but the world that I live in, the world around me. How I think, how I feel, how I breathe. You're in my heart, now. You're my home."

His voice caught, and he had to pause. "You're my home, and for as much of your life that you let me, it would be my honor to be that for you."

And then it was my turn, which wasn't fair, because I was tearing up, and if he'd done this, if he'd made up these vows on the spot just to get a reaction from me, then it worked. Everyone in the room would be fooled—including me.

But if he really meant them...

God, I *hoped* he meant them.

"Elizabeth," the officiant prodded.

"Yeah, I got this," I said, and the audience laughed. I took a deep breath and tried to find words that would equal his. "Weston, you knock me off my feet every time I walk into a room. You frazzle my head and you make my insides do somersaults and somehow you make me braver than anyone I've ever known. I've never felt more wanted and important and worthy than I do when I look at myself through your eyes. And how you make me feel about myself is only a fraction of how I feel about you. I don't want you to ever let me go. I want to serve all my days beside you as your queen."

The rest of the ceremony went by in a daze. We exchanged rings and it didn't feel awkward or pretend—it felt real.

It *was* real.

And when it came time to kiss the bride, we reached for each other like we were starving and a kiss was the only thing that would nourish and bring us back to life.

Afterward, there was chaos and confusion and hubbub, and LeeAnn was rushing us along to our next destination. The ballroom was being changed over to fit our reception in the very same space, and we were hurried out to take photographs. Some of these were to be alone and some with family, including Darrell, and I knew there wasn't time for chatting or trying to figure out what had just happened on that podium in front of everybody.

Nevertheless, Weston pulled me into the event room across the foyer, an area we had reserved for breakfast earlier in the day, and when LeeAnn scolded him, saying she needed us right then, he said, "One minute with my wife," with such finality that she backed off.

And a shiver ran through my entire body because *I* was his *wife*.

He closed the door and I wanted to jump into his arms and kiss him some more, wanted to tear him out of his so carefully fitted clothes and ravage his body, but even more I wanted to ask him, needed to know, "Did you mean it?"

"I meant it. Every word," he said practically speaking over me.

Just like the ceremony, we were standing face to face, our hands held in each other's, this time with new matching rings on our left hands.

"I meant it too, Weston, I meant it too. I want to be with you."

"I want to be with you, too," he said kissing my face everywhere, quick and urgent. "I want my home with you. I want a life with you."

"I do too. I was so scared that you didn't. I thought—"

"I know. I should've—"

"No, I should've told *you*."

We were talking at the same time, kissing and laughing and apologizing. And everything inside me threatened to burst. I wanted to throw open the door and yell to the whole room, *Everyone, it's real. Weston and I are real!*

"You make me so happy," I told him instead, knowing I only had a second, and I couldn't say anything out there.

"When you don't want to kill me that is," he added, joking.

I nodded and laughed. Another explosion of joy went off inside of me as I imagined our life ahead, us living together, taking over my father's company. "You're going to love life in France."

"Sure," he said. "I've been there before. When are we going to France?"

"Well, we'll live there. To run the company."

Weston chuckled. "What do you mean, *we'll live in France?*"

It was my turn to chuckle. His forgetfulness was becoming legendary. "You're kidding, right? It's always been the plan that I'll live in France. Dyson Media is headquartered in France. My father lived in France."

He took a cautious step back from me, dropping my hands, and sticking one of his in his pocket. "No, no. You can be a shareholder without having to live in the country."

"But you know that I want to be more than a shareholder. I want to be on the board. I want to be an officer." His expression didn't budge. "Weston, you *know* that was always the plan. That's what you've been training me for all these months."

He shook his head slowly.

"You'll have the subsidiary. You'll merge with Reach and you can still have the business there. Is that what this is about? We can still live there and you can still have your company." We'd just found each other. And he was saying we couldn't be together already?

No, I wouldn't lose him this fast.

"Elizabeth, I can't. I—"

LeeAnn knocked on the door, and came in without being invited. "You guys, the photographer is waiting! And your guests! We have to go!"

"Weston?" I asked, not caring that LeeAnn was still standing there. I was begging, pleading with everything I had, by saying just his name.

He looked at our wedding planner and back to me, and shook his head one final time. "I'm sorry, Elizabeth. I can't go with you."

The photographer was waiting to capture my heartbreak; there was no more time left for this. No more time left for *us*.

We walked as one out of the room and into our separate lives.

DIRTY SEXY GAMES

ONE
ELIZABETH

"YOU'RE MARRIED!" exclaimed my grandmother—Nana—embracing me, as I walked into the hotel foyer. She was happy and joyful, as was her daughter Becky, who was waiting behind her to hug me.

I was blinking rapidly, trying to stop the frustrated tears from rolling down my cheeks. I could probably pass off a few as sentimental, but the wave threatening was bigger than that. My family would certainly recognize it as more if it broke.

I had to swallow it back, had to rein it in somehow.

I focused on the sound of Nana's voice and the smell of her, warm and comforting and familiar, and tried to forget about the confusion and the war between me and my new husband.

It wasn't so easy when it was my mother in front of me. She could see right through the mask.

"What's wrong?" she whispered in my ear as she gave me the required mother/bride embrace.

I was saved from answering by LeeAnn Gregori, our wedding planner.

"Elizabeth!" she called, summoning me towards her. "We're waiting!"

I glanced over my mother's shoulder toward the *we* that LeeAnn referred to—the wedding photographer and my groom, Weston King. They were only thirty feet away from me, but it felt like a continent.

The ceremony that had concluded less than half an hour before made Weston and me closer than we ever had been, in theory. And yet, after the words he'd just said to me—*I can't go with you*—he might as well already be an ocean away.

I wiped at the stray tear and squeezed my mother. "Everything's fine," I lied. I should've been good at this by now, after five months of pretending, but right now it felt harder than ever. Perhaps because I didn't know anymore which parts I was faking and which I wasn't. The wedding was real. The feelings were real. For both of us, I'd learned.

The relationship, though?

Apparently that was still up for debate.

But if I wanted to convince my cousin this was all legitimate so he didn't challenge my claim to my inheritance, I had to pretend the relationship was solid as well.

I crossed the room with my head held high, a smile on my lips, making damn sure no one besides my mother could see the struggle inside.

"One in front of the Christmas tree would be absolutely spectacular," LeeAnn suggested, and the photographer agreed, posing Weston and me there. We did several variations of holding hands and embracing. I couldn't look directly into his eyes, had to force myself to look at his nose instead, or his eyebrows, knowing I'd be unable to handle what I would find if I looked at him for real.

He seemed to feel the same. Just as awkward around me.

"They're sort of stiff, aren't they?" I heard the photographer whisper to LeeAnn.

"They're very formal," LeeAnn said, making up an excuse for us on the spot. The poor lady probably didn't know *what* to think of us with all the bickering we'd done in her presence over the last few months.

Maybe Weston had heard him too, because all of a sudden he *did* loosen up, and in the next picture he pulled me to him and improvised a kiss. I wanted to push him away, because I was frustrated and angry at him for keeping me in the dark and confusing me and yanking me up and down like a yo-yo.

But even if it wasn't for the show we were putting on, I couldn't resist him. I'd never been able to resist him. I threw my arms around his neck and let him kiss away my worry. *He'll explain later,* I told myself while his lips were bruising mine. *He wants to be with me, just like I want to be with him. We'll make it work. Somehow.*

He pulled away and I searched for that same reassurance in his face that I'd felt in his kiss, but his eyes seemed to be trying to tell me something different than what I was asking.

"Weston? We can still figure—"

He shook his head. "Not now," he whispered harshly.

"Where do you want us?" a familiar voice came from behind the photographer.

I pried my gaze away from Weston and found my cousin Darrell had joined my mother and Nana and Weston's family, all gathering for the group pictures to be taken.

This whole charade had been for him. If I hadn't been afraid he'd contest the validity of my nuptials, I would have eloped with Weston at City Hall.

Which meant Weston may have just been performing again. He could have seen Darrell and thrown in the kiss to make the photo seem more authentic.

At least I could count on him for that.

As to whether or not he would tell me what was holding him in New York, what would keep him from having a relationship with me and moving to France, I could hope he would tell me later, but why would he, when he'd never opened up before? He'd never even bothered explaining his strained family dynamics to me.

It was probably safer not to hold my breath waiting for more.

The group pictures were easier to endure. Even though I still had Weston at my side, could still feel his heat in the press of his body against mine, there were others around me and their energy helped bring a genuine smile to my face.

Soon the pictures were finished. "Let's go!" LeeAnn said, in full drill sergeant mode. "The schedule has us back at the reception by now."

Weston followed after her, eager to be away from his clingy parents, but before I could escape, Darrell caught me by the elbow. The hair stood up at the nape of my neck. The last time he and I had been alone he hadn't been very nice to me, and I didn't expect that he'd be any kinder today.

He surprised me, though. "I must say, Elizabeth, I was very impressed with the sincerity of the ceremony. You and the King boy seem to have feelings for each other. It was hard to tell in the porno I watched from that nightclub footage of the two of you."

Turned out I was less in the mood for this than for his bullying. It made me feel more like a fraud than when he'd accused me of spreading my legs like a prostitute in the video he'd referred to as a porno. And when I'd grinded on Weston hoping to be caught on camera it *had been* pretend. So that was saying something.

But of everyone on the guest list for the day, Darrell was my number one priority. If I didn't fool him, there was no point in trying to fool anyone else.

With a sigh, I turned toward him. "What is it going to take for you to believe that I'm really happy and in love with Weston?" I certainly didn't sound like a bride who was happy and in love, but being harassed by my cousin on my wedding day certainly warranted some agitation on my part.

"I'm sure I won't be truly convinced until you're both settled in together and the transfer of ownership has gone smoothly," Darrell said. "But today was a good start."

My already empty stomach clenched like I was going to retch. Because from the last word Weston had given me, there was going to be no settling in together.

But it had never been the plan to actually settle in with him. Everything was on course, even if it felt like the train had run off the tracks and there were mass casualties, the only one hurting was me.

"Then you have nothing to worry about," I said with the fakest smile I'd ever given. I spun on my heel and went to find my groom so we could be announced to our guests as Mr. and Mrs. King.

Inside the ballroom, I forced myself to forget about what was on the line and the questions in my head. Weston and I separated, each of us to say hello and mingle with guests on our own, and while that hadn't been the plan, it turned out to be for the best. I could forget better when he wasn't standing next to me, forget that he'd declared feelings for me out of the blue during our ceremony. I could forget that he told me how he'd meant them as soon as we were alone together. I could forget that he then told me we couldn't have a life together and that none of it mattered.

I could forget, until I came to Jepson Arndt, an old friend of my father's and the current treasurer for Dyson Media, the company that I would soon be taking over.

"I'm eager to hear what your plans are for the company," he said, which sent me spiraling in a new round of dizzy nerves.

Was I ready for this kind of questioning? Was I ready for this company? Weston had been training me for the last several months, but there was still so much that I was ignorant about, so many areas where I was naïve. Jepson was a man well into his fifties with a whole career of experience behind him. I was less than half his age, my only experience in business gleaned from Weston's old text books and pop quizzes—and I would now be his boss. How did I ever think I could manage this?

Thankfully, he didn't continue the conversation in the direction that I thought he would.

But the new avenue he took was just as bad.

"I don't want to bog you down, though, with business details on your wedding day. We can leave that for another time. Perhaps we could meet privately some time soon. What are your living arrangements going to be? Will you be staying here? Or are you moving to France, like your father did?"

"I...we..." It was really stupid to not be prepared for this. I'd expected people to ask about our honeymoon, not about after. Weston and I hadn't planned an *after* together. We'd come back to New York, of course, and I would begin the process of taking over the company. At some point, I'd go on to France. Weston would stay in the States, and I would tell people he would come later.

And that would be a lie.

Instead of joining me, we'd get divorced.

Now I wasn't sure of any of it. Because if Weston wouldn't come with me to France...was there a chance I'd stay in New York for him?

"I'm putting my penthouse up for sale," I said, because that was one thing I was sure of. Even if I stayed in New York, Weston preferred living near his office.

Jesus, I couldn't believe I was even considering an alternate future, one where I gave up my dreams to be with him. But more than anything, I hated that I didn't know what came next.

"Then you're planning to come to France?" Jepson asked.

I turned my head to look for Weston, wondering again why he wouldn't come with me, wondering if I could change his mind.

When I found him in the crowd of people at our reception, I was hit in the stomach like a crash in stock prices.

He was dancing. We hadn't even had a first dance together—we hadn't put one on the agenda, but that wasn't the point—and he was dancing with Sabrina Lind, his ex-girlfriend and current employee.

Was that why Weston didn't want to come to France with me? Because he'd have to leave *her*?

My ribs felt as if they were suddenly squeezing together. I'd been jealous of her for months, and Weston had never given me any reason not to be. Donovan had brought Sabrina as his date, and I knew that Donovan was interested in her for himself, but that didn't say anything about Weston or Sabrina's feelings. I'd never had the impression other people's feelings were terribly important to Donovan Kincaid.

From this angle, I couldn't see Weston's face well, but it was impossible to miss the way Sabrina was clinging to my husband. She seemed almost desperate, like she needed him to stand.

Yeah, that was the way I felt about him too.

I was so frustrated. So confused. So unsettled. The tears that had threatened earlier pressed against the dam, hot and angry.

"Yes, I'll be moving to France," I said, because I needed the security of my plans. "Excuse me, Jepson, I need a moment please."

I didn't even care what it looked like, or what he thought of me, this giant in the empire that I was taking over. This moment felt so small and pale compared to the vast wilderness of betrayal and pain inside of me, a wilderness brought on by Weston King.

I had to get away.

And there was nowhere for brides to escape, I'd learned. All eyes had been on me from the minute the celebration had begun. Even trips to the restroom were nearly impossible with people swarming to compliment and praise and give their well wishes. But I needed someplace, a spot I could hide, if even for just a minute.

Desperately, I looked around and noticed the divider that had been set up to wall off the reception during the ceremony was nearby. It wasn't perfect, but it would do.

I slipped around the corner and finally, I was alone.

I made my way to the small stage that was now pushed all the way up against the wall, where Weston and I had so recently stood and made vows to each other. He'd looked me in the eyes and told me I'd changed his life for the better. He'd called me his home.

If I really was his home, why did it feel so much like I was spinning aimlessly?

With no one watching me, I could throw my head back and let the tears fall—not too many, just a few. I wasn't even sure what I was crying about, really. Everything. Nothing.

I was tired, that was it.

Tired of pretending my feelings for Weston weren't real. Tired of pretending my marriage was. Tired of guessing what was in his head. Tired of justifying what was in mine. Of not knowing if I could pull this off and tired of worrying about what happened next. Of wondering if my father would approve. Of being jealous of Sabrina. Of wearing these heels. Tired of men making me question my worth and my value and my place in the world.

I was a queen.

That was my place in the world.

With or without a king, I was a queen. I'd be a queen no matter how this ended. I had to remember that.

"Elizabeth?"

I startled, glancing at the source of the voice, simultaneously trying to hide my face while I frantically wiped the moisture off my cheeks. "Clarence," I said, my voice breaking. "I'm..."

He was at my side before I could figure out how to finish the statement. "You're crying. What's wrong?"

"I needed some air," I said pushing the emotions inside me, boxing them up. "It was so crowded in there." I couldn't look at him yet. Too frazzled. Too obviously lying.

"These aren't the *just-needed-space* kind of tears, Bitsy. Come on. I know you. Remember?"

I turned to look at him finally, to study him. He was just as attractive as he'd been in high school, with his broad shoulders and defined jawline. His slicked-back brunette hair and light brown eyes were maybe nothing special on their own, but the whole package came together quite nicely, tied with a Henry-Cavill-type bow.

But even though he still looked *good*, he didn't look the *same*. We weren't the same.

"You *don't* know me anymore. It's been years." Years since we'd been together. Seven, to be exact, and we'd barely seen each other since. I wasn't Bitsy anymore. The ways I had changed could be written in volumes.

"I think I still know you," he said sweetly rather than patronizingly. He reached his hand out to brush my face where tears had gathered along my jawline. "I really wish you'd tell me what's wrong."

And for half a second I considered it, considered telling him everything, not because I still had feelings for him or because I wanted him now, but because he was gentle and kind and there, and I really did want someone to talk to in the moment.

But the person I wanted wasn't Clarence Sheridan. And it wasn't just a shoulder to cry on. I wanted Weston King.

And confessing things to this old friend, practically a stranger now, would do nothing to get me the man I wanted.

"Really, it's silly. I was just sad that my father isn't here for my big day."

"Of course. What was I thinking? He died a little more than a year ago, didn't he? I heard about his passing. I'm so sorry." He rubbed his hand up and down my arm. He was trying to be comforting, but his fingers felt like sandpaper on my skin. Rough and wrong.

"Thank you. I didn't think I'd be so emotional about it." And now that I was already emotional and thinking about my father, I actually was sad about his absence too. "But, hey," I continued. "Let's not think about it anymore. I need to cheer up. Change the subject."

"Okay." He stood back and looked me over. "You're married! I can't believe it."

I almost wished I could take it back and keep talking about my father.

"Yep. I'm married." It would take a while before I got used to that. Probably just about the time my divorce was finalized.

"You're a beautiful bride. Stunning. I have to say Weston King is a really lucky guy."

Tell that to him, I thought. "Thank you."

Clarence sobered. "Are you sure there isn't anything else going on?"

I'd forgotten how persistent he had always been. "I'm positive. It's been a long day. I haven't eaten. I need to get back out there, though. Maybe we can catch up some other time?"

"Sure. But if there's anything you need, Elizabeth, you can tell me. You know that, right?"

I nodded. "Of course. I appreciate that."

"I mean it," he insisted. "Promise you'll tell me if you need me."

"I promise." I forced a smile, the seventy billionth of the day, and gestured to the ballroom behind the divider that was hiding us. "I've really got to get out there before they miss me."

"Right. I'll go with you."

Clarence put his arm out to escort me. I started to put my hand on his bicep but then hesitated when he started to walk. "Does my makeup…?"

"Look up." He scrubbed at the corner of my eye with his thumb. "There. You're perfect."

No. I wasn't perfect. I was a mess.

I was married.

And I'd never felt so alone in all my life.

TWO
WESTON

SHE WAS the most beautiful woman in the room.

She was the most beautiful woman in the world.

I couldn't take my eyes off of her for more than two minutes all night, which was how I noticed right away when she disappeared.

And then, ten minutes later, the most beautiful woman in the world—my *wife*—walked out from behind the partition arm in arm with her fucking ex-boyfriend. He was giving her the eyes of a lover, and suddenly I saw red.

The day was definitely not going how I'd imagined.

I'd been a nervous wreck in the beginning, reeling from the revelation that I had a son. But then, while I stood there at the end of the aisle waiting for Elizabeth to appear, it felt like the strings were finally coming together, knotting into a perfect bow instead of falling apart and unraveling like they had been for the past several weeks.

There she was, walking toward me with the simple strains of a cello accompanying her as she made her way. And it didn't matter anymore that I had less to offer than she had to give, that I was from a family of fuck-ups, that I could never be as selfless and noble as she was. She brought me up to her level just by allowing me to be in her presence. The name I was given at birth, King—it had always been a joke. Until Elizabeth Dyson stood beside me and finally made me royalty.

I was in love with her.

She was a beginning for me, and I never wanted her to end. If she did, if she walked away, if she didn't feel the same, I was pretty sure that I would end. During the ceremony though, with her hand held in mine, I wasn't worried about her leaving. And I wasn't just trying to clutch onto her because I felt like I needed her in order to be a father to Sebastian—this wedding, this fake wedding, had become the most real thing in my life. *Elizabeth* had become the most real thing in my life, and finding out about Sebastian had just kicked me into gear, made me understand I had to own what I was feeling.

So right there, in front of all our friends and family, I told her. And I meant it.

And I knew in my bones that she meant it when she said her vows to me, too.

When we walked back down that aisle together, as man and wife, I thought our lives were starting together.

How the fuck had I forgotten to factor in France?

It was my gut reaction to instantly say that I couldn't go with her, to say that moving out of the country was out of the question. The last words Callie had given me about our son were still so fresh in my mind—she'd offered me a place in his life, but only if I could be there. How could I possibly be there if I was halfway across the world?

I couldn't lose him. Not when I'd just found out about him.

And I couldn't lose her. I wouldn't have a home to give Sebastian without her. I couldn't be a man who could be a father without her.

Maybe it was something that could be sorted out without Elizabeth having to lose her dreams, without me having to lose a relationship with my child, but it wasn't something we could discuss in thirty seconds in a side room at our wedding. It would have to wait, even though it was a fucking tug of war between them inside me, and that perfect bow that my life had been tied up in? I was now desperately holding on to both strings as my arms were being torn in different directions.

The worst part was the look on Elizabeth's face, the plea in her voice. I hated not being able to give her an explanation yet, but I couldn't drop the same bomb on her that Callie had dropped on me. Not today.

It all had to wait.

So I compartmentalized as much as I could, put Sebastian in one corner of my heart and Elizabeth in another and focused on getting through. Today the goal was to fool Darrell. We were so close to pulling this off, we couldn't let him see the tension between us.

I'd thought I'd done a pretty good job of it too—we posed for pictures together, then mingled separately at the reception. I flirted with the older women. I let my bachelor friends harass me. When Sabrina mistakenly thought she'd seen someone that had scared her, and Donovan wasn't around to comfort her, I calmed her down by taking her for a spin on the dance floor. She wasn't who I wanted to be dancing with, but she'd become a good friend, and it was nice to have something else to think about.

The trick was, I realized, to not be too near Elizabeth. She made me impetuous and passionate, made me say too much. Distracted me from the agenda because I wanted the point of the day to be *us*. I wanted to take off her garter and cut the cake and have a first dance with her, wanted all the wedding traditions we'd left out of the reception since we weren't a *real* couple.

But now we *were* a real couple.

And it was harder to be next to her, worrying things might not work out now that I actually cared.

But just because it was hard didn't mean I was going to stand by and let Douchebag Sheridan make his moves on her. She was mine. End of story.

I made my way over there so fast, Clarence was still with her when I got there.

"Where have you been?" I asked, my eyes darting between the two of them.

Her bright blues widened as though surprised that I'd caught her. Did that mean she was guilty of something?

"I just...I needed...air," she answered, her cheeks pink.

"I saw her disappear and went to check on her. I noticed you were busy with other...guests," Douchebag said. Other guests. As though I should've been with Elizabeth instead. As though he knew anything about what was going on between us.

But maybe he did. I didn't know if they'd had contact with each other in the recent weeks since they'd reconnected. She had his phone number—I knew that because I'd given it to her myself. She might've even told him just now. Had she been gone long enough? How much time would it take to say none of this was real, that she'd thought it was, but Weston King had played her?

But I hadn't bailed on her. Not yet. Not ever, if I could help it. And I would help it.

I just couldn't fix it right now.

I put my arm around her waist, pulling her to me possessively. "Let's talk." I might not be able to fix it right now, but I had to be able to tell her enough to keep her, before she went running off to someone else.

She looked around, not just at Douchebag but at all of our guests. "We can't right now."

Okay, so there was no way we were getting across the ballroom with all these people. But I had an idea. "Come with me." I tugged her onto the dance floor, away from her past to a place we could be alone. Into my arms, where I'd wanted her all evening.

"Weston, I don't feel like dancing," she said through her teeth as she smiled at a passing couple.

"I don't fucking care if you feel like dancing. I need to hold you right now." That shut her up for a moment, and as I spun her on the floor to the slow song, she relaxed into my embrace.

I rested my head right next to her ear, intent on telling her...something. I just didn't know what would be the right thing to say. There was so much to share. So much to tell her. I still hadn't actually told her I loved her. And now I had to tell her I had a kid. Would she still want me now that I came with baggage? I didn't even know how she felt about the prospect of children. We hadn't even discussed what country we'd live in, much less what could happen down the road.

"I saw you dancing with Sabrina," she said before I had a chance to tell her anything.

I stiffened, because this was another drama of my own making. How long had I let her be jealous of my employee? There was nothing going on with her—hadn't been since Elizabeth had walked into Reach's lounge and into my life.

"I wanted to be dancing with you," I told her, feeling the weight of its inadequacy even as I said it. But I wasn't certain Sabrina's past was my story to tell.

"There was nothing stopping you," she hissed. "You could easily have asked me."

"You didn't want to do the first dance ritual."

"We said that months ago. Back when we said we were going to do scripted vows." She pulled her head back so she could look at me. "You have me on a roller coaster. One minute you care, the next you don't. How am I supposed to know what's real and what isn't?"

Her voice was thick with emotion and it slammed me with the want to make it better.

"I have you on a roller coaster so you turn to Clarence for consolation?" Well, maybe I *wanted* to make it better, but I was better at being an asshole. It came more naturally.

"You were dancing with Sabrina," she reminded me.

"In front of everyone. Not alone in a corner where no one could see us. Her cheeks weren't rosy when we were finished." The more I thought about this, the angrier I legitimately became. I didn't truly think Elizabeth would cheat on me, if for no other reason than she didn't like to break rules. But to run straight to him instead of coming to me was not okay.

"She was clinging to you the whole time. Is she the reason you won't leave New York?"

"I can't believe you even—" I cut off sharply as I noticed that there were eyes on us. Lots of eyes on us. The entire room was watching us, not necessarily because we looked like we were arguing—I was pretty sure we'd managed to cover that up. Most likely, they were just watching the wedding couple sharing a moment on the dance floor.

Elizabeth followed my gaze. "Oh, shit."

"Just keep dancing."

"We're continuing this discussion later," she warned quietly. She smiled again. She was so good at it, putting that fake dazzle on, but I was really getting good at telling the difference between the fraudulent and the authentic. Strangely, the real one was never quite as bright.

I would have given anything to have seen that dimmer smile right then.

IT SEEMED like decades before LeeAnn was summoning us over to her. "You need to make a big exit," she said. "That means you need to leave before your guests do. It's time to say your goodbyes."

"Thank God," Elizabeth said, her relief evident in her sigh.

LeeAnn raised an eyebrow.

"My feet hurt," Elizabeth said, and though I was sure it was true, I was also sure it wasn't the reason she was glad this was almost over.

"Of course," LeeAnn said, like she should've known all along, though her own shoes were two inches taller than Elizabeth's. I had a feeling LeeAnn wasn't the type of woman who would complain about her feet hurting. It was the price you had to pay for looking good.

I preferred Elizabeth's honesty, as inappropriate as it may have been at the moment. I attempted to share a smile with her, but she missed it, and perhaps that was for the best. I was in a pissy mood from our fight, from Douchebag, from the frustration of being at an utter loss for how to solve these problems, and I wasn't sure my expression was even worth sharing.

Elizabeth headed over to her family to make her farewells. Most of my friends had already left—Donovan and Nate had both brought dates for the evening and had ducked out early. The last people on Earth I wanted to see at the moment were my own parents, but it was still a performance, and they were the ones I was most expected to say good night to.

"She really is a lovely woman," my mother said as I let her hug me. "I hope we get the chance to know her better."

I'd done so well keeping walls up all day, but at my mother's mention of a future with Elizabeth, my chest felt tight. "I do too," I said.

My mother's expression brightened, and too late I realized she thought that I meant that I would let Elizabeth into their lives, when what I really meant was I hoped that Elizabeth would be in *mine*. It wasn't something I could take back after the fact, either. Especially as my mother's eyes brimmed with tears, happy at the mere suggestion that I'd spend time with her.

"Oh, Weston. You can't imagine how much I've missed you." She pulled me into another hug. "One day, you'll have your own son, and before you know it he'll be grown up too, and you'll be saying goodbye to him on his own wedding day, and then you'll understand." She was blubbering now.

My throat got tight and I was afraid if I spoke I would blubber too. Because now I wasn't just thinking about Elizabeth and a future with her, but also how much I had missed my mother. And also the added knowledge that I now *did* have a son. Her grandson.

I hadn't even met him yet, and I felt like I'd missed so much. Two years of his life, I'd missed. It was going on seven years that things had been strained with my family. How many years was I going to let my mother lose?

There wasn't room for this inside of me. Not tonight.

"I love you, Mom," I whispered, not even sure she heard it.

I hugged my dad too, but nothing was amended when they walked away. There was still a massive chasm between us, but for just one moment, we'd both found a bridge and met in the middle.

My best man, Brett, a friend from college, announced our departure from the reception. There was a round of applause and cheers and it felt like the kind of standing ovation one got at the end of a performance. I took Elizabeth's hand in mine and waved to everyone as we walked into the hotel lobby toward the bank of elevators that would take us to the honeymoon suite.

As soon as the doors closed and we were alone in the car, she dropped my hand and folded her arms across her chest.

So that was how the evening was going to be.

I rolled my eyes and pushed the button to our floor. We rode up in silence, the tension growing thick and hot around us. I was used to the friction, the way it sparked and flashed between our eyes. I'd grown accustomed to the ticking time bomb. The space surrounding us had always been a warzone. Why should it be any different now?

I probably shouldn't have found that realization as comforting as I did. It probably shouldn't have turned me on so much.

As soon as we were in our suite, the bomb exploded, the bomb being Elizabeth. "We're alone now, so just tell me straight. You knew I was always going to France. If you wanted to be with me, you had to know it would involve living there. Is that not something you'll even consider? Is it Sabrina? Is it Reach? Is it Donovan? Because if it's fucking Donovan who's keeping you from—"

I grabbed her hands, which were flying in midair as she yelled, and pulled them behind her back at her waist as I cut her off with a searing kiss, my tongue plunging into her open mouth, robbing her of oxygen.

When she was thoroughly kissed, her lips pliable, her body sagging in my arms, I let her go.

"I'm tired, Elizabeth. I'm not discussing fucking anything tonight." I took off my tuxedo jacket and threw it on the desk. Then I began working on my cufflinks. "What I think we both need now is to release some tension."

Her spine straightened, her neck growing longer as she stared at me in shock. "You think we're going to have *sex* now?"

I loved how she made it sound disgusting, like she wasn't interested, even when I'd just been kissing her and had felt the lean in her body, had tasted the desire in her mouth.

Two could play the indifference game.

I shrugged. "I'm fucking someone tonight. If you want it to be you, you better take off your dress."

Her mouth slammed shut, and she only seemed to consider it for two seconds before she was fumbling with the zipper at her back. She struggled with it, but I didn't help her. It made me stiff to watch her frantically trying to strip down, just because I told her to. Just because she thought I might find a better offer if she didn't.

Like there was a better offer than her.

Like there was anyone but her.

I didn't take my eyes off her as I unbuttoned my vest and tossed it to the side with my jacket. I'd loosened my tie by the time she got her dress undone. It fell to the floor and she was left wearing a strapless corseted bra, one that had a low back so it couldn't be seen with her dress on, and matching lace panties—both in a white ivory so virginal and bridal it seemed dirty.

Jesus, she was a fucking wet dream.

And she was my *wife*.

I was so goddamned hard at that thought, my cock was a brick. I had to stroke myself through my pants, just to get some relief.

Elizabeth was watching me as closely as I was watching her. She saw what she did to me. She loved it, that little demon. That witch. That spiteful angel. Her lips quirked up the tiniest bit, taking pleasure in my misery, as she reached behind herself to undo the corset.

But I stopped her. "Leave it."

"Can I take off my shoes, at least?" she asked, her tone full of sass and sauce.

"Fuck no." So her feet were hurting, but that was part of the turn-on. That she was suffering. Suffering like I was inside.

I wanted to make her suffer more.

Suffer *and* feel good. The way she made me suffer and feel good and wish that I could only ever feel exactly that way all the time.

I unclipped my suspenders then undid the fly of my pants. My boxer briefs were damp from my dick leaking inside them, begging to be released, aching for Elizabeth's pussy. But I wasn't ready to bring it out yet. Not until she was aching for me too.

Scanning the room, I quickly found where I wanted to be.

"I'm already not in the mood to be good to you; I really don't think you want to push me."

Her head shifted back toward me quickly, her mouth opening with a slight gasp. "What are you going to—"

"I said no talking." Before she could say anything else or challenge me or make me want to throttle her, I moved to kneel in front of her pussy, hooked my arms around each of her thighs, and began licking at the lace barrier.

She responded with a series of moans and grunts. I kept it up, licking at her through the material, swiping up her slit, using the lace to create friction. I'd been sleeping with her long enough to know how to get her worked up now, how to read her signs. And every time she got a little bit close, every time her gasps got louder and her breathing more rapid, I pulled away, changed my tactic.

It wasn't too long before she was writhing, still dressed in her bridal underwear, wound up from my torturous tongue. So desperate, she started to beg, remembering my order that the only word she could speak was my name. "Weston, Weston," she pled.

She wasn't worked up enough. Wasn't destroyed yet. Wasn't torn apart inside like I was over her.

I pushed aside the panel at her crotch. My fingers found her wet and slippery as I slid inside her. She bucked up with her hips, urging me in deeper. But I continued my torture, fucking her shallowly with just my fingertips, licking in wide circles around her clit.

She was sweating, tears were trailing down her cheeks when she finally broke the rule I'd given her and spoke. "I don't know if you're trying to make me feel good or miserable," she said.

"That's the point," I said against her.

"Please, fuck me now."

I nodded, unable to take watching her squirm any longer. My balls already ached with the need to release inside her. "I'll close the curtains," I offered.

"No, I like them open."

"Follow me." I led her to the bench in front of the [window]. She watched me, and I could feel her curiosity as I turned [lights] on and then opened the curtains all the way. With th[em open,] anyone who was looking in the building across from us [would be] able to see us pretty well.

"You and those damn floor-to-ceiling windows," Eliz[a said,] her voice raspy and eager.

Yeah, she liked the windows too.

"You want me to close them?" I asked, but I was alre[ady rolling] up my shirt sleeves, moving on to the next part of my pre[paration].

She shrugged with one shoulder. "Whatever turns yo[u on."]

"Lie down on the bench," I commanded.

She lay back, tentatively, as though she were conce[rned with] getting it right, not as though she didn't want to do it.

"All the way, flat on your back," I instructed. "Th[en spread] your legs, as far as you can."

I stepped back to look at her, imagining what some[one would] see from the other side—this beautiful redheaded bride, [spread on] a table in front of her groom, a banquet feast just for [me. The] bench was the perfect size for her; it fit her from her h[ead to the] bottom of her ass, so when she spread her legs, her puss[y dangled] at the other end, clothed in delicate lace.

I rubbed myself as I gazed upon her. "You're the mo[st sexy] woman I know," I told her, massaging my crown throug[h my pants]. She turned her head on the bench to look at me, her lips [parted,] eyelashes fluttering.

I continued. "You were so fucking sexy when you [walked] into that aisle, I was almost pissed that anybody else go[t to see] you."

Her breathing quickened, but she parried m[y words,] turning to look out the window. "That's a guy thing to [say,] so—"

"Stop talking unless you're screaming my name," I s[aid.]

God, she was divine. I pushed my pants down with my briefs just as far as necessary, and pulled her panties from her gorgeous legs. Then I was climbing on top of her, fucking into her hard, harder, so hard. She wrapped her legs around me at my waist, hooking us together, and when I looked in the window I could see our reflection there, could see what the neighbors saw, and it spurred me on more, drove me to pound into her faster and deeper and harder, harder.

It was the final dirty encore to our earlier performance.

We came together, both of us tortured and miserable and in desperate need of the release.

When I was calm enough, I pulled out of her and gathered her in my arms, carried her to her bed where I held her and made love to her the rest of the night. We didn't talk about the mountains between us.

We were married now. We had the rest of our lives for talking.

Or, at least we had tomorrow.

THREE
ELIZABETH

WESTON WAS STILL ASLEEP when I woke up the next morning. I spent several minutes tracing the dips and curves of his bare torso with my eyes, his abs so toned that six-pack didn't even cover it. My mouth watered as I gazed lower at the V-lines that peeked out from under the sheet—two short roads leading to pleasureland. But it was the sweet gentle rise and fall of his chest that had me hypnotized. I thought about how easy it would be to roll into his arms and fall back asleep, or wake him up with a kiss and urge him to make love to me again.

But there was a giant wall between us, invisible, yet I believed it was surmountable, and that had to be dealt with before I could truly be as close to him as I wanted to be.

I forced myself out of bed and into the bathroom. One look in the mirror said that the beautiful bride from the day before had gone, leaving a faded beauty queen in the wreckage. I needed a shower and breakfast, needed to pull myself together, needed to make myself look like a decent human being—needed to feel like a decent human being before facing my groom.

My husband.

How long would I be able to keep calling him that?

The shower did wonders for my mood. I washed off the makeup and the traces of the extraordinary day I'd had before. I felt melancholy as I washed away the sticky leftovers of sex between my legs, as though a little water and soap would take away the memory of Weston's mouth and cock. But those memories were forever seared into my mind, deep, like ink into flesh. Whatever I left this marriage with, at least I'd have that.

When I was clean and fresh, I turned off the water and wrapped a towel around my body and another around my hair. I brushed my teeth and put makeup on my face until I looked like someone whom I recognized again. When I walked back into the bedroom, I found the bed empty.

Sounds from the other room said Weston was up and moving around. Hopefully he'd ordered breakfast, or at least coffee. I found a robe in my suitcase and traded the towel for that, then padded out to the main room of our suite.

My spirits dropped at what I found. Weston was dressed. Seeing him with clothes on was always somewhat disappointing, but more disappointing was that he was dressed to go out. He had shoes on and his coat in hand.

"Are you going somewhere?" I hated how weak my voice sounded.

His eyes darted around the room, looking anywhere but at me. "Yeah. I have an appointment. It shouldn't take too long. I'm just looking for my wallet."

"You have an appointment? We're on our honeymoon." Technically we didn't leave for our trip until tomorrow, and of course when all this had been planned, our entire marriage was a farce. But then suddenly it wasn't. And we needed to be together if we had any shot at all of figuring this out.

"There it is," he said to himself, finding his wallet in his jacket from the night before. As though I hadn't said anything at all.

I didn't even care anymore what it looked like for him to be leaving his bride less than twenty-four hours after our nuptials. I didn't care about putting on a show anymore. I cared about *us*.

"Weston," I called as he headed toward the door.

He turned this time and looked at me, really looked at me. His expression, which had seemed distracted before, focused and softened.

He crossed the room and pulled me into his arms, cupping my cheek with his hand. "I promise I won't be gone very long." He kissed the side of my lips.

I clutched onto his jacket. "But we need to talk."

"We do. We will. We have two weeks and I'm all yours. But first I just have to do this one thing. Okay?" His thumb grazed along my chin, sending goosebumps down my arms.

"Okay," I said when it really wasn't okay at all, but what choice did I have but to trust him? He kissed me again, for real, the kind of kiss that made my knees weak and my toes curl.

"Don't be dressed when I get back," he said half teasing, half commanding.

I nodded, though for the kinds of things we needed to discuss, being dressed was probably the wisest decision. As he headed for the door again, it felt like he was leaving, leaving for real, and his name came out of my lips again involuntarily. "Weston!"

He stopped, the door half-open, and looked at me longingly. "Two weeks," he promised again. "I'm all yours." Then he shut the door and was gone.

It wasn't the two weeks I was worried about. It was the whole lifetime after.

I stood staring at the door for a long moment after he left, sorting through the banquet of emotions I was feeling inside. He'd meant to comfort me with his words and his kiss—and he had, momentarily.

But now that he was gone, and I was left alone in the bridal suite of the Park Hyatt with nothing but questions and a brand-new diamond-lined wedding band under my engagement ring, his well-meant intentions vanished and were replaced with a brewing storm.

Alone, his comfort felt like rejection.

Alone, his words sounded like empty promises.

Frustration swept through me like a gale wind and I reached for the nearest object I could find, an empty water glass on the desk, and threw it as hard as I could against the door. It smashed at once into pieces, unleashing a dam of tears inside me. What the hell had I gotten myself into? I cried as I hugged myself, asking myself the same question over and over. Why did it hurt so much? I didn't even know who to blame—myself, my father, Weston, or Donovan.

And maybe all of this was stupid and dramatic and there was nothing even to cry over. I would get my company. That was what I'd wanted, right? And maybe I would even get Weston, but if I had him, then why was he rushing off to secret places on a Sunday morning at 10:00 a.m.? Why did he leave me in the dark? Why would he never let me in?

I bent over in an attempt to control the sobs racking my body, when suddenly there was a knock on the door. My crying halted, my body froze.

It was probably housekeeping. We'd forgotten the stupid do not disturb sign.

The knock came again, and I knew I had to answer it or they would walk right in. I crossed to the door, careful not to step on the glass, and opened it just to say, "We don't—"

But it wasn't housekeeping.

"Clarence?" I wiped the tears from my cheeks with the whole of my hand. God, this was the second time in two days he'd seen me crying. "What are you doing here?"

"Can I come in?" he asked.

"Weston is..." I didn't necessarily want to tell him that my husband wasn't there, and it seemed just as odd to invite an ex-boyfriend into my bridal suite when I was alone.

"He just left," Clarence finished for me. "I saw him."

My brows furrowed. "Did you know he had an appointment today?"

Clarence shook his head. "I just got lucky."

I processed what he'd just said, understanding that he'd meant he wanted to see me alone.

I couldn't think of any reason to tell him to leave. Honestly, I wasn't thinking very well at all. "Be careful. There's glass by the door."

I opened the door farther so that Clarence could step in, then let the door go so it could slam shut on its own, and I wouldn't have to dance over the glass again. Clarence looked at the mess on the floor.

"Did something happen here, Elizabeth?" he asked anxiously.

"I just dropped a glass," I said, tightening my robe around myself, conscious that I was naked underneath. "It's really silly how upset I got about dropping the glass. You must think I'm really emotional these days." Such a lame excuse. I picked up the hotel magazine and headed for the door to start cleaning it up.

Clarence took the magazine from my hand. "Let me." He bent down and swept the broken pieces onto the magazine, glancing up at me furtively. "You just happened to drop a glass right in front of the door, huh? It really seems more like it was thrown."

I turned away from him to the Kleenex box and cleaned up my nose before turning back to him. "I really don't know what you're suggesting, but maybe you could tell me why you are here today."

"Not trying to upset you, Bitsy," he said using his old nickname for me again. He dumped the glass into the trash can under the desk, set the magazine down, and faced me head-on. "I came because I want to make sure you're okay. Yesterday I was worried that you weren't. And now that I see you today, I'm even more concerned that you're not doing well."

More tears leaked from the corners of my eyes. Because I *wasn't* okay, and because Clarence had been the first person to notice. "You know, weddings are just really hard," I said holding my arms across my chest. "And relationships are really hard. Being an adult is really hard."

He crossed to me and put his arms around me, hugging me. "Do you want to tell me about it? Because you can tell me anything. You always can." He ran his hand up and down my back, soothing me as I cried on his shoulder. It felt like I imagined a father would comfort his child. A normal father, anyway. Not mine.

"I had a crazy idea about you actually. Want to hear it?"

I nodded into his neck, unable to talk.

"After I saw you a couple months ago, at the restaurant with Weston, when you told me you were engaged, I kept thinking about you. My father's in the television business here in the States, you know, and I asked him about you. Asked about Dyson Media and what was going on with it after your father's death. I heard about the terms of your inheritance. It got me wondering, and I might be crossing the line here. This is a total shot in the dark."

My heart sped up as I listened. I could see where this was heading.

"Well, I just wondered if you were getting married just so you could get control of your father's business."

I pushed out of Clarence's arms and swallowed hard. "That's really inappropriate for you to ask," I said, choking on my words.

"I know. It is. Truthfully, it's probably just wishful thinking."

I looked up at him quizzically. "Wishful thinking?"

"I still think about you, Bitsy. When I saw you again I realized I still have feelings for you. If you're happy with this King guy, then good for you. I'm ready to let you go. But if you're not..." He took a step toward me. "If this marriage is under false pretenses, then I really wish you would've told me."

"And what would you have done if I would have told you?" I asked, despite myself, knowing it was better to leave it alone. "I mean, if it were all under false pretenses, I mean."

"I would've offered to marry you instead."

FOUR
WESTON

I PAID the cab driver and stepped onto the sidewalk outside the brownstone in Brooklyn. I didn't want to be here. I wanted to be back in bed with my wife, wanted to spend the day making love to her, planning our future.

But as much as I wanted to be there, I needed to be here.

There would be time to discuss everything later, once I knew more about the baby. I climbed the six steps up to the front door and walked inside to the tiny foyer, looking for the number I wanted to press. And I tried not to think about Elizabeth's lips, her warmth, the way she looked at me when I told her I was leaving today.

There it was—*Callie Tannen and Dana Steadman*, apartment four. I bristled for a moment at the additional name on the plate. Callie had said that Sebastian didn't have another father in his life. Was Dana a man or woman? Would he be a father to Sebastian if I chose not to be?

I pushed the button and waited for Callie's voice. It didn't come, but a moment later, a buzz indicated that the door was unlocked. I walked in and made my way to unit number four, an easy route because it was on the first floor. Units one and two, it turned out, were garden level units. First floor was good. Not too many stairs. A good apartment in which to raise a child.

I lifted my hand to knock on the door, but Callie opened it immediately. She was dressed in yoga pants and a sweatshirt, her hair tied up in a ponytail. She seemed slightly out of breath, like she'd been rushing around, and from the look at the items in her hands—a stuffed puppy, a toy dinosaur, and the remote control—I guessed that she was doing some last-minute straightening.

"Come in," she said. "I'm just cleaning a bit. It's impossible to keep up."

I stepped in and shut the door behind me as she walked over to a basket in the corner and dropped the toys inside, then she took the remote and set it on the coffee table before turning her attention to me. "Can I take your coat?"

I nodded as I began to take it off, my attention on examining every detail of the room. It was nothing like the minimalistic design of my apartment or the highbrow furnished penthouse that Elizabeth lived in. Callie's apartment was stuffed and cozy. Toy boxes and tables and toys to climb on were shoved in between every bit of furniture. The bookshelves had classics on the top shelves, but the bottom shelves were dedicated to kid-friendly objects and *The Very Hungry Caterpillar*. There was a miniature armchair next to the grown-up armchair, and as Callie took my coat for me I noticed there was also a potty training stool set up in front of the television.

This was a house where a kid lived.

This was a house where *my* kid lived.

"Is he here?" It was too quiet. I already knew the answer.

"Dana took him to the store."

"Dana's your...nanny?" I asked hopefully.

"She's my...friend. She lives here."

That was a relief then. Not a potential daddy substitute. And a relief that Callie had someone to help her, too. Someone who lived with her.

"I have some coffee brewed," she offered. "Would you like some?"

I nodded again, still not completely sure of myself.

She headed to the kitchen, which was connected to the living room in an open layout, and I followed her, finding my thoughts on the way. "Look, I'm still really pissed at you."

"Mmm." She poured the coffee into a mug and looked up at me. "How do you take it?"

"Cream, if you have some. I'm serious here. You stole two years from me."

She opened the fridge and grabbed the container of cream, the real stuff, like Elizabeth got, and poured it into my cup before handing it to me. Then she gestured that I should take a seat at the dining room table.

I sat. "Are you even listening to anything I say?"

She put her own coffee cup on the table, picked up a photo book off the counter, and put it on the table in front of me. She opened it to the front page and scooted it toward me. Then she sat down, too.

I looked at the first image in front of me, a picture of a newborn wearing one of those striped caps they put on babies at the hospital. His face was red and blotchy, but the rest of his skin was white and peeling. Next to the picture was a printout that read *Sebastian Maximilian King, weight: 8 lbs. 1 oz. length: 21 inches.*

Sebastian. My kid.

She'd given him my name. My ribs felt tight like they were pressed against my lungs. It was hard to breathe in. I couldn't stop staring.

A couple of other photos filled out the page, one where Callie held him to her bare chest, her expression one of exhaustion and joy. Another photo of him bundled up like a burrito laying in one of those plastic baby boxes hospitals put newborns in.

"I was climbing the stairs of the West Virginia state Capitol Building when I went into labor," Callie said, as I studied the pictures, memorizing every detail. "I was already four days past due, and it seemed nothing was going to get him out of me. There weren't any stairs in the duplex I was renting—I didn't live here yet. I'd already walked all over the mall, but it wasn't challenging enough. Politics were already in the family. So the Capitol it was."

I chuckled. I barely knew her, but from what I did know, her story was exactly what I'd expect. "Were you worried about making it to the hospital in time?"

"My sister was with me. She's a doctor. She drove the car and coached me through the whole birth." She leaned forward. "It took about twenty times up and down those stairs before I had any intense contractions. If I'd been living here already, I would have gone to the Empire. Or the Statue of Liberty. And then I might have been in trouble, because I had a fast delivery."

"I guess I'm glad you weren't here, then," I said, not sure if I meant it.

I turned the page, wondering if she saw my hand trembling when I did. Here were pictures of a newborn at home, various snapshots of the life of a woman raising a child on her own. Callie explained them all to me, narrating Sebastian's life. This was when he first rolled over. This was when he first smiled. This was when he first crawled. This was when he tried peas. This was when he tried cake. This was when he said his first word.

"What was it?" I asked, completely riveted by her stories.

"Mama."

She said it proudly and I hated myself for feeling jealous. Hated the bitter way the envy sat between my muscles and my bones, making it impossible to stay comfortably in one position for long.

I turned another page, unable to look at her.

"I know I can't give you those two years back, Weston. But they're in the past now, and there's nothing I can do about it. Except tell you his stories. Except share him with you now." She was sincere, and I could feel her genuine desire to connect with me, like the fingers of a fire reaching out to new kindling.

I was already burning for this kid. She didn't realize she didn't need to try that hard.

"What's this?" I asked, pointing at the doll that Sebastian held in many of the last pictures in the book.

"That's Bella. His baby. It's his favorite toy."

I looked up with surprise. "My son's favorite toy is a doll?"

"He chose it. He knows his mommy snuggles up with him and he likes the idea of being able to be like me. I hope you're not suggesting that he shouldn't play with a doll because of gender stereotypes or cultural standards, because—" she sat up straighter, ready for a fight.

"No, definitely not," I said, cutting her off. I really couldn't give a rat's ass about the gender bullshit. I'd liked cars as a kid. And superheroes. But I'd liked Barbie dolls too, mostly because they had boobs, but sometimes I dressed them up for fun.

I looked closer at the picture where Sebastian was hugging Bella like she was everything in the world. Had my father ever held me that way? "That's really sweet that he wants to love so young."

Callie relaxed. "Thank you," she said on a sigh.

I looked up at her, saw that her expression was more anxious than I'd realized.

"I really appreciate you not making judgments about this. About how I've done things with him."

"This is hard for you," I said, as I realized it.

She met my eyes and nodded, her eyes watery. I reached across the table and put my hand over hers.

It helped, because it was hard for me too.

"Want to see his room?" she asked, suddenly excited.

"Yeah, I do." I was equally excited, like it was Christmas day. I wanted to see everything of his, wanted to see his clothes, wanted to see his bed, wanted to see the food he ate and where he played. I was aching to fill myself up with him, like a starving man, only I didn't know how hungry I'd been until now. Each little piece of him I got only reminded me how much I didn't know.

"Who stays with him?" I asked as we stood from the table.

"I do. I don't work outside the home."

"Nice." The benefits of being a sorority princess, I supposed. Usually I rolled my eyes at my peers who lived off their trust funds, but this time it was a relief that she had that, because she had this option. I liked that she'd been the one caring for Sebastian. She'd kept my son from me, but not just to hand him to someone else.

She led me down a small hallway, past one bedroom that I assumed was hers to a second smaller room next to the bathroom. It was decorated in green and yellow, with a thick, plush, dark blue rug. There were toys everywhere along the walls, and in one corner a tiny bed. Another corner held a dresser. There was also a rocking chair and one of those LEGO tables with the big blocks, the non-swallowable precursor to the regular kind.

"I loved LEGOs," I told her, smiling at the memory of all the sets I used to build. Alone, and later with Donovan. How I'd shown those to my father when he'd come home at night.

"Sebastian adores those blocks, but he's not strong enough to pull them apart yet by himself. So he builds, and we tear down."

I nodded because I didn't know anything about child development and when they could do this or that. There was so much I needed to learn.

"And that's where he sleeps?" Would it be weird if I leaned down and sniffed the blankets?

"Naps only in here. I co-sleep." When I looked at her questioningly she went on. "That means he sleeps with me. It was easier when I was nursing and then he just got used to being next to me. Or I just got used to him being next to me."

"It's not dangerous? I'm not judging, I'm asking." Because I honestly didn't know.

"Like anything, there's mixed opinions."

So much I didn't know.

The weight suddenly felt too much to hold, like carrying rocks, and I sank down onto the floor, my back braced against his tiny bed.

Callie followed suit, sliding down along the wall opposite me so that we were face to face.

"Did you want him?" It suddenly felt like the most important question to ask. I had to know—as if knowing if he was wanted by her would change how I would feel about him. I hated to think of how alone she must have been. Knowing she was happy about his existence made it better.

"Oh, yes," she said and I had no doubt that she had. "Very much. Wait—are you asking did I try to get pregnant? With you?"

"No, but...? We used condoms."

"We did. One broke."

"One broke," I said, remembering just as she said it. "Why hadn't I been concerned about that?"

"I was due to have my period any day. I told you it was the wrong time of the month for anything to happen."

That was right. She'd assured me it would be fine. I'd been tested for STDs since then, and I'd never heard from her again so I'd never thought about it again.

"And it should have been fine. I *wasn't* trying to get pregnant. And when I got back home, I waited for the period that didn't come and didn't come, and then I realized I was pregnant. I just *knew*. Without even taking a test I knew. Not because I had sore breasts or because I was feeling sick but because I've always been really regular and, I don't know, I just knew I felt different. Inside."

"And right away, you knew you wanted to keep him?"

She threw her head back against the wall. "I suppose I weighed my options. But I realized that I wanted to be a parent so I could give Sebastian a better life than the one that had been given to me," she said. And in that moment, I believed that she would, regardless of whether I was present in Sebastian's life or not.

"Yeah, I know exactly what you mean." God, this day was stirring so much inside me.

Callie tilted her head, studying me. "We're probably more alike than I realized, you and I. I'm sorry I didn't give you a chance earlier. Imagine what we could've found out about each other if we'd spent more time talking during that week we spent together." She smiled.

"Right? We might've even ended up friends." A thought occurred to me all of a sudden. "You know I'm not looking to make a family here. I like you and everything—what I know of you—but I am just not..."

She rolled her eyes at me. "I'm not flirting with you, you narcissist. Didn't you just get married?"

"I did. I did just get married." Thinking about Elizabeth was like the sun breaking through clouds on a stormy day. I wanted to be with her, wanted her light, wanted her warmth. I wanted the calm that I felt in her presence, inside her. "I need to get back to her."

"Of course."

I wrinkled my brow and tried to smooth it over with two fingers. I still had decisions to make and questions to ask—but I didn't want any of my questions to take away any of my choices. "I can send money. I'll figure out what the right amount is for child support and make arrangements to start paying that, as well as back pay, as soon as I get back from my honeymoon."

"Weston, I don't need money. I didn't come after you for that."

"I know. But ignoring a financial responsibility is not something I'm going to do. As for the rest—being a father. It's not that easy.

You say you want someone who's around, but my company is located all around the world. We have offices on three continents—so far. What if I had to move? Would leaving the country mean leaving all of this?" I gestured around the room.

She put a hand on her neck and circled her head as though her muscles were tense and bothering her.

"I don't know, Weston. I know I told you that I only wanted you in his life if you could be here. But logistically—legally—I can't really hold you to that." She sat forward, spreading her legs open in a V. "I want Sebastian to have a good relationship with you. I want him to know his father and not be disappointed and feel rejected. And whatever things keep you from him, even if they're legitimate things like work and life—they're going to have real consequences, and he's going to feel heartbroken. And I'm going to feel heartbroken because he does. But I can't force you to be anything that you are not willing or ready to be."

"Then you're willing to accept me as his father in his life, whatever I'm able to give?" It sounded terrible asking that, after what she just said. Because I didn't want to break her heart, and I didn't want to break this kid's heart either. Didn't want to destroy the foundation Callie had built for him out of love and stability.

Didn't want to recreate my own childhood in his.

But I had to know my options, had to know the choices before me.

"Yeah. He's a King." She didn't seem too happy with her answer though.

"Because you know that even if you don't tell him about me, if you let him grow up fatherless, he's going to notice that too. He's going to notice he doesn't have a dad like the other kids at school, whether he knows my name or not." I said that more for me than for her. Because it was time that I was responsible. Because I had to stop behaving like a child myself.

Because Elizabeth had made me want to be better.

"Do you wish I hadn't told you at all?" Callie asked.

I didn't answer because I was afraid of what I would say.

"I really have to go." I stood up, and she did as well, rushing to get my coat for me. At the door I turned to her again.

"I have a lot of things I want to say to you, but they are conflicting. Part of me is really angry at you, part of me really resents you, and I'm trying to come to grips with that. With all the things I've missed. I can't rewind time and be present for his first steps, first words. But another part of me is really grateful that you've done all this on your own, that you looked after our kid when I know it's probably been pretty hard, and with my reputation..." I trailed off. In her shoes, I likely wouldn't have told me, either.

She gave me a faint smile. "Maybe they can cancel each other out, and we can say we're even."

It didn't work that way, but I nodded, wishing that it did. "I have to go on my honeymoon. I have to tell my wife." Would Elizabeth even want to add a child to the mix? And would she want to do so badly enough to find a way to run her company remotely? My stomach sank again at the thought.

"I don't even know how she's going to react to all this."

"I understand. I'd like to meet her."

"I'd like to meet *him*," I countered.

"Okay. Next time."

My heart leapt at the idea.

And the only reason it was easy to walk away from this woman—practically a stranger—and her life, which was so foreign and unreal to me, was because I knew Elizabeth was waiting for me. And now more than ever, I needed her to give me roots.

FIVE
ELIZABETH

I TOLD CLARENCE EVERYTHING.

He didn't pressure me to, and I didn't feel trapped or caught, like I had to confess, but I suddenly wanted to tell someone. Weston had Sabrina, and I didn't know how much he talked to her about our arrangement, but even if he didn't, he had Donovan. And Nate.

I had my mother, who smiled and patted me on the head and said things like "let's try a full-body cryotherapy treatment," and asked how good the sex was.

Clarence understood the arrangement for business reasons. He understood my motivations, why I wouldn't tell anyone, why I would choose someone like Weston King. And though I didn't talk to him about the gooey parts, or the naughty parts in much explicit detail, I could even tell him a little about that. That I'd fallen for Weston along the way.

That I was in love with Weston now.

"This marriage is real then?" he asked, when I'd finished telling him everything.

I tucked my feet underneath me and covered my knees with the robe. I was sitting on the couch, and Clarence had been a gentleman and sat far away on the armchair, careful to treat me like a friend and nothing more. Which was good, because I wouldn't have welcomed anything more. After falling for Weston, the thought of being hit on by another man left me cold.

"Yes," I said, because I was thinking positively. "I want this marriage to work. If it can—I don't even know if it's possible. We have obstacles between us that we haven't even explored because we never talked about us like a real thing."

"That's tough, I'm sure. But not impossible. Every relationship has obstacles. We did."

I peered over at him, jolted by the reminder of our past. What we had didn't compare to what Weston and I had. We'd been in high school. But come to think of it, the obstacles that broke us up hadn't been all that different from the situation I was in now. Clarence had been headed to college at Harvard and I had been going to Penn State, and though they weren't far from each other, we'd decided they were too far to make things work.

We'd been younger, of course. Inexperienced. Ready to move on and add more to our repertoire.

I hadn't really loved Clarence. Not in my bones and my toes and in the ends of my hair the way that I loved Weston.

But the similarities were still troublesome.

"I don't know if that makes me feel better or worse," I admitted.

"I'm sorry. I shouldn't have brought us into this." He leaned forward and put his palms on his thighs, staring at the back of his hands. "I guess I'm still wondering why you didn't ask *me* to marry you."

I took a deep breath in and let it out, thinking before I answered. "Honestly, Clarence, I thought it was too big of a favor to ask of anyone without having something to offer in exchange. I didn't think I had anything you would have been interested in bartering with."

He stared at me, pointedly. "You seriously thought you had nothing I'd want?"

My spine tingled as I realized he meant he would have been interested in me. It was sweet of him, and it surprised me to hear it, but I was over him. I'd grown out of him a long time ago.

"Too much time had passed," I said mindfully.

"Got it. That's fair." He chuckled to himself. "And it doesn't matter now because you found the right man for the job all around."

My entire body pulsed at the thought of Weston. "I hope so. But I mean, he's not even here right now."

"He's not," Clarence said standing up. "But if he wants to fight for you too—and Weston King's a smart man, he's going to want to fight for you—then he's not going to want to see me here when he gets back."

"I'm sure you're worrying over nothing." I started walking him to the door despite my words, just in case.

"I don't think so. I've seen the way he looks at you. Plus, I texted him about a month ago asking for your phone number, and he never replied. It all makes sense now." He buttoned up his coat, both of us standing by the door.

"You asked him for my number? And he didn't give it to you?" This was the first time I was hearing about it. "How does that make sense? It's not making sense to me."

"Obviously he didn't give it to me because he sees me as a threat. He wants you to be his alone, Bitsy."

I cringed at his use of the old nickname, and he corrected himself.

"Elizabeth. It suits you better anyway."

"I don't know if what you're saying is the only reason he wouldn't give you my number. Maybe he forgot. Maybe he's not good at answering texts." But I wanted to believe what he said. And I did believe Weston cared for me. "Anyway, thank you for telling me. And thank you for listening. And thank you for checking up on me."

"I'm glad I did. A little sorry you didn't choose me, but content to know you're happy." He smiled, and I knew he meant it. He was a good man.

"Next time I have to get married in order to get my inheritance, I'll definitely call you first," I teased.

I leaned in to hug him goodbye, and as I did I heard the digital beep of the lock, but before I could fully grasp what was happening, the door swung open.

And Weston was standing there, a deli bag under one arm and a tray with two coffee cups balanced in the opposite hand.

"Hi," I said, jumping away from Clarence. "You're back."

The door slammed shut behind Weston as his eyes carefully swung from one of us to the other. "I brought breakfast burritos and coffee. I hope you haven't eaten yet. I didn't realize we had a guest." His tone was flat and hard to decipher.

I took advantage of the fact that he didn't know that Clarence was in on the arrangement, and rushed to help, treating Weston like I would if we were keeping up our performance. It was a way to buffer the strange tension that had suddenly filled the air around all three of us.

"Let me help you. I'm starving. Thank God you brought food." I grabbed the bag and the coffees and set them on the desk while he attended to his coat.

"I was just in the area and decided to stop by. I didn't really get a chance to talk to Elizabeth at the wedding," Clarence said, trying to diffuse the friction.

"How thoughtful," Weston said coldly. He propped his coat on the back of the desk chair and turned to stare at my ex-boyfriend.

"I was on my way out," Clarence said. "Bye, Elizabeth."

I rushed to the door and opened it for him. I waved goodbye as he disappeared down the hall, then shut it again, but I didn't turn back to face my husband right away, worried he was, as Clarence had predicted, not happy about the circumstances he'd walked into. Honestly, if he *was* upset, I wanted to say fuck him. Because he'd left with no explanation today. And I was still pissed about that myself.

But I didn't want to fight anymore.

Taking a deep breath, I turned around, my back pressed to the hotel room door, and wrapped my arms around myself. "Thanks for getting food. I'm starving."

"You said that." He looked at me, a fist on his hips, examining my expression.

"Weston," I asked tentatively, still unable to get a read on him. "Are you mad?"

He tilted his head, his jaw working as he thought about it. "Mad? No. I'm not mad." He took four steps, even and bold until he was standing just in front of me, then placed his palms on the wood of the door next to my head, caging me in. "What I am is curious."

I swallowed, my pulse picking up. This close, I could see that his pupils were dilated, could see the flick of his gaze to my lips.

"What is it you're curious about?" I splayed my palms on the door beside me, as if that could hold me up. No other man could turn me on instantly like this. No other man could make me wet with just his presence. Make my body vibrate and hum and stir.

He brought one hand down and reached into the divide of my robe, sliding it up the front of my thigh.

"Are you mine?" he asked, his voice steady, and waited, as though everything that mattered between us rested upon the answer to this one question.

I couldn't answer fast enough, and yet the word came out choked, strangled by emotion. "Yes. I'm yours."

The strain in his face seemed to ease the slightest bit as his fingers found their way to the space between my legs. "Is this pussy mine?"

I nodded, spreading my legs farther apart to give him better access.

"Not good enough. I need to hear the words."

"This pussy is yours. It's only yours."

His fingers massaged my clit until I was gasping, then went down farther to where I was wet and aching. "This is mine? All this? Is it for me?"

As if I could have been wet from Clarence Sheridan.

"Every drop," I moaned, and he pushed two fingers deep inside me, twisting them so that I bucked against his hand.

He moved his free hand then to anchor me at my neck, and reached up to my lips with his thumb, rubbing roughly against them. "What about this mouth? This mouth is mine?"

"This is your mouth."

He leaned forward to tease my lips with his, brushing against me, sharing space and breath. It was hot. Hotter than actually kissing, somehow. With the way he was still finger fucking me below, claiming and taking ownership of me, I was going to come any minute.

Except this was only one-sided. I had my own stakes to claim.

I reached for him with my hand, fumbling until I found the thick bulge in his jeans. I covered it with my palm. "Is this...mine?"

He leaned his head back just slightly so he could look at my eyes, could gauge whether I was sincere or taunting him.

I might've been taunting him, only a few weeks ago I would have been. But now, I was so sincere.

"It's yours."

It was more of a relief than I realized it would be to hear him admit it. "Say it again," I whispered.

"It's only yours. I'm only hard for you. Only ever fucking hard for you."

I undid his jeans and stuck my hand under the band of his briefs. His cock felt solid and powerful in my hand. Like a staff. Like a scepter.

"Mine," I said, stroking him up and down.

His breaths grew thicker. "Whose ring's on your finger?"

"Yours," I answered, growing more confident in the game now. "Whose body am I touching?"

"Yours."

I pushed down his pants and briefs, freeing his cock, telling him what I wanted from him without words.

He moved both of his hands under my ass, and I threw my arms around his neck so he could lift me up, lining himself up at my hole.

"Who are you?" he asked again, just before he thrust in.

"I'm Mrs. King. I'm your wife. I'm your home. I'm yours."

He drove into me, slowly enough that I felt every inch of him, but with full power, so that I was sure he was there, really there. With his eyes locked on mine he pulled out again, almost to the tip before pushing in again. And again. Each thrust purposeful and distinct. Each one defining his place inside me.

As he fucked me, he laid down the law.

"You're mine. I'm yours. I won't share you. And I don't expect you to share me. As long as this works, as long as you wear my ring, we are an *us*. We are a *we*. If that doesn't work for you, then you need to get off my cock right now because I'm not playing the pretend game with you anymore." He pushed my thighs up higher so that he hit me deeper, and the angle was just right, getting me in a spot that would have me exploding any second. "You got it?"

I couldn't speak, could only make a sort of mewling sound, high-pitched and breathy, which I knew he wouldn't accept, and he didn't.

"You got it?" he asked again, meaner, more intense.

"I got it. No games. We're together, and it's real."

"You better never doubt *this* is real," he said, glancing down at where we were joined. He slowed for a moment to watch as he worked himself in and out of me, then brought his gaze back to mine and increased his pace, driving me, riding me, urging me to release.

I fell over the other side like I'd been pushed. Tumbled into the bliss of my orgasm, growling out his name and digging my fingernails into his shoulders while he continued to stab into me at a frenetic pace. And in the bliss, the warmth, it wasn't just the explosion of endorphins. It was the words he'd said, the relief he'd settled in me. They didn't solve any of the problems between us, but they let me know where he stood. He wanted to fight for us too. He wanted us to be together, and if we both wanted that, then it was a good start.

There was hope.

I could feel him as he got close, as he slowed and stuttered, then suddenly he set me down and pulled out, and began stroking himself in front of me. With his free hand, he untied my robe and spread it open so my torso was bare in front of him. I watched, eyes wide, the same way that I had the night I'd spied on him in the living room. This time it was so much more fascinating because I was up close, so much harder because he was right in front of me, so much more arousing because I knew what he was about to do.

I felt another orgasm building in me, at the very idea, and reached down between my legs to touch myself, massaging my clit rapidly so that I could get there with him.

"Good girl," he praised. "Touch that pussy of mine. Come with me."

He got there first, freezing and then shooting strings of cum over my tits and belly. The sight was so hot. So fucking hot, I came immediately afterward.

Weston stood back, watching proudly as I shuddered through my second orgasm.

When I was finished, he pulled me into his arms, not seeming to care that I was sticky and covered with his cum. He kissed me slowly, languidly.

"Let's get you in the shower and clean you up," he said when he broke away.

I nodded and let him lead me to the bathroom, let him undress me and wash me and take care of me, because I was his. And even though he was mine, too, even though I was still a queen on my own—Weston King was the one who ruled me.

SIX
WESTON

I TOOK my time washing Elizabeth. I thoroughly shampooed her hair, rinsing it out then washing it again just so I could have the luxury of listening to her moans while I massaged her scalp. I liked the freedom to keep touching her too, without any questions or explanations.

I'd have to give them soon enough, and I wasn't ready.

When I'd shown up at our room, brunch in hand, I'd been carrying the baggage of the morning. I was still thinking of Sebastian, and my primary focus was on how to make my life fit into his.

But when I walked in the door and saw Clarence holding my wife, everything changed.

It was a sharp reminder that I needed to think about things the other way around. My life with Elizabeth came first. My life with Elizabeth was the foundation. Before I could figure out how my kid fit into that, how to build him room and space, I had to be sure she and I were solid.

Were we?

How did I begin to find out?

It wasn't as simple as figuring out where we'd live or choosing whether to follow her to France. Even if I didn't have a son to think about, could I say that Elizabeth and I were ready for that? That was serious commitment, and while I was sure I knew enough about her to follow her anywhere, I wasn't sure she knew enough about me to just let me.

We had to draw up some plans. And I had to tell her things about me, show her everything before we laid down cement.

Except, we'd done it all backwards.

We'd already laid the cement. I'd already put a ring on her finger—twice.

And I didn't know where to go from here. Did we tear it all down? Start over from the ground up? Did we redesign and build on, like an addition? Did we piece floorboards and walls on top of what we'd already laid out and hope it was strong enough to bear whatever we put on top?

They were questions with hard answers, and it was easier to listen to Elizabeth's quiet murmurs as I gently took a washcloth to her most private areas than to confront the obstacles in our way.

But eventually the water got cold, and Elizabeth got clean. I turned off the shower and pulled her into the bathroom where I continued to dote on her, rubbing her down with a thick, plush towel.

She was dry and warm when she placed a hand over mine. "What now?" she asked, her eyes catching mine.

"We can heat up the burritos in the microwave. And the coffee. We should get some food in you."

"That's not what I meant," she said, her impatience showing in her tone.

"I know." I reluctantly let go of her so I could wrap a towel around my hips. "But let's eat. You're less cranky with food in you."

She scowled, but she couldn't argue because I wasn't wrong, and I had to fight the urge to pull her into the bedroom for another round of lovemaking because her pouty face was so adorable.

But as good as it would feel to be inside of her, I forced myself to look at the bigger picture. If I wanted to have the right to her body forever—and I did—sex was definitely not the answer.

Holy shit, I was a grown-up.

A grown-up with a kid. That thought never failed to punch me in the gut.

Since I was an adult now, apparently, I had to start acting it. I pulled my jeans back on and threw on a T-shirt, and as much as I wanted her to stay naked, I encouraged her to change into something non-accessible while I heated up our food. After we ate, I had things to tell her, hard things, and I didn't need to be distracted.

Ten minutes later, we were sitting on the couch in our suite, Elizabeth's legs thrown over mine while we ate our burritos.

"These are spicy," she said midway through her second bite. "Tasty, but spicy."

I raised an eyebrow. "Spicy? They have like zero kick. You're such a gringo."

"Weston!" she exclaimed. "You can't say things like that! It's not P.C.! Besides, you're almost as white as I am. Why isn't it bothering you?" She downed some coffee, chasing away the spice from her tongue.

"I don't know," I shrugged, taking another bite. I thought about it while I chewed. "It might be from all the chili peppers that Donovan had me eat as a pre-teen. He used to dare me, and I can never turn down a dare."

She laughed. "I didn't know that about you." She seemed to store that information away for later. "Do you like spicy foods a lot?"

"Yes, actually. The spicier the better. Why do you think I like you so much?" I cupped her neck with my free hand and ran my thumb along her jaw.

This was easy—touching and talking. This light banter was the way I'd always communicated with women, skirting any real issues, wading in shallow waters. It tended to get boring after a while, but whenever a girl beckoned me in deeper, I took off for another pond.

I didn't want to do that with Elizabeth. I wanted the courage to swim in her ocean, even if it meant getting all the way wet. Even if it meant I might drown.

She leaned into my palm, closing her eyes and savoring the contact. When she opened her eyes, she asked, "What's going on between us, Weston?"

Her voice was soft, her expression vulnerable, and I realized that she didn't get that I was already in deeper with her than I'd been with anyone ever before. She didn't know me, not like I wanted her to know me. And I didn't know her. I needed to learn her before I could trust her enough to walk blindly into the crashing waves. She needed to learn me. We needed time.

Fortunately, we had two weeks.

"Let's find out," I said, an idea forming.

She tilted her head, her gaze questioning.

This was good though. We couldn't really start again, but maybe we kind of could.

I dropped my hand from her neck and shifted to face her. "I meant everything I said to you, Elizabeth. In front of all those people, when I put that ring on your finger, I meant it. You changed my life, you changed who I am, and I want to be that man. For you. I want you to be my home. You are my home. But the truth of the matter is that while I was falling for you, I was trying my damnedest not to. And that meant that I was holding parts of me back, pieces of me that I never wanted you to see. Pieces of who I am that I never thought you would have to see because we weren't real."

I reached out to caress her cheek again. "We're real now. I don't want to lose that. But before we can move forward, I have to step back and show you things that we skipped. I've been trying to figure out the best way to do that, and I think maybe the best way is really the simplest. We just find out."

She took a deep breath in. "I really loved about ninety-nine percent of what you said there until the part where I didn't understand it. What do you mean by let's find out?"

"I mean," I dropped my hand from her face and leaned forward, excited by the idea. "Let's go on a honeymoon and take these two weeks to learn each other. Without the world around us to interfere. Without the mask of pretending. Without work. Without the internet. Without Darrell. Without having to put on the show. Without Donovan. Without Clarence."

"Without Sabrina," she interjected.

I grinned. "Without *any* of the things that distract us here in the real world." I couldn't help thinking that included Sebastian. And Mr. and Mrs. Clemmons and the money I paid out in retribution for my father. "By the time the two weeks are over, I promise you will know everything about me. Hopefully by then we'll have all the information we need about each other to figure out what happens next."

She bit her lip in that funny way that she did sometimes and didn't say anything for a minute.

Which made me suddenly doubt everything I'd suggested. "Did that all sound stupid?"

"No, I think it sounds actually really nice. I like the idea of it very much."

I leaned into her and kissed her once, twice. Then longer, because I liked her taste and because she was mine and I could.

It felt too good, though. Too much of a relief, like I was getting away with something by not telling her everything up front. And that wasn't what I wanted. I wanted to take our time getting to know each other for real, but I had to tell her about Sebastian now.

Except when I tried to break away, she pulled me back to her.

"We still get to have lots of sex too, right?" she asked, her mouth hovering near mine.

"That's definitely a given. Definitely, definitely a given." *She* kissed *me* this time. "We could start that right now, actually."

"Good, because I'm not hungry anymore for food."

Then I'd tell her about Sebastian tomorrow. Waiting one more day wouldn't hurt anything.

THE NEXT DAY STARTED EARLY. We had to be at the airport by seven, and I didn't get coffee until we were seated in the plane, which meant I wasn't fully caffeinated when I noticed the price on our tickets.

I'd come to terms with Elizabeth paying for the wedding. It was her farce, but also, her family was traditional and the bride's side took care of that expense.

I hadn't thought about the price of the honeymoon. That was usually the groom's responsibility, wasn't it? Elizabeth had made all the arrangements months ago. She'd been the one with the time while I was working, and the one with the money. Back then, when the whole thing had been fake, I hadn't had any qualms with her putting out for a honeymoon that was only meant to fool her cousin. Now I felt differently.

"It's our money," she said, rolling her eyes when I apologized for not contributing.

For some reason, that ruffled my feathers even more. "It's not *our* money. It's *your* money. You are the one with lots and lots of it."

"Right. So much that this plane flight is nothing. In fact, I would've booked a private jet except that I wanted our names on the roster so it would be easy for Darrell to track us down and know we went together." She fluffed her pillow and set it behind her back before fastening her seatbelt.

"That doesn't make me feel better."

My wife had a lot of money.

Fuck.

My wife had a shit-ton of money.

She turned her head to study my profile. "Is this going to be a problem for you? This was always who I was, you know. What's the difference now?"

I thought about it for a minute. Did it make me an inferior man because she had more dollars to her name than I did? Did it make me any less attracted to her? What did it really change?

"I guess the difference now is that I want to give you the world, but you can already buy it for yourself. So what do you need me for?"

She smiled in a way that made me feel like I was both charming and ridiculous. "Oh, Weston. I need you because the world you give me can't be bought."

She laced her hand in mine. It was the one with her rings sparkling proudly on her fourth finger. I thought about "my world," the world that I gave her. I loved the sentiment, but she didn't know everything about my world. She didn't realize there was an embarassing financial scandal and a secret child.

Maybe she'd want that world too, but in case she didn't, I wanted to keep her smiling at me the way she was now. That meant putting off telling her my secrets until the end of the honeymoon. She'd promised me she would stay offline and not worry about Dyson for two weeks. This was the same thing, wasn't it? It would let us enjoy each other without anything else pressing in on us. Let us get to know each other without the baggage.

I would tell her—I'd said that I would, and I meant it. Just not right away.

The flight was long. And boring. And did I mention long? Eleven hours. Even in first class it was too much time to spend in a plane. Particularly one we couldn't join the Mile-High Club in.

The only benefits to the flight were that I could catch up on my sleep—something I'd been lacking the last two nights since I'd wed the beautiful lady sitting next to me, and it gave me enough time to properly explain the difference between the Marvel and DC universes, something Elizabeth was clearly confused about.

When we landed in Honolulu, we still had another short flight to Kauai, then finally we'd arrived. It was early evening by the time we rolled into the five-star resort Elizabeth had booked. We checked in and were told we had been given the honeymoon suite, and shown where to find the private bungalow on the beach. Our bed was covered with rose petals, and a bottle of champagne and chocolate-covered strawberries awaited us. Everything was top-notch and first rate. Truly, she'd planned a romantic and decadent honeymoon.

"This is amazing," I said to my bride, awed. I glanced down at the sheet of activities that she had reserved for us already: island hike, massage, windsailing.

Actually, this was a really, really *romantic* honeymoon.

My brow wrinkled. "Elizabeth, you booked this before we even started sleeping together. What exactly did you think would happen between us on this trip?"

"What do you mean?" she asked not meeting my eyes.

"I mean, these activities are incredibly romantic. A lover's trip to the waterfalls? A spa day for two?"

"It's basically just stuff for parties of two. A pretty hike. A massage. I thought we could both enjoy having the tension rubbed away. I don't understand what you're getting at."

"It's a *couples* massage. We're going to be naked in the same room together. I'm not sure that would have helped the tension." I stared at her, a shit-eating grin on my face.

"Just say what you're saying, Weston. Stop beating around the bush." She sighed at her own use of the word *bush*, knowing exactly where my mind would go.

I gave her a break about the bush remark, and instead attacked the real matter at hand. "Were you planning to make a move on me during this two-week trip?" Her cheeks reddened. "You were! You were planning to come on to me, Elizabeth Dyson!"

"I said no such thing. I admit nothing. Just...we were both going to be here, and all the pretend stuff was going to be over and if whatever happened happened, and you let loose, and I let loose, I don't know!"

She was turning adorably red, and I tossed down the activity sheet so I could grab both her hands, and pulled her close to me. With my mouth pressed near her temple, I told her the honest truth. "If I had somehow made it through those five months without jumping you, there is no way I would've made it one night in this room, sleeping in the bed next to you without having to fuck the living daylights out of you."

She hid her head in the crook of my neck. "You're just saying that."

"Swear to God. I would've jumped you so hard. You wouldn't have been able to walk when you got back to the mainland."

She looked up at me, her eyes blue and liquid like the ocean. "I worried about it sometimes. When I was still just *wanting* you all the time, and not sure what to do with it. I worried we would get here, and you would find some woman at the bar, that you would disappear for two weeks into someone else's bed."

I could feel her anxiety about it, how it once had plagued her, and I wished more than anything I could find a way to go back in time and let her know back then how much I'd wanted her too.

"And then sometimes," she continued, "I'd imagine I was the girl at the bar. I wondered what that would feel like, to be picked up by Weston King."

I leaned in to brush my nose against hers. I'd planned for us to order dinner to our room so that we could be alone, start getting to truly know each other, but suddenly I liked the idea of playing this game with her instead. It could be a much sexier way to accomplish the same thing. "Want to find out? Want to go be a girl at the bar, and I'll be Weston King?"

She perked up suddenly, leaning back, her eyes wide. "Can we do that? Oh, let's do that!"

She dropped my hands and started scurrying around the room, opening our suitcases, looking for things.

"You get ready first, and then go out to the main bar and order drinks and be you, and I'll get ready and then come down whenever. You be Weston and I'll be Elizabeth, and we'll meet each other for the first time. As though we never had this arrangement. As though there was never an inheritance on the line. We'll meet here in Hawaii, and we can learn all about each other and fall for each other. We can treat this whole trip like a do-over. Or not. You know. Whatever. What do you think?"

I tilted my head in amazement. It was like she'd read my mind, putting our real lives on hold while we dedicated this time to just us. In a way, this game gave me permission to put off the truth.

Was that an excuse?

Maybe. But she looked so excited and happy about the game, I was eager to cling to it, excuse or not.

So when she asked, "What is it?" I answered with a questioning lift of my brow.

"I still get to bang you, right?"

She giggled. "Everything is unscripted, but I'll tell you now that I am definitely going to put out."

"Then yeah. I like this plan a lot. I'll get changed and then game on."

"Oh!" She lifted her hand and wiggled her ring finger. "And I'm not taking this off. Everyone else gets to know I'm unavailable. You keep yours on too," she added sternly.

"Mine stays," I said, agreeing, wiggling my own wedding-banded finger. As far as I was concerned, I would be happy to never take it off.

Hopefully this honeymoon made her feel the same, and when I told her about my kid, she'd decide she wanted both of us.

SEVEN
ELIZABETH

I DISAPPEARED into the bathroom to get ready. I left my hair down, working with the humidity, letting it fall into its natural waves. I left my makeup soft and natural.

When I came back out, Weston had already left, so I could get into my dress without him seeing me. I chose a patterned maxi dress in mostly blues and browns with a halter top, two long slits up the sides, and a price tag that would make Weston flinch. A final look in the mirror told me I looked good, but casual. Perfect for an island resort. I finished the look with strappy beige sandals with a chunky heel, transferred everything to a small clutch purse, and made my way toward the center bar.

The weather was nice, the breeze perfect. It was fantastic to be outside without a coat after the cold winter months back in New York. Normally I would feel awkward walking alone at a place like this, but knowing I was going to meet someone made me walk with an assurance and confidence that I normally only felt in familiar circles. I caught a couple of men looking at me as I walked by, and normally their gazes would send me spiraling into awkwardness, but tonight they just lifted my head higher.

When I got to the entrance, though, I paused. I'd never been a woman who hung out in bars just waiting for a man to pick her up. I'd barely even gone with a girlfriend to this sort of venue. I felt much more comfortable in lounges and places that served only wine.

I scanned the crowd from afar and quickly spotted Weston alone at a high top. He already had a drink, some island concoction in a fun glass that was a specialty of the resort's bar, and was sipping it while glancing around, probably looking for me. He looked breathtaking as always, even wearing khakis and an untucked white button-down shirt. Part of me wanted to forget this entire ruse and just walk up to him directly, stick my hands up under his shirt and find the warm skin beneath.

He hadn't shaved since the wedding, and his face had gotten scruffy the last couple of days. He looked different this way. The rugged look somehow made me feel wild with him. As though I could be wild and rugged like that just by proxy. As though this wasn't a game at all, but a real chance at meeting the man of my dreams.

I knew what to do, what my mother would do, what all my friends would do. But I was still nervous. It was so out of character for me to go in there, beelining for the gorgeous, scruffy man alone in the bar. To stand next to him, take a sip of his island drink, and wait for him to offer to buy me one. This was how *he* picked up dates, not me.

Even though it was my idea, I hesitated.

He caught my eye from across the room, held it like a stranger who had just seen someone interesting. It was my cue to follow through, walk in, and introduce myself.

But just then drums began playing, and an overhead announcement said that the luau was now open for dinner.

I turned my head to the left where visitors were lining up to attend the feast. A bar wasn't my scene, but a luau was something that Elizabeth Dyson could get behind. And if Weston and I were here to meet each other on real terms, with our real characters—no more pretending, no more acting, no more playing a part—then I would never have walked into the bar where he was seated.

I looked back to him where he was now watching me with a curious expression, then I headed over to the luau and got in line.

Other people got in line behind me, and I knew it would take a while before Weston caught up—he had to pay for his drink and make his way over, so I entertained myself by playing a game of Candy Crush on my phone. I didn't look up again until I was at the cash register.

"One please," I told the hostess, a dark-skinned woman dressed in a Hawaiian print dress.

"What a coincidence," came a voice from behind me. "I'm by myself as well. I'll pay for both of us."

I lowered my phone as Weston handed over his credit card. Somehow he'd managed to sneak his way up through the line.

I looked him over from head to toe, taking him in as though I'd never seen him before. I remembered that even the first time I'd seen him he'd sent my pulse racing, and was surprised he could still do it with no more than a glimpse of those blue eyes. "Thank you," I said, hesitantly. "That's truly not necessary—"

"It's not necessary, but it's done." He flashed his dimple as he took back his credit card and put it in his wallet, then stuffed it in his back pocket. "It's my good deed for the day."

"Well, I can't argue with that."

Another hostess led us through an arbor where luau employees were waiting with fresh leis. A stout island man placed one around the neck of the woman in front of us, then turned to grab another one and looked in my direction.

"Let me," Weston said, reaching to take it from the man's hands. He then came around in front of me and dropped the fresh chain of flowers around my neck. "You've been lei-d," he said, waggling his eyebrows.

I couldn't help but grin. He really was charming. If I'd met him just like this, I would've been mesmerized.

I *was* mesmerized.

"Allow me the same honor." I grabbed another one from the man, who smiled at us, and placed it around Weston's neck. "You look good freshly lei-d."

"I can't possibly look as good as you. Getting lei-d suits you."

I rolled my eyes, but I was still smiling.

Next we were ushered in front of a beautiful tropical floral spot where a photographer was waiting to take our picture.

"Oh, we're not together," I said, because we weren't playing a part anymore, but in some way, we *were*. An alternate timeline part. As though we'd met here instead of months ago, and our matching rings were mere coincidence.

"The ticket was purchased together," the photographer's assistant said, confused.

I couldn't help the laugh that escaped me at how silly we were being, but Weston kept it up, looking at me and shrugging. "What's the point of a picture alone? Seems rather boring to me. I don't mind if you don't."

"I suppose if you put it that way."

He stood next to me and put his hand on my waist in a way that could have been considered overly friendly from someone I'd just met, or casual for someone I'd just married. The photographer said he would give us a countdown. On three I turned to glance at Weston and found him already looking at me, his eyes blue and clear, as though no secrets hid behind them.

The lightbulb flashed, and without having seen the proof, Weston said, "I'll buy two."

He arranged for the pictures to be sent to our room before leading us down a path to yet another host who offered to seat us.

"Two?" the gentleman asked.

I turned to Weston. "You know, just because you paid for me tonight doesn't mean that I feel obligated to be your date."

"I can respect that," he said, a smile playing on his lips.

"But you lei-d me. And I take that seriously. So now I think you're kind of stuck with me for the evening."

The host tried not to laugh.

Weston's smirk bloomed into a full dimpled grin. "As a gentleman, I feel as though you're my responsibility now. I am not the kind of guy to lei and run. I definitely have to have dinner with the girl afterwards."

I turned back to our host. "Yes. Two."

We followed him side by side past several long banquet tables already filled with people crammed in and chatting, getting to know those around them. My hand brushed against Weston's, and I felt the urge to lace my fingers through his. I wondered if he felt the same pull, that magnetic tug drawing us to always face the same way, forcing us together.

I liked this. I'd missed this—the part of a budding new relationship where you wanted to touch but didn't know if it was too forward. From the very first minute that I'd wanted him, I'd been forced to touch him, whether he wanted it or not. Whether he'd wanted *me* or not. I got what he meant about having skipped so many things. We'd skipped the uncertainty part.

It was erotic, the wonder. When would he touch me? When would our fingers finally meet? Would our whole bodies feel shock from the spark of electricity?

The hostess sat us together at the end of a long bench. I scooted in first, with Weston on the end, and I caught him checking out my bare thigh as my skirt rode up when I sat down. Normally I'd appreciate my husband checking me out like that, but in this game we were playing, I pretended to be a little shocked.

"You can keep your eyes above the table," I scolded him. "Thank you very much."

"I could. Maybe I'll even try." He scooted in next to me and we made stupid small talk about the blue-tinted rolls, childish banter that edged toward sexual innuendo and nearly sent me into a fit of giggles when he asked me to butter his blue ball of bread.

When there was a lull, the couple across from us asked how long we'd been together.

"We're not," Weston said, taking my cue from what I'd told the host earlier.

The woman frowned, her brows meeting above her nose. "But you're both wearing wedding rings. Aren't you...?"

"Are we? I'm married, obviously. But we just met tonight. Are you married?" I asked Weston, improvising. Not caring what other people thought about us wasn't necessarily an Elizabeth thing, but I was having too much fun to break the scene.

"I guess I am," he said looking down at his ring finger. "Hey, that's another thing we have in common."

"This really is turning into kismet, meeting you here this way."

The woman across from me looked to her date, then back at us, even more confused than she'd been just a moment before. "I don't understand. Where's your husband?"

I sat forward, leaning across the table and whispered conspiratorially. "I'd rather not discuss it, if you don't mind. I came here to specifically *not* think about my husband, if you get my drift."

"Me too!" Weston exclaimed. "Or not think about my wife, I mean. I don't have a husband. It's definitely a wife."

"So much in common." I nodded winking at my husband/not husband.

"But," the woman started to say again, "the waiter mentioned when he brought your drinks that he was billing them to the honeymoon suite."

"Honey," her date said, "leave them alone. You don't want to pry into those open-relationship things. This generation does things much differently than ours."

I had to stuff a blue ball of bread into my mouth so I didn't dissolve into another fit of laughter.

For the rest of the dinner, Weston and I kept our conversation light, mostly joking about superficial things—commentary on the entertainment and the people sitting around us. The show broke for us to fill our plates with various island recipes—shellfish, salads, pork from the pig that had slow-roasted all day in a pit in the ground, poke, and the juiciest fruits I'd ever tasted.

Here we began to really talk, began to learn new details about each other.

"You have to try the lobster, it's so fresh it doesn't even need butter." Weston held out a piece of the meat he'd broken from a claw on his own plate.

I backed away. "I can't. I'm sure it's delicious, but I'm allergic."

"You are? That is the saddest thing I've ever heard."

"To all shellfish. I break out in the wickedest rash all over."

His mouth actually gaped. "How did I not know—?" he caught himself with a shake of his head. "How do you go on living?"

"Since I haven't had any shellfish for years and don't remember how it tastes, I thought I was living just fine. But maybe I need to reevaluate my misery levels."

"It's not fair. Not fair, I'm telling you." He shook his head again, then swallowed the piece of lobster himself. He wore an expression that said the taste was divine, but he kindly said, "It's so disgusting. You're not missing anything at all. Worst thing ever."

"I'm sure it tastes better than the poi."

"Burnt tapioca tastes better than the poi. Old caviar tastes better than the poi. Soy yogurt tastes better than the poi." Then he had to let me feed him the poi, the way the true Islanders did it, from their fingers, because he was very smugly making fun of my own soy yogurt habit.

He licked the mushy substance from each of my fingers until there wasn't a trace left, and I could feel each swipe of his tongue along my skin as though he were licking the full of my pussy, each heated trace notching up my desire.

"I take it back," he said when my fingers were clean, his hand still wrapped around mine. "Poi tastes pretty damn good."

Midway through dinner, I spotted Weston looking around the crowd.

"Are you checking out other women while you're on a sort-of date with me?"

"No," he laughed. "I was making a work observation. I'm off the clock, but it gets in your blood. Becomes a habit."

I set down my fork and patted at my mouth with my napkin. "Now I must hear this. What was the observation, and how does it get into your blood?" In all the months that Weston had taught me about business, he'd rarely put the spotlight on his own work. I knew he knew his job inside and out, but I'd never seen him in action.

"I was observing that nearly everyone at the luau is an adult. Likely because this is an adult-friendly resort. But the dinner still didn't sell out, so I was thinking that if they marketed this as adults only, or couples only, they might get better bang for their buck. It would seem more attractive, more exclusive. Might even be able to raise their prices a little, charge extra for the frou-frou drinks. Right now it's just a luau, same as everywhere else on the island. It wouldn't really change their clientele, but it would seem cooler."

"Oh. I see. That's a very astute observation." I rubbed my lips together as I considered everything that I knew about Weston and everything that I could glean from him just during tonight's interaction. "So you are an idea man?"

"I wouldn't say that. I'm all about the magic tricks. I like the sleight of hand." He took the plastic flower that was on the center of the table as decoration and held it in the air with his left hand.

Then after a bit of flash and choreography, suddenly it had disappeared. Then—presto! He was pulling it from behind my ear.

"How the fuck did you do that? Do not tell me that that gets you girls?" Though I knew for certain it got him girls. Because it was totally dorky, but he was also totally hot. "Do it again."

"I'm not going to do it again. You're just trying to find out how I did it. And yes, it has totally gotten me girls." He stuck the flower behind my ear for real this time, perching it against my hair. "It looks nice there."

I held his gaze then flicked my eyes to his lips, wanting to kiss him, knowing it was too early, not wanting to break the spell. "You think of marketing like magic?"

"Yeah. It's telling people one thing while you're doing something else. It's just showing them what you want them to see." I nodded, encouraging him to go on.

"When Donovan—my good friend—came to me with the idea of starting an advertising company, he wanted me to be the salesman, the one who pitched to clients, sold the campaigns and the creative. He always teased me, said I had the face for it. The personality. But I wasn't really interested in that. I liked the idea of advertising, but I wanted to be the magic. The guy behind the scenes, planning the tricks. Scheming. So I agreed to come on, but only if we found another face."

I knew that there were five people in total running Reach, Inc., but I wasn't quite clear on everyone's roles within it. I used the opportunity to play dumb and hear the story of the company's formation. "Then you found another face?"

"Yeah. Donovan had another friend, Nate Sinclair. He was an art dealer, so he knew creative. A very good salesman. We didn't quite have the capital to go into it as large as we wanted to—as large as *Donovan* wanted to, so we got a couple of other guys. Even then, Donovan and I came with the most cash." Weston took a breath, then corrected himself. "Donovan came with the most cash. He loaned me a significant portion to come in as his partner fifty-fifty; the other three have smaller shares in the company."

And that was something I hadn't known. Something that didn't fully make sense, considering what I'd learned about Weston King and the amount he should be worth. "You borrowed money from Donovan to invest in Reach?"

He looked down at his plate and nodded. He swallowed—I could see the bob of his Adam's apple, even though he hadn't taken a bite of anything. It bothered him, this transaction that he had made with his friend. It bothered him to tell me.

"I think it's awesome that you have someone you feel comfortable enough with to have an arrangement like that," I said, and it was true. I'd never had to borrow money from anyone in my life, but there had been several times that I'd wanted to help out friends, and no one had ever been comfortable enough to ask me. It's a strange dynamic being the one with the money, maybe as strange as being the one without.

"That's a great way to look at it," Weston said, finally looking at me. "He knew I was good for it, anyway. I do have a trust fund I haven't touched that could more than pay him back if I ever wanted to dig into it."

I sat quietly, in case he wanted to tell me more, but when he didn't, I let it go, knowing he would tell me when he was ready. This was only day one in our tropical paradise, day one of getting to know each other, and he'd already confessed something that was obviously difficult for him.

We already had one less wall between us. We were already so much closer.

The second round of entertainment began then, and talk gave way to singing along to "Tiny Bubbles" and learning familiar Hawaiian phrases. When the emcee asked for a volunteer to come up to learn how to hula, I joked about taking the stage.

"You wouldn't do it. You're too classy for that."

I wasn't sure if he was challenging me or if he really thought that I was too much of a prude, too serious to have any fun.

Either way, it pushed me to raise my hand.

"The redhead in the back," the emcee said, calling on me. I really had given him no choice since I was practically standing and waving my arm like I was on a sinking ship trying to hail a lifeboat.

"No way," Weston said with a smile as I smugly took to the stage.

A couple of assistant dancers led me behind the backdrop while the main singer sang another traditional Hawaiian song. I was dressed in a coconut bra over my maxi dress, and a hula skirt—a genuine one, not one of those plastic things that came from a costume store—was put on over my head and pulled down to my waist. When the song was over, I was led back on stage and in front of everyone, I was taught the simple movements of a basic hula love story.

It was easy enough to catch on to, for me anyway. I'd taken ballet for so long that I was good at picking up new choreography. Isolating my hip muscles was a bit of a challenge, but when I looked into the audience and saw the expression on Weston's face, saw him hypnotized and practically drooling, I was more determined to get it right. For him.

Afterward I was congratulated with applause and praised by the artists. I was given both the coconut bra and the skirt to keep as a prize for volunteering.

Weston met me at the side of the stage with my purse. He took the bag that contained my hula outfit for me and gestured to a pathway that led away from the dinner crowd.

"Do you mind? I don't think any of the entertainment can top what I've just seen."

That damn dimple again. Made my stomach do the flip-flop. Even if I had just met him tonight, yeah, I would let this stranger lead me away. Stupid, maybe. Crazy, definitely.

"I don't mind," I said.

We started walking, our hands dangling near each other again, sometimes brushing so slightly I wondered if it was just the breeze.

"You looked good up there," he said, his face tilted toward me.

"No I didn't. It was silly."

"You did. You, really did. Your hips can really move."

We followed the path around the garden toward the sound of the ocean waves. Just around some larger bushes was a hidden nook where a group of palm trees were surrounded by thick green bushes with bright tropical flowers.

"Years of ballet had you fooled."

"You took ballet?"

"All my life."

"That explains so much," he mumbled to himself. More loudly, he said, "You seem flexible."

He'd been thinking about some of the ways he'd fucked me, I could see it on his face. We had done some rather advanced positions in terms of bending and twisting.

I stopped and turned to face him. "I've kept my body up through yoga. But I felt off, doing the hula. I was distracted. They tied the bra so loose, I kept worrying it was going to fall down. Did you notice I kept pulling on the strap?" I leaned back on the tree behind me, gazing up at him.

"I didn't notice. I was too busy wondering what was under your skirt." He put his hand on the tree behind me, dropped the bag on the ground at my feet, and took a step closer, erasing the space between us.

My breath sped up at his proximity. I squinted my eyes up at him. "Would you really say that to a girl you just met?"

"I just said it, didn't I?" His eyes flicked to my lips.

I glanced around, to be sure we were alone, then grabbed the hem of my skirt and pulled it up toward my waist. "Go ahead and find out."

"Would you really say that to someone you just met?" he teased.

"Do you care?"

He lifted my skirt the last few inches to discover that I hadn't worn panties.

"What a pleasant surprise." He rubbed two fingers along the bare skin of my pussy. "I can't believe you went out alone like this. So brave. To think that this treasure could have gone unworshipped."

"I guess it's a really good thing, then, that we met."

"I'm not going to argue with that." He removed his hand from my pussy and brought it to my lips. "Open." I opened. "Suck." He slipped two fingers inside. "You have a really pretty mouth. Big, full, gorgeous lips," he said, his voice low and raspy, as I sucked on him until his fingers felt as wet as I did down below.

He returned his hand to the space between my thighs, parting me with his fingers. "You're beautiful here too. I can tell just by touching. Soft and wet and plump." He squeezed my clit with an expert amount of pressure, and I closed my eyes, surrendering to him.

His head lowered, and I could feel his mouth next to my ear, hear his breathing get heavier as my own breaths became more rapid. I clutched onto him as the tension within me began to build. He slid one finger lower, inside my eager body.

"You're so wet. And snug." He pulled out and thrust back in. Added another finger. My body bowed, begging for more. "Do you hear the rush of the ocean?" He paused, waiting for an answer. "Do you?"

I had to concentrate really hard to be aware of anything outside of Weston and my body and what he was currently doing to me, but somewhere nearby behind us, the ocean roared. "Yes. I hear it."

"The way the waves come in fast and sudden and overpowering, crashing on the sand, then pull out, taking everything in their wake with them? That's how it's going to be when I fuck you."

Holy shit.

I moaned, my hips bucking into his hand, greedy for more of his words and this feeling. Not sure how much I could take.

"Shh. It's okay. Keep listening. Surrender to that sound." He put his free hand around my waist to hold me up. "I'm going to fuck you fast like that ocean. Big like those waves. I'm going to overpower you. I'm going to make you come, make you crash. I'm going to take everything you give me and steal it away with me."

My pussy rippled around his fingers, which were stroking in and out of me, his dirty promises driving me crazy, partly because I knew he was good for them. Partly because I truly believed he *would* talk to me like this if we were indeed strangers, and that was so deliriously sexy.

But his words stoked something deeper, something I believed was probably also true. He really did want to win me over, really wanted to take everything I had to give. Really did want to steal it away with him.

Forever?

God, I hoped so.

"You know it, don't you?" he asked. "You can feel how it's going to be between us."

"Yes, yes. Please." I needed to release. I was so close, so desperate.

"Look at me when you come." He massaged my clit in small, tight circles with the pad of his thumb while he pushed his fingers in and out in a steady, unhurried rhythm.

I locked my eyes onto his, and everything tightened in my core. I let out a jagged cry as the wave crashed through me, my hips pumping onto his hand, mindless about our location and the possibility that someone could come upon us at any moment. His own gaze was feral and fiercely triumphant, and if I hadn't already been panting and breathless, that look alone would have stolen the air from my lungs.

I wanted to say something, when I could find the words, when I could speak again, but before either of those things happened, Weston fell to his knees and threw one of my legs over his shoulder so quickly I had to grab onto the tree for balance.

"Oh my God, I can't," I said as his tongue lapped at my clit. I was too sensitive. Too raw.

But I was also wrong. The need was already winding again, faster and tighter than before. He circled my rim with his finger as he sucked greedily at my tender, swollen nub, teasing me. Taunting me. When he licked down my slit and speared me with his tongue, I was lost. I came a second time, gasping and weeping, my orgasm tearing through me violently as he fucked me like this—with his mouth and his fingers and his tongue.

I was weak and boneless as he lowered my leg from his shoulder back to the ground. He kissed my upper thigh and then my belly, then tugged my dress free from where it was gathered between my back and the tree trunk. When he stood again, his face was flushed, his eyes dark. He pressed in close, but not so close that I could feel the erection that he surely had by now or felt obligated to kiss him.

He was a gentlemanly player, then. A decent guy. It was nice to learn that about him.

I dug into my purse and pulled out my room key and handed it to him, even though he had one of his own. "You're an overachiever. One orgasm would have earned you this."

"Maybe I want more than just the key to your room."

A warm rush of pleasure shot through me almost like an aftershock from my orgasms, just at the idea of this man trying to win my heart—a heart he already owned.

I wrapped my fingers in his shirt and held on, suddenly afraid he wasn't really real, that he'd disappear if I didn't touch him.

"Should I be worried about how good you are at this?" I wasn't sure if I was asking as a woman he'd just met or as a woman he'd just married.

With a sigh, he settled his hands on my hips and leaned his forehead on mine. "I used to worry about that sometimes," he confessed. "But what's the story of Cinderella and the prince? Didn't he put the slipper on every woman's foot in the kingdom before he found the one who fit the shoe?"

I burst into laughter. "Are you using a children's fairy tale to explain your expertise at oral sex?"

He smiled—that full-dimple, little boy mischievous grin. "If you buy it, I am."

I laughed again. "I'm not buying it."

"Okay, okay. How about this—I'm good at giving this. Giving sex. Giving my body. I'm not so good at giving my time or my thoughts or my energy. My heart. I've given my body to a lot of women, but I want to give you more than that. If you'll take it. But you have to take my body, too—it's part of the package."

I sobered. He'd definitely answered the question for the woman he'd married, and it was exactly what I needed to hear.

And now I wanted to get back to the game.

"Take me to my room?" I asked.

He nodded then slipped his hand into mine and led me on the path toward our bungalow.

"Oh, by the way, I'm Weston," he said. "Weston King."

Oh yeah. We hadn't ever introduced ourselves formally.

"Nice to meet you, Weston. I'm Elizabeth."

EIGHT
WESTON

I SAT in the wicker chair next to the bed watching her sleep, imagining her reaction when I finally told her about Sebastian. Would she be angry? Would she be thrilled? Would she be as excited and curious about this little person as I was?

I still worried about telling her, but after our first night on the island, when I'd opened up to her about Donovan and the money he loaned me to start Reach, I felt less concerned about it. She'd accepted that confession with no judgment, and it had been freeing to share that baggage with her.

I was starting to get excited with the idea of telling her about my son. I needed someone to talk to about this incredible new discovery in my life and she was the only person I wanted to tell.

But we were playing our game. It was only our second day in Hawaii, the sun was just peeking out over the ocean horizon, and our agenda included nothing but hiking through the tropical island wilderness. We were still practically strangers in this version of us. It wasn't time to bring in other players yet.

A knock startled me, even though I was expecting our breakfast order. I threw on last night's pants and hurried to the door, signing for the meal and taking over the cart in just a few short minutes.

"Thank God, you ordered breakfast," Elizabeth said as I wheeled the cart toward the bed. She sat up, stretching, the sheet falling to her waist as she covered her mouth to yawn.

I freely ogled her bare breasts as I pulled the cart's leaf out and extended it over her. Her nipples perked from my attention. "Island fruit and yogurt," I said lifting the cover off her dish.

"Exactly what I would've ordered." She looked pleased that I knew her tastes, and I resisted the urge to point out that she'd infiltrated my every waking thought, that knowing what she'd want to eat had become as natural to me as knowing what I wanted.

I grabbed my plate of eggs and bacon and moved around the other side of the bed, hopping back in and scooting up next to her. Before I dug into my food, I set my plate on my lap and turned to her, wrapping my hand around her neck to pull her mouth toward mine. When I kissed her, she tasted like the pineapple she'd already snuck into her mouth, sweet and tangy. I kissed her again. "How did you sleep?"

"Really well. I think I sleep better with a body next to me. It's a good thing I met you last night." She grinned.

"I had a lot of fun," I admitted.

"If I were really a stranger, would I still be here?" she asked, her eyes narrowing suspiciously.

I let go of her neck and sat back against the wall. "You are here, aren't you?" I said, teasing.

She took a sip of her coffee then planted her eyes on me. "We're still playing, right? I like this—this just-meeting-you game. But I really do want to know if it's plausible that a girl would still be in your bed the next morning."

"Sure, I'm up for it. And yes, many women have been here the next morning. Which is usually when I say goodbye. I would not have said goodbye to you."

"What would you have done with me? Tried to convince me to stay in this bed all day?" She fluttered her eyelashes as though getting into the character she thought I wanted her to be.

"Well, yes. Probably. And if you insisted that we climb up to Hanakapi'ai Valley to see the falls instead, I'd be right behind you, but I would try to convince you not to wear any panties for the adventure."

"Then this is a legitimate scenario. Right on."

"Does that mean *you're* planning to go without panties?" God, this woman was perfect.

She didn't answer, but she grinned before turning back to her meal. I was glad she did, that she removed her focus from me, because I was feeling things for her at that moment, deep fuzzy feelings that likely showed on my face. And this level of adoration was definitely too soon if we were playing strangers.

But by the last day of our trip, there wouldn't be any games left to hide behind. And I could only hope we were still looking at each other with adoration then.

AN HOUR LATER, we were on the bus headed to Ke'e Beach, backpacks on our laps stuffed with towels, a change of clothes, and plenty of water and snacks for the hike.

"We're taking the shuttle instead of driving," she explained as she rummaged through her own backpack, "because parking is tremendously hard to find. Even at this time of morning." She pulled out a bottle of sunscreen and handed it to me. SPF 60. "Would you mind?"

She unbuttoned her denim shirt so that I could apply the lotion generously to her skin. She had a bikini top underneath, but the shirt was long-sleeved and her hair was knotted up high on her head to fit under a wide-brimmed sun hat. I put some sunscreen in my hand and then began working it into her creamy white skin, and it occurred to me she wasn't really cut out for the tropical sun.

"Tell me something. Why did you choose a vacation in the tropics? I'm guessing you burn easily." I *knew* she burned easily from the one time she'd forgotten sunscreen when we'd ended up at a Labor Day event earlier in the summer. But we were playing that game, the game where we didn't know things about each other, and I really *didn't* know why she'd chosen Hawaii. "Why not a vacation somewhere in Europe?"

"Well, it's December, and I knew I'd be tired of the cold when I planned it." She was facing the window but I could see her skin pinking up at her neck and collarbone as though she was embarrassed.

That meant there was more to the story. "But there are probably other warm places that don't require putting your skin at risk." I moved my hands down her torso, enjoying the goosebumps that sprouted at my touch.

She shrugged with one shoulder. "I was hoping to meet someone," she said cautiously. "There are only so many romantics spots. Paris was out of the question." She turned and looked at me, daring me to ask her why she wouldn't go to France—I wasn't touching that with a ten-foot pole. I wasn't ready to talk about the future, how she was planning to live there. When I didn't say anything, she went on. "And I figured resorts where I could show a lot of skin were my best bet. You know. In attracting a member of the opposite sex."

Her words registered. "This was about seducing me again," I said with a laugh. "You thought showing more skin, flaunting yourself in a bikini was the way to seduce me?" God, if she'd only known how turned on I'd been even when she was fully covered in those pantsuits.

She turned her head toward mine, her face fully red now. "Shut up," she giggled. "You're breaking character."

I kissed her, sweeping my tongue into her mouth with luscious deep strokes. I would've told her I loved her, it was on the tip of my tongue, natural the way that it wanted to spill out, but after she'd just admonished me for not playing by the rules, I felt I had to keep it inside. I hoped my kiss said it instead, told her all the ways I wanted her, eased every one of those anxieties about winning my heart.

It was hers.

Somehow, after a fair amount of making out, I managed to cover her with enough sunscreen to satisfy her by the time we arrived at the end of the road, quite literally. When we climbed off the bus, I saw that the road didn't go any farther from this point on the north side of the island, and as Elizabeth had warned, the sides of the road were full of parked cars, even at this time of morning. It wasn't even eight o'clock yet.

"See why we took the bus?" she asked. "Come on. The trail's this way." I followed her—as well as the entire crowd from the bus—to the trailhead, swinging my backpack onto my shoulders as I walked. I was looking out at the ocean, at the blue mixing with the pink in the sky, admiring the swirl of colors when she shrieked in front of me.

"What's going on?" I asked as she jumped into my arms.

"It's attacking me!"

I looked down to where she pointed. There was a brightly colored rooster on the path in front of us, crowing proudly as though guarding the way. I tried, and failed, to swallow a roar of laughter. "It's a chicken. You're scared of the chicken?"

"It's feral! It's coming right for me!" She clutched onto me tighter.

"It's actually just...standing there. But don't worry, I'll save you." I put a hand out in front of me, as though I meant to ward it off. Then, with her still clutching my side, I made a generous sidestep around it. "That was close," I teased.

Without letting go of my arm, she craned her head to watch the bird behind us. "He's still looking at me."

"He has an eye on each side of his head. He's looking at everything." I shook my head as I pulled her along the trail. "Brave, fearless woman wants to tackle Dyson Media. Afraid of a little chicken."

She pushed me, letting go. We were far enough away from the bird for her to seem less wary, even though she kept looking back after him. "You didn't see him when I did," she said defensively. "He attacked me."

"Whatever you say." I kept smiling, following after her cute ass, tight and curvy in her jean shorts. It was an easy target, something I wanted to follow, and I had to remind myself to look out at the stunning views every now and then along the two-mile walk to Hanakapi'ai Beach. We didn't talk much on this part of the route, walking single file, mostly because there were so many other people headed up with us. So much for getting a chance to talk to her alone.

Once when we stopped to take a break and drink some water, she seemed to notice my fretting as I watched a group of Boy Scouts pass us by.

"What's wrong?" she asked, passing the water bottle.

I took a swallow before I answered. "Nothing. I just didn't expect there to be so many people up here."

"It's a really popular trail. There will be less people climbing all the way into the falls."

So I'd have time to talk to her then. I could wait.

We made it to the beach in about forty-five minutes. The climb hadn't been too strenuous as we'd walked along the cliff walls that bordered the ocean. Hanakapi'ai Beach, however, surprisingly didn't have any sand, though the inlet was breathtaking. Like an undiscovered cove, untouched by modern vehicles.

"There's sand in the summer months," Elizabeth explained. "In the winter the tides come in too far."

"You sure did a lot of research. I'm impressed."

"I like to learn about the adventures I'm tackling," she said confidently. I studied her, recognizing the student inside. She did thirst for knowledge, eagerly wanting to know everything about the ventures she meant to tackle. I'd discovered that as I'd taught her business over the last several months. She was a quick study too, and I wondered how much she actually knew about me that I didn't realize she knew. How many secrets I was holding that she'd already uncovered on her own, simply by spending time with me.

It didn't make me feel as uncomfortable as I thought it would to be known the way I suspected she might know me.

And that did freak me out.

"Ready to head to the falls?" she asked.

I wanted to tell her that I would follow her anywhere. But I still wasn't sure it was true. Wasn't sure I would follow her to France. Wasn't sure that I *could*. So I just said, "Lead the way."

Elizabeth had been right—there were fewer people on the trail inland to the falls. It was hard to even call it a trail in some places. The path was so grown over and untrodden that there were several times I wasn't even sure that we were actually on the designated trail. It was nice to be alone, but the difficulty of the hike made conversation impossible. It took all our concentration to figure out where we were going and worry about not sliding through mud. And even on the parts that were easy, we didn't talk. We were too busy taking in the sights. Beautiful, strange flora and fauna I'd never seen before surrounded us. Breathtaking scenery that was lush and green and so patently different from the environment in which I lived, it was hard to believe that these plants were from the same planet that I was, let alone the same country.

It was another two miles from the beach to the falls, and I

sensed we were getting near, only to take another break. Elizabeth climbed on top of a big boulder just off the path. When I took off my backpack and set it at my feet and bent down to get the water bottle out of it, I had to look up to meet her eyes. So perfect and beautiful and stunning. She'd taken the denim shirt off and stuffed it into her backpack, and beads of sweat rolled down her pale décolletage, gathering at her cleavage. I wanted to climb up the rock and lick every drop of sweat off of her, peel off her jean shorts, and find out if she was wearing a bikini bottom. Wanted to take her and claim her in this jungle.

I stood and handed her the water bottle, just to get closer to her.

She took it, her fingers brushing mine. "There is another reason I chose Hawaii," she said.

"Tell me."

"I told you I'd never been. But that's not entirely true. I came once with my mother when I was thirteen years old. She'd been dating this guy for a while—Victor—and it was getting kind of serious. Like maybe Mom was going to make a go at another marriage. At least, it was serious enough to try to blend her little family with him. He suggested we all go on a trip together to get to know each other, and he took us to Kauai. It was supposed to be a month-long getaway for the summer. He had a condo here and came every year."

She handed the water bottle back to me and I took it, too intrigued by her story to take a sip for myself.

"I was really excited. My father had promised to take me to Hawaii, I don't know, seventy-billion times, and he never came through. That was my dad, though. Lots of broken promises. So when Victor suggested we go, it felt like maybe he was going to be a brand-new dad. Like, a chance to do it all over. I mean, I was excited about seeing the island too. I was really into the idea of waterfalls, and my mom used to like that Fantasy Island show. We watched it together all the time. I wanted to go to a luau. It was all so exotic and just really in my zone at the time."

I'd never been that into the tropical islands myself, but my sister had gone through a phase, so I could picture what she talked about. I took a swig from the bottle. "Go on."

"Anyway. We were here one night. And I'd come out looking for my mother wearing just my T-shirt and underwear. I don't know what exactly happened, but the next day my mother packed us up early in the morning and put us on a flight back to the mainland. She said that Victor had looked at me in a lewd way. She'd seen him staring at me in my underwear, and she'd recognized his lustful look. And she wasn't going to stand for it. She'd argued with him. I guess. I didn't hear this, she just told me about it later. He didn't deny anything. And Mom decided there was no coming back from that. Once a guy looked at your daughter lustfully, he was never going to get over that. She ended their whole relationship."

She brought her knees to her chest and hugged them in tight. "And the thing is—I was mad at her. I was mad because she took me away from Hawaii when I'd been looking forward to the trip. And I was really mad that she denied me a chance at having another father. For a long time I really resented her for it. It took me several years before I understood that she'd actually made a sacrifice for me. She'd given up a guy that she'd maybe really loved, because she loved me more."

"Well. Are you okay?" The thought of a guy even looking at Elizabeth the wrong way made my primal male brain react. I wanted to cut someone's throat. Wanted to string the guy up by his nuts.

"Like I said, he didn't touch me. I didn't even really notice. After the fact, it did seem a little creepy how he'd looked at me, but it wasn't traumatic. Which is why it took so long to realize what my mother had done for me. When I did finally understand? You know, that that's the way a parent *should* be. Not like my dad who made promise after promise, laying out dreams and visions of the world that he never really intended to give me. A good parent sacrificed. A good parent took away those dreams and promises because it was what was in my best interest. I spend a lot of time talking about how shitty my dad is. But I don't spend enough time saying how awesome my mom is." She smiled, a shaky smile. "That's why I wanted to go to Kauai. Because I was only here for a day. And I wanted a do-over."

I reached out my hand to her and pulled her down the rock until she was standing in front of me, then wrapped my arms around her. "I'm really glad I'm the one who gets to finally have this adventure with you," I said, and I just held her.

After a few minutes, I said, "You do have a really good mom." It made me think about how I wanted to be like that. How I wanted to be a good dad.

A rustling down the path stole our attention.

"Don't stop now. You're almost there!" an older man said, coming toward us returning from our destination. He was about my father's age, and the woman next to him seemed to be about my mother's age. "If you listen, you can hear the falls."

Elizabeth picked her head up. "I can hear them. Race you!" She was gathering her pack and bounding down the trail before I could stop her.

"Thanks for the encouragement," I said to the couple, then headed after the woman I was pretending wasn't my wife.

It was only a hundred feet or so later before we came upon the falls. They were majestic and gorgeous, the kind of thing you imagined in paradise but never actually saw for yourself. There were people swimming in the lagoon of water at the base of the falls, and Elizabeth was already stripping her clothes before I even had time to get my backpack off my shoulders. She dove in, fearless, shrieking as she hit the water.

I watched her splashing around, taking my time as I untied my shoes. How did she do that? How did she live so open and free, her feelings so exposed to all the world?

I envied her.

And I loved her.

And maybe it was selfish and self-centered to wish that we could live in this tiny paradise forever, just me and her, but right now that's what I wanted more than anything else. Even if it meant sacrificing everything waiting for me at home. In this moment, I loved her *that* much.

Not able to stand being apart from her a second longer, I finished undressing and jumped in the water. She swam up to me immediately, throwing her arms around my neck and wrapping her legs around my waist. We bobbed around in the water like this, holding onto each other and kissing. It didn't even matter that there were other people nearby. We kissed like we were alone, and soon my cock was hard, pushing against the seam of her pussy, outlined clearly through her thin bikini.

"I could be fucking you right now, and no one would know," I said quietly at her ear. It was hot thinking about it, about being inside her with all of these people nearby. And I needed it all of a sudden, needed it desperately. Needed to mold myself to her, prove how well we fit together.

"We can't," she said, her breath hitching. She met my eyes and hers were dark and dilated.

"We could. It would be so easy to slip inside you."

She rubbed her pussy against my cock, which was thickening at the thought of being nestled warm in her tight channel.

I let go of her so I could push my swim trunks down far enough to pull out my cock, all of it underneath the water where no one could see. I nudged along the outline of her pussy lips with my crown, showing her how easy it would be. "Let me," I said huskily.

She nodded, slightly, just the tiniest jerk of her head, but it was all the permission I needed. I pulled aside the crotch panel to her bikini bottoms and lined my tip at her entrance. "You're going to have to be quiet. You can't give us away."

She bit her lip and nodded again, more vigorously as though begging for it. I pushed into her, slow and evenly, exhaling at the sudden cloak of heat around my cock. I grabbed her hips and pressed her tighter against me, so that I was as deep as I could go, stretching into the most sacred parts of her.

I stayed like that, without moving, just locked inside her, feeling the flutter of her pussy around me, watching the shallowness of her breath as we tread water. Elizabeth peered at the people around us, showering under the falls and playing in the lagoon.

"No one knows," she whispered, wrapping her arms tighter around my neck. "That's so hot that no one knows."

My cock twitched inside her, that's how hot it was.

"This is probably against a million health recommendations," I said, hoping that if I expressed concern it would erase the sin of having absolutely no guilt.

"I'll take an antibiotic when we're back in the mainland—don't you dare pull out."

"I'm not going anywhere."

I was content to stay just like that, fastened together and nothing else, but she pivoted her hips, pulling off of me, then tilted them in sinking back on my shaft with a whimper.

"Oh, it feels good." Her eyes teared and her lips quivered.

I kissed her, kissed her and rocked with her, memorizing the taste of her mouth and the grip of her pussy and the feel of her arms and her legs wrapped around me like a pretzel. It wasn't even about climaxing or release—it was about holding on. It was about being as close to a person as possible and not letting go. It was about hoping she didn't notice that I still had walls up, and praying to God that the ones I'd knocked down were enough. It was about loving her with everything I was, without the baggage that came with me.

And I would tell her about Sebastian—of course I would. I had promised myself I would tell her everything before we left this island. But I was leaving that story for last, in case she wanted me to be the man her father wasn't. The kind of parent her mother was. The kind of person I kept telling myself I could be.

Truth was, I wasn't sure I was strong enough to be the guy a woman like her deserved.

NINE
ELIZABETH

WESTON EMERGED FROM THE OCEAN, an Adonis shining in the sun. He traipsed across the sand, seemingly unaware of the women nearby ogling him. It was impossible not to. He'd bronzed during our nine days in the tropics, and wearing only his swim trunks, his finest assets were displayed. His washboard abs. His perfectly sculpted biceps. His sun-bleached hair. That wicked grin. Not to mention that dimple that practically caused ovulation just by looking at it.

And it was mine.

His body, anyway. He told me in every way he could. With words, with actions. He'd given himself to me physically, and more and more he'd revealed parts of the man inside the perfect casing.

But there was still so much more inside him that I hadn't yet seen. Who did *that* belong to?

I watched him from my safe spot in the shade on the hammock swing behind our bungalow as he rubbed the towel up and down his arms, walking toward me the whole time. When he reached me, he dropped the towel on the sand, and bent down to kiss me, his wet hair dripping onto me and making me shiver.

"You look so serious," he said, plopping down on the deck chair next to me. "What are you thinking about?"

I twisted my lip and caught it between my teeth. We'd continued playing the stranger game since the first night we'd arrived, and the baggage-free personas we'd brought to our island paradise had enjoyed getting to know each other. I'd learned everything about Weston's love of graphic novels and his secret adoration of the art of magic while horseback riding on the beach and kayaking together. I discovered his secret love for grunge music while driving up a canyon. I'd learned he was just the slightest bit afraid of heights when we took a helicopter tour of the island. I discovered his amazing massage technique at our couples spa treatment, when after our massage therapists had given us each a rubdown, they'd left us alone in the room with an edible sugar scrub.

Who knew sugar could be so erotic?

But now I felt that game was played out. That we were stuck and not moving forward. As much as I'd learned about this wonderful, amazing man—as much as I fell harder for him every day—I was nowhere nearer to resolution for the future. We'd shared our pasts, but nothing of our present.

It was time for some honesty.

I pushed my sunglasses on top of my head and angled myself so I could face him. "I was thinking that in five days we go home. And I'm not really sure where home is."

His jaw tensed ever so slightly, and I worried I'd jumped too fast without warning, but he surprised me with his response. "Does that mean you're considering that your home could be somewhere other than France?"

The hesitant note of hope in his voice gutted me. "Of course I am. Just like I hope you are considering that France could be yours."

"Yeah." He took a deep breath and repeated himself. "Yeah, I really am."

I wanted to grab onto his arm and pull it, pull him like a taut fishing line until he sprang up from the deep and displayed the treasure he was hiding under the surface. But when I'd agreed to the trip, he'd promised to show me all of his insides by the time we left. I wanted to trust that. So I wouldn't push him.

Yet.

I covered his hand with mine instead. "Okay."

That night we ate dinner at the five-star seafood restaurant at the resort. The meal was amazing. I'd never had fish that tasted so fresh and divine, melting in my mouth with such succulent briny sweetness.

But without the stranger game between us, there was a new tension that hummed quietly around Weston and me, butting in and spiking up whenever the conversation turned anywhere serious. We were polite—too polite—and gone were the simple discoveries and easy stories that had flowed between us over the previous week.

Still, there wasn't anywhere I'd rather be. Wasn't anyone I would rather be with.

A piece of bread hitting my shoulder alerted me to the table next to us, a young mother already apologizing for her toddler even as I turned around. Undeterred, the child threw another piece. I laughed out loud at the mischievous look on her little face.

"Do you like kids?" Weston asked, a tentative edge in his voice.

I glanced at him, surprised.

"I like some kids," I said. "I don't have a lot of experience around them, but from what I have gleaned, they are pretty much just like tiny people. Some are amazingly wonderful to know. Some are assholes."

He laughed, full and hearty. "I guess what I'm asking is...do you want kids?"

I peered over at him, studied the strange edge in his features. Maybe it was just the candlelight playing tricks on me. But it *was* strange we hadn't had this conversation, looking at our situation on paper, anyway. How could two people get married and not know the other's stance on procreation?

Of course, our marriage had been under false pretenses. And so we were only just getting to this now.

"Yeah, I do. I definitely want kids."

His shoulders seemed to ease, the shadows disappearing from his expression, and I felt that I had answered correctly.

"You?" I asked to be sure.

"I hadn't really thought about it until...recently. But I do."

Good. This was good. With that, I felt the last remaining tension flow out of my body. I hadn't realized how much I wanted to be on the same page with him on this.

"I mean," I qualified, "not right now. Not for another ten years."

"Ten years?"

"Right. I am only twenty-five now, so I have time. Thirty-five is not too late."

"And you're set on that?" The hardness from before was creeping back into his tone.

"Well, yeah. I really am. I want to focus on my business right now. Dyson Media is an important legacy and I'm determined to make something of it. You know that. My father spent so much of his life dedicated to the business, and I learned from him that it was a job too big to have with children. He didn't have enough time to give to me and his work. Which wasn't fair to me. I don't want to make that same mistake with my kids. So I want ten years devoted to my business, then I'll be able to step away. Probably won't ever be a stay-at-home type, but I will definitely be an involved mother. It was one of the reasons I wanted to get my hands on my company *now*, and not wait. Because I recognize my biological clock is ticking, and I really need these things to be separate."

"Just because your father couldn't manage both doesn't mean that *people* can't manage both. Maybe your father was just...not a good parent."

I considered. "Maybe. But part of being a good parent is making good choices about how you build your life. And before I have kids, I want to build my life so that I have time to devote to them." It wasn't something I would back down on. It was more important to me even than living in France.

Weston didn't seem to like my answer though. He crossed his arms over his chest and scowled. "But what if you got pregnant sooner? What if you had a baby right now?"

"Right now? If I had a baby right now, it would be yours. And I would want it *so* much." I stared into his eyes, willing him to see exactly how much I meant what I was saying. "I'd welcome it into my life with completely open arms. And I would change my priorities where Dyson Media was concerned. I'd probably let Darrell stay where he is. I wouldn't be so involved, I don't know. It's not how I want things to be, so I am making every effort to not have to be in that situation. Because I want the best circumstances when I have a baby—when I have *your* baby." It made me feel vulnerable to say that last part, to admit that I wanted kids with him, but it also felt freeing and right.

"So you're saying that you would have a kid now, if you *had* to, but it's not what you want, which means one day you might even grow to resent it. Or me. Because it kept you from doing and being the thing that you really wanted to be first." His words were sharp, his body language almost hostile.

"Are you mad at me?" I couldn't understand why he was so upset over a hypothetical situation. He himself had said he only recently decided he wanted kids. He couldn't have some dying need to have a baby now, could he?

"No. I'm not mad." He turned back to picking at the remainders of his food, definitely seeming like he was mad.

I could feel him slipping away from me. "Can you tell me what it is I need to say then? Because I feel like I've said the wrong thing, but I can't say the right thing if you won't tell me what it is."

He shook his head, his eyes now watching the young couple with the toddler as they packed up their table, getting ready to leave. "Never mind. It was a stupid conversation."

I placed a hand on his forearm, felt it tense beneath my fingers. He was close enough to touch, but somehow it felt like he had a wall around him, some barrier I couldn't reach through. "It's not stupid. It's important, and I wanted to talk about it."

He shot me a glance. "We talked about it. There's not much else to say."

I set my jaw, actively conscious of the string of wrong things I could say that were rolling through my mind, wishing I could find the one right thing to say.

Finally, with tears threatening at the corner of my eyes, I swallowed back the ball lodged in my throat, and tried one more time. "I want to be inside you, Weston. In all the ways you're inside me. But I feel like I'm up against a door that I can't open unless you give me the key." I paused to steady my voice. "Give me the key."

His eyes closed briefly, my words settling over him, before he turned again to face me. "You're so far inside me, Elizabeth, that I don't know where you end and I begin anymore."

He opened up his arms, and I was instantly in them, moving from my chair to his lap, kissing up his jaw, licking at his salty skin until his mouth found mine. He held me close and tight, his lips locked with mine, unmoving, clutching onto me with a fierceness I'd never seen in him before. Like he was keeping me in place. Like he was afraid I'd leave, or let go first, or not love him enough.

I let him grip onto me like that, wishing his words and his embrace were enough to make me feel sure of our future together.

But they weren't.

I was just as desperate and scared as his kiss told me *he* was. Because if I was truly inside him, like he said I was, he wouldn't be holding on like he was about to lose me.

TEN
WESTON

I QUIETLY SLID the back door to the bungalow shut, making sure not to wake Elizabeth, and stepped out into the muggy night air. A couple of footsteps and I was in the sand, cool against the bottom of my feet. I stood in the silent night, gazing off into the dark distance, my thoughts rolling and loud as the waves against the shore. The time on my phone read two thirty-eight. I hadn't slept a wink.

I was a giant asshole.

With a disconcerted sigh, I ran a frustrated hand through my hair and wandered over to the hammock swing. It was better to be out here sorting through the wreckage in my mind than tossing and turning next to the warm body in my bed. I couldn't help but think I'd made a mess of everything. That I would be far less burdened in this moment if I'd just been clear and honest with my wife from the day of our wedding.

But I hadn't been.

And now, before I'd finished laying my groundwork, before I'd gotten brave enough and secure enough to tell her I was a father, she'd told me she didn't want children of her own—not anytime soon, anyway—and I'd blown up at her. All I could think was, how is she possibly going to want me now? Now that I come with a plus one?

All I could think was, I'm going to lose her, and I freaked out.

Hours of staring into the darkness while I listened to the sweet rhythm of her breath as she slept made me realize I might be overreacting. Made me realize I was definitely being a prick, not giving her a chance to embrace my son. I'd given her a hypothetical situation and taken her hypothetical response—a response aimed at biological children of her own—and decided that it meant something that it didn't have to. *Callie* was raising Sebastian. Callie was Sebastian's mother. My paternal relationship with this little boy didn't mean Elizabeth had to lose her dreams. What kind of blockhead assumed it meant otherwise?

This blockhead, apparently.

I groaned as I leaned back into the hammock, pushing off with the balls of my feet into a gentle swing. I had to tell her. I had to tell her everything. Every last thing I'd been storing inside of me, not willing to expose, had to be shared with her now. There wasn't any more putting it off.

As though the universe were intent on making me commit, it was then that Elizabeth chose to open the sliding door and interrupt my solitude. She stepped down onto the beach wearing the button-down linen shirt I'd had on earlier, her hair tangled from when I'd bent her over the vanity in the bathroom and fucked her hard, mercilessly, watching us both in the mirror as we rode through our climaxes.

With her hair tousled and the moonlight hitting her, she looked like an angel, maybe even an angel of death. An angel who was about to put me out of my misery, if I'd let her.

She found me quickly and started over to me before I'd even fully gestured for her to come over. I was still caught up in my self-made hell, but not so distracted that I wasn't wondering if she was wearing nothing underneath the shirt. My cock was already twitching against the drawstring of the pajama pants that I'd pulled on before I came outside, and when she sat across my lap, her long creamy legs stretched over me, I definitely got stiff.

"What are you doing out here? It's late." She wrapped her arms around my neck and I nestled my face into the curve of her shoulder. I kissed the delicate strip of skin that was bared there, sending more blood down to my cock.

"Couldn't sleep." I trailed my tongue along the spot I'd just pressed my mouth to.

"You should've woken me up." Her sultry voice was an invitation and I was ready to RSVP. I wouldn't even have to have her straddle me. I was sure I could press into her at this angle and imagined how good and tight it would feel to bury into her soft, sweet pussy while she continued to sit on me sideways.

But that was a guilty temptation I was intent on not taking advantage of. Not right now—I wouldn't feel good about myself afterward. I'd been given a moment of clarity, followed by the opportunity to talk to her for a reason. I needed to be better than I had been. Needed to be the guy who didn't blow it.

With a heavy sigh, I sat back away from her.

She ran her fingers through my hair and studied my features. "What are you thinking about?"

The tone of her voice held that note of hopeful longing, a distinct giveaway that she wasn't sure I would tell her anything.

Which made me only feel like a bigger asshat.

But also made me a thousand times more committed to baring something meaningful to her. I took a second to answer, gathering my words and confidence. "I was thinking about how stupid it is that I can't just tell you everything that's inside me. Why is that? They're only words. They're only sentences. And yet each time I think about bringing them through me, they snag at the back of my throat."

She curled her knees up against my bare chest, and I could hear the slightest uptick in the speed of her breathing—an indication that this conversation thrilled her? Scared her? Possibly both, but for the most part she played it cool, continuing to lightly stroke my hair.

"Are you afraid of what I'll think about you?" she asked, raw honesty layered in her tone.

"Yes. I guess that's the biggest reason why it's hard to say these things."

"I want to tell you that there can't be anything that you would say that would change how I feel about you. Because I believe that's true. You couldn't have even really cheated on me, and that's the worst I can think you could do, since we were never really—"

I turned my head to face her, cutting her off abruptly. "I haven't cheated on you. Nothing has been directly against you. I haven't betrayed you, not really. Or maybe I have by not sharing with you earlier, but I haven't cheated on you."

"That's vaguely clear. But I feel even more confident in saying that nothing you can tell me is going to change how I feel about you, Weston. I also understand that you can't know that until you tell me. And I also understand that whatever you're keeping from me is a big enough part of you to matter. That you have to tell me before we can move on in this relationship. So you're just going to have to try me to find out that I mean it when I say it's going to be okay. Try me, and let me prove it to you."

"I'm trying. I really am. I haven't done this before. Never talked to a woman about anything real. Never talked to anyone, really, about anything real. Donovan sometimes. But mostly that was because he just already seems to know everything." I could do this, though. Even sharing this—this fear, the anxiety surrounding opening up to her—that was a brave beginning, as far as I was concerned. I got points for that, didn't I?

Points or not, I was scrambling trying to figure out where to go next. What to *say* next. Telling her was going to happen, but how to do it was another matter entirely.

"Maybe you could make it like a game of sorts. Maybe that would make it better," Elizabeth suggested. "It was so easy to get to know each other when we first got here when we played strangers. Should we play that game again?"

I ran my hand along the outside of her thigh, loving the feel of her skin underneath my palm. "Some of these things I would never tell a stranger." But maybe there was another game we could play. "Truth or dare?"

"Are you sure you won't just pick dare every time?"

God, she knew me too well. "Fair. Another game then...?" Part of me was trying to find a way to involve stripping when a real answer came. "Two truths and a lie."

"Two truths and a lie. That's an excellent game."

It was dangerous because I would be able to gauge her reaction to my truths beforehand, making it tempting to change my mind and tell her the wrong thing was a lie if I didn't like how she responded.

No. I couldn't do that. Mostly because she wouldn't react terribly, I was almost certain.

"Let's play then. You go first." Because I was still a dick, after all. "Make it about sex. It's always good when it's about sex." Because I was still a guy.

Because I was still scared.

She chuckled. "Okay. All right. Let me think a second."

I continued to rub my hand up and down her leg while she thought, not letting myself get too worked up about what my turn would be. I needed to stay here, in the moment. If I thought about it too much, I'd end up running.

"I got it. I got it," she said sitting up a little, twisting her tight little ass to get more comfortable as she did, sending jolts of electric pleasure straight to my groin.

"Careful, Lizzie."

She ignored me and went right into her turn. "I lost my virginity to Clarence Sheridan."

"Oh," I groaned. "Please let that be the lie."

"I've never watched porn with another person. Or the Lelo vibrator is my tool of choice when it comes to masturbation."

She tilted her chin up as though she was proud of herself.

The smug little look on her face, the very close proximity of her ass to my cock—I had to briefly pretend there were zombies about to come crawling out of the ocean before I could concentrate on her three statements and try to decide which one wasn't true.

"I really wish the first one was a lie," I said. "But I have a feeling, a deep dark feeling that it's not. You don't have a vibrator. I'd know about that by now, and there's no way you've watched porn with another person. You blush too easily. *I* haven't even watched porn with another person."

"*You* haven't watched porn with another person? How can you not have watched porn with someone?"

"Who needs to watch porn when you're making it, baby?"

Even in the darkness, I could see her roll her eyes. "Anyway, you're wrong."

My heart lifted suddenly. Maybe she had never slept with Clarence Sheridan.

"I've totally watched porn with people. Multiple times. It's amazing."

"So you *have* fucked Clarence."

"And watched porn with him!"

Gross. The guy probably needed it to get a woman turned on. I took that as comfort.

I turned my thoughts away from Clarence for a moment. "Does that mean you have a vibrator?" I hope I didn't sound too eager.

"I didn't bring it on my honeymoon." She leaned down to run

her nose along my ear. "But we can play with it when we get home, if that's what you're suggesting."

So much for calming down my dick.

Though, thinking about our ambiguous future did make for a boner killer. What if we never had a chance to play with her vibrator together? What if we never got to watch porn? I couldn't stand the idea of Clarence Sheridan going down in history as her best lover.

I needed more details about him.

"Was Clarence good to you at least?" I paused a second. "Actually, tell me he was an amateur. That's what I want to hear. That he didn't know what he was doing, and he was a total loser. With a tiny dick."

She laughed, the side of her breast jiggling against my chest. "He had a normal dick. Whatever that is. And he was...sweet. It was his first time too."

Oh, fuck. That meant it was a big deal for both of them.

It also meant he was brainless when it happened. "So he didn't know what he was doing. At all. That's what you're saying."

"He didn't know what he was doing," she confirmed. "It was over within seconds."

"That's what I wanted to hear. Thank you, Mrs. King."

"I have to be totally forthcoming, though—"

"Do you?"

She continued. "And tell you he did get better. We both did."

"I think I could've lived without knowing that." To make matters worse, my boner wasn't gone. In fact, now my cock wanted to go prove itself. Like, remind my wife that I was the best she'd ever have.

As if sensing the turmoil I was going through, Elizabeth brushed her lips against my jaw. "I don't need to tell you how good of a lover you are, Weston. You already know you own the title of Best in Bed. Best against any hard surface, actually."

"I don't necessarily know that." I mean, I did. "And, even if I do. It is nice to hear every once in a while."

She chuckled again, her body curling tighter against me as she did.

"I think you're a pretty hot lover too," I said softly. "Feisty and kinky and loud and soft all wrapped into one."

"Please don't say that was the beginning of your turn. Because I would have to guess that that was your lie."

"It's not a lie." I tickled her until she squirmed and my cock felt miserable again.

"Your turn, your turn," she sang, poking her index finger into my chest.

Yeah. My turn. My fucking turn.

I was tempted to take this round as a warm-up, give her some bullshit statements that didn't really mean anything, but I also needed to get this over with, get inside Elizabeth, get her inside me as soon as possible.

Three statements: *I'm a father. I'm going to do better than my father. My father fucked up big time.*

The lie was the middle one—I already wasn't sure I was going to do better than anyone. I worried I couldn't even do better than my father. And maybe that was the hang-up with me where Sebastian was concerned—I had daddy issues. Big time.

Where did I begin to get over the failures of Nash King?

By talking about it, I supposed.

The next sentence that came out of my mouth was thought as it was spoken. "My father encouraged unethical packaging and approval of housing loans even after the financial crisis."

There it was. Out there. My most embarrassing family secret told to another human being. Told to the most important human I knew.

And all I could do was go on. "Statement two: He let one of his employees—Daniel Clemmons—practically a family friend, take the fall and go to jail for him. And statement three: I don't care at all what you think about me after you hear this, that I'm not afraid you'll think I'm like him or that I condone this, or that I worry you'll be appalled when I tell you that I feel so guilty that I haven't touched my trust fund—money that was made by squandering other people's life savings—or that I've been giving money monthly to the Clemmons family to try to make up for...everything."

I swallowed. "Obviously the last one's the lie. I care very much what you think about me. I worry very much that you think I'm like him—like my dad. Maybe because *I'm* afraid that I'm like him."

She was still for a moment on my lap. Then she was moving, adjusting herself to straddle me so she could take my face in her hands and look at me directly, and I held onto her, clutching her with shaking hands.

"Weston," she began.

But I couldn't lift my eyes to meet hers. I could just go on, could just blunder through the whole tale of it until it was told. "I found out when I was working at my father's office one summer. I was still in college. It was about seven years ago. Before the allegations even came out publicly. And I was mad. I was really mad. And hurt, but mostly mad. Because why did he have to do something unethical? Weren't we already making enough? Donovan didn't see it so black and white. We didn't have to go into business with our parents, he said, and we could do things differently, but we didn't necessarily need to be so judgmental about how things had been done before us. It wasn't exactly illegal. Which, okay. Sure. Fine. Everyone was doing shitty business deals."

"Weston," she said again, patiently.

"But then the charges came out and it really became an issue, because that's when my dad had the opportunity to make things better. And he didn't. I told him he needed to take the fall. He'd ruined people's lives. To build *our* life. That wasn't right, and I told him he needed to take responsibility. I think he might've even considered it, except my mother—my mother..." I lost myself in the vivid memory of that day, her usually perfect makeup smeared down her cheeks.

"She begged and cried and said she couldn't live without him and there was no way he could turn himself in. But what about the Clemmonses? What about *their* children and his family? Daniel Clemmons was only following orders. He shouldn't have had to pay the price for everyone else. I do everything I can, give them everything I can, and I just feel like it's not ever enough. It's never going to be enough—"

"Weston, look at me."

Her insistence was sharp. I lifted my eyes toward her face. Her beautiful, angelic face.

She ran her thumb gently across my cheekbone. "This is not your fault. Okay? I am so sorry this happened, and it has to hurt so bad. But I don't think a fraction of an inch less of you for this. I probably think a whole hell of a lot more of you, if that's even possible." She tilted her head slightly. "Are you hearing me?"

I nodded, a ball lodged in the back of my throat that I couldn't seem to swallow down.

"I mean it. Are you really hearing me? Because I'm going to tell you again—your father's sins are not your sins. Who your father is is not who you are. I'm sorry that he's hurt you. You never deserved that. But it's not your fault."

I nodded again, hearing her. Accepting it. Knowing it, because I did already know it somewhere inside of me, and yet I'd still sought so valiantly to undo the damage done by my father. How many years had I wasted trying to erase his errors? How much time and money and energy had I spent feeling guilty for things I hadn't done?

Too much. That's how much.

Besides being my life, the whole scenario sounded obvious and oddly familiar, like I'd been on the other side of it before. Like I'd stood outside and looked in. And of course I had, I'd been looking outside at the same scene ever since I'd met Elizabeth. I'd been where she was, watching her lament the things her father had done in his business, hearing her tear herself apart, wanting to make it better while she put all the weight on her own shoulders.

I brought my hands to her neck and stroked my thumbs along her jaw. "Your father's sins are not your sins," I repeated her words to her, wondering if she could hear them now the way I just heard them from her.

Her eyes glistened in the moonlight and her lips trembled as she nodded tightly. "I know. I'm trying to know that."

She kissed me, or I kissed her, fierce and reassuring. When she pulled away, she said, "Let's go inside." She was already climbing off my lap, already tugging at my hand.

"I'm not done. I have more rounds to go," I protested.

"No more games tonight. I need to feel you inside me." She let go of me and started toward the bungalow door, peering over her shoulder at me with a beckoning glance.

I followed after her, because I needed that too.

The rest of my confessions would have to wait.

ELEVEN
ELIZABETH

FUCKING FATHERS.

I could write a thesis paper on douchebag dads, and that was just based on the experience with my own. Now there was Weston's to add to the list. At least mine had never done anything criminal. Not that I knew of, anyway.

I'd been naïve and ignorant not to consider that Weston had good reasons to not get along with his parents. I'd looked at the family portrait, not realizing there was dust and cobwebs hanging on the frame. Not understanding the reason for the pointed pinpricks made from darts thrown at the perfect face of the patriarch. I owed my husband an apology for that. Later, when he was able to hear it.

I did know that all men weren't like this, that there were *good* men in the world—men who didn't prey on weaker people. Men who didn't put themselves above everyone else.

Men who wanted their children and loved them and attended to them. Were part of their lives.

I believed that Weston was a good man. Everything he'd shown me about himself, his character, led me to believe that he was decent through and through, even if he didn't see it about himself. I was sure he would even make a good father—a feeling so strong inside me that it made my ovaries squirm and plead to do their biological job. *Someday.*

Someday.

If we made it through this, and more and more I was thinking that we would, we would make it to that someday. We would settle together and eventually raise children. Raise a family. Prove to each other that we didn't have to follow in our parents' footsteps.

But we weren't ready for that yet. Especially with the walls still between us, walls I could feel crumbling down. I could sense the last of Weston's secrets coming out of him. Like a magician pulling a string of handkerchiefs from a hat, I wouldn't have been surprised if he had kept divulging round after round of secrets in our game the night before.

It had just already been so much. Not for me—for him. I wondered if he even knew how deep these scars ran through him, how badly the betrayal from his father had damaged him. I'd been coming to terms for a long time where my dad was concerned, and I still felt like I was barely getting a grip on it. Weston, the way he kept it all bottled inside, I wasn't sure he'd even scratched the surface of his pain.

So I'd cut him off. I'd put the confessions on pause and brought him inside where I could comfort him with my body. I'd held him while he stretched out over me, wrapping my legs around his hips, taking every bit of anguish that he gave me.

It had drained him, and this morning he'd slept past his normal waking time. He didn't even stir when the waiter brought breakfast. So I'd thrown on a robe and curled up in the wicker armchair next to my sleeping spouse with my iPad.

We had sort of had an unspoken rule for our entire honeymoon to not get on the internet. We were leaving the real world behind, after all. But alone and curious I looked up everything I could find about King–Kincaid and the scandals they'd been implicated in. There were quite a few articles about several different improprieties, but the major headlines pointed to a loan-bundling scheme not unlike the housing default crisis of the early part of the century. Though he repeatedly stated he was only following orders, the blame of this scandal was mostly placed on CFO Daniel Clemmons who had twin adult autistic children, both unable to function outside the home. His wife cared for them full-time.

No wonder Weston felt guilty about it. It was terrible.

I wondered if Weston also realized that Daniel had done what he'd done willingly. That he'd also known it was wrong. My gut said that Weston did understand that, and likely his need to support the Clemmons family while Daniel was in jail had a lot to do with Weston feeling like they were in the same boat—that they were all a sort of club of orphans who'd been destroyed by the bad business choices of their fathers. Perhaps his monthly contributions made him feel less alone in that betrayal.

God, it must have been such a heavy weight for him.

After I'd read everything I could find on the subject, and I wearied of the tight, heavy feeling in my chest, I did a casual check up on all things Dyson Media. There wasn't a lot that I wasn't already up to date on, but I did find a few interesting things.

"What's got your attention so riveted?" Weston asked.

I glanced over to find him sitting up against the headboard, his arms stretching up above his head, showing off his toned torso. It was distracting, but not so distracting that I'd forgotten what I'd been so intensely focused on.

"Did you know that France just changed the regulations regarding pricing structures for children's media?"

Weston rubbed a hand over his scruffy chin. "I feel slightly embarrassed to say that I didn't know that." He was mocking me.

I didn't care. I was too excited about this. "They did. And because they did, everyone's business structures are going to have to change if anyone's going to make any money. Do you think Darrell knew this? Do you think that's why he sold off the children's portion of Dyson Media? I'd chalked it up to him making a malicious decision, but maybe he was actually acting based on insight."

"I don't see that there's anyway you could really know without asking him."

"Mmm hmm. And remember the guy who was rumored to take over as chief programming director? Marc Laurent?"

"Vaguely," he said, his brows knit into a frown. "Wait, are you working? Because I thought this was our honeymoon."

"Just for a second. You were sleeping." I grabbed the iPad and jumped onto the bed, moving up next to him.

"Hell yes. This is what I like to see. Put some porn on that thing. We can watch it together. Be my first."

I felt my cheeks heat but didn't respond. "Word was that Marc Laurent was going to take over as the programming director. It was all but announced. Everywhere. I was totally behind that move. Actually looking forward to it. The guy had great recommendations. And his resume? It was insane. He was beyond well-qualified, he's like a god in the French business world."

"Right, right. Then Darrell hired some nobody instead. Right?"

I'd already fussed to Weston about that several times, as part of my ongoing rant about how my company was being run into the ground while lining my cousin's pockets. "Exactly. But look." I tilted the iPad so that he could see the screen to read the headline: *Famed Television Executive Caught Up in Child Pornography Scandal.*

"Holy shit. Marc Laurent is a pedophile?"

"Innocent until proven guilty, but he's at least embroiled in a pretty major uproar. You think Darrell might've found out about that early on? And didn't want to be tied to it when it went down? It would have caused our stock to tank, I'm sure."

"Again, I can't guess what the guy was thinking. But it's possible. It's possible he made two really good decisions. Or, he just got really lucky."

I put my back against the headboard next to Weston and dropped the tablet in my lap. "One time is coincidental. But twice?"

"Are you starting to change your mind about what you think of your cousin?"

That was going a bit too far. Darrell had iced me out and blocked me from the company on too many occasions for that. But, to be fair, he didn't really know much more about me than I knew about him. "I just wonder if there's more to him than meets the eye."

"There's more to me than meets the eye under this blanket," Weston teased. "If you'd put the work away."

"Your breakfast is waiting," I said. It was already cold, but I thought I should at least mention it to the guy.

Before he could decide if he wanted to eat it now or let it get even colder, my phone rang. "Well, speak of the devil," I said. My phone's ID showed the number was French, and it was one I'd long since memorized—the day he took over my father's company, in fact.

"Darrell. I was just thinking about you," I answered.

"Likewise," he said. Well, that was never good. But in this case, I was hopeful that since my marriage, he was planning on looping me in more on the decisions he was making overseas. He was probably calling to break the Laurent news, so I could praise him on a job well done. Or just to lord it over me that he clearly had inside connections I was not yet privy to.

"If you'd like to set up a time to talk, I'd love to chat when I get back from my honeymoon." I winked at Weston. "But we're a little busy."

"Oh, I'd say so. *We* have been very busy indeed. And I'm not so sure you're going to want to wait on this chat. How much do you actually know about this so-called husband of yours, anyway?"

More than Darrell knew, that was for sure.

"Look. I'm well aware of what went on at King-Kincaid. And I fail to see how that has any bearing on my future with Dyson Media." Annoyance made my voice sharp.

"Call me after you open the email I just sent you, and tell me then just exactly what your plans for the future are, won't you?" I rolled my eyes and navigated over to my inbox. A link popped up on the same business gossip site that was reporting Marc Laurent, only this one had a different headline: *Dyson Media Princess Fairytale Marriage Shattered By Double-Timing King.*

I only clicked on the headline out of curiosity. Both Weston and I were famous enough in our circles to have a gossip spread about us now and then. Most of it was easily dismissible. I was ready to scoff at this.

He'd promised he hadn't cheated, after all.

"Go on," Darrell said, the hint of a smile in his voice. "I'll wait."

The new page that loaded came with pictures of Weston walking into a brownstone somewhere in Brooklyn, from the looks of the neighborhood. There are several shots of him in different angles coming and going. Then a picture of a woman carrying a toddler walking out the same door. "*Less than two weeks after their nuptials, Weston King seems to be stepping out on his new bride, Elizabeth Dyson. Does he have a secret family no one's talking about?*"

I rolled my eyes, not interested in continuing on. There wasn't even any proof the woman came out of the same door that Weston did. There were probably a lot of apartments in the building. This was fake news. Clickbait. That was all.

Until Weston saw the page over my shoulder, and said, "I can explain."

I looked back at the screen. Studied the pictures more closely. It was the outfit that Weston had worn the day he'd left me in the hotel. And the toddler...it couldn't be. But those dimples were unmistakable.

I scanned the rest of the article. *"...a senator's daughter...love child with Weston King."*

My stomach dropped.

"Darrell, we can discuss this after my honeymoon. I have nothing to tell you or anyone else right now." It took every single ounce of determination I'd inherited from my father to say it in a crisp, professional voice. Because inside I was boiling and twisting in knots. Twisted, boiling knots.

When I hung up, I turned to my husband.

"It's true?" It couldn't be. But my heart was hammering, and my mouth suddenly felt like it had so much cotton in it that it could barely open.

"I was going to tell you."

I jumped off the bed, suddenly needing to be away from Weston. From the man I'd so arrogantly thought I knew only moments ago. "Tell me...what? That you have a secret life? You've had a super-secret wife and kid? A secret other family? You said you didn't betray me! You said you didn't cheat!"

"No!" He moved to his knees, and his adamant tone made me hopeful that I had this all wrong. "No, I didn't cheat! I don't have a secret wife. I don't have a secret other family. Just a secret kid."

"Just a kid!" I could feel my eyes widen, could feel my blood vessels opening as indignant adrenaline surged through my body. "You have *a kid*?"

"Yes. I do. A son. He's two."

"You have a two-year-old son and you didn't think that maybe I'd like to know?" My voice cracked. I was surprised, most of all. And outraged. And hurt.

"I was going to tell you," he said hitting the bed emphatically with his palm.

"When?"

"I..." He faltered, but went on. "I was going to tell you today. After last night, I was ready. Before we left—before we went home—you would have known. There was the game we were playing and, and...I just wasn't ready to—"

I cut him off. "You know what I wasn't ready for, Weston? I wasn't ready for the entire internet to know more about my husband than I do." He started to protest, but I put my hand up, stopping him from saying whatever it was he wanted to say. "Did it never even cross your mind that maybe I should have known this *before* we exchanged vows? We had plenty of time during our engagement for you to mention him, or were you too busy pining for Sabrina and arguing about not getting a maid?"

Sometimes I got mean when I got mad. It was a trait I'd inherited from both my parents.

"First of all, I never pined for Sabrina, and you know that." His stern glare dissolved quickly. "And I only found out I had a kid on the day of our wedding."

"You only found out you had a *two-year-old child* on the day of our wedding? I don't understand." I was pacing now, making long, wide arcs around the bed as I rubbed either side of my temple with my index fingers.

"Callie came to me in my dressing room."

"Callie is the senator's daughter?" My belly ached with the familiar way he said this stranger's name. "Are you sleeping with her now?"

"No." Then he said it again, louder. "No! I don't even know her. I hadn't seen her in almost three years, I'm telling you. She just showed up." He was talking fast and frantically, as though he thought I could disappear at any moment. He wasn't wrong. "I thought she was there for the wedding, and she dropped by my dressing room—"

"An ex drops by your dressing room on your wedding day," I muttered. "Only you would think that could be innocent."

Never mind that mine dropped by the honeymoon suite. *We* didn't have a child.

He scooted on his knees closer to me. "I was a wreck of nerves thinking about marrying you. All of my thoughts were tangled in *you*. All my feelings. Everything. Then half an hour before the wedding she shows up—Nate let her in, I think—and she dropped this bomb on me. I didn't have any time to react. Didn't have time to think. Didn't have time to do anything. I had no one to tell—"

I stopped abruptly, leaning forward. I placed both hands on the bed. "You should have told *me*!"

He reached for my wrist but I pulled away before he could grab it. "I know! I was going to. I wanted to. I did, I really did. You were the only person I wanted to tell and I've been dying not to share it. But then you dropped this new bomb about France. About *moving* to France, Elizabeth, and here's Callie who's just told me that I have a kid, and that the only way that I can be part of his life is to actually *be in* his life. A kid that I might love, and I probably do love so much, and I haven't even met him yet. And on the other hand there's you—this woman that I *already* love with everything that I am and couldn't imagine a minute of my life living without, and now I have to choose? I didn't know what to do, Lizzy. I didn't know what to do." There was torment and exasperation in his voice, in his body. In his movement, as he ran his hand through his already tousled hair.

My chest squeezed and pinched, my breath knocked so far out of my lungs it took a moment to speak. "You love me?"

His head tilted to the side, his expression ridiculously soft and warm. "Isn't it the most obvious thing in the world?"

"Maybe. I didn't know, though. You never said."

"I guess I didn't know how to tell you that either. I've never told a woman I love her before."

I could've guessed that about him. But hearing it confirmed made my heart skip and ache all at once. "Well, you picked a fine time to mention it. And by fine time I mean a really terrible time. I don't even know how to deal with those words right now. I'm still trying to deal with this other thing. And I'm mad at you, you asshole! You hurt me by not telling me this." I sniffled, tears close. "But for what it's worth, I love you too."

He smiled, just enough to let that amazing dimple show. "Yeah, that was definitely obvious."

Even now he could be such a fucking charmer. "Whatever. So I wear my heart on my sleeve. Not a bad thing."

"One of the things I love most about you, actually."

"Weston..." A sudden urge to cry crept up along my spine, but I tamped it down. Barely. Wondered if he could hear every bit of confusion and anguish inside me.

"Lizzy. I'm sorry. I'm sorry I hurt you. I never wanted that." He held a hand out in my direction then dropped it, his fist folding tightly. "I want to hold you right now. So bad."

It was tempting. I wanted that too. Wanted to crawl up into the bed and kiss him and let him apologize to me in earnest. Wanted to hear him tell me he loved me a million more times before it became real.

I shook my head. "Fuck. What about Darrell?" We'd worked so hard to make this marriage look believable. "He's aware of the situation already, clearly. What will happen to my claim on Dyson? This makes our marriage look as false as he always suspected it was."

"Tell him that you married a guy who has a kid from a previous relationship. There's nothing unusual about that in this day and age."

He was trying to reassure me, but I was spinning. "It's unusual when the bride doesn't know anything about it. It's going to look like I know nothing about *you*! I *feel* like I know nothing about you."

"You know everything. Everything there is to know about me. I swear. Everything inside me belongs to you now. What else do you want me to tell you?"

"Tell me again why you didn't think you could tell me this as soon as you found out. Because I still don't get that. Like you just said, people come to marriages with children all the time these days. Why did you think you would have to choose between me and your child?" It didn't make any sense. I wasn't going to keep him from his child. Why would he even think that?

"Because..." He sat back on his heels and took a deep breath. "I want to be with you, Elizabeth. I mean that. I want to follow you wherever you go. And you've made it clear that being with you means being in France. But now I have a kid—a kid who needs a father in his life not just on occasion. A kid who lives with his mother. In the United States."

Oh.

Now I saw it.

It was a big problem.

"I think I need to sit down." I made it over to the wicker chair and sank down into it. My father's biggest sin had been not being there. How much of his absence from my life had to do with the fact that he'd resided on a different continent? Maybe if he'd been a different man, it wouldn't have mattered where he'd lived, but it sure had to have been a big part of it.

I certainly wouldn't wish that parental separation on another kid.

Weston stood and wrapped the bedsheet around his waist, then he came and knelt in front of me. "Do you see why I couldn't tell you?" he asked.

I looked down into his blue eyes. "Because you didn't think I would understand this?"

"Because I know you, baby. And you would have told me to choose Sebastian."

Sebastian. The little boy had a name.

I could picture him—the photo from the article only showed him in profile—but even with just that I could see he had Weston's features. His eyes. That dimple.

My husband was right. I would have told him to choose his child. There wouldn't have been any room for discussion. I wouldn't have even bothered with this honeymoon. I'd have sent Weston in the direction of his son's door and told him not to look back.

And, yes, it would have hurt like hell. But parents are supposed to sacrifice for their kids. I'd learned that from my mother.

"I can't tell you to walk away from him," I said, confirming what he already knew.

Weston gathered my hands in his. "But I will. To be with you."

"No, you won't. Because if you were the kind of guy who would do that, you wouldn't be the kind of guy that I'd be in love with. And I am in love with you. Obvious and stupid as it is."

"I know, Lizzy. Me too."

I bit my lip hard, trying to trap the sob inside.

With the sweetest of sighs, Weston pulled me down to the ground and into his arms. "We'll figure something out. This isn't over. We're going to work it out."

I listened while he said, "We're going to figure something out." And then I got up, and I walked into the bathroom.

I listened, but I didn't let myself believe it. I'd learned long ago not to trust men's vague assurances.

I knew who to thank for that lesson.

Fucking fathers.

TWELVE
WESTON

"IT'S NOT a secret that I had a baby out of wedlock, but my father isn't really going to appreciate major press about it." Callie's clipped tone buzzed in my ear like an annoying fly.

I stretched my feet out and propped them on the bed and sank down further into the wicker chair. Just what I needed—two women mad at me. "It's not a major news site. It's a stupid little gossip pit. No one will see it. It's not going to grab network attention."

"It's obviously worrisome enough that you called me about it. And I never had to worry about any of this shit before you came into Sebastian's life."

I rubbed a hand over my face and willed myself not to throw the phone across the room. "It isn't a big deal. I only wanted to make sure that you weren't going to say anything until we had a chance to say something together. Just in case anyone came knocking on your door asking for more information." I could hear my voice getting tight with irritation. "And let's not forget that it was *you* who came into *my* life."

That last bit hadn't been fair, and the timing had been particularly bad since that was when Elizabeth had decided to finally come out of the bathroom. After she'd heard me out, even encouraged me a bit, she'd gotten suddenly cold and sullen and had retreated to the en-suite for a long bath. I'd heard the click of the lock before she got in, signaling that I was not invited to interrupt.

It had probably been about two hours since that door had shut in my face, and now she approached fully made-up, her hair dried and styled in luscious waves that dripped down her shoulders and back. She was wearing a sundress or, a midi dress was what she'd called it when she'd unpacked, a long straight thing without sleeves that hugged around her curves and fell all the way to her ankles. It was crimson and low cut with a giant slit up the middle, and even though I'd been under her skirt many times now, it was the kind of dress that made me want to pull it up and look again.

But her lips were still turned into a frown, and I doubted she appreciated walking out and hearing me talk to my ex-lover. The mother of my child.

I stood up, striding away from my wife. "Look, Callie, like I said, it's not a big deal. Just don't talk to anyone. I'll contact you when I get back to the mainland. Cool?"

"Fine. I wouldn't talk to anyone anyway."

I wasn't really expecting anyone to reach out to her, but, just in case Darrell sent someone, I didn't want anything she said to be misconstrued or twisted in a way that would harm Elizabeth.

I paused now, wanting to say something else, not sure how to ask about someone that I'd never met before.

"Is there anything else?" Callie asked brusquely, and then I could hear it, the gentle sweet chatter of a toddler in the background.

"Is that...him?" It was so weird that my chest could feel both tighter and lighter all at the same time.

"Yeah, he's supposed to be asleep, the goofball." Callie's voice got softer as well, I noticed.

My eyes darted to Elizabeth, because she was the one I always wanted to share things with, which just came naturally. But though her head was tilted and she was obviously watching me, she wasn't glowing the way I felt like I was glowing. But she wasn't hearing what I was hearing either.

And it wasn't her kid.

Could Sebastian ever be part of her family?

The thought that he might never have a place in her life put a damper on the moment. "I'll let you go so you can get him to sleep. Good luck with that. And...him... Give him a hug for me."

"Okay, Weston. I will." She hung up, and again I looked to Elizabeth to see her reaction. This time she gave me a tight smile.

"That was good," she said. "You did good."

I let out a sigh of tension that I didn't realize had been knotting through my muscles. "I just don't have any idea what to do. I don't know how to be a dad. I need you, Elizabeth. I need you to—"

Her expression shadowed. "I can't talk about this right now, please. I need a break from it. I need to get out of this room."

"Oh. Sure. Whatever you need." I hoped I sounded supportive rather than punched in the gut. Which is how I felt. She was always so open and engaging. I didn't like seeing her like this, didn't know how to interact with her when she was closed off. And I definitely didn't want to let her out of my sight, even just for a few hours, but if that's what she needed, I would give it to her.

I would give her anything.

"We have tickets for the harbor cruise tonight. We can still make it if we leave now. You'll want to hurry up and change."

"You want me to go with you?" This time I definitely sounded too eager.

"I said I wanted to get away from *it*, not *you*. It's our honeymoon, you dork." She stepped over to the bed and sat on the edge so she could begin putting on her strappy sandals. "Plus, it would be kind of embarrassing to go on a romantic sunset cruise by myself. So hurry up."

She didn't have to ask again.

GETTING out of the bungalow seemed to lighten the mood, but Elizabeth remained quiet and aloof for the rest of the evening. Neither of us had really eaten during the course of the day, and while I didn't have much of an appetite either, I forced us both to take a full plate of appetizers. The first glass of champagne was served as soon as we'd taken our seats, and with the gentle rocking of the boat and empty stomachs, alcohol didn't make a great addition. Elizabeth nibbled her food, getting down some cheese and pineapple before pushing her plate away.

"You're going to get seasick if you don't eat more than that," I prodded.

But she waved me away dismissively and kept her focus on the guy who was telling us stories about the island and the state of Hawaii in general.

As the sun set, and the night got cooler, Elizabeth wrapped her cardigan around herself. A couple of times I attempted to pull her into my arms under the guise of warming her up, but both times she only leaned on me momentarily before finding a reason to push away: to stretch her neck and peer at a splash in the distance, to reach down and tighten the buckle on her shoe.

I got the hint after that. I left my arm draped along the back of the seat behind her, accepting that she'd wanted me near, but she wasn't ready to let me in. I certainly was the last person to fault her for that.

She relaxed more as we made our way back toward the shore and the entertainment turned from the storyteller to a lone singer with a ukulele, his rich baritone singing the familiar songs of the

Pacific islands. Her muscles relaxed as her thigh finally pressed against mine. Then her arm nudged against my rib cage, and I wondered how I'd ever lived without the heat of her body. How I could ever exist without hers close to mine.

Back at the dock, I climbed down from the boat first, then turned to give her my hand, helping escort her down the stairs. I'd used that as an excuse to hold her hand—since when did I need an excuse?—and then I wrapped my fingers through hers and didn't let go, holding on tightly as we walked back to the beach.

When she didn't pull away, I took it as a sign, and I plunged into the subject we'd been avoiding all evening, the one that had sat like a third person between us throughout the entire harbor outing. "I've never met him, you know," I said, sure without a doubt that she would understand who I was talking about. "It isn't like you, who lived with your father and then he suddenly went away. Sebastian has no idea about me. If he never meets me, it's not going to be the same sort of loss."

She stiffened, attempting to yank her arm away, but I held firm, dead set on keeping this little bit of contact.

Once she realized she was trapped, she sighed and looked out over the water. "He will still miss his father. Orphans, kids who were put up for adoption, children who were abandoned—all the research says they have abandonment issues because a parent has left them. It doesn't matter the circumstances. You would forever change the scope of his life."

I had probably heard that somewhere before. It wasn't the sort of thing I took note of. But I believed her, if she said that it was true.

"And, besides, Weston—I saw you. I saw your face when you just heard him on the phone. Your entire being lit up. You *want* him. Why would you deny yourself that?"

She was looking at me now, hard and deep. So hard and so deep that I thought she could probably see into my pores and capillaries. Behind my eyes and into the very lobes and neurons of my brain.

"Because I want you too," I said, sure that she could see that in all the things that she was looking at inside of me. Sure that it was as plain as the midnight blue sky above us. "I want you that much, too."

We'd reached the sand, and she stopped and faced me with her whole body. "I know that." She squeezed my hand, as though that simple gesture could amount to understanding all the feelings that I contained for her.

I would find a solution. I had to.

"Callie doesn't have a job," I said, suddenly remembering that. "Maybe she could come to France with us. Who doesn't want to live in Paris?"

"You can't just expect someone to pick up and move to another country!" She smiled at herself, hearing the words as they came out of her mouth. "You can't just expect someone who's *not* married to you, I mean. Someone who has no investment or commitment. And do you think that I really want that? My husband's ex-lover, moving across the ocean just because he said so? That's kind of creepy. I would always question why she would be willing to do that for you. It would just be icky all around."

"You sound jealous," I said with a grin that was completely inappropriate for the moment. But jealousy meant she still cared, so I couldn't help myself.

While I was busy gloating, she tugged her hand away and started walking. I trotted right after her, about to apologize when she spoke first. "Hell, yes, I'm jealous. She has a part of you that I don't have. It's not fair."

"Oh, Lizzie." I wrapped my arm around her, even as she bristled. "You think I don't wish it were yours? I would give anything that my first child was with you." I kissed her shoulders and along her neck.

"Really? You want babies with me?" She was pouty and unsure. So vulnerable, and I realized that with all her confessions of when and how she wanted to have children I'd never confessed this to her.

I felt like a vulnerable teenager myself when I said it. "Yes. I want babies with you. I definitely want babies with you. I get this really strange fuzzy feeling all down my spine every time I think about it."

Her lower lip was still pushed out, but her body eased into mine. "Me too. I feel that way when I think about having babies with you too."

We walked quietly for a bit, just enjoying the sand and the beach and the beautiful island night. After a bit, she asked, "How did you know her?"

I was glad she'd asked. Part of me felt guilty for not telling her all this already, but I hadn't known if she'd wanted to hear it. I didn't want to tell it, to be honest. It made me feel shallow and promiscuous. Probably because I *had* been shallow and promiscuous. And though it wasn't news to Elizabeth, I didn't love reliving the details.

Still, it was fair that she knew. I wanted her to know.

"I met her at a rich kid's party in Aspen. She was on a ski trip, but she sprained her ankle their first day in town. I occupied her time while her friends hit the slopes." I paused, considering how best to say the next part. "We didn't leave my hotel room much."

"Got it." She was quiet and I could practically hear the wheels turning in her head. "I...thought you always used condoms."

Ah. "I do. I did. There was a...condom malfunction."

Elizabeth nodded. "I suppose that was bound to happen with your lifestyle."

With that tone, she obviously meant it to be a dig—I could feel the barbs piercing and twisting as the words settled on me.

But I probably owed her at least that one. So I took it, and swallowed the urge to respond.

"Why did she wait until now to tell you? Did she say?"

"She didn't know me. She made an assumption about how I'd react, and didn't even try to tell me. Also, she has issues with dads. I guess that's the 'in' thing these days."

She half-smiled. "And now she's changed her mind just out of the blue?"

I shrugged. "Maybe seeing I was getting married made her think I might actually be family material. I don't really know. I didn't ask. I was pretty overwhelmed with everything going on that day."

"That makes sense." She kicked at a branch of seaweed in our path. "What do you think you would've done if she'd told you before? If you had found out when she was pregnant?"

God, I hated to even think about it. My stomach soured with the acidic honesty. "I think she was smart not to give me the chance to find out. I wasn't ready to be a father until you came along. You're the person who made me finally think about having a home. Finally made me think that I could maybe be good for that. That maybe I *wanted* to be part of one."

"Of course you're good for being part of a home, you silly." She turned her head and placed an open mouth kiss on my neck.

She was right—I was good for being part of a home—but my home was with her. I wasn't anything but scraps of a shallow, promiscuous man without her, and I couldn't be good for anyone—let alone be a good father—in that condition. If I had a future with my son, it simply had to be with her at my side.

"I'll fly back and forth. It will work," I said, determined to figure out the solution to the twenty-ton dilemma weighing down on us.

"That's not going to work," she said immediately. "My father said the same thing. It lasted about three months."

"Elizabeth, I'm not your father."

"I didn't mean to imply that you were. I'm sorry. And I know that you would do better than him." She came up along the steps to the lifeguard station and paused against the railing. "But realistically, Weston. How can you manage a company and spend so much time in the air? Those are long flights. And if you're going to manage the advertising division in France, they're going to need you there."

I stuffed my hands in my pockets. "So I won't manage. I'll take a lower position. I can take a pay cut. Haven't you heard? My wife is, like, a billionaire, and apparently what's hers is mine." Jesus, that felt terrible to say, even in jest.

I immediately regretted it, though I knew Elizabeth would agree to it without batting an eye if I genuinely asked her to.

She furrowed her brows disapprovingly. "Do you really want to give up control of your company? I thought you loved what you do."

"I do. But a beautiful woman told me about making sacrifices, so..."

"I think that's very noble of you. But even with less work, I don't think you understand what you're committing to, going back and forth like that. It's going to get real old, real fast." She hesitated, and before I plunged in with a new argument, she continued. "No. This is not the best option for us. I don't want to be away from you that long. It's not the best way to start a marriage, either."

"You're not helping me here, honey. You keep shooting down everything I suggest."

"I'm sorry. I don't mean to seem so impossible." She swung around the railing to the steps and sat down on the fourth one up. "I've just already thought everything through myself. I've been thinking about every option, all day long—why do you think I spent so many hours in the bath? It's the only thing that's run through my mind since I found out, and it all comes down to the same thing. There's really only one good solution—"

"Do not say that it's splitting up."

"It is an option." Her gaze crashed into mine, holding it with earnest. "At least, for a while. Until you've established a relationship with Sebastian, and I get a better handle on things at Dyson headquarters, it could be—"

"No," I said, adamant. "Not even for a little while. Not an option."

She chuckled. "Just throwing it out there. Anyway, it wasn't what I was going to say. I was going to say that the best option would be for me to get a different CEO to run Dyson. My place is up for sale, but we still have your apartment. We can live there. I don't need to be hands-on with the corporation. It's gone this long without me. I can let the board run it. Maybe Darrell can even stay in charge? If he's doing it under my authority, maybe he'll stop padding his accounts at my expense and pad both of ours."

God, I loved her. I loved her so much. It felt like a living thing inside me, this love, the way that it would stretch and poke at me, the way that it would kick and squirm.

I squatted on the stair below her until I was at her eye level. "There is no possible way to tell you how much it means to me that you would offer that for me. There's also no way that I'm going to let you do it."

"It's not really giving up anything," she protested.

"Elizabeth, everything that you have done since I've met you, everything that you have been working for and toward has been to one day get you to the top of that company. There is no way in fucking hell that I am letting you give that up, especially for a child that isn't even biologically yours."

"It doesn't matter that he isn't from my womb." She reached her hand out and cupped my cheek, the spark of her touch sending a jolt through my nervous system. "He's part of you. That means he's part of me too. That means I want to be there for him. If you let me."

Heat spread through my body, like the sun was out and shining on me instead of the moon. "You undo me, Elizabeth Dyson." It took me a minute before I could say more. "I'm really very moved by that. I didn't know it was possible to love you more, but that right there. That would've done it. But it doesn't change the fact that I can't let you do that. I can't let you leave your dreams behind. You'd get resentful. I don't want to give you a future you resent. That is not what I'm bringing to this marriage."

"You don't know that. I might be perfectly happy. We could have a family of our own, now, too. Instead of waiting, I could get pregnant right away. Maybe this is the universe's way of saying we should start earlier."

I leaned forward and kissed her quick, because having a baby with her was an amazing and beautiful concept, but the timing was so wrong. And I didn't know how many kisses were left before she realized it, too.

"As eager as I am to knock you up, Lizzie, I'm not keeping you from France. We are picking another option. End of story." To further prove that I was done discussing this particular solution, I stood up and scooted past her up the stairs.

This lifeguard stand had the typical lookout chair at the top, but there was a larger enclosure all around it, with a roof and walls that came up mid-torso. I went to the farthest one and looked out at the island behind. A group of people were seated around a firepit about one hundred feet away, laughing and enjoying their evening. Other than that, the beach was quiet and empty.

Elizabeth came up behind me, and placed one hand on my arm as she nestled up to my side.

"It's beautiful tonight," she said.

I turned to look at her profile, studied the way her hair was tossed by the gentle breeze, zeroed in on the spot underneath her ear that I loved to suck on. It was a spot that always made her limp and boneless in my arms.

I was half hard just staring at this gorgeous woman.

Who was I kidding? I was fully hard. A heavy lead bar pressed against the linen of my pants. I was busy working out how I could convince her that we were alone enough to fool around when she grabbed my shirt into her fists and pulled me closer.

"Kiss me," she said, her voice thick and raspy, the way it got when she was aroused.

Fuck, yeah. This was exactly what I wanted to be talking about.

I turned her so that her back was against the wall and trapped her with my hands on either side of her. "Kiss you? Where do you want me to kiss you? Do you want me to kiss you here?"

I bent down to press my lips along her jaw, and she tilted her head back, granting me access to her neck.

"Or do you want me to kiss you here?" I bent lower, sucking at the delicate hollow at the bottom of her throat.

She let out a soft whimper, and my hips pressed against her, my aching cock searching for relief. When the rigid center of my itch rubbed her lower belly, her breath cut sharply.

Jesus, that only made me harder.

I reached up and undid the one button on her cardigan and slipped it off her shoulders, leaving it loose on her lower arms. Then I unbuttoned the top few buttons of her dress, peeling down the red fabric until her breasts stood up white and perky in the dim moonlight. Her nipples were furled knots, sharp and steepled. So tight and aroused, and I could imagine her clit plump and swollen, a perfect companion to the two peaks in front of me.

I leaned in and took one nipple into my mouth, licking my tongue along the tip before sucking the whole of it. "Is that where you want me to kiss you?"

"Mmm," she said, barely a response, as if the words were too much effort.

"Where? Here?" I gave the other nipple the same attention, following it up with a few extra flicks of my tongue against the tender tip. Her knees buckled, and my arms slid around her waist to hold her up.

"Should I get on my knees to kiss you?" I started trailing kisses down her belly, but she tugged at my collar, pulling me up.

"I want to kiss you here," she said, just before her mouth lifted up and closed over mine.

We kissed. With long, luscious strokes, I licked into her mouth as I palmed her breasts, savoring the gasps of pleasure that formed in the back of her throat. I could taste them. Who knew that sound had a taste? This sound did. A taste of hunger and vulnerability and pure fucking lust mixed with straight-up Elizabeth. That's what her gasps tasted like.

Her hands found the bulge imprisoned in my pants. Frantically, she began working at my buckle, magically undoing the belt and the zipper without ever looking down.

That amazing girl, that goddamn brilliant girl, got my pants undone and my cock free before I'd even lifted her skirt, the skirt I'd been dying to get underneath ever since I first saw her wearing it.

"You're in such a hurry," I said, wanting to slow her down, wanting to hold this moment.

"I need to. Need this. Hurry." She massaged my cock in her hand, and there wasn't a way I could argue with her. What Elizabeth wanted, Elizabeth got.

Hurrying my pace, I gathered up the bottom of her dress and flung it over the sides of the wall behind her, and found her pussy bare and glistening. "You've been so good to me, baby. Leaving your panties off. Just like I like it."

She'd done that so often on our honeymoon trip. She was such a good, perfect wife.

"Want to make you happy," she said, tugging mercilessly at my cock with one hand while pulling me nearer with her other at my shoulder.

"Put your elbows on the wall behind you," I told her, wanting to gain control.

With her lips in a slight pout, she did as I ordered. I stepped closer, looking down at her beautiful pussy. Even in the darkness, I could see how wet she was. I took my cock in my hand, and rubbed my crown up and down her folds, splitting her opening so I could see the pink, shining and greedy as it clenched around my tip.

Fuck, she was a goddamn erotic sight. Her tits plump and primed, her dress pulled down just enough to put them on display, her shoulders back, pushing them forward even more. Her skirt thrown up around her waist and over the wall left everything below her midriff naked and exposed to me. My erection was angry and throbbing now, sliding up and down through the wet arousal of her seams.

And she was mine. Forever mine.

It was the first time that I really believed that. The first time I really felt that we were sure. The first time that I was fucking her and feeling like it wasn't about trying to hold onto her, but about knowing we were going to last. Somehow the vision of a future with this sensual, breathtaking creature made me want to not rush through it, but also made me feel spun up with need I could barely contain.

I dragged the head of my cock up to her clit once more and circled it, pressing on her nub until I could see her muscles tense. "You have such a good pussy, Lizzie. This pretty, pretty pussy? One day, I'm going to put a baby in here. Would you like that? If I put a baby inside your pretty pussy?"

"Weston," she begged, her lids heavy. "Please."

Her entire body quivered, and I couldn't take it anymore. I had to be inside her.

Once more, I drew my head back down along her lips until I found her hole, waiting and hot. "Here? Here, Lizzie? This is where I'll put a baby. Would you like that?"

"Yes, please. Do it now. Put it in me now."

It was sex talk. She was on birth control, and she wanted me inside of her—not the baby, not now—but the idea of it, the knowledge that one day I would... It was overwhelming and intense and so incredibly hot.

I thrust inside her. Hard. Again. And again.

"Like that? Right there? Is that where you want me to put the baby?"

She clenched around me immediately, erupting into an orgasm that appeared fierce and mind-blowing, all the while stuttering over and over again, "Yes, yes, yes, yes."

"I'm going to. I will. Right there. Your belly will be so round with my kid. Your pussy will be spoiled with my seed." I told her all this, thrusting into her madly, defining our future, how I would make babies with her, and fuck her, and love her, day after day, night after night. Over and over and over, again and again.

I came with an explosion, white hot and terrifying. It shot through my body, stiffening every muscle, and I grunted as I ground into her, desperate to spill every last drop of myself into her.

When I was done, I held her and kissed her and promised her again that everything would be okay. That I would find a way to keep her and the child that I'd made.

This time, thank God, she didn't push away.

"No, Mom. Gross. Hey, how did you get past the doorman?" I wasn't just trying to change the subject. I actually was curious if I should be concerned about security.

"I have my ways," she said, waggling her brows as I took my seat again next to her. "But seriously. The honeymoon was good? The wedding was gorgeous. Everyone bought it as the real deal. It didn't seem fake at all."

"When that boy made his vows..." Marie paused from pouring the coffee to clutch her heart. "I swooned. I swear on my mother's grave. I actually swooned. I don't care if it was scripted. I don't want to know if it was. Because I swooned."

"He did a really good job," my mother concurred.

And it suddenly occurred to me that there was so much I needed to catch my mother up on.

I took a bite of chicken, deciding that I needed fuel before I tackled the debriefing. After I swallowed, I dabbed at my mouth with a napkin. "The wedding *was* good. I think it did what it needed to do. And the honeymoon was also really nice. Both of us had a really nice time."

"*Really nice time* is code for lots and lots of fucking, Marie," my mother said, exchanging a playful glance with her friend.

"Mom. Stop." I could feel my face heating as Marie set a steaming mug in front of me. "Thank you. You didn't have to do that. You didn't have to bring me lunch either." I offered the last statement to my mother since I knew she was behind it.

"I told you, honey. I missed you!" She smiled fondly at me, studying me too closely, the way mothers do. "You do look good. A little rosy in the cheeks, but otherwise you didn't get too burned, I see."

"I wore lots of sunscreen. And hats. And I stayed in the shade a bunch too."

"Good girl. No skin cancer for you."

"This is a fabulous apartment," Marie said from the kitchen

where she was cleaning out the sink, likely washing up after Weston's breakfast.

"Marie! Don't do that!" I jumped up and swiped the bowl out of her hand.

"It was one dish. I was putting it in the washer for you."

I squinted at her, doubtful she was going to stop at one dish, as I loaded it into the dishwasher myself. "It is a nice place," I said with a sigh as I closed the dishwasher door afterward, looking out over the living room where the sun was shining through the giant windows. As much as I'd bitched about the place, I'd grown to love it. The layout was refreshing. The natural light, spectacular. The memories, irreplaceable. "It's too bad Weston might sell it when we go to France."

Weston's latest plan was to feel out Callie's interest in moving to another country, despite my hesitancy about wanting his ex anywhere near me, and if that didn't work, he was set on traveling back and forth, living a week every month in the States. In that scenario, he wanted an apartment in Brooklyn, closer to Sebastian.

Truthfully, I'd rather have his ex close to me all the time then have Weston alone with her on a regular basis.

But, really, none of it felt like a long-term solution. Nothing felt figured out. Nothing felt settled.

"Sell it?" my mother asked from the table, her mouth half-full of spring roll. She finished chewing before she went on. "Won't Weston want to move back here after the divorce?"

I wiped my hands on the dish towel and pivoted toward her. "There's actually probably not going to be a divorce."

"Heavens, it *was* real!" Marie exclaimed behind me.

"Elizabeth! Are you saying—?" my mother put her hands to her face, a frequent reaction when she was flustered or excited.

"I'm saying that Weston and I are in love." It still felt strange to say that. Strange and dizzying and bright. As though there was a secret light switch hidden somewhere inside me and when it was flicked on, it burst forth a megawatt ray of solar brilliance. And all it took to turn it on was to think of how much I loved Weston. To think of how much he loved me.

My mother squealed and jumped up from her seat so I took the few steps to meet her in yet another embrace.

"Oh my God, that's so wonderful! I'm so happy for you! You're happy, right?" She leaned back to look at me. "Yes, you're so happy. This is amazing. Marie, our baby is really married! I should have worn a better dress for the photos. Thank goodness you looked as spectacular as you did. My God, you really got married!" She swept me up in her arms. Again.

"Yes, Mother. We're happy. It's real. *I'm* happy."

I was also terribly confused. But wasn't that the way with love?

"So then you'll be settling down in France together seriously. You're really going to make a home there." When she let go of me this time, she put her hand to her chest and rubbed the spot right below her throat. "I'm going to have to consider moving overseas. I don't know if I can live so far away from you if you're actually putting down roots."

Though I appreciated that my happiness was a priority for my mother, it was more than mildly annoying that even she didn't consider my move as real without a husband attached. Sometimes she was just as much of a traditionalist as my father had been.

But that battle was pointless considering the thing I was going to say next.

"About putting down roots..." Though Weston had his ideas of what we should do, I still thought my idea was better. "What would you think if we didn't move to France? And we stayed here, instead."

"You know I'd love that, darling. But what about the company?" She tugged at my shirt, straightening it on my shoulders. "Why are you even thinking about this? Does Weston not want to move?"

"No, he's willing to move." I brushed past her and headed back to my seat at the table, wanting to be have space between us so I could talk without feeling so "mom'd." "Just. Imagine that. If we settled down here...we could start a family."

"Angela! Babies!" Marie exclaimed from behind me.

"Elizabeth, are you pregnant?" My mother didn't seem quite as excited as her friend.

"No!"

"You promise? You can tell me if you're in trouble. I don't even think they call it 'in trouble' anymore. But you know I'll understand." She came and sat down at the seat Marie had set for herself, directing her focus completely on me.

"I told you. I'm not pregnant. I'm just saying I could get pregnant. I could put someone else in charge of the company. I could be less hands-on and raise kids instead. I could be a full-time mom. Like you."

Her face scrunched up as much as her Botox and fillers allowed. "Oh, honey. I don't know about that."

That had not been the reaction I'd expected. "Why not? Don't you want grandkids? You were happy not working, raising me. Weren't you?" My heart thumped in my chest, afraid she'd say no and turn my whole image of my childhood upside down.

"Yes. I was," she said to my relief. "Very happy. But you are not me. You would be bored out of your mind. And you fought so hard for your company. You should go to France. You've said for years that you were planning to wait to have kids. I think you should stick with that plan, if you ask me. Is Weston pressuring you otherwise?"

"No. He's not. Sometimes plans change, though. With a new person in my life, I thought I should rethink everything."

"You shouldn't have to rethink your dreams if you've really found the right man. Don't rethink this. You will regret it. Go to France, do your thing, win big, or fail even, and then have your family. You have years for that."

"But, Angela! Babies!"

I glanced up to find Marie had paused from dusting the appliances in the kitchen to make her comment. "Stop cleaning!" I scolded, knowing it was hopeless.

"Babies can wait," my mom said. She smoothed her mostly drawn-in eyebrow with her pinky. "I'm not old enough to be a grandma yet anyway. Unless you're already pregnant. You're sure you're not?"

"I'm sure. Geez."

She narrowed her eyes. "Then what is it? There's something. I can tell. I know you, Elizabeth. What's going on?"

I threw my body back against the chair in a frustrated huff. My mother always managed to bring out teenage behavior from me. "Fine. There's something else. It's Weston. Sort of. He..." There was a part of me that wanted to really throw him under the bus, wanted to make him the bad guy for keeping the secret that he'd kept.

But a bigger part of me realized that if we were going to make our marriage work, I had to treat us like a team.

So I stuck to what was relevant. "He just found out that he has a two-year-old son that he was unaware of until now."

"Oh my God," Marie said, dropping the duster and stepping closer for the gossip.

"I know. It's been complicated, to say the least. He found out on our wedding day."

"Oh my God." From my mother this time.

"Right?" I filled them both in on Callie and her surprise visit, on the bomb she dropped and the dilemma about Weston wanting to be part of Sebastian's life yet also wanting to be with me in France.

When I'd finished, they were both sitting at the table on either side of me, staring at me with wide eyes.

"Are you going to say anything?" I asked, looking at my mother.

I hadn't intended to ask her for advice, but now that I'd spilled everything, I realized I wanted it. Especially since she'd shot down the only solution I'd thought was viable.

"I'm not sure," my mom said glancing to Marie, as though seeking some support before saying something difficult.

I tensed. My mother didn't usually give hard words. I gave her hard words more than she delivered them to me.

"Spit it out, Mom. What are you thinking? Are you thinking it's never going to work? Daddy couldn't handle seeing me and being part of my life so how the hell is Weston going to make it work?"

"I don't think that's fair to say," my mother said, surprising me. "Your father would probably have been a lousy father even if he was on the same continent. He was simply more invested in his business than he was in a family. It's just the sort of man he was. If Weston intends to be a father who is devoted to his son, I'm sure he could work it out."

Again, I felt relief.

But... "Then why are you so hesitant? You seem hesitant. What am I missing?" The way she was cautiously staring at me, I felt like I was missing a whole lot.

She answered with a question, which I hated. "What are the terms of the inheritance again? How long do you have to be married?"

"They're vague. It just says I have to get married. I wanted a solid marriage so that Darrell had nothing to stand on if he chose to fight it in court. What are you thinking?"

"That Weston's secret love child gives you a good reason to want a divorce."

"Mom!" I scooted away from her. "Why would you even say that?"

"Because I know you were worried the marriage might not look real if you got divorced too soon, and I'm seeing this as a way out of that worry. It's actually kind of a lucky break."

"It's not a lucky break if I'm not intending to get divorced anymore. Did you forget that part? Where I said I loved him? And he loved me?" It was my turn to steal a glance with Marie, as I checked to see if she thought my mother was being as insensitive as I currently thought she was.

But Marie looked as though she thought my mother's idea wasn't so bad. "Maybe you should hear your mother out," she said, nodding toward the woman who'd raised me.

"Then tell me already. Quit dragging this out. What is it I'm not thinking of?"

My mother tapped her pink-painted nails on the table, seeming reluctant or unsure of how to proceed.

Then she shifted in her chair and dove right in. "I'm going to just be real honest with you, honey. Marriage is hard. Whoever you are. Whatever circumstances you are in. Especially the first year of marriage. And here you are trying to add a really big job on top of that new marriage. And on top of that, you're adding the additional stressor of moving to a completely new country, which isn't too big of a deal for you because you've spent so much of your life in France, but what about Weston? Then again, on top of all of that, Weston is trying to form a new relationship with a son he just found out about? You will have to build a relationship with that child too, you know. Plus you're adding the stressor of being apart so much. That's a whole hell of a lot of stressors. I'm pretty sure that any good marriage counselor would tell you it's *too many* stressors. How can any marriage work under those circumstances?"

"That is an awful lot of stressors," Marie said, nodding.

I hadn't thought of it exactly like that. Some of it, but not all of it. Not in quite those terms.

I didn't like those terms.

"That's why I suggested living here. It would take out half of the things you just said." My throat was tight though, because I'd already heard her opinion on me living in the U.S., and because I really didn't want to give up being a major part of Dyson Media. And that only left one real option.

"I see," my mother said, patting my hand. She tilted her head and nodded understandingly. "You know that's not going to make you happy, though. You know you're going to be miserable like that."

"But I love him, Mom," my voice cracked and a stupid tear surprised me by rolling down the side of my cheek. "And Weston has never loved a woman until me. It's like we're meant to be. Like we're supposed to have found each other. Supposed to have taught each other how to love. What's it all for if we don't end up together?"

"That's amazingly beautiful. And so very special. Even if it ends, it doesn't mean it won't have been special. Remember that Hollywood movie that came out a couple of years ago? It won the Academy Award. Where the two artists were really in love and they split up because they knew they had to go follow their dream and that they couldn't be together while they did that. They didn't end up together, but in the end they were both really happy because they lived for their dream, and they found other love and it all worked out in the end."

"I hated that movie," I said, my lip trembling.

"It is a really heartbreaking movie, Angela," Marie agreed.

"The point is," my mother said, raising her voice to drown out Marie, "you may very well have been meant to find each other. You may very well have been meant to teach each other how to love. But you might not have been meant to live together forever. I was meant to find your father, and I was meant to have you. But I was not meant to live with that man forever."

"No one was meant to live with that man forever," I said, wiping at my nose.

"You know, honey. If you and Weston have something real, something that's really meant to last, then he'll still be here when you're ready. Go off and run your business for five years or so. Come back and then see if he's waiting. If he is, then you'll know. And if he isn't, then you'll know that too. Real life isn't like a romance novel. You don't always have to end up with the guy."

"I don't think I like real life anymore." I was definitely wishing my real life didn't include a know-it-all mother.

That wasn't true—I was grateful for my mom and glad she'd stopped by. I needed to hear what she had to say, even if I didn't decide to listen to her.

Was I actually thinking of taking her advice?

Nothing she'd said had been wrong. In fact, she'd been very right. About everything. That was the worst part. I wouldn't—couldn't—accept that her plan was the only way forward.

"I need Weston," I said, refusing to give him up so easily. "I need him to help me run the business. He's taught me a lot, but I'm not ready to do this on my own. I need him by my side!"

"Pfft." She waved her hand, dismissing the notion. "You'll hire advisors. You were planning to run the company before you fell in love with him, so why not now? Do you really think Weston's going to have time to give you the kind of attention you think you need when he's focused on being a new dad? Besides, I bet you know more than you think you do. All you need is little confidence."

I rolled my eyes. Confidence would fix everything. Right. She was talking like I was preparing to give a lecture, not run a multibillion-dollar corporation.

She had a point about Weston, though—could I really rely on him to be my pillar of strength, my backbone, and my right hand when he was going to have his hands full figuring out this fatherhood thing? It wasn't fair to him to even expect that. And it wasn't fair to me to not have someone to rely on.

"I don't know what to do," I said, my voice tight with emotion.

"This is a lot, I know," Mom said. "Think about it. Think about all of it. One thing your father was good at was making plans. He looked at every angle, thoroughly researched every option before putting any plan in motion. Follow his lead and do the same."

"It just feels so...cold," I said. "I don't like following his lead."

"Honey, it's your *heart*. Making plans to keep it safe is the opposite of cold. Besides, your dad isn't here to threaten Weston into safeguarding it. Which he certainly would have. I know this inheritance thing feels archaic, but I can tell you—when he put it into place, it was because he assumed you'd be more like me. He thought you'd fall in love and want to spend your time on that. And you have. So now it's time to channel him and make a logical decision about that love, whatever it is."

"Thank you, Momma." I sat with her words for a minute, then added, "I like it when you say nice things about Daddy. I really didn't know him that well, and I forget that he was a good person too, until you remind me. I appreciate that you remind me."

It made it a lot easier to deal with the fact that I was my father's daughter, knowing that he wasn't all bad after all. Knowing that if I made that choice, the choice my mother had suggested, it would make me like my father, but that wouldn't be the worst thing in the world.

AFTER MY MOTHER and Marie left, leaving me with lots to think about, I decided to take at least part of her advice and research all my options thoroughly. I picked up my phone, feeling the weight of the call that I knew I needed to make to Darrell, having promised I would get in touch with him when I was back on the mainland. I still hadn't cleared up Weston's double family. As soon as I did, it took away the option of using Sebastian as a reason for a divorce.

I couldn't do that.

Could I?

I didn't know yet. Maybe. I needed more time to sort out all my alternatives.

So it wasn't Darrell that I called.

"Elizabeth, what a surprise." Clarence sounded genuinely happy to hear from me. "To what do I owe this pleasure?"

"Well, I was wondering something. Did you mean it before, when you offered to help me in any way I needed?" My stomach curled as the words came out of my mouth, feeling as though I were committing some sort of betrayal just by having the conversation.

"Yeah. I definitely did. What do you need?"

"I'm not sure yet."

FOURTEEN
WESTON

I PICKED at a piece of tape on the package sitting on my lap for the fiftieth time then smoothed it back down before pulling out my phone and looking at the clock on the screen. "We're going to be early," I said.

Elizabeth didn't answer, seemingly lost in her own thoughts as she stared out the window of the cab driving over the Brooklyn Bridge.

I understood. This was a lot. A lot to ask of her when she already had so much on her plate. But that was marriage—sharing everything. Sharing the little and the lot, even when the "lot" wasn't bargained for.

It was Saturday. Three weeks since I'd married her. Three weeks since I'd found out I was a father to a little boy. And today, together, we were finally meeting him.

I couldn't decide if I was excited or nervous or was coming down with the flu. I definitely felt like I wanted to throw up.

My knee started bouncing and the present slid onto the seat next to me, bringing my attention to it once more. "Did we get the right gift? I should've gotten the construction set. It had three times the pieces."

I was met with silence. "Elizabeth?"

She turned her head toward me. "What? No. That set was made for a five-year-old. This is perfect. It's age-appropriate."

Age-appropriate. That was a term used at the ad office. Not in my actual life. Not before now, anyway.

Elizabeth covered her hand with mine. "He's going to love it."

I laced my fingers through hers and held on. It was soothing to touch her. And shocking, as though I hadn't touched her in a long time. Since we'd been back from the honeymoon, we hadn't been as connected as we had been before. She seemed more distant, more guarded, but I was sure she was just preoccupied with the overwhelming obligations to the outside world that we now had to face.

There was also much for me to catch up on at Reach, and I still hadn't broken the news to Donovan that I was leaving—mostly because I wanted to have my exact arrangements in place before I did, not because I was afraid of telling him. Not that at all. And Elizabeth was busy packing and arranging the transfer of business. She wanted to be in France before the New Year. Christmas was in two days. It was all happening so fast.

And I still wasn't sure how to be enough. Enough for Donovan. Enough for Sebastian. Enough for Elizabeth.

But I loved her. And I knew she loved me.

And I knew I loved this kid.

And somehow, *that* would be enough. I just hadn't yet figured out how.

I fiddled again with the gift. "Should we have asked for it not to be wrapped with a ribbon? Is that dangerous? Could he choke on it?"

Elizabeth twisted her lip. "I can't remember the exact age that strings stop being a concern. But it's not going to be a problem. We're going to throw away the wrapping as soon as he opens it.

Stop worrying, honey. He's going to love the present and he's going to love you." Her phone buzzed, and she looked down at the cell, her face falling at whatever she read on the screen.

"Is it him again?" I asked, grateful for the distraction of something else toward which to aim my anxiety.

"Yeah." She slid her fingers across the screen, declining the call, and tucked the phone away. "I told him I'd get back to him when we were done with the honeymoon, and I still haven't."

She was talking about her cousin, Darrell. He'd called a few times since he dropped the news about the gossip site that had outed me as a dad, but she'd declined all the calls. "Why don't you just respond to him? Let him know it's not a concern."

She hesitated, taking a slow breath, then letting it out before she answered. "I don't know."

I could understand. How long had I waited to tell her things because it was easier not to deal with it? She already had so much on her mind, it made sense that she didn't want to have a confrontation with her cousin right now as well. "Give yourself a few days then. Talk to him after the holidays."

She opened her mouth, but the car was slowing, so she asked, "Are we here?"

"We are." I looked again at the time. "We're really early. Almost half an hour early." I must've been really anxious when we left.

"Well, we can't sit in here. And it's too cold to stand outside."

"I'll let her know we're here."

Elizabeth settled up the cab fare while I texted Callie. We climbed out of the car and stood on the sidewalk, waiting for her to respond. A tall, muscular woman with thick, straight, dirty blond hair brushed past us and headed up the steps of the brownstone, her arms full of groceries. She glanced back at us, her expression wary.

"You're right that we can't just hang out here. This is the kind of neighborhood where people call the cops on loiterers," I said. Luckily, just then Callie responded.

> No problem. Come on in.

"Here we go, Mrs. King." I shifted the gift under my arm so I could take her hand again.

"Here we go. *Daddy*." Her smile was the confidence I needed. We walked up the steps together.

"SORRY AGAIN THAT we're so early," I apologized as we walked across the threshold into Callie's apartment a few minutes later.

"It's fine. Really. Let me take that, then I can get your coats." She reached for the gift in my hand and set it on the coffee table.

I turned to help Elizabeth with her coat, covertly checking out the room for Sebastian. I didn't see him but saw the woman from outside, the one who'd been carrying the groceries. She was in the kitchen now, putting them away. She must be Dana—Callie's roommate.

I handed Elizabeth's coat over to our hostess, then began to work on taking off my own jacket as I continued to take in my surroundings. When I caught Callie's eye, she said, "He's not up from his nap yet. He should be awake any minute. I can go get him, but he might be cranky."

Maybe I hadn't been so sly in my search for him after all. "Let him sleep," I said, hard as it was to let even another second go by without meeting him. "It will give us time to get the introductions out of the way. Callie, this is my wife, Elizabeth." I put my hand on Elizabeth's lower back, where her waist cinched in just above her luscious ass, and displayed her proudly. I still wasn't used to her being *my wife*. Wasn't used to *having* a wife. I liked saying it as often as I could.

I noticed Elizabeth checking Callie out, her gaze moving up the length of my ex-lover's body before it hit her face. I was sure it was supposed to be as covert as my own examination of the room, and I hoped that Callie hadn't seen it, but my chest broadened and puffed at the obvious hint of jealousy.

"It's such a pleasure to meet you," Callie said, shifting the coats to her other arm so that she could shake Elizabeth's hand. "You must hate me. Showing up in your life the way I did."

"I don't hate you. I don't know you." Elizabeth's honest answer was somehow warm with honesty rather than snappy. "I hope that we can get to know each other, though."

"I'd like that." Callie smiled, then slipped inside the coat closet to hang up our things. When she turned back, she said, "I really hope I didn't ruin the honeymoon. I've had a lot of regret about the way that I approached Weston. I really didn't think I had another way of reaching him, but in hindsight, it was a crappy thing to do to you."

"I suppose..." Elizabeth glanced from Callie to me. "It did change the dynamic of the trip, in a way. But I didn't know about any of this until the internet article came up."

Callie's jaw dropped, and I could feel my neck heat with embarrassment. "Weston! You didn't tell her?" Her eyes cut back to my wife. "And you didn't murder him? Maybe my father is right—miracles do happen."

"I was a coward and an asshole. I didn't want to—" I broke off, realizing that Callie didn't need my excuses, and Elizabeth had already heard enough of them. "Let's just leave it at—cowardly asshole. Thank God, Elizabeth is the most amazing woman I know, and she's been very supportive about all of this." I tugged that amazing woman to my side, wrapping my arm around her waist, hoping she could feel just how much I loved her, how much I appreciated her in this moment.

"You *must* be an amazing woman to have tamed this notorious player," Callie said, agreeing.

The woman in the kitchen snorted, as if trying to hold back a laugh.

"Oh. That's Dana." She twisted her neck toward the kitchen. "Get out here and be friendly, will you?"

"Fine." Dana hung up her reusable grocery bag on a hook on the wall, and then headed over to us. "Nice to finally meet you," she said shaking my hand, eyeing me much the same way that Elizabeth had eyed Callie.

Callie had said she'd been a big help to her, and very supportive. Nannied a bit, if I was recalling correctly. It was nice to see that the mother of my child had someone on her side, so I tried not to take offense.

Elizabeth had a different reaction. "Oh," she said suddenly, as if understanding something that she didn't before. Then her lips pursed together tightly, as though hiding a smile, until it was her turn to shake Dana's hand.

"A real pleasure to meet you," she said to her, even more enthusiastically than she had to Callie. Maybe she was relaxing into the situation. I was too. Though my nerves hadn't calmed completely, the pleasant introductions combined with the scent of fresh coffee brewing made me feel better. It felt like one by one, the unknown factors were fading, and now there was really just the one left.

One big one.

But this was good. Really good, getting all the adult stuff out of the way before Sebastian woke up.

"You haven't had any trouble because of the article, have you?" I asked, since we'd recently been on the topic. "No one tried to bother you or ask more questions?"

"Only person I know who saw it was my father," Callie said.

"He's left me two messages, which I haven't returned yet. *'That's the King who knocked you up?'* I hadn't bothered giving him details before so he'd assumed you were no one he'd know of."

I cleared my throat, trying not to appear too concerned while simultaneously offering up a prayer that our fathers had never done business together. "It doesn't necessarily sound like he's happy now that he *does* know."

"Nah. He's probably glad the press is linking me to a father at all, for once. Especially a guy as reputable as you. It's like a Christmas present for him. Better than whatever no-name 'loser' everyone is assuming knocked me up and left me to do this alone. Or, just as bad in his eyes, getting pregnant from a sperm bank."

Yikes. Her conservative senator father had more issues than *Forbes* magazine. That had to be tough to deal with for Callie in this day and age, where so many children came without a wedding first. Where women chose to become single mothers for no other reason than the fact that they wanted a child. The man really needed to loosen up.

"Can I get you something to drink?" Callie offered. "We have coffee, tea, eggnog—"

"Is it too early for hot toddies?" Dana asked, already heading back to the kitchen.

"It's two in the afternoon, so yes," Callie said.

"But it's the holidays. Anyone interested?"

A little alcohol sure did sound like a nice way to ease the rest of the knots in my shoulders, but I wanted to be a responsible parent.

"I'd like one," Elizabeth said, surprising me.

"Fine. I'll have one too," Callie conceded.

Well, if everyone else was doing it... "Me too."

Dana grinned triumphantly as she put the kettle on.

"Since you opened the door to the conversation," Elizabeth said, crossing one jeans-clad leg over the other as she sat on the couch, "might I ask why you decided to tell Weston at all? He's explained to me your reasons for not telling him in the beginning. What made you change your mind?"

I appreciated my wife for this question. I knew it had to be hard for her to understand Callie's decision. Elizabeth would have been eager to unite a father with his baby, and keeping her pregnancy away from me was not a choice she could easily relate to.

Callie tucked one leg underneath her on the loveseat as she sat down, then glanced at her roommate. "Actually, Dana convinced me."

Elizabeth and I both looked toward Dana, who beamed and said, "Guilty."

"She pointed out that I was being selfish by not giving you a chance," Callie continued. "She also reminded me that this was the age that Sebastian would start realizing that other kids have dads. The most helpful thing she said, probably, was when she pointed out that keeping Sebastian from his father wouldn't change any of the things that happened with me and *my* father. Which, I guess was when I realized I was thinking of myself. Not of Sebastian. And not about Weston. So I reached out." She smiled knowingly again at Dana before changing her focus back to me.

Me, with my own problem father. To think how close I was to never knowing...

"I'm really grateful that you changed your mind. And really grateful to you, Dana, for being such a positive influence, and I can tell you're very important in Callie and Sebastian's life. I'm very grateful to that. For what it's worth."

Next to me, Elizabeth made a little sound, but I didn't understand what she was trying to say, or what she might've been trying to warn me about, so I just took her hand again and squeezed it, guessing maybe she was just moved by the whole situation, much like I was.

"Then this means you're on board? That you're going to be part of Sebastian's life?" Dana was the one who asked, as she brought the first two mugs of hot honeyed bourbon over to us.

I let go of Elizabeth's hand to take my drink, then lifted it to my lips for a sip, delaying my answer. Of course, it was too hot, and I burned my mouth. I had to put it down on the coffee table right away to fan my tongue.

Also, since I'd been asked a question, all eyes were on me through the entire mishap. Dana stood with her arms crossed across her chest, biting back a laugh.

"When they say hot, they mean *hot*. Thank you. I'll let that cool." I watched as Elizabeth wisely set hers down right away. "And yes, I definitely want to do the dad thing." I still was not quite ready to talk about all the details. My dream was to ask Callie to come back to France with us, but I needed to feel out her situation first. As tight as she was with her friend Dana, it was starting to seem like maybe that wasn't the route to go. Besides, it wouldn't be very nice of me to take my son away from his favorite babysitter.

And that left the option of once a month, full-week visits. I wasn't sure how Callie was going to feel about that one either.

"I'd like to try to work out some arrangements before we leave today. But that doesn't necessarily have to be right this second." I looked around the room, at the faces of all the women, hoping someone would be able to steer the conversation in a different direction.

But nobody had anything to say. "Or we can do it now. First of all, though, I want to be able to reassure Elizabeth." My wife sat up straighter next to me, and it almost seemed as though she shook her head, but the movement was so slight I might've misread it. "We are newlyweds and all. I need her to realize that there isn't going to be anything between you and me, Callie. That you have no intentions of creating the family that the internet scandal says exists."

"Weston," Elizabeth said quietly.

I couldn't ignore that; she definitely was trying to get my attention.

"Honey, this is important. I want you to hear it from Callie. You don't mind reassuring her, do you?" Callie had told me to my face that I was a narcissistic asshole. All she had to do was repeat that for Elizabeth.

It even seemed she'd be happy to say it, considering the laugh she was stifling.

Dana was also stifling a laugh, not so successfully.

Elizabeth shook her head more noticeably now.

"What? What's going on?" I asked.

"Weston," Elizabeth said. "I'm not worried."

I smiled patiently. "You say that now. But you'll feel better if you hear it."

Elizabeth sighed. "I mean, Dana and Callie are together."

Right. Together. Good friends.

"*Together*, Weston."

Oh.

More than friends.

No way. "No way," I said. "You're a lesbian?"

Callie nodded.

That explained why there was only one other bedroom besides Sebastian's. "Or, I guess, bi. Because you slept with me." It was important to get the labels correct these days. And bi made me feel better, for some reason.

"Lesbian is really more accurate," Callie said.

"You were the last guy she was with," Dana said proudly. "And she's not going back."

"I—turned you lesbian?" No, no. This was not happening.

Elizabeth took one look at my face and started laughing so hard she was shaking.

"This is terrible. Really, really terrible." I'd never felt so much a champion for the disenfranchised minority as I did right then in a room full of women laughing at me and my sexuality.

"No, it's not," Elizabeth reassured me, through her mirth. "This is good."

"Yeah," Dana confirmed. "I guess I owe you too, Weston King." She pivoted on her boot heel and headed back to the kitchen to pour another two mugs of toddies.

Thankfully mine had cooled enough to drink because, goddammit, I needed it.

As I brought the mug to my lips, I realized what else Dana and Callie's "together" meant—Callie was tied to Dana in a way that was far stronger than friendship. And Dana was a lot more to Sebastian than his favorite babysitter. That meant that asking them to move to France for me was a lot harder. Impossible, probably.

Not that I was ready to give up the idea.

"Dana, so, do you...work?" It wasn't the best attempt at casual conversation, but it was what I had.

"Look at him; he's seeing if you're worthy of me," Callie said. "Better than my father who won't even acknowledge Dana's existence."

I felt a painful stab between my ribs of sympathy for her situation, for being so estranged from her family. I could definitely relate to that. At least they didn't see any ulterior motives in the question.

"Yes, I do." Dana returned with a mug for her partner then sat down next to her on the loveseat. "I work for the State Department. It's actually how we met." She looked at Callie the same way I was sure I looked at Elizabeth. "We were at a party hosted by the state for the senators and representatives and their families."

"Ironic, isn't it?" Callie said. "My father actually brought us together in a way. I'd probably cut off all ties if it wasn't for Sebastian. It's seemed really important to have my family around since he's been born, whether we all get along or not."

The pain in my ribs increased and twisted. My parents still

didn't know about Sebastian. I had to tell them, too. Add that to the list of issues to deal with.

"I'm so sorry your family isn't understanding or supportive. My father was a misogynistic asshole," Elizabeth said, "if that helps. He wouldn't let me have my company until I was married."

The women exchanged appropriate sounds of horror and sympathy while I silently tucked away the idea of having *my* family all together in one country. The State Department was not the kind of job where you could just fill out some papers and transfer from one place to another. You went where they sent you. Besides, people who worked in politics generally liked their politics. It wasn't like Dana could find an easy replacement for that in France.

"Now that she's going to run the company though," I said, using the opportunity to drop the next bombshell, "we have to move to where Dyson Media is headquartered. Which is Paris." I paused a moment, letting that settle. "I know that throws a wrench in what you want in terms of me being available as a father. But I *do* still want to be involved in his life."

Callie stiffened, and next to her, so did Dana. "How do you intend to make this work from a different country?" Callie asked. "Skype? That's not really the kind of involvement I was thinking when I said I wanted you involved in his life, Weston."

"I know. I know," I rushed to calm her. "I've already thought about that and talked it over with Elizabeth. We've decided that I will travel back and forth frequently. I'm going to get an apartment in Brooklyn and spend a week here each month. I was hoping you would agree to let Sebastian be in my care for the full week. After he gets to know me better, of course."

Callie wrapped her arms around herself and bit her lip, glaring at Dana. "That's not really what I'm comfortable with."

"He'll be nearby," Dana said comfortingly. "If he has an apartment in Brooklyn. You will have him for three weeks every month.

That's still the majority. And think of all the extra time we'll get to spend alone together!"

"I can't be away from him for more than a few *hours* at a time already. That's too long. It's too soon. He won't like it either; he needs me. I was thinking more like weekends. A couple days at a time." Callie was visibly rattled.

"Sure, I understand." I *did* understand. I was taking away her child, in a sense.

But he was my child, too.

"Then maybe we could at least agree to share him every day for a week? I could take him during the days and bring him back at night?" It wasn't exactly what I'd been planning or hoping for. Flying across the ocean every month, I really wanted to have as much time as I could with him.

But she'd made a good point about his preparedness. Having almost no experience with kids except that I once was one, I really didn't know what kind of emotional attachment was normal for a two-year-old.

"Yeah, maybe. Maybe that would work." She didn't have time to sit with the idea, because just then a burst of chattering sounded over the baby monitor. "Look who's up. I'll go get him. Be right back."

She rushed off, and I rolled my shoulders back, trying to loosen the sudden tension that had crept up from the conversation and the renewed anxiety about meeting my kid.

My kid.

What if he didn't like me? What if I didn't like *him*?

What if I saw him and couldn't let him go?

"We'll figure it out," Dana said, encouragingly. "Just give her some time. Remember, it's just been her and him. She needs to get used to the idea of sharing that."

I nodded, willing to believe her, but too focused on the terrifying moment approaching.

As Callie walked back into the room, I stood up, unable to sit any longer. My heart was beating so fast I could feel it in my throat. My hands felt clammy and my muscles jittered.

But as anxious as I was, my focus was locked on the little boy in her arms. From the second I caught sight of him, my vision tunneled, and he was the only thing I could see. Nothing anyone said or did could make me look away. The house could be burning down, and I would still be focused on this wonderful, amazing, beautiful little boy.

His hair was long, with curls at the end, similar to pictures I'd seen of myself as a child. So blond in some places it was almost white. His eyes were bright blue under the longest lashes. His lips were incredibly thick and pouty, his face angelic. His outfit looked like something a grown-up would wear—a plaid button-down shirt with khaki pants. One sock was half-falling off his foot.

Elizabeth stood and automatically reached to fix the sock. Sebastian looked down at the woman touching him.

"Sock," he exclaimed, pointing with a pudgy finger.

At the sound of his high, light, tiny voice, it felt like pieces of my chest broke off inside and scattered everywhere, spreading through me like no drug I'd ever known.

Elizabeth watched me with a curious smile on her face, stepping out of the way so that Callie could continue her path toward me to show me my son. "Yep. Sock. That's your sock. And this is your daddy. You see your daddy, Sebastian?"

Sebastian took a second to draw his eyes from his sock to his mother's pointed finger, and then finally to me. He met my eyes and smiled.

I tried to smile back, but my throat felt so tight all of a sudden, it was hard. Inside, my chest did that weird thing again, breaking and spreading throughout me. And my voice was shaking when I asked, "Can I?" I was already holding my arms out toward him.

"Of course," she said. "Want to go to Daddy?"

Sebastian was even smaller than I'd pictured, and I suddenly realized exactly why Callie was so protective. He was hardly more than a baby—I didn't expect him to welcome a strange man. But he surprised me, opening his arms and reaching for me the way I was reaching for him.

I held my breath as Callie let him go, and then I was holding him on my own. Holding my son. He was lighter than I'd thought he'd be. So very light. How could something so little and tiny be big enough to permanently change my life?

My eyes pricked.

He studied me as closely as I was studying him, and the quick rise and fall of his chest reminded me to take my own breath. I let air into my lungs, slowly, taking in every detail of the moment with my indrawn breath. Memorizing this first moment—the first of a lifetime—with my son.

Sebastian reached out with his pointer finger, all his fingers splayed, and touched my chin. "Chin," he said. Then reached higher to try to stick them in between my lips. "Mouf."

"Sebastian!" his mother scolded. "Don't stick your fingers in people's faces!"

I took his arm, pulling it gently away in accordance with his mother's words. "That's right. That's my mouth." I was practically trembling. My kid knew where my mouth was, and it rocked my world. Surely other two-year-olds weren't this smart. He was a genius. A miracle.

I swiveled so he could see Elizabeth. "Look here, Sebastian. This is...Lizzie," I said, quickly deciding that was the easiest thing for him to call her. "Can you say Lizzie?" I didn't know if he could repeat words at this stage in his development, and I didn't care. I was making conversation. *With my son.* We could speak complete nonsense, and I'd be happy.

"Izzie," Sebastian said, pointing to my wife as she stepped up next to him. "Izzie mouf."

Elizabeth let out a happy, tearful sound that made my skin tingle. "He said my name!"

"He did! I want him to say my name." I was greedy and content all at once.

"He'll say it, I bet. Ask him," Callie prompted.

Fuck, my knees were shaking. "Sebastian, can you say, Daddy? I'm Daddy."

The room was silent, all of us waiting and watching for him to perform—poor kid.

Sebastian looked back to his mother who nodded in reassurance. "Go on. Can you say Daddy?"

"Daddy," he said, looking back at me, the d's so light in the middle of the word they were barely there. And when everyone applauded and cheered, he said it again, stronger. "Daddy."

"That's right. I'm your daddy. That's me." I hugged him to me tight, pressing my mouth against his hair. He smelled like baby powder and wet wipes and baby shampoo and by God I was ready to declare the combination my favorite scent in the world.

Except then I looked over at my wife standing next to me, her eyes brimming, and I knew her tropical body wash/perfume scent so well now that I could almost pick it out on the air, and I remembered that *it* was my favorite scent in the world. Especially when it was mixed with the musk of her arousal or the after-smell of sex.

I guess now I had two favorite scents. Two favorite people. Two favorite worlds to build my own around.

Why the hell did loving them both have to be so complicated?

Today wasn't for the complicated parts, though. Today was for the good parts.

I brushed away the worry of the future and sat down on the ground with Sebastian in front of the coffee table. "I brought you something. A present. Do you want to open it?"

I reached over for the gift before he could answer and handed it to him.

His eyes lit up, big and bright. His mouth formed a perfect O shape. "P'esent!" he exclaimed in that toddler voice. He immediately started grabbing at the ribbon, and I looked to Callie to make sure it was okay.

She nodded reassuringly, and sat down on the ground near us.

There was no way he was getting that ribbon off without help, so I tugged it off for him, but then he only wanted to play with it.

"Give it to Mama," Callie said, calling to him.

Sebastian looked at the red ribbon in his hand, contemplating before he happily flung it over to his mother. Then she pointed him back toward me and the gift. I nudged a corner of the wrapping paper up so he could grab it and together we tore all of the paper off.

"Oh!" Sebastian said, pointing to the picture. He was so surprised and pleased, it was written all over his little face. I swelled with pride as he examined it. The box contained a big block LEGO train set.

"I hope he doesn't already have it," I said.

"Nope. He'll love it." Callie gathered the rest of the paper and Dana took it, along with the ribbon, to the kitchen to throw away.

"Tain! Daddy, tain!"

Every time he said *daddy*, my heart did that ricochet, shocking new parts of me to life that I didn't even know had been dead.

"You want to open it? Let's open it." I started to open the box, which turned out not to be as easy as it looked.

"Yeah, they make these things impossible," Callie said.

She was right. Once I got inside the box, it was even worse. All the pieces were fixed to the plastic backing with elastic ties. It was going to take forever to get all fifty-six pieces out of the box.

"Tain. I want tain," Sebastian said, tugging at the pieces unsuccessfully, as his little voice rose in volume.

I managed to get one piece out while Sebastian was grabbing at the others. "Give it to me," Callie said, "I'll work on the rest."

Elizabeth knelt down beside her. "I'll help."

I handed the box over Sebastian's head to his mother. He followed, trying to get at the other pieces while they were working on them.

"Sebastian," I called. "Over here. Look at this." I rolled the single train car back and forth along the coffee table. Somehow that only brought his attention to the bourbon that I'd left there, and his eyes once again widened in delight.

Thankfully Dana swept in and grabbed my mug as well as Elizabeth's, just before Sebastian stuck his hand in. "I'll take those," she said, sticking her tongue out at him.

"Sebastian," I said again. "Look." I ran the train piece again along the table and he watched, mildly interested, but also torn between wanting to find out more about what was going on with his mother and the other pieces. Before I lost his attention totally, I decided to do a little sleight of hand—taking the car, waving it around, and then I made it disappear. "Uh-oh! Where'd it go?"

Sebastian's look of surprise was comical. He grabbed my hand and turned it over, but there was nothing there. Then he grabbed my other hand and examined it with equal intensity. He walked around my entire body looking everywhere for the train car.

"It disappeared!" I said, wiggling my fingers to show that it was nowhere.

Immediately, he started to cry.

"No. No. Don't cry. It's right here." I grabbed it from between my legs where I'd dropped it. "It disappeared but now it's back. See?"

"Disappeared," Sebastian said, his lips still quivering. "Come back."

"Right. It disappeared, but it came back. I'll do it again." I did the trick again, waving my hands, distracting him so he didn't notice the drop. Once again, the tears started the minute the object was out of sight.

"I don't like dis'peared," Sebastian said.

This time, I brought it back quicker. "But it comes right back." He stopped fussing. The third time I did it there were no tears at all, only a big smile when I brought the object back into sight.

"Come back!" he said, taking the car from my hand. He ran the train along the table himself then. "You made come back."

"I did. I made it come back," I told him. Then I pulled him into my arms again, hugging him, tight. Tighter than a squirmy little toddler wanted to be held, because it felt like I had so many hugs to make up for, so much time that I'd missed. I hugged him and I held him, and I breathed him in. And I whispered in his ear, "I'm going to be a good dad, Sebastian. I promise you. Whatever it takes. Whatever you need. And sometimes, maybe I'm going to disappear. But I promise, I'll come back. I'll always come back."

He pulled away, rushing over to claim the new cars Callie and Elizabeth had freed, bringing them back to me. I showed him how they hooked together, feeling the pride swell again when he did it himself. He was so smart. So perfect. And *I made him*.

Yes, I would always come back.

I didn't know how everything was going to work out with all of us just yet, how we would survive the lengths we had to go to in order to all stay together, but I could promise him that at least, and mean it.

Couldn't I?

FIFTEEN
ELIZABETH

WESTON WAS A NATURAL FATHER.

I knew it even before I'd seen him play with my cousin's child back in Utah. And why wouldn't he be? He was a charmer, loved games, and had an easy smile. And a heart so big it was made for parenting.

I was jealous of him, in a way. I didn't know that I had that natural instinct in me—the desire to give and sacrifice for others, especially a creature that could barely communicate. I appreciated conversations with intelligent human beings. I didn't like messes. I liked things neat and orderly.

But how could I not fall in love with that child, that baby boy that looked exactly like the man that I loved so much? Was it just because Sebastian belonged to Weston? Or because he was such an amazing kid in his own right, which he certainly was? Or was it that I wanted a baby of my own, more than I realized?

I didn't know. But I really did want to be part of his life, part of Sebastian's life.

And the shitty thing, the terrible, rotten, incredibly certain thing that I knew after seeing Weston with Sebastian was that I *wouldn't* be a part of his life.

Weston needed to be with his child.

And since I couldn't keep them from each other, I would have to let them go.

It took everything I had not to let the heartbreak show on my face while I watched Weston's heart grow fuller.

We drove back to the city, my husband as talkative and excited as when we'd driven to Brooklyn. He relived every moment with Sebastian, commenting on every single thing the child had said and done, relating the entire afternoon to me as though I hadn't even been there. I understood, and I was happy for him, *so happy for him*, and his endless stream of narration made it easy for me to hide away the turbulent storm of emotion inside me.

Yes, it would have to be faced. Eventually. But I understood now more than ever why Weston had pushed away telling me about Sebastian in the first place, how he'd kept stretching the days of our honeymoon before disclosing the information that would change everything. My frustration over that had drained completely. Because now I was the one keeping my secret plans to myself.

It would wait another couple of days. Until after Christmas. I wasn't going to ruin that for him.

For us.

Before we left Callie and Dana's, we'd made arrangements to see Sebastian again. Dana, it turned out, didn't have any family living close by, her parents both long deceased. Callie's family celebrated the holiday on Christmas Eve. Weston and I had plans to spend the twenty-fourth with my mother and Marie, and we had a standing invitation to his parents' for Christmas Day, which we hadn't yet committed to.

Now we were going to get to spend the holiday with Sebastian, and, with that change in the agenda, Weston wanted to take him to meet his folks. Callie and Dana had agreed, even finding a restaurant in Larchmont that served Christmas dinner so they could drive up with us and have a nice meal out together while we were with the Kings, then we'd all return together. That way, Sebastian wouldn't be too uncomfortable during such a long day without his mother.

All of it had worked out perfectly, everyone agreeing easily, all the stars aligning as though it were meant to be, and with each piece that fell into place I felt more and more secure in the path I had set forth.

If only it didn't have to hurt so much.

But I'd been hurt before, and I would hurt again. At least this time the hurt came from a father who was doing the *right* thing.

It wasn't until we were back at our apartment, after we'd had dinner and Weston had opened a bottle of wine for the two of us that he noticed I was unusually quiet.

"You know, you haven't said much since we left Brooklyn," he said, stretching out on the sofa in the living room. "What's going on in that head of yours, Lizzie?"

I flipped on the lights to the artificial tree, the one Christmas decoration we'd had time to put up. It didn't even have ornaments on it, just a string of white lights, but it set the mood nicely with all the overheads dimmed. Then I turned to face my husband.

"I don't know. Today was a lot, you know? In a good way. I guess I'm just tired now."

"Come be tired on my lap." He set his wine glass down so he could tug off his pullover sweater and toss it to the ground. Now he was just wearing his button-down long-sleeved shirt. Plaid, not unlike the one that Sebastian had worn in miniature form.

Jesus, one day that kid would grow up and look like him. It was almost unfathomable. To imagine those tiny limbs growing and forming into long, muscular, strong, toned arms and legs. Hands that were soft and sweet now, but would become large and capable.

I took him all in once more before wandering over, then I curled up onto his lap, tucking my head under his neck and bending my knees up against us.

Automatically his arms came around me, wrapping me up tight. "That's better," he said.

Weston started kissing along my neck and I leaned my head against my shoulder to give him better access, wondering how many more times I would feel his lips on my skin, how many times I had left where simple kisses would give way to abandoned clothes and tangled bodies.

However many times it was, it wouldn't be enough.

I had to *make* it be enough.

"Tell me something," I asked, as a shiver rolled through my body from his light nip on my earlobe.

"Right now?" His tongue traced along the shell of my ear, sending me into a dizzy wave of euphoria.

"Yeah." I was breathless. But determined. "Tell me what it's going to be like."

He paused to look at me, trying to read my mind by studying my eyes. "What *what's* going to be like, baby?" He slipped his hand under my sweater, the warmth of his fingers against my skin shocking me into a moan. "What it's going to be like when I fuck you? Don't you think it will be better if I show you?"

He bent to kiss me, but I put my finger up to stop him.

"What it's going to be like in the future. Like...this day next year. When our routine is all settled in. When Sebastian knows you and Callie's comfortable with your arrangement and I know what I'm doing with my company and your trips back and forth have just become a normal part of our lives." It was a fantasy, that life was. And I wanted to hear about it anyway. Wanted to live in the fantasy for one night. "Tell me what it's going to be like this day next year."

"Ah," he said. "Well, first, it's going to be amazing. And incredible, mostly because it'll be hard, but hard things are worth it."

He emphasized the word *hard* by lifting up his hips and rubbing the stiff rod of his erection along the curve of my ass.

"They are," I said with a grin. "But tell me the details."

He paused for a minute, thinking. "We'll fly together to the states that month. I'll be so happy to have you with me, instead of the usual long flights by myself. It's so nice to have you next to me instead. Even when we just fall asleep for the entire flight, it feels less lonely."

I nodded. He was already getting into it, switching into present tense and imagining the moment as if it were happening right now.

"We get into town on the twenty-second and sleep most of the day because of jet lag. And we fuck, because you've been working so hard I've barely gotten time to see you. Plus, I just like fucking you. So I'm taking advantage of our vacation before we're intruded upon by the kid."

"Good thinking."

He curled his arm tighter around me and started fiddling with the button on my jeans as he spoke, undoing it and pulling down my zipper. "Then the twenty-third, today—a year from today—we go over to Callie's in the morning to pick up Sebastian. She has a long list of orders and instructions. Even after a year of this, she's still overprotective. But she lets us go eventually. Sebastian is bundled up in a snowsuit from head to toe. One of those outfits that are hard to walk in, his hands are covered and we can barely see his face. He's all puffy like a tiny marshmallow man. Because we're going over to Prospect Park. To go sledding."

"Sledding?" My voice hitched as I said the word, Weston's hand slipping in underneath my panties at the same time. "It's been years since I've been sledding."

"It's fun. Though, you might get wet." He slipped a finger down the seams of my pussy, sledding through the wetness down to my hole before dragging two fingers up again to tease my clit in large lazy circles.

"Go on," I urged, meaning both his story and his hand.

"After the sledding, we go back to our apartment, which is not too far from the park, to get dried off. Sebastian takes his nap. We fool around. Obviously." He smirked, dipping his fingers back to my hole, then returning them to my clit to resume his slow torturous pattern.

I let out a soft moan, the pressure already building and tightening inside me. "What next? What's after his nap?"

"Then we go into the city and see the trains at the botanical garden. Sebastian's so excited by that. It's better than meeting Santa Claus. We have dinner next. Somewhere family friendly. When we get home, Sebastian's wiped out. But he's not too tired to examine all the presents under the Christmas tree."

"When did we get presents? And a Christmas tree?" It was hard to talk with Weston's assault on my pussy. Hard to even think, but the fantasy had to be perfect in my head.

"I had the tree put up the month before. The gifts..." He thought about it a minute, creating a likely scenario. "We enlisted Callie and Dana for that." He was quiet for a few seconds. "Still can't believe they're lesbians."

I nudged him with my elbow. "Stay focused. Go on."

"Go on like this?" he asked, trailing his fingers back to my hole. This time instead of just teasing me at the rim, he stuck them inside, long and deep, curving them until he hit the spot that made my back arch.

"Yes," I hissed. "And the story."

"We're total pushovers, you and I, as parents."

I managed to glare at him—I didn't particularly picture myself as a pushover for anything.

"Okay, *I'm* a total pushover. So we let Sebastian open one gift. It's a stuffed giraffe that he names Dog Man because I'm raising him right. He loves it so much, we can't get him to let go of it, even to get him changed into his pajamas. He wants to sleep with it. So we let him."

"Ahhh." It was really hard to focus on the story now. Weston's hands were too good, the way they plunged in and out of me, his palm rubbing against my clit.

"He doesn't want to stay in his room now, and like I said—pushover—so we bring him in with us. He likes to snuggle. He cuddles up with his head under your chin. I hold you both to me, sniffing his head and his fresh new scent, and kissing your beautiful pouty lips." He added a third finger then, stretching me, filling me the way his dream story of our future was filling me, warming me with this beautiful lie.

"When we're sure he's knocked out, you and I slip out to the living room. You remember to move the elf on the shelf. Thank God. Because I always forget the damn thing."

I giggled, but it came out as a whimper, my orgasm reaching the threshold.

"And then I curl up with you on the couch, and finger fuck you until you're coming all over my hand like the dirty, sexy girl you are."

My body started to shake, and I closed my eyes, ready to lose myself to the entire fantasy.

"Eyes on me, Lizzie."

I turned my head, opening my eyes, my gaze crashing into his, eyes so blue and unwavering.

He sped up the thrust of his fingers and slid his other hand up under my shirt, pulled down my bra cup, and teased my nipple, the whole time keeping his stare locked on mine.

"Just like that, baby. You're almost there. You're so good and tight on my fingers," he praised. "Fuck, when you make those sounds—I could also come on that alone." He rubbed his erection on my ass again, and my eyelids started to flutter, the intensity of the coming climax bearing down on me.

"Stay with me, Lizzie. Stay here."

My eyes shot open again, and this time I pinned my eyes to his. I didn't want to look away. Wanted to keep looking and looking at what I saw there.

Jesus, he loved me. It was written everywhere in his expression, in his face, in his stare, in his voice and hands.

"I love you," I whispered, knowing he heard me. So much. Like his soul was my own soul. Like his heart was my own heart. "I love you," I cried over and over as my orgasm rocked through me, shaking me, tearing me apart, destroying the vision he'd planted in my head with its vibrancy. The words he'd said were false, a dream we'd never have, but these words, this passion, was raw and honest and surging through me.

This was truth. This moment. This feeling. It was truth and it was fleeting. It couldn't last. It wouldn't.

But for this moment, at least, I could look at him, could love him. Could stay with him before I let him go.

SIXTEEN
WESTON

"OKAY?" Elizabeth asked, her head tilted, studying my features as she waited for my response.

It was one word, a simple question, but difficult to answer. We had already had an eventful morning—opening presents with Sebastian at Callie and Dana's had been even more exciting than getting presents myself. It had been hard not to spoil the kid, but luckily the short amount of time had limited us to five wrapped packages.

Even that number of gifts had turned out to be overwhelming, particularly when my little boy wanted each and every one set up immediately. Thank God for four adults buzzing around to help cater to his every whim. The fresh mimosas that Dana made didn't hurt either. I was really starting to appreciate what she brought to our little family.

Then we'd all loaded into the car. Like the first time I'd taken Elizabeth to my parents' house, I borrowed Donovan's Tesla. It was strange how it seemed like an entirely different vehicle with a booster seat in the back, lodged between two mothers. Less sports-car, more practical. Sebastian napped the entire ride to Larchmont clutching onto his baby doll, still his favorite toy despite all his new loot.

Now the five of us stood on my parents' front step, and after several deep breaths, I still hadn't gotten the nerve to knock.

I'd told them I was coming—that Elizabeth and I were coming—but I hadn't told them I was bringing anyone else. I still hadn't told them about Sebastian. I thought that was a conversation better had face to face. Now, however, I was nervous about my decision.

And there were so many other things to say today. My shoulders were tight and tired from carrying all the loads that I needed to lay down.

So was I okay? God only knew.

"Don't you have a key?" Dana asked impatiently behind me.

"Yeah." The last time I'd come, I'd used it. That trip, I hadn't wanted to see anyone. Now it seemed more appropriate to be open about my entrance. "I think it might be more polite, though, to knock."

"Well...?" She pushed again.

I looked to Callie, who was rocking her weight from one foot to the other, Sebastian's head resting on her shoulder, not quite awake from his nap. Then I turned to Elizabeth, who merely shrugged.

I paused too long. With a huff, Dana brushed between me and Elizabeth and knocked herself.

"Well, okay then," I muttered under my breath.

Elizabeth again shrugged, but I saw the smile she was trying to hide.

A moment later, the door opened and there was my sister, dressed in black leggings and a red dress, her blond hair pulled behind her into a low ponytail.

She squealed at the sight of me. "Weston!" Before I could even cross the threshold, she flung herself into my arms, wrapping me into a giant little sister embrace. "I can't believe you came! I'm so happy!"

"I'd be happy too, if you'd let us in the house and out of the cold," I said into her neck.

"Oh yeah! Of course. Come in." She let me go and scuttled backward so that we could walk into the foyer, her brow knitting slightly in confusion when it wasn't just two of us that entered, but four adults and one adorable toddler.

"Elizabeth, I'm so glad you came! I've been dying to get to know you better. I've always wanted a sister. It's not fair that Weston's kept you from me." Noelle lunged at my wife as soon as the door was closed, not even letting her take her coat off first.

Teenagers.

Thankfully, I'd married the most amazing woman on the planet. "I've always wanted a sister too. Only child here. Let's make sure to talk all the shit on Weston before I leave today."

"And every day," Noelle said, conspiratorially.

"But let's get in most of it today," Elizabeth insisted. Probably because she knew we were moving soon and that we wouldn't be around much, no matter what happened with my parents at dinner.

God, I loved this lady.

Next, Noelle turned to the women behind me. "And, I'm sorry. Weston didn't say that he was bringing anyone else. At least, Mom didn't tell me?" Her voice lilted up in a question, leaving room for me to introduce the rest of the guests.

Like on the doorstep, I hesitated again. I had no problem introducing Callie and Dana, but I didn't want to tell Noelle who Sebastian was without Mom and Dad.

"These are some friends of mine. Callie, Dana, this is my sister Noelle." I turned to my sibling. "We drove up together, and now they are going to have dinner at a nice little place in town."

Callie took the cue. "We'd better get going if we're going to make our reservation." She began to hand over Sebastian, so I dropped my coat into Noelle's hands and took him from her.

"Here's the diaper bag. He's at the stage where he sticks his fingers into everything," Dana said. "I left a Ziploc bag inside with some outlet protectors. Make sure you put them in around whatever room you're going to be in if you're going to have him on the floor. Here's his booster seat for the dining room table. There are snacks in the bag as well as wipes and diapers. You have our number. You know how to reach us if you need anything. But, please—" she paused, her eyes suddenly taking on a pleading expression. "Don't need anything. I can't tell you how long it's been since someone else has poured our wine."

"Got it. We'll be fine. I promise." I even sort of meant it. With Elizabeth at my side and in my family home surrounded by my parents and sister I was sure that we could handle a two-year-old.

I turned to Callie. "Thank you so much for trusting me."

She gave me a tight smile that made me wonder if she actually did trust me, but she left in the end, taking the keys to Donovan's Tesla (I may not have told him that was part of the bargain when I borrowed it).

Then I turned back to my sister and Elizabeth. Our coats were hung up now, except for Sebastian's. I stood him up on the bench near the door and began unzipping his jacket.

"So...you're babysitting?" Noelle asked, her face squinting in confusion. "On Christmas?"

"Uh...where's Mom and Dad?"

"In the kitchen. Finishing up with dinner. Seriously. What's with the kid? Practice baby?"

My sister was tenacious.

"Sebastian, this is Noe," I said, introducing my sister with her longtime nickname as I took his baby doll from him and maneuvered his coat off. "Want to say hi to Noe?"

Sebastian's face grew concerned at the meeting of a new stranger while in the midst of a strange house and he sidled up closer to me. "Daddy," he said reaching up for me.

"Is that something he says to all guys?" Noelle asked, "or...?

Weston. Holy shit. Mom's gonna freak." Then she called louder. "Mom!"

"Hey, hey!" I shushed her. "Let's just go in and do this all together. Okay?" I was about to seriously bribe her to get her to shut her mouth.

But Noelle surprised me. "Fine. If this is what got you to come home for Christmas, then fine. But I definitely want to be in the room when you tell Mom she's old enough to be a grandma."

A wave of nausea rolled through my stomach, and I had the sudden urge to flee, but then there was Elizabeth, slipping her hand through mine. Warm, comforting, reassuring.

"You've got this," she said.

And because of her, I knew that I did.

With my free arm, I hoisted Sebastian up onto my hip, and the three of us trailed after my sister into the kitchen to find my parents.

We saw my mother before she saw us, bent over a platter of ham, artistically garnishing it with parsley and cranberries, humming a Christmas carol off-key.

My throat tightened.

I hadn't realized how much I'd missed my mother until I saw her in her element, cooking for her family, the house spruced up to look like a page out of a Martha Stewart catalog. She was happy, and I knew that a good part of it was because she knew I was coming for dinner. How easy it was to give this woman joy. How much had I hurt her these past years by keeping my distance, whether it was justified or not?

Was the pain she'd caused me worth the pain I gave back?

Noelle, impatient and intent on stirring up shit, cleared her throat, announcing our presence.

Mom looked up. "Weston! Elizabeth—is it Elizabeth?" She turned from the meat to wipe her hands on a dishtowel. "Or do you prefer something else? Liz? Beth?"

"Elizabeth is fine," my wife said after glancing at me. I was glad we were on the same page—Lizzie was a name that belonged to me. And Sebastian.

"I was just finishing up here. You're right on time! Dinner is ready, and as soon as my hands are all clean and I get this off, I can give you both a hug." She tugged at the strings of her apron, then threw it on the counter. "There's a bottle of wine chilling on the sideboard in the dining room, and your father is already loading up the table with dishes so we can...oh!" She'd started around the kitchen island to greet us properly, and finally, she'd noticed Sebastian. "Well, who's this little cutie pie?"

"Just wait," Noelle said, saucy and snide as she leaned a hip against the island.

My father chose that moment to enter from the dining room. "I thought I heard you all in here. You shouldn't be in the kitchen. You're the guests! You should be around the table."

His jubilant smile faltered only slightly when he followed my mother's gaze and discovered the little boy in my arms. "It looks like I need to put another table setting out," he said calmly, as though there was nothing out of place with me holding a child.

That helped me to *feel* less out of place holding a child.

"Before you do that, Dad, I was just about to...um..." I looked from one parent to the other, not sure where to start, as always.

Elizabeth leaned over to whisper in my ear. "Should they be sitting for this?"

"Probably." I seriously didn't know what I'd do without that woman. "Do you guys want to sit down?"

"Why don't you just spill it? I'm sure we can handle it." My father was obviously unconcerned with the gravity of what I had to say.

Alrighty then. "Mom, Dad—this is Sebastian. How's this for a Christmas present? He's your grandson."

MY MOTHER DIDN'T FAINT, thank God, but she did cry. So much so that it took twenty minutes of hugging her and letting her hug me and Sebastian before we could finally sit down at the table. By then, much of the food was lukewarm, but no one complained.

Most of the meal was spent explaining how Sebastian had come into my life, what little I knew about him and his mother, plus delivering the blow that I was soon moving to France. The last bit of news set off a new round of tears from my mother, but fortunately we had Sebastian at the table with us. His adorable antics made it hard to be upset about anything for long.

I loved watching my parents dote on my kid. My mother had always been attentive, but I'd forgotten my father's ability to be imaginative and playful. Or maybe he'd just matured. Maybe he was different with a grandchild than he had been with me and Noelle. It was hard to say. Either way, it was possible to overlook a whole lot of grievances in order to be in a room with both my parents and my child.

It occurred to me, in a stupid sort of epiphany, one of those kinds of epiphanies that really should not even be an epiphany, but somehow it shatters the earth when it falls into place, that my father was just a man. A man who had tried the best that he could to be a good father. And maybe on a lot of days he got it wrong, but at least he was there, trying. Unlike Elizabeth's father, who hadn't even bothered to show up.

And here I was, about ready to divide my life between a child and a woman, between two continents. The reasoning made sense perfectly inside me, but one day when Sebastian looked back on it, would he resent me for not doing more for him? For not giving more? Was he going to hold me to the same standard of perfection that I had so long held my dad to?

God, I sure hoped not.

Sometimes we fathers needed to be given a break.

After dinner, we all helped clear the table—well, everyone except my mother, who was too busy oohing and awing over her grandson. Then everyone headed to the living room, but halfway there, I stopped my parents.

"Mom and Dad, can I talk to you for a few minutes?"

Elizabeth picked up the hint immediately. "Maggie, let me take Sebastian and see if he needs a diaper change." She somehow got my mother to relinquish the little boy, and then asked Noelle to show her to a place where she could change him.

Alone, my parents and I headed to the library.

It was strange being in my father's favorite room, not because I hadn't been in there a million times before. In fact, the last time I'd been there I'd been with Elizabeth. Right now, how I longed to be alone with her again, longed to pull her into my lap and bury myself inside her, thank her for always being a warm, safe place.

But I had things to say. Things to get off my chest, and that was what was strange about being in there now. I'd never felt like this room was a place where people actually talked. It was meant for studying and reading. Meant for silence. And here I was about ready to say the most important words I'd ever said in this house. Ever said to my parents.

This time I did make sure they were sitting, and I took the armchair next to my father. I leaned forward, my elbows on my thighs, and gathered my thoughts before I began.

"When I first found out about Sebastian, I freaked out," I said. "I couldn't be a dad. I didn't know the first thing about being a father. And the only people who've taught me about parenting—my own parents—were a million miles away from me, in so many ways. I didn't feel like I could even ask you for help."

My mother shifted on the couch, but she didn't say anything.

"Of course, the reason you were a million miles away was because I put you there. And the reasons I put you there were because of mistakes that Dad made in business. Not because you were actually all that bad of a dad."

My father hung his head and studied his hands. It was progress, considering that the last time we'd talked about the corruption at King-Kincaid, he'd wanted only to defend himself and barely let me get a word in edgewise.

I supposed that was a natural response to being accused of being a terrible person by your son. I couldn't imagine hearing the things I'd said to my dad coming at me from Sebastian. Silently, I promised to make sure he'd never have to.

Could my dad promise that I'd never have to say them again to him?

"The thing is, I don't want to spend forever..." There were a million ways I could finish that sentence. I didn't want to spend forever hating them, blaming them, defending them. Without them.

"I miss you," my voice cracked. I swallowed. Swallowed again when the ball was still lodged at the back of my throat. "But I'm still really mad at you, too."

"Weston, I—"

My mother put a hand on my father's back. "Nash, let him talk."

"I understand some of it, Dad. I understand that you couldn't just leave the company. If you'd taken the fall, everyone who works for you would have lost their jobs when the company fell apart. Maybe you were actually doing the noble thing by staying in charge and helming the ship through the scandal.

"But I don't understand why you would need to have used such unethical practices in the first place. And I don't understand why you let Daniel be the one who suffered for it. It was wrong, Dad. It was a big mistake."

I straightened, letting my pronouncement fall on the room and settle. "It was a mistake," I repeated, "but I get that you're not perfect, that you are doing the best you can. And I forgive you."

God, that felt good to say.

Like a two-ton boulder had been lifted from my back, and I hadn't even realized I'd been carrying it. I'd had no idea how much I needed to say it.

I'd needed to say it so much, I said it again. "I forgive you, Dad. And you, too, Mom."

A choked sob erupted from the couch, but when I looked at my mother, who was indeed tearing up, I realized the sound had come from the person at her side. From the man I'd never seen shed a tear in my entire life. The King of the financial world, my father, was crying.

My mother wrapped her arms around her husband and held him.

My own eyes stung as I fell to the floor in front of them and placed my hands on his knees. "I forgive you, Dad." Apparently he'd needed to hear it as much as I'd needed to say it.

"Thank you, son," he choked out. "That means a lot."

"But forgiving you doesn't fix everything. It doesn't make amends."

He looked at me, intently focused.

"I've been giving the Clemmons family money every month, trying to help them out, but it's not enough. I'm going to give them my trust fund. It doesn't feel right for me to have all that when they've had to sacrifice everything for me to keep it."

"No," he said. "That's your money. I saved that for you."

"I know you did. And I'm giving it to the Clemmonses. Because they suffered for *you*."

He wiped his eye with the flat of his large palm as he shook his head. "No, please. Don't do that. It's not your job to fix this. It's mine."

The ball thickened in my throat. "This was your money. You wanted me to have it. I figure you suffer by me giving it to them."

"That's very noble of you," he chuckled. "But I'd rather suffer by giving your trust fund to Sebastian, if you refuse to touch it. And I'll donate the same amount that's in your fund to the Clemmonses. It's what I should have done all along. I'm sorry I didn't offer it sooner."

"You did have that settlement drawn up for after Daniel got out of jail," my mother said. "Don't forget that."

"You were planning to give him a settlement?" I was more than a little surprised.

"Maggie insisted," he said, looking at my mother. "As soon as she heard the verdict. She also made me put up an anonymous scholarship at the day school that helps care for the twins."

"I hadn't realized," I said feeling the last bit of tension roll off my shoulders. "I didn't realize you were looking out for them."

"You didn't think your compassionate side came out of nowhere, did you?" my mother asked, teasing.

"Eh, let's be clear—he didn't get it from me."

I laughed. At least my dad was honest.

And maybe a better man than I'd given him credit for.

"I'm sorry, Weston," he said. "For a lot of things, but mostly for disappointing you. You're already a better father than I was because you've learned from my mistakes. And you're a good father because you're willing to build your life around him. I'm proud of you."

"Thank you, Dad." My chest burned. "Thank you both. For raising me. For being there, as much as you were. I wasn't there for two entire years of Sebastian's life, and I can't stand how much time I missed with him. It guts me to think of how much of my life I've kept from you." Jesus, I didn't want to be crying.

My mother leaned forward and wrapped her arms around me. "Please just say you won't let us miss anything else."

"I won't," I promised, hugging her. "I won't."

I made other promises too, silent promises, about being a better son and a good dad. Promises to be a good husband and a better human. Not to be perfect—no one could be perfect—but I promised to keep trying.

Because try was all we could do for sure. We could try, and we could forgive.

If we managed that much, then, yeah, we were going to be okay.

SEVENTEEN
ELIZABETH

I TOOK A DEEP BREATH, adjusted my teardrop necklace, then stepped out of the elevator onto the floor of Reach's executive offices. I'd been here a hundred times since that first day almost six months ago. How was it possible to feel so lost when I knew exactly where I was going? So out of place in a setting so familiar?

It was only the day after Christmas, but Weston and I couldn't afford any more time off. We had too much to do. Too much to get caught up on. He'd gone into the office early, and I'd started straightaway into my list of tasks. Movers had headed to his apartment today to pack up and collect my things and prepare them for shipment to France. Then I'd had errands, all in preparation for this afternoon's meeting. Everything had been set in motion, each carefully laid out detail now put in place.

All that was left was this.

And this was going to be the hardest part.

Hard things didn't get easier by dragging feet, I'd learned in my short life. So while I dreaded the upcoming conversation, I still forced myself to head toward Weston's office at a rapid clip, smiling and nodding greetings to his coworkers who acknowledged me on my way.

"Mrs. King! What a pleasure to see you. He knows you are coming?" Roxie stood to greet me and gestured for me to hand her my jacket.

"He doesn't. It's a surprise." And not a very nice surprise. But I didn't mention that.

Roxie frowned. "I'm sure he'd like to see you. He has a four o'clock though. They haven't arrived yet—late. You could probably sneak in a few minutes."

"Actually, I'm the four o'clock," I confessed. "I had my assistant make the appointment so that you wouldn't recognize my voice. To make it a true surprise."

"You have an assistant now! How fancy. I like to see women in power." She hung up my coat in the closet behind her desk and then sat back down.

I just smiled, because I didn't feel very powerful, and though I was sure to have an assistant when I got to Paris, I didn't have one yet. Advisor was his official title. And he'd made the phone call to get the appointment as a favor, not because it was his job duty.

"Can I go in?" I asked, nodding toward the half-closed door.

"Oh. Yes. Should I announce you?" Roxie's hand hovered above the receiver of her phone.

"No. I'm sure he knows who I am."

It took more strength to walk to his doors then I would've thought necessary, and, truthfully, if Roxie hadn't been behind me watching me, I might've turned around and fled. But with her eyes on my back, a sort of unwilling, unwitting cheerleader, I made it past the threshold, and shut the doors behind me.

Weston looked up at the sound of the door click. And the way his face changed when he saw me—it was like finally getting to the Hallelujah chorus of the Messiah with his bright smile and lit eyes.

He looked at me like I was royalty. Like I was fit to bow down to. Fit to kneel in front of.

"Elizabeth, what are you doing here?" He was already up and out of his seat and coming to me. But when he leaned in to greet me with a kiss, I turned my face at the last minute, so his lips landed on my cheek.

I could be cruel, I'd learned. Especially where my love was concerned.

I brushed the incident off, talking quickly as if that was why I'd moved my face. "I have an appointment with you."

"An appointment? You're my four o'clock?" If he was hurt or worried about my rejection, he was now distracted by this latest news.

"Yep. Surprise."

His mouth morphed into a mischievous grin. "Why, Mrs. King. Did you book me for office sex? What a terribly kinky and amazing idea. Why didn't I think of it?" He rushed to his desk and hit the button that changed the windows that looked out into the office from clear to opaque.

I stepped forward, eager to clear up his mistake. "No, no." Though, now I was regretting that we'd never gotten to have office sex. "I have some other things to discuss. Business things. Formality things. I thought this was the best setting for them."

His smile dissolved into a concerned frown. "Okay. Sure. What's up?"

"Why don't you have a seat." God, why did I say that? Everything terrible began with *have a seat*.

But he unbuttoned his jacket and sat down, so I smoothed my hands over the thighs of my pantsuit and then sat in the seat facing him.

It was so weird, sitting with something so big and bulky between us. It hadn't been that long since we'd finally shed our last secrets, since he'd torn down his last walls. After being that close to someone, it was hard to go back.

No. Not going back. We were going forward—toward where we were both supposed to be. I needed to remember that.

I looked around the room, letting nostalgia take me over for a moment.

"Your office is a whole lot less intimidating than the first time I was in here," I said, because it was true. It was the words that were intimidating, not the office. Not the man.

Weston leaned back, relaxing a bit. "I don't know why I was intimidating. I kept my hands to myself."

It hadn't stopped me from imagining them on me. "I meant that I was so naïve."

"You were ambitious."

"*Overly* ambitious?"

He considered. I was sure if someone had asked him then, he would've said yes. Now, he said, "I underestimated you. You've come a long way. You've learned a lot. Your passion alone will take you far, but your knowledge will make you a force to be reckoned with."

"But you were right—I *had* been in over my head. I had no idea what I was talking about when I walked into that meeting with you and Nate and Donovan. It was all show. You had no reason to stand behind a pushy, overzealous poli-sci major. And yet you did."

I caught his eyes across the desk, and they felt penetrating.

Abruptly, he sat up straight and started fiddling with the pen in front of him. "Elizabeth, why exactly are you here today?"

I wasn't ready.

I jumped up and walked over to the bookcases, the ones that opened to reveal the dartboard behind them. When he'd opened them that day and shown me the board, his father's face had been pinned to it.

I chuckled at the face there now. "Donovan?" I wouldn't mind throwing a dart or two at the man myself.

Weston rose and came over to the board with me. Not bothering to remove the staples, he ripped the photo down. "He's the most recent person I've been mad at, I guess. But I'm not really mad at him right now. Not really mad at anyone at the moment."

Not yet.

"Lizzie...?" It was a repeat of the question he'd asked at his desk. Why was I here?

He anchored his hand on my cheek, and I was very aware that he knew something was off, that he wanted to fix it. I could feel his anxiety creeping up like a spider crawling on my pant leg.

"What you did that day—letting me throw darts at my father's face? I don't know that I ever thanked you for that. It was sort of life-changing," I said.

"No, it wasn't."

"It really was. And not just because you told me to throw darts at my father's face, but because you got down on your knee and put a ring on my finger. Not because you loved me, but because you thought I was cool enough to fight the stupid demands of his will. And cool enough to give up your Friday nights to teach me basic business, knowledge that you spent a fortune to learn. All my life, I always thought I wasn't the kind of girl who'd ever find someone who would want to give me that much attention."

His expression was baffled. "Are you kidding me? You were made to be worshipped."

"No one ever treated me like I was until you. Maybe that was my fault, because I hid behind my father, but that's what started to change that day. I started to realize that I didn't have to live in his shadow anymore. *You* did that for me. Pulled me into the sun. And I'm so grateful, Weston."

The words came out slower than I usually spoke. I was choked up saying them. But these were things I really wanted him to know, and what I'd said had only scratched the surface of the universe of gratitude that dwelled within me.

But this was all I knew how to express. It would have to do.

I put my hand over Weston's and twisted my face to kiss his palm before I dropped my arm again.

His eyes sparked as he rubbed his thumb along my cheek. "How come all this feels like something someone says when they're about to die? Are you trying to tell me you're dying, Lizzie?"

Feels like it. "I'm not dying, you jerk. I'm grateful. You changed me. I wanted to be sure you knew."

"Okay. I know." He still seemed hesitant. He wasn't dumb. Then, after thinking a second, he added, "You've changed me too."

"I know," I answered with a smug smile.

"Of course you do. My smart girl. It was your hot brains that I fell in love with, the minute I saw you." He dropped his arm and stuffed both his hands in his pockets. "But this isn't what you came to tell me. And if you didn't come to have sex on my desk, then..."

God, it already hurt. And I hadn't even gotten to the part where I slashed us both open yet.

I walked back to my seat and sat down so I could lean over and dig into my purse on the floor. Weston followed, strolling back to his side, then sinking slowly into his chair.

I can do this. I can do this, I told myself.

"I called Darrell today," I said out loud, still bent over. "Finally. I told him that I hadn't known about your child before we got married." When my fingers closed around the paper I'd carefully folded into thirds earlier, I pulled it out, sat up, and set it on the desk between us. "I explained to him that it was a big blow, naturally—"

"Elizabeth," Weston warned, sensing where I was headed. Trying to head it off.

I raised my voice, undeterred. "And that I couldn't continue to be in a relationship, let alone a marriage, with a man who had lied about something so important. Which he understood."

"No. No, no," Weston said quietly, shaking his head.

He continued repeating the same word, over and over, as I went on. "I went to my lawyer's office next, and filed for an annulment. Marriage based on fraud."

There. I'd said it.

This part I'd rehearsed, though, so it was supposed to be the easy part, and it wasn't easy at all. It was the hardest thing I'd ever told a person in my life.

Now I had to stay strong while the man I loved tried to change my mind.

"Here." I pushed the folded paper across the table toward him.

"I said no." He didn't look at it. He didn't have to. I'd just told him what it was—the proof that I'd begun the process to end our marriage. "Did you hear me?"

I let out a breath. "You can't just say no. That's not how annulments work."

"I don't care how annulments work. We're not getting one." He shoved the paper back toward me. "We've discussed this. This was not an option. You can't get one anyway without losing your inheritance," he added with smug relief.

I had an answer for that. "I worried that was true as well. But my lawyer feels that since the dissolution has occurred through no fault of my own, we have a leg to stand on. He's sure there's enough precedent for me to take charge of the company for the time being, and if it goes to court, we'll likely be nearing my twenty-ninth birthday by settlement anyway."

"That's an awful lot of maybes. What happened to doing everything so carefully, being on guard every minute, taking no chances, so there was no way in hell you'd lose your company? There are possible holes in this route, Lizzie."

I didn't want to say it, but he left me no choice. "The holes are unlikely, but if it comes to that, I'll have to remarry. The court battle will buy me time."

He looked as though I'd slapped him. "You won't do that. You won't marry someone you don't love. Not after us."

"I'll do what I have to, Weston. For both of us."

"I don't accept this."

"Don't make this harder than it has to be." My voice was thinner than usual.

"Elizabeth, don't do this." He gave a pleading smile, just enough to show his dimple.

The sight increased the tightness in my chest. Made me feel like clawing at the air in frustration. Made me feel like shouting from the rooftops that I wasn't doing this because I wanted to.

I picked up the damn paper and held it toward him, my hands shaking. "It's already done. See? Look." He didn't move. "Look!" When he didn't take it I threw it back into my purse. "Whether you look at it or not, it doesn't change the fact that I filed it. It's done."

He leaned forward, putting all his weight on his forearms on the desk. "Then we'll get remarried. The first ceremony was for show anyway. This time we'll do it for real. We'll do the first dance, and we'll cut the cake."

Jesus, he was breaking my heart. "Don't," I said. It was all I could manage. "Please, don't."

Showing him my hurt was the wrong move. He clung to my pain. "You want that, don't you? You can't tell me you don't want that. I can see it in your face. Marry me again. I'll even pick out the ring this time. Just marry me."

I couldn't help myself. "I loved this ring," I said softly.

"Then marry me."

I closed my eyes. Shut them tight against the threatening tears and focused on why I was doing this—for *him*. For Sebastian. I couldn't let that out of my sight.

When I opened my eyes again, I felt stronger. "I wouldn't need another wedding, Weston. The one we had was perfect, and I'll cherish it forever. Now it's time to move on." I wasn't sure how I'd gotten through that statement without my voice cracking when my insides were shattered.

He pushed his lips together in a straight line while he processed.

Then he was done processing and back to refuting. His gaze flew around the room, as though looking for another angle to come at me, then zoomed back to land on me when he'd found one.

"What about the company?" he asked, a spiteful glint in his eyes. "You've learned a lot, but you need someone to help advise you. You're not ready to lead."

"Fuck you," I said, despite knowing his words came from a hurt place. "And I've already thought of that. I've asked Clarence to come to France with me. As an advisor—"

"Clarence Sheridan?" His face puffed up and went red.

"Yes, and he agreed. It's a paid position, of course, a really good opportunity—"

"A really good opportunity to get in your pants." He was mad, and I couldn't blame him.

But I couldn't help defending myself, anyway. "That's assuming I can't take care of myself. That I'd let him into my bed. And if I *do* let him into my bed, that won't be your business anymore. We have to be over, Weston. I'm leaving tomorrow. Clarence will meet me later. You need to be here for your son. And I need to put all of my focus into my company."

He slammed his hand on the desk. "Dammit, we can do both!"

"Maybe we could." I was purposefully quieter in comparison. "But odds are that we can't. And we could do a lot of damage to a lot of innocent people while we're trying."

"So you're just going to give up?" He spit the words at me.

"I'm not giving up. I'm giving us both a better chance." I met his eyes and held his stare for long seconds. They were cold and hard like ice, but I could glimpse the sea underneath and it was rocked with turbulent waves.

I was rocking his ocean. I was the storm on his main.

Fuck, I hated this. *Hated* this. Hated hurting him and me. But mostly him.

Storms pass. He's going to have a better life because of this. With his child. Now was his chance to do right by his son, and I couldn't stand in the way.

"You are going to be an amazing father. You already are. And I want you to know that in an alternate world where my dad was still alive and his company wasn't up for grabs, I know I would have found a way to you anyway. And I would have married you and had a hundred of your babies, and we'd be happy together." Yeah, I was definitely crying now. "I know you'd make me happy forever. I know you would. In a timeline where there isn't this other thing pulling at me. This other obligation. This other responsibility. I'm sorry that we can't be in that world, but it helps for me to believe that somewhere it might exist."

"An alternate timeline, Elizabeth? Let's talk about *this* fucking timeline, okay?"

I cowered at his volume.

"In this timeline, we work best when you're my wife, when I'm beside you. You say I'm going to be a good dad? That's only when you're there. You're my home, remember? You're my queen. I don't work without you next to me."

I shook my head. "Now you're not giving yourself enough credit."

"Elizabeth, don't do this." He got up from his chair and came around to me. "You're reacting too quickly. We haven't even tried anything out yet. You don't know what it's going to be like." He crouched down next to me, but I refused to turn toward him, keeping my body angled forward.

"I *do* know what it's going to be like," I said. "You'd try to make it work for everyone. You're going to try to fix things for me and for Sebastian and you're going to end up sacrificing yourself. Just the same way that you don't want to watch me stay here and give up the things that I want, I can't watch you tear yourself into pieces trying to be everything to everyone."

"I won't. I can do it. I'm stronger than you know."

He tried to swivel me toward him, so I stood up and walked out of the chair the opposite way. "You're strong now. But it will break you down. Give yourself the best shot at fatherhood, Weston. Think about Sebastian. We have to do this for him."

Of course he followed me. "How can I be a good father when I'm a miserable wreck because you've left me?"

He was just a few steps away from me.

I put my hand out to stop him. "I've made up my mind, Weston."

He stopped and stared at me, pleading with his eyes. I could feel his body aching to reach me, just as mine was aching for him.

I couldn't let him get to me. It would undo everything.

It would undo me.

I forced myself to look away, forced myself to go on, finish up. Cut the cord and get out. "I'm not going to pretend this is easy. I'm not going to say that I don't love you. Because of course I do. You know that I do. It's *because* I do that I'm doing this. It's because I love you that I have to let you go."

He took another step toward me, and he was close enough to pull me into his arms.

I took a step back, out of his reach. "Let me go, Weston. If you love me, let me go."

And because I couldn't stand to be there anymore, because I

couldn't take the way his eyes felt on me, and the weight of his love pressing, pressing, pressing on me, I rushed over to grab my bag, then hurried out before he could say anything else. Before he could stop me.

Before he could truly see me break down.

EIGHTEEN
WESTON

I WATCHED her walk out the door.

I stood there, dumbfounded, frozen in place while rage and pain and disbelief swirled through my veins, a wild tempest within me. I heard the muted sound of her voice as she spoke to Roxie, and then it was quiet. Too quiet.

I should have known.

Everything had been too perfect. And she had felt distant. Closed off. And I blamed it on the chaos and the circumstances because I hadn't wanted to believe it was something else. Because I was determined to believe she couldn't be considering this. Never this.

I let the rage and fury have free rein as I swept my arm across the desk, throwing everything on top of it to the floor.

That crash, that explosion breaking through the silence—that was what it felt like was going on inside me. Like noise and thunder and wreckage.

Roxie ran in through the door. "Are you all right?"

I didn't answer her. I just pushed her aside and ran out of the office, hoping I wasn't too late.

I ran down the halls, but when I reached the elevator, the doors were already shutting. I pressed the call button, I pounded on the steel, but she was gone. Unlike that first day I had run after her, this time I didn't catch her.

I turned and leaned against the closed elevator door. I could try to run down the stairs, but that was a long shot. She was gone. I had let her go.

I trod back down the hall, ignoring the looks from the staff, but instead of heading toward my office, I went straight for the lounge. There was a liquor cart there, and I poured myself a drink. I swigged it back in one gulp, then poured another. I snatched my glass and started to leave, had second thoughts and went back for the bottle, taking it with me to my office. If she was gone, I was going to be drunk. There was no way in hell I was going to deal with it sober.

Back in my office, I found Roxie on the floor trying to clean up my mess. "I won't ask what happened, but do you really need to take it out on the office equipment?"

She lifted up the computer monitor and set it on the desk.

"Go home," I growled. And that was an attempt to be friendly.

"I'll finish cleaning this mess up first." Roxie was never afraid of my moods.

She'd never seen this mood though. I shook my head, my whole body moving with the action, and this time I roared. "Go home!"

I'd hired Roxie because she was smart. She proved it when she didn't say another word, just stood up and silently left, shutting the door behind her.

Alone, I sank into my chair and took a big gulp of my drink.

Fuck her.

Not Roxie. Elizabeth.

And not really. I didn't really mean fuck her, I meant fuck her decision. Fuck the idea that she could choose this without me having any say in it.

If she could plan our lives out without my input, then why couldn't I? Why couldn't I choose what happened between us, what our future looked like? I took another swallow, finishing off my glass and then refilled it.

I could. I could choose. Why not?

I could stick with the plan I had before. Move to France. Travel back and forth. What was she going to do if I showed up there anyway? Refuse to see me? If I was living in France three weeks out of the month anyway, would she just refuse to acknowledge my existence?

Not a chance.

I was going, and that's all there was to it.

I marched out of my office toward Roxie's desk. She'd gone now—it was almost closing time anyway, and, like I'd said, she was smart. I was pretty certain she stored unused boxes in the closet behind where she sat.

Turned out, she did.

I grabbed a couple, then returned to my office and began packing things up. I started with my books, the business-related ones. I wanted to have those, especially for Elizabeth, in case she needed to look up some professional information. She could use them in her resource library.

Then I moved on to my desk drawers, cleaning out files and binders. When I'd filled the two boxes, I went and got two more.

I kept packing and drinking until the office was quiet, and I was sure most everyone had gone home. I'd made it to my graphic novels by then, my collectibles. My first edition of The Walking Dead was missing. I tried to remember if I'd loaned it to anyone.

I hadn't. That left one person to blame—Donovan. He was the only one who would mess with my shit.

Speaking of Donovan—I needed to tell him I was leaving.

I tramped out of my office and started toward his, but the dark hallway said he wasn't there. I was desperate to tell him anyway, eager to make it known, so I shouted it out. "I'm moving to France."

"You are?"

I looked to my side and found Nate was still here. I'd missed *his* light on.

"No," I said, sullenly, feeling the loss of my wife all over again. Then I remembered I was going to move to France anyway. "Yes. I mean yes."

Moving to France. It was laughable. *I* was laughable. She didn't want me, and I was chasing after her.

What the fuck was I even doing?

Except she *did* want me. She'd just decided we were better apart.

Lies.

Lies, lies, lies.

I needed to find her. Needed to tell her she was wrong about her decision. Convince her we belonged together.

"I have to go," I said, heading back for my coat.

"To France?" Nate called.

"God, I hope so." I put my coat on as I walked toward the elevator, wondering if I should call for an Uber or if there'd be a cab.

I looked at my phone, meaning to pull up the Uber app, but got distracted when I saw my wallpaper—a picture of Sebastian that I'd taken the day before. "Did I tell you I'm a dad?" I called back to Nate.

I didn't even know if he could hear me anymore; I was almost at the elevator, and I couldn't see him past the dark sections of the hallway.

"That sounds about right," he yelled back.

It did sound right. But it didn't *feel* right without Elizabeth. I had to make her see that, too.

I USED my key to get into her apartment, then shut the door and pressed my back against it while I let my eyes adjust to the dark.

It was only a little after eight o'clock. Fuck, was she even here?

I didn't want to turn on the light and announce my presence in case she was. Not yet, anyway.

I started through the foyer into the interior of the apartment and bumped into the end table, knocking into the boxes stacked on top of it. "Shh," I told them as they rattled, afraid they would crash to the floor. "Shh." Fumbling, I managed to steady them just as the light flicked on.

"What are you doing here, Weston?"

Well, at least now I knew she was home.

I ran a hand through my hair and straightened my jacket, which was rumpled from packing, a general day's wear, and my drunken state. I'd lost my tie hours ago, probably left behind at the office.

A quick once-over of my soon-to-be ex said she'd taken a bath. The bottom half of her hair was limp and damp. She was wearing one of those nighties that always drove me crazy in the early days because of how sexy she looked in them.

They still drove me crazy.

Her eyes were swollen and puffy, and maybe should have been a comfort to know that she was also miserable, but if she was really miserable, then why the fuck was she doing this?

I stormed past her into the living room, pulling the string of another lamp. Everything was gone. The walls were empty, her knickknacks missing. All that was left were a few pieces of furniture and some miscellaneous boxes.

"It's bare in here," I declared. "Like my insides. Scraped out. Gutted." I pivoted to see her reaction.

"I know. I'm sorry," she said wrapping her arms around herself.

Sorry? I was empty. I was hollow, and she was just *sorry?*

"I don't know how you manage that—that—that *ice queen* bit of yours, but lucky you. It's sexy as fuck, how you don't have feelings."

"I have feelings. This is killing me." She said it so quietly it was almost a whisper.

It didn't matter what she said. What she'd done erased anything else, so I pretended I didn't hear her. "It will come in handy when you're ruling your empire. Not having to care about anyone else. Your father seemed to have that figured out. You really are daddy's little girl, aren't you?"

"Fuck you." Her hands were fists now at her sides, her entire body trembling with rage. And with pain, probably.

Good.

I needed to see her hurt. I needed to see her devastated. Like I was.

"You did fuck me. You did." I spun around to take another look at the stark surroundings and tripped on the edge of the couch.

"Are you drunk?" she asked behind me, the sentence lilting in that way that said my actions might be forgivable if I were.

I shrugged. "Sobering up." I ran my hand along the arm of the couch, realizing she was likely getting rid of it. That I also had to make my goodbyes with her belongings and the memories they held. I wouldn't even be able to picture her somewhere far away remembering us when she sat on her sofa or curled up in her bed. She was erasing our entire life together.

"What's going to happen to all this stuff?"

"My personal belongings have already been shipped. Everything that's left is going to be sold or donated." She paused, and I had to give her credit—she was being really patient with me, considering. "Is there anything here you want?"

"You." I twisted to see her response. The deep frown and the creases in her expression, signs she was on the edge of tears, was almost worth it.

"Weston, you should go," she was nearly begging. "This is only making us both miserable."

I stepped—stumbled, maybe—toward her. She backed up. I took another step, steadier this time. She backed up again, hitting the wall behind her. I stopped, a foot in front of her, pleased with how she cowered under my size and dominating posture.

"Tell me you don't love me," I demanded, studying her eyes and her lips.

"I told you I wouldn't say that."

"Tell me it won't feel like a hundred razor blades cutting into you every morning to wake up without me next to you."

She tilted her chin up slightly. "Tell me it won't slice away a piece of your heart every day that you don't get to see Sebastian."

She had me there.

"Look me in the eye, Weston, and tell me a handful of stolen moments every month is going to be enough for you with him. With your parents."

I almost lied to her. Because there was a part of me that believed it *could* be enough. That seeing my kid's face a few hours a day for five days before disappearing again would be plenty.

But the reality was I was already struggling to catch up from my two-week honeymoon at my job. Balancing work and cross-country and intercontinental flights seemed exhaustingly hopeless when I tried to picture it. And after only seeing Sebastian on two occasions, I already missed him like he was a piece of myself that I'd left behind. I supposed he *was*.

But so was she.

And I was just as hollow inside at the thought of how much I was going to miss her.

It was madness. Fucking impossible. I wanted it all, and not because I was an ambitious guy—that had never been me—but because I *loved* too much. I'd never imagined that as my destiny. An ironic ending for a player like me.

Maybe it was better to ice it over like Elizabeth, to go numb, but right now I resented her for being able to shut me out. Resented that she could put up barbed fences and stone walls and live safely alone inside her encampment.

I wanted back in.

I inched closer, careful not to touch her. I studied every feature of her face, every tiny freckle, every tiny pore, features I'd already memorized a thousand times over. My eyes traced down the length of her lashes, past the swollen bags under her eyes, along the slope of her nose to the curve of her lips, down her chin and jaw to her neck where I could see her swallow. I lingered at the neckline of her nightgown, silently cursing its presence for obstructing the view of her beautiful, gorgeous form.

"Take it off," I ordered, wanting it gone, wanting there to be no barriers between us, no oceans, no walls, no flimsy silk material.

"Weston..." She trailed off. She didn't say no.

"I said, take it off."

Her hands moved up to push the spaghetti-thin straps from first one shoulder, then the other. She had to shimmy to get it to fall past her breasts, but a few seconds later it was pooled at her feet.

Her chest rose and fell more quickly now, her nipples perked up as though reaching for me. As though begging for my tongue to lave along their peaks, to ease their ache.

I wanted to touch her, to cup her breasts, to squeeze them and fill my palms with them, wanted to hear her moan and gasp and give her relief.

But she'd said she wasn't mine anymore.

So I kept my hands at my sides, and trailed my gaze down further past the swell of her abdomen to the band of her silk white panties.

"Take them off," I said nodding to them.

She didn't hesitate this time, pulling her panties down her long, slim legs, then kicking them and the nightie aside before standing up to her full height.

I stared at the V between her thighs, the sacred cave I'd buried myself in so many times. There was a glint of moisture along her folds—she was wet. Just from my eyes. Just from my proximity.

How could she really say she could live without me? Without me with her? *In* her?

I placed my palms on the wall at either side of her head, and her breath hitched.

"Undo my buckle. Undo my pants."

Her eyes were sad and dilated, but her hands began the work immediately, quickly loosening my buckle and unzipping my pants, then pulling down my briefs to expose the rigid steel underneath. See? I *had* sobered up.

I slid my hands down, and grabbed her under her thighs, the touch of her skin searing my palms as I hoisted her up around my waist, trapping my cock between us. Using the wall I pushed her high and tilted my hips so that my crown was pointed right at her entrance, so that I could thrust right in, but I didn't do it.

"Put my cock inside you," I told her.

"What?" Her voice was shaking with need.

"Put my cock inside you, Elizabeth. Put me inside you."

Her small hands came to circle around my dick, she angled me the way she needed, then pushed her hips forward, filling herself entirely.

Bright lights smeared across my vision, warmth shot through my body, and I had to force myself to breathe in order not to come right then. She felt so good, warm and tight like sex but also like home. She felt like the warm, tight security of home.

I hugged her closer to me, kissed her face—her jaw, her lips, her chin. Kissed her mouth as I moved in her, frantically trying to plant myself as deep inside her as possible. So deep that she could never get rid of me.

I took each whimper and moan from her, swallowed them into my own body, absorbed her sounds and scent and taste. And when she came, my cock vice-gripped by her pussy, I continued to plunge in and in and in. She could push me out all she wanted, try and try, and I would come right back. And I would stay.

I would stay.

I was sure I muttered that as I ground out my own orgasm, bucking into her with a fierceness that I'd never before used on her body. Shooting stars of light and pleasure exploded through me, and I was almost certain that I was putting every bit of my soul inside her with my semen as I rode out my climax.

But then it was over, and the adrenaline and the hormones settled. And I realized I was still a little drunk, and we were still just Elizabeth and Weston. I still had my soul inside me. It was dwelling right alongside my broken heart.

I set her down, hoping that this had changed something, afraid that it hadn't.

"Don't go," I said selfishly. Because even I couldn't pretend anymore that I was going to be happy dividing my life between France and New York. "This proves we belong together. That we shouldn't be apart. So don't go."

She sighed as she leaned down to gather her clothes. "The only thing this proves is that I know how to spread my legs."

She really was an ice queen. I'd always known she was royalty.

I stepped backwards in a daze as I put myself away, not quite sure what to do next.

Of course *she* knew.

"This isn't mine," she said taking the engagement ring off her finger. She came to me, turned my hand over, and set it in my palm. "You can keep your wedding band. I don't want it back."

She'd paid for the wedding bands. What was I supposed to do with mine now?

Obviously I was going to keep it forever.

I looked down at the engagement ring in my hand. "This is Donovan's, actually," I said, my head foggy.

"Then give it to Donovan." She pulled her nightie over her head, replacing the barrier between us. "You'll be happy together."

With her panties in her hand she turned on her heel and headed toward her bedroom. Over her shoulder she called, "Turn the lights off when you leave, please."

She went into her bedroom, and for the second time that day, she shut the door between us.

NINETEEN
ELIZABETH

EVEN AFTER WALKING into the lobby, waiting for an elevator, and taking it all the way up to my mother's floor, I still felt as cold as I was when I was outside. It wasn't even a particularly chilly day, but my fingers and toes felt numb. And no matter what I did, I couldn't get warm.

Come to think of it, I hadn't really felt warm since I'd left Weston's office the day before. Even a hot bath and the strange goodbye sex had done very little to ease my chill. Was this just how I was now? Permanently cold? Ice through and through? Dead inside?

I wouldn't mind so much if I were really dead inside. If it didn't feel like my chest was being stretched and pulled like taffy at the same time.

Crying didn't help. Sleeping didn't help—I hadn't slept well as it was. I'd tossed and turned all night, missing Weston's body next to me, feeling alone in a deserted bed much too big for one person. I was sure that flying across an ocean wasn't going to help either, but it was next on the agenda, after saying goodbye to my mother.

It took me a few minutes to find her in her apartment. I'd

checked all the usual places before sticking my head into the barely used office.

"What are you doing in *here*?" I asked, as I pushed through the French doors.

She was out of place behind the giant redwood desk. My mother was not the type to do any work that required a flat surface. My mother wasn't the type to do any work period.

She looked up from what she was doing and smiled brightly. "I'm signing checks!"

"You don't have people for that?" I walked deeper into the room, still perplexed by this image of my mother.

She turned the page in her book of checks and went to the next entry, which had already been filled out for her—all except for the signature. "I have people for everything but this. You should always sign your own checks. Oprah says so." She signed another one in a big flourish of cursive handwriting then paused to admire it. "I like doing it. It makes me feel like a celebrity. Signing my autograph over and over again."

I laughed. *My mother*.

She signed a couple more, then shut the book and turned to face me. "How are you feeling today?" she asked, her elbows propped on the desk.

I'd called her, of course, after I'd left Weston's office, and I'd told her everything. And I'd cried, because somehow mothers made it easy to let the tears out. She'd understood and supported me. Was proud of me, in fact. I hadn't told her about his later visit, and I didn't see the need to. It hadn't changed anything, though I was sure she'd understand it too.

I ambled in and sat on the edge of the desk, facing her. "Okay, I guess. Tired." I shrugged in case she wanted more of an answer. I didn't have one to give.

"You can sleep on the plane today. You're still meeting with Darrell tomorrow?"

"Friday."

"Good. It will give you a day to recover. Maybe the swelling in your face will go down by then." She reached up to touch the tender skin underneath my eyes; I batted her hand away.

"Mom," I groaned.

"Wear an ice mask as much as possible. And remind me to give you my cream. It will help." She really was genuinely trying to be helpful.

"Maybe I don't want the help," I said, pouting. "Maybe I like the souvenir." Something to prove to the outside world that my heart was breaking inside.

"Sure. If that's what you'd like." She patted my hand and sat back and looked at me with an inquisitive eye. "Are you really taking Clarence Sheridan with you?"

"You don't think I should?"

"I don't think you need to."

"That's sweet, Mom." It was hard not to laugh. She thought I was Wonder Woman sometimes, that I could do anything. "But even though I know things now, I still don't have any experience. I'm not going to fuck this up by going in green."

"You're trying to be wise. I get it. But Clarence isn't any older than you. Have you looked at his credentials? Does he really know a lot more than you? Is he going as an advisor or a security blanket?"

Hmm. Well.

I hadn't really thought about that. I'd just assumed everybody had more experience than I did. And Clarence had been so eager to do anything I asked.

"If you need an advisor," my mother went on, "hire a *real* advisor. You don't need anyone to help you stand on your own two feet. That's what was stupid about your father and his will in the first place—it showed he didn't value *you*. You all on your own. Don't make the same mistake he did." She pushed her chair back and stood. "Think about it."

"I...will." It was a lot to chew on for some reason. Even though she hadn't said very much, it felt like her words had a lot of meat.

"And Elizabeth," she added, "if you are still miserable when you get over there, then turn back around and come be with Weston."

"Mom!"

"What?"

"You're the one who said to let him go!" Who was this woman? Giving me one line of advice one day and steering me in another direction the next. She had me twisting and turning and chasing my tail.

"I want you to be happy!" she said as though that explained everything. "That's all. And if *this* doesn't make you happy, and Weston does, it's okay to change your mind."

I blew out a puff of frustrated air. "You drive me crazy."

"Well, now I'm going to have to drive you crazy on FaceTime." She put her hand up to bop my nose. I grabbed it and held onto it so that when I jumped off the desk I could easily pull her in for a hug.

"I love you," I said into her neck. I held her for a long time, hugging her tighter than I usually did, letting her hold me tighter than I usually did.

For the first time that I could remember, she was the first to let go.

"You've given me a lot to think about, Mom. Thank you."

"You're welcome, and I love you too." She circled around me and started to walk around the desk. I turned around, meaning to follow her, but stopped to run my hand across the redwood surface, remembering all my years that I'd spent doing homework sitting in that very spot. I'd moved out of my mother's apartment years ago, but I'd still been nearby. Leaving the country was the first time I really felt like I was leaving home.

"You want me to have it sent to you?" she asked.

I looked up. "What? The desk?" I hadn't been considering it. But now that she'd mentioned it... "It was Daddy's."

"Once upon a time. I think you've used it more over your lifetime than he did over his." She fiddled with her earring while she talked. "When he first moved out, you used to sit there for hours. You were so little. The desk was so big in comparison, it practically swallowed you up. I think you were waiting for him to come back."

Always waiting for him. How much of my life had I spent waiting for him?

"Do you remember that?"

"Sort of." It was vague. I'd been really young when he'd left and all the memories after blended together. "I used to write him letters. A ton of them. And I begged you to send them as soon as I'd finished."

"I did, too. I was very good about that. You told him everything in those notes to him. Don't think I didn't read them before I put them in the mail."

Thank God I started mailing them myself when I got older. Half the things I wrote to him were complaints about her. They'd almost been more of a diary than for him. "He never wrote back. I wonder if he even read them. Probably not. I don't even know why I kept writing them. I guess it made me feel close to him somehow. Made it feel like it wasn't my fault. At least I was making an effort even if he wasn't. You know?"

She gave me a sympathetic frown, one that said *I feel bad because you feel bad.* "I'm sorry he couldn't be the man you wanted him to be, sweetie. He disappointed me a lot too. But he made you! So I've always been fond of him for that."

I guess he had done that. And not just biologically. In so many ways I wouldn't be who I was if it weren't for him—for the person he'd been to me.

"Is it time for you to go yet?" she asked.

I looked up at the clock on the wall, an antique with a cuckoo that ticked audibly. "Almost. I'm just going to make sure I got everything I wanted out of here first."

That was code for I needed a few minutes.

She translated the message perfectly. "Okay. Make sure you leave enough time to give me a proper goodbye. I'll be in the living room with my feet up. Maybe I'll get Marie to fill a bowl with warm sudsy water so I can soak my tired hands. Being a celebrity is so much work." She winked, wiggling her fingers in the air, then she turned and disappeared out the doors and down the hall.

Chuckling, I plopped down in the big chair and rolled up close to the redwood desk. It was majestic and sturdy, very masculine in its design and ornamentation. It was probably worth a fortune. I was a full-grown adult, and I still felt so small sitting behind it. So overwhelmed.

Had my father ever felt that way? Had he ever felt tiny in his place? Had his ambition ever scared him the way mine scared me all the time? The way it scared me now?

There was a lifetime of questions I'd wanted to ask him and never got the chance. An encyclopedia of things I'd never get to tell him. So many words left unsaid.

On a whim, I opened up the top drawer and found my mother still kept a box of stationery there. Just like in the old days. I'd usually picked something simple with a modern design, but the light lavender floral would do. What I was intending to write wasn't getting sent anyway.

I took out a single sheet and picked up the pen my mother had used to sign her checks. Then, without thinking too much about it, I set the tip to the paper and let everything out, the words flowing once I started.

DEAR DAD,

There's been a hole inside me since the day you moved away.

Each day we were apart, every year that went by without spending real time with you, that hole grew wider and deeper, leaving a cavernous empty space, so big it left little room for anything else. That was all I was—the shell that you left behind. The little girl you didn't want.

For the longest time, I believed the only way to fill that emptiness would be to get you to notice me. Then, when you died, I thought I could fill it by filling your shoes. By taking your place at the head of your kingdom.

But I've learned I was wrong. I don't need your company to be fixed. I don't need a man at my side or a marriage certificate. The way to fill the hole was learning my worth.

I've learned my worth, Daddy. I've learned my value, something that you couldn't ever quite see. But I can't be mad at you anymore because your ignorance and the way you treated me have forged my path as much as your DNA. You made me who I am, with every missed phone call and forgotten birthday. With every canceled vacation. With every stipulation on my inheritance.

You made me, and I like who I've turned out to be.

Maybe I won't run the company with the same cut-throat ambition and maybe my mistakes will be obvious and irreparable, but I'm going to be okay because I know who I am. I'm a queen. Not because my father was the King of Media—though that too. Not because I married into royalty.

I'm a queen because I decided I would be one.

I love you. I've always loved you.

But I love me now too.

Your daughter, Elizabeth

WHEN I WAS DONE, I dropped the pen and laid my palms flat on the desktop for support. I was out of breath, like I'd just finished an advanced ballet class, and it took several seconds before my heart rate had settled.

But then I felt...good.

Really good.

Like, I really believed what I'd written. That I was going to be okay.

I mean, I still felt heartbroken and devastated about Weston, but it felt like maybe even that might be okay eventually, somehow. With these words written, the future felt less set in stone. More malleable. And instead of being terrified about that unknown, the vagueness of it made it seem less impossible to figure out how to fit Weston into my happy ending.

Mostly, it felt like the chill in my bones was beginning to thaw, and that the anger and resentment I'd been holding against my father for so long no longer fit inside of me. I could finally let it go, and I wouldn't even notice it wasn't there anymore.

The cuckoo came out of the clock then, chirping one o'clock. Quickly, I folded the letter in half and then wondered where to put it. My purse? My pocket? I didn't want to take it with me, though. That didn't seem quite right.

Finally I tucked it in the bottom of the stationery box and shut the drawer again.

Then I ran out to find my mother so I could tell her goodbye. My cab would be here soon to take me to the airport.

"Oh, and, yes," I told her first, before we got all emotional, and I forgot to mention it. "I do want the desk."

"Good!" she exclaimed. "It suits you."

"I know," I said, because I finally did.

TWENTY
WESTON

"BIRD!" Sebastian squealed, slapping his hands emphatically on the tray of the stroller. The few pigeons scrounging for food in the snow nearby ignored his exclamations, apparently too accustomed to the sounds of city life to be disturbed by an excited toddler.

"He's never going to fall asleep," Callie complained, studying him covertly as she walked next to us.

"Yes he is," Dana insisted. She reached over and flicked the canopy down on the stroller, obstructing his view. "Sebastian," she warned. "Lie down. Close your eyes."

"You're supposed to be ignoring him," Callie said through gritted teeth.

"Does this usually work?" I asked, veering the stroller around a slick piece of ice then centering it again on the sidewalk. It was Wednesday, and rather than sit at my desk and dwell on the fact that my wife—soon-to-be never-was wife—was likely boarding a plane and leaving the country at that very moment, I'd texted Callie and asked if I could crash her day.

Dana's office was still closed for the holiday, so she also had the day off. We'd planned to take Sebastian to the park to play in the snow, but he was supposed to have napped and been up by the time I got there. Instead, I'd arrived to find two mothers stressed and frenzied from dealing with an overtired two-year-old who refused to nap.

At her wit's end, Callie had suggested we take him for a walk, bundling him up in his snowsuit and a quilt on top of that.

"The motion usually knocks him out," she said now. "If he's not too distracted."

I wasn't the one distracting him. I'd hoped he'd be the one distracting me. Pushing the stroller, we couldn't even see each other. But there were plenty of other things in the park for him to be interested in—the birds, a bunch of older children building an emaciated snowman, the *squeak squeak* of the stroller tire as it went round and round over the uneven ground.

Actually, that last one was rather mesmerizing. If someone were pushing me in a giant-sized stroller, maybe it would even help *me* fall asleep. I hadn't slept well the night before without Elizabeth, tossing and turning, missing her warmth, my mind replaying every word she'd said, wondering if letting her walk away was the right thing to do. Scared that I was failing a test. Knowing I didn't have any better answers, even if I was failing.

Except I hadn't failed anything. I hadn't given up yet. I was just on hold for the moment. Until I figured out my next move.

"Are you looking for apartments yet?" Dana asked, interrupting me from my broody thoughts. "There's some amazing units in Park Slope over on Union."

I hadn't yet told the women about me and Elizabeth, mostly because once I said it, said that we were over, it meant that I believed it was true. So right now they thought I still needed a place closer to them for my travels back and forth across the pond. I didn't want to lie, but I didn't want to tell the truth either.

So I hesitated.

"Are those two bedrooms over there?" Callie asked while I tried to figure out how to answer.

"I think so. Maybe not available right now. But Claire and Karen are over there and they have the twins so they can't all be one bedroom."

"That's the building with the amazing playroom, isn't it? And oh my God that roof terrace!"

"I'd give my left tit for that terrace."

Turned out if I just paused, I didn't have to say much at all with Callie and Dana around.

A notification from a phone went off, and Callie reached inside her coat pocket to pull hers out. She unlocked her screen and after a few seconds of staring at her phone, she groaned.

"Is it him again?" Dana asked.

"It's not even from him. It's his secretary," Callie answered, stuffing her phone back in her coat pocket.

I slowed the stroller to prevent it from jumping over a bump, then hurried to catch up. "What's going on?" I asked, because I was nosy. And because I'd rather talk about whatever the unwanted notification was than why I wasn't looking for an apartment in Brooklyn.

Callie let out a deep breath, her air forming a cloud as she exhaled. "My father's been picked for the president's Cabinet." She bent down to peer inside the stroller. "He's asleep by the way."

Dana gave a silent golf clap with her gloved hands.

"Congratulations! On both your father and Sebastian. Do we need to head back now?" I could turn around if we needed to, but I was enjoying the crisp air, enjoying being somewhere other than stuffed inside where my thoughts were stifling.

"No, we need to keep going for at least thirty minutes to make sure it sticks," Callie said.

"And no congrats on her dad," Dana added. "When we heard

he was being considered, we were happy at first—it would get him out of the state, and we wouldn't have to see him as much."

The two exchanged a glance over the stroller that I didn't have to see to understand. Though I'd recently reconciled with my parents, it had definitely been tough to rebuild that bridge.

"It's always a strain when we have to do family events, you know?" Callie offered. "Dana always comes with me, and she's so, so gracious, even though he ignores her the entire time. Or worse, says things about gays being the abomination of the Earth."

"That doesn't just affect me," Dana pointed out.

"I know." Callie looked away, and even from behind her, I could sense she felt guilty and torn. "I don't care so much when it affects me. It bothers me that he says it about *you*. And eventually Sebastian is going to get older and hear all this about both of us. It's messy. But I don't want to officially divorce myself from the family, and you don't tell my father how to act or what to say. That's not how he rolls."

"No," Dana agreed.

I thought about that, thought about Sebastian learning how to treat women, how to treat his mother from this terrible role model. It bothered me. My skin pricked, as though I had feathers and they were ruffling, and I debated whether I needed to stomp my foot and make some demands about how much time he spent with his grandfather. Was that even something I could do?

I wasn't sure. It was definitely something we were going to have to talk about more.

"Anyway," Callie said, deciding for me that we were discussing it now, "the president's office is asking for a ton of publicity with this Cabinet position. From the entire family. They want me and Sebastian to go to New Year's parties and campaign events and fundraisers. It's not even my political party. Like, I voted independent." She whispered *independent*, as though some secret government official would hear her and take away her membership to her family. "And since New York is so close to DC, a lot of these events are in town, so we aren't really getting away from him at all."

"It's ridiculous what they expect of you," Dana complained.

"I know. I'm going to have to start telling them no—except that's just going to break my mother's heart and cause a whole scene. I don't know how to avoid upsetting people either way."

Dana turned to face me. "I'm not very helpful. I can't go to any of these. The media thinks Callie is an unwed mother. Be careful, now some of them think *you* are in the picture, thanks to that article. They may start trying to grab you for these."

Callie laughed. "Good thing you have Elizabeth. Tell them *you're* married to someone else, and they won't try to hook us up." She laughed again, and this time Dana joined her.

I definitely didn't laugh. Though, maybe I should have. To someone else, it could be quite a funny situation.

"What's wrong, Weston? You don't find the idea of arranged marriages amusing?" Dana's eyes sparkled.

God, if she only knew.

I cleared my throat, unable to let the truth remain burrowed inside any longer. "Quite amusing, actually. Except, Elizabeth filed for an annulment."

There were exactly four seconds of silence before both of them started speaking at once.

"Oh my God!"

"What? When?"

"You two are ridiculous around each other! So obviously in love! You can't be breaking up!"

"I think I got knocked up just from being in the same room with you together."

Their shock made me feel both better and worse. It validated that Elizabeth and I belonged together, and also made me feel truly shitty for not fighting harder for her.

And now they were both looking at me for an explanation, an

explanation that I felt hard-pressed to give when I barely knew how to explain it to myself.

"It's complicated," I said defensively.

But that was a lie. "Okay, it's not. She has her company in France, as you know. I want to be here for Sebastian, and I'm sure you both realized how terrible the idea of going back and forth is—though I was willing to make it work. I really was. She thought it would be too much pressure on our relationship. And on both of you. And on him."

The silence that followed said that as much as the mothers of my child believed in my marriage, they also understood why Elizabeth did what she did.

For several long moments, the only sound was the fall of our steps on the sidewalk, the hypnotizing squeak of the wheel, and the imagined voice in my head yelling for everything to just stop.

Dana eventually broke the silence. "So why don't we all move to France?"

"Don't joke about that. Please." I was too depressed to even imagine the scenario anymore.

"I'm serious," she said. "Give me a job there, and I'm on board."

"Um!" Her wife exclaimed.

Um! I echoed silently, though I was much more excited about the prospect than Callie sounded. "What do you do exactly? You work for the State Department?"

"I do. I'm in public relations."

She was in fucking PR?

I'd assumed she was a bureaucrat—*but PR?* I owned an advertising firm. "I can totally get you a job! A really good job."

On the other side of me, I could feel Callie nervously fidgeting. "Dana! Shouldn't we *talk* about this?"

"We're talking about it right now. You don't want to move to France?" she asked as though everyone wanted to move to France, which was totally not the way I'd looked at it when I'd first heard the idea.

"I don't know," Callie said, with a tone that said she'd never really thought about it.

"It would get you off the hook with your parents. Get me out of this job—which we both hate. They legalized same-sex marriage there years before the U.S. did."

Callie's head bobbed back and forth, considering. "Universal healthcare," she said dreamily.

"No school shootings." Dana spoke the words as though they were candy.

To be honest, that sounded enticing to me, too.

"I don't think the education system is that good, I'm sure I read that somewhere." Callie pulled her phone out of her pocket, and I assumed she was looking this fact up.

"We'll do private school. *Everyone* does private school in Europe. It's all the rage."

"Are you speaking out of your ass or do you know this?" Callie glared at her spouse.

"Does it matter?"

Callie turned to face me. "It's all good, Weston. The education will be fine. Dana's right. We'll do private school."

I shrugged. Education was the last thing on my mind. The kid was two. "I'm still so new to this parenting thing, I barely have time to realize I should be worrying about something before you guys are telling me it's okay."

"This one *is* okay. I'm generally always in a state of worry," Callie told me.

"Noted." I paused for a fraction of a second. "Can we go back to talking about moving to France? Because you guys can't just yank my chain on this one. I was seriously going to ask if you'd consider it before, but when I realized you were together, and that you had a job, Dana, I didn't think it would even be an option." I was getting excited. Too excited for something that we were just bouncing around.

"You should always ask, Weston," Dana said seriously. "For no other reason than because I love shooting people down. Especially Callie's ex-lovers."

Callie stifled a giggle.

I was not laughing about this. "Are you shooting me down right now?" I asked, staring Dana straight in the eyes.

She stared across the stroller. "Callie?"

They were taking it seriously. I could feel the brevity of the moment, the weight of this decision pressing down on me, knowing that if they just said *yes*, every bit of pressure that had been piled onto my shoulders would immediately evaporate.

"I'd pay for all moving expenses," I said, desperate. "And help you find a place to live. You could stay with me and Elizabeth until you found your own apartment. I haven't seen ours yet, but she says it's humongous, and I'm guessing it's probably quite nice. Used to be her father's. I'm sure there's more than enough room for everyone."

Callie made a humming noise like she couldn't believe she was even thinking about this. "This isn't something we should be deciding on a whim."

Dana's eyes were bright, excited, the way I felt inside, bubbling like a lava lamp. "No, we probably shouldn't. But isn't it awesome that we have the means to be impulsive? If we want to be?"

I stopped the stroller, unable to move until this tension was unraveled.

"I don't know when we'd have the chance to be this impulsive again," Callie said, coming to that conclusion slowly.

Dana nodded. "We should do it. Raise our kid in France and open ourselves up to new experiences and adventures. We should totally do it."

She and I both looked to Callie, waiting with bated breath.

Slowly, Callie's indecisive expression eased into a smile. "You only live once," she said.

I suppose that meant yes, because then Dana and Callie were hugging each other and kissing, and it was probably pretty hot, but all I could think about was turning the stroller around, getting back to my apartment, packing up, and getting on a plane so I could get to my wife as soon as humanly possible.

When the two of them finally broke apart, they held hands and looked at me. "What do we do next?" Callie asked.

I didn't hesitate for a second. "We go to France and get my wife back."

I CAUGHT a cab and headed back to the city, but instead of going to my house to pack a bag and make arrangements, I went to the office first. There was someone I had to deal with, someone I should have dealt with a while ago.

It was still early in the afternoon, so fortunately Donovan was in his office. I could see him through the clear glass, and he wasn't on the phone, so I strode right by his secretary, walked in, and shut the door behind me.

"I'm in love with Elizabeth. I married her for real, and we're going to stay together." I probably could have called, but I wanted to see the look on his face when I told him this.

Except he just leaned back in his chair, crossed one leg over the other, ankle resting on the opposite knee, and said, "I know."

"What do you mean you know?" How could he possibly know? Even Elizabeth didn't know as of right now.

"You went off-script at the wedding. Said your own vows. That had to mean something. Had to mean you'd fallen for her. And doesn't every woman fall for you?" He cocked his head, smugly.

"Every woman doesn't...no." *Did they?* I wondered. *Didn't matter*. Elizabeth did. "Yes. She's in love with me too." It irritated me that he had this figured out already. But not enough to dim my mood. "Invoice me for your ring. I'm keeping it." I'd debated getting her a new one, but there was sentimental attachment to this. It was the one I'd already proposed to her with, and she'd told me she loved it. It was part of our history, and I was eager to put it back on her finger and didn't have time to get another one.

"Sure thing." He raised a brow. "Anything else?"

"And I have a kid." He *definitely* didn't know about that.

"I know."

Fuck him.

"How? I haven't told anyone?" I mean, I told some people. Nate—did Nate tell him?

"I read an article about it online," he explained matter-of-factly.

"But that was... How did you... That was a gossip site! Why would you even think that was real? How did you even see it?" Jesus, did this man know *everything*?

"I've had Google alerts set for both you and Elizabeth since you got engaged. I've told you that. I wanted to get ahead of any bad press or rumors if need be. When that came up, I remembered you telling me about hooking up with that senator's daughter. Plus, a player like you was bound to knock a girl up eventually."

Fuck him again.

"Okay. Fair." I definitely had something that would throw him a curveball though. "And we're moving to France. I'm taking over the new company there." No way he could have guessed that one.

"I know," he said, again. And before I could ask how, he added, "Of course you are. You were always going to move to France. Elizabeth's company is there. Why did you think I wanted this merger to take place so badly?"

"Oh, don't pretend you thought we were going to get together the whole time. That you were arranging the whole situation so I could have something to do in a foreign country." He might be a puppetmaster, but surely that was taking it too far.

He only shrugged. "Sabrina will be better at your job here. She knows more about your accounts than you do at this point."

I tilted my head, unsure whether I wanted to punch him or give the guy a hug.

I settled for a smile. "This thing you do? This big brother thing, where you fix everything in my life, save the day every time?" I let him think about it for a minute. "You don't have to do it anymore. I've got it together now. I can take care of things from here on out."

"You sure about that?"

He was a righteous little asshole, but deep down I was sure he knew I was saying thank you.

"Yeah, I'm sure."

"You're welcome."

I turned to leave, then remembered. "Hey, I want my Walking Dead comic back."

His eyes narrowed. "Did you watch the security tape?"

I shook my head, baffled. "I don't need to watch the security tape. I know you're the only one who takes my shit. Hand it over."

He paused, reluctant. Then he tugged open a drawer and pulled out my revered issue and handed it over.

"Thank you. For everything." I backed out of the room, still looking at him. "Oh, and Donovan, one more thing."

"Yes?"

"Can I borrow your plane?"

TWENTY-ONE
ELIZABETH

MY FATHER'S house was ridiculous. A private mansion with a sprawling landscape and wooded garden. The twenty thousand square-foot residence included an indoor swimming pool, extensive wine cellars, roof terrace, and staff apartments. There was even an actual petrol pump on the grounds.

As a child it had felt large and overwhelming and hollow, even with its fully decked out playroom and million-and-one places to hide. I'd only ever wanted to just crawl up in the library. And that was the one room I'd always been kicked out of, not because I was too young or because my father forbade children from touching his books, but simply because there were always so many other adults ambling over and through the rooms and offices that my presence in the library was always a nuisance.

Even with the bustle of his fully staffed house, it had felt like a lonely place. So when I landed in Paris at 7:00 a.m. on Thursday, I chose not to drive the twenty minutes to Neuilly to change and settle into the house, which was kept up by two live-in staff members, and instead made my way to his much smaller, six thousand square-foot apartment in the heart of the city.

My apartment now.

The five-bedroom penthouse apartment overlooking the Eiffel Tower was also too quiet, even with the live-in maid who greeted me when I arrived. My feet echoed on the wood floors, and while I had the entire library to myself, I'd never wanted to be anywhere less.

How was I ever going to make a home here?

Those weren't thoughts for dwelling on when I was jet-lagged and miserable from missing Weston. And this was only day one without him. I had the rest of my life to get used to my new reality.

I had a feeling I'd need that long to adjust.

"MR. HUBER ISN'T QUITE BACK from lunch yet. I do apologize he's not here to greet you." Darrell's secretary was overly kind and penitent, speaking so quickly I almost missed some of her words in her accent. I was glad, though, that she chose to speak English since my French was rusty.

I looked at the time on my phone. It was a little before one and my meeting was set for half past.

"I'm early. It's my fault." I tried to put the woman at ease.

"I am sincerely sorry, Ms. Dyson. He really wanted to make a good impression. Can I get you some tea? Coffee? Pastries? Something else to drink or snack on?"

I'd been attended to my entire life and still had never had anyone fall over me as she was doing.

"Nothing, please. Though, I could use a place to make a phone call. International."

"Please. Use Mr. Huber's office." She was already up and headed toward Darrell's door with her key before I could stop her.

"I don't want to intrude on his personal space," I attempted anyway.

"It's no trouble. He would want this. It will be your office soon anyway," she said, smiling over her shoulder as she pushed the door open.

I had to take a deep breath then to steady myself, my legs all of a sudden feeling wobbly on my heels. It hadn't occurred to me that I would be taking over Darrell's spaces, places he belonged and worked in. Lived in. I wondered what his staff—what *my* staff—thought about that.

I didn't linger on the thought too long, because the door was open now, and I could see into the office that had once been my father's, a place I'd visited often as a child when I'd made trips to France. It had always seemed like a secret cavern. Like the holiest of holies, a place in which I'd never been fit to truly dwell. I'd always been excited and thrilled and honored when I'd gotten to visit my father there, even if it was only for a few minutes to kiss him on the cheek before being bustled away to a nanny.

I stepped into the room reverently, shutting the door behind me so I could make my call in private. While I hadn't meant to arrive early, and I certainly hadn't meant to overtake my father's former office on my own, I was glad now that I got this chance. There was an emotional element to being in the Dyson Media headquarters that I hadn't quite counted on. Sentimental nostalgia and the first true sense of grief at the loss of my father that I'd had since his death. I took another deep breath and let the emotions settle in me as I took in the room.

It was large, spacious. Not much had changed since the last time I had been there. The couch and chairs that surrounded the fireplace and bookshelves were still exactly the same. My father's oversized executive desk still sat ominously near the windows where he could look out at the park while he thought. A second, more modern desk sat perpendicular to it now. This was the one that was stacked with files and papers and Post-it notes with memos jotted down in illegible handwriting. I assumed that was where

Darrell worked, and I made my way over to my father's leather wing chair—his throne—preparing to make my call.

It was only 8:00 a.m. in New York. Early still, but business people were already at their offices. As I dialed the United States country code, I tried not to think about Weston or wonder what he was doing. This conversation wasn't about him. It was about me, and it was short and brief. My mother had been right—I had hired an advisor as a crutch. It was much easier to tell Clarence I didn't need him in France, it turned out, then it had been to tell my husband.

My soon-to-be former husband.

Of course, that was because I *did* need Weston in France. When I'd told him I didn't, it was a lie.

I felt the loneliness and sorrow of missing him prick at my eyes, and I tried to distract myself, running my hands along the top of the desk, focusing on how different the feel of this oak was to my palm from the one in my mother's apartment, the one that would soon be shipped to me.

"Teach me how you did it, Daddy," I said quietly to the desk, to the office, to his ghost. "Teach me how you learned to cut your ties."

I was answered with silence.

I hadn't remembered wishing I could talk to my father like this in a long time. And I'd wished so many times.

With Darrell still gone, I searched for something to occupy my mind. I opened one of the desk drawers, looking to see if it still contained my father's items inside.

The first drawer had miscellaneous desk supplies and didn't give me any true hint as to whether they were of a personal nature or not. The second seemed to hold frequently used files. Many were missing and I assumed Darrell had pulled them out as he needed them. The top drawer on the left-hand side was a different story. As soon as I opened it, a single piece of paper fell to the floor. Which was sure to happen, because the drawer was crammed full of folded papers, not at all organized like the other drawers had been.

When I bent to pick up the dropped note, my heart skipped.

I recognized the paper stationery.

With shaky fingers, I picked it up and unfolded the item, scanning through the carefully written words to be sure, but only took one glance to recognize it as mine. I pulled more from the drawer, unfolding each of them, checking them one by one. All of them were from me. My letters—the ones I'd mailed him throughout my life, stuffed here in his left-hand drawer, the one at the very top, overflowing, some of the papers so worn they'd obviously been read many times.

Maybe letting go of attachments wasn't a lesson my father could teach me after all.

If there wasn't a sudden ball at the back of my throat, I might've muttered a thank you to the air. An *I love you*. An *I forgive you*. But, if he was out there somewhere, I had a feeling he already knew what I was trying to say better than I did.

"That was the only drawer I didn't go through," a deep voice said, pulling my attention.

Darrell had walked in without my noticing.

"We cleaned out most of his other stuff, but I thought you'd want to do that when you got here, personally."

I nodded. Swallowed hard, then thanked him.

Awkward silence fell between us. I sat in my father's chair and Darrell stood there looming in the doorway of his office—my office? —my *father's* office, unmoving. He was a tall man, and I'd always felt small in his presence.

But today, even in my sitting position, he didn't feel so overwhelming.

Perhaps it was the power of Daddy's throne.

We both seemed to realize that one of us needed to talk at the same time. "I'll just sit—" he began gesturing to the seat nearby while I simultaneously said "I could move over to your desk—" since there weren't other chairs around my father's.

We both smiled.

"Shall we sit on the sofas?" I asked.

"After you." He held his hand out toward the seating area, but we fell in step together walking toward the arrangement of couches and chairs as though we were equals.

It was only twenty feet to our destination, but while we crossed I had a sudden flashback to the first meeting I'd had with the men at Reach, when I'd gone in with false bravado, determined to run the show, intent on proving that I had "balls."

I planned on leading today as well. Strangely, these six months later, I felt more aware of all the things I didn't know—about business, about life—but the confidence I wore was genuine. After everything that had happened, it was validation to recognize I'd grown. If it was the only thing I walked away with, it wasn't nothing.

"Your marriage—" Darrell began as soon as we were seated, quick to get to the heart of things.

I interrupted him. "—Is being annulled, but should not stand as a barrier to my inheritance, according to my lawyer. If you wish to contest, I will fight its validity considering the circumstances surrounding the ending of my marriage. You should also know that I'm not above staying married in name only if it's how I hold on to the reins of my company."

He opened his mouth to speak, but I lifted my hand to silence him. "I'm happy to discuss that matter further and at length, though, before I do, I have a question for you. You may find that the subject of my marriage or my inheritance isn't as entertaining once we've talked."

His forehead wrinkled in a single spot, a section of muscle that was due for more Botox. Then he settled back into the couch, his mouth in a straight line. "Go on, then."

I hadn't needed his permission, but it was a relief not to battle. Hopefully we could stay on friendly terms. "I've been watching you since you've taken over the company," I began. "Many of your decisions have seemed in line with my father's vision at first glance, but on further inspection, it appears you may have different intentions for Dyson Media. What is your overall agenda as CEO?"

"Well." His lip quirked up in a snide smile. "You may not enjoy hearing this, Elizabeth, but your father, good businessman that he was, was not exactly a saint in terms of his human relations, and he was not quite on the cutting edge of the new era of technology. Knowing that this company would only be in my hands for a short time, but that I would still hold shares after Dyson's inexperienced, overzealous daughter took over, I've been trying to make changes that will have long-term impact for good. I've changed the hiring policies to bring on more diverse employees, cut off dead weight, and invested in contracted relationships with partner companies that will bring beneficial change to how media is viewed in Europe and possibly worldwide."

He was smug and boastful in his delivery, as though he thought this might be his last chance to passionately speak his mind about the business he cared for deeply.

I could see it from his side, actually. Darrell had twenty years on me. He'd spent his life on his career, and a twenty-five-year-old rich bitch had shown up to pull the rug out from under everything he'd worked so hard to earn.

I imagined I'd be sour about it as well. Though, I doubted I'd be so nasty.

Temperament aside, his answer had been the one I'd been hoping for. "I appreciate your candor, Darrell. And I'm in full agreement about your assessment of my father's outdated business vision. Which is why I'd like to ask you to continue on as the CEO of the company. I do hope you'll say yes."

He blinked several times, his eyes wide. "I thought... It seemed that... You aren't planning on taking the job for yourself?"

It was awfully delightful to see Darrell Huber at a loss for words.

"I'll retain my executive position, and I do expect to be very involved."

"Sure, sure."

"I won't be here full-time, though. I plan to be traveling back and forth between here and New York every month."

The crease in his forehead returned. "What's in New York?"

"My husband." I grinned so hard my cheeks hurt. I hadn't let myself get my hopes up so this was the first time I was admitting my plan to anyone. It hadn't made sense for Weston to be gone so long from his son, and it wouldn't have worked if Darrell had turned out to have ill intentions for the company. I would have put Dyson first because I was responsible for all the employees and the legacy and the entire billion-dollar corporation.

But Darrell shared my vision, and I was desperately relieved, because in the wretched endless few days without Weston I'd realized I couldn't live without my kingdom *or* my king. With my cousin at the helm, my kingdom could wait. I couldn't wait for my king.

"I'm confused... You said you were getting an annulment."

I waved Darrell's comment away with my hand. "A minor technicality. I know I'm not making any sense. Just..." God, how did I explain this?

"No worries. I understand. You love him." This time my cousin's expression was warm and empathetic.

"Yeah. I do." My eyes burned with threatening tears. I blinked them back. "I understand that an annulment puts my inheritance in a grey area. I'm hoping that with our arrangement, working side by side, you'll find the idea of years in court just as tiring and wasteful as I do?"

"I can certainly think of better ways to spend my time," he said with a chuckle, and I finally was able to take a full breath, sure that things between he and I were going to work out fine.

"Thank you, Darrell. I value your years of experience, and I want to learn and apprentice at your side so that when you're ready to retire, perhaps, then, I can take over."

"Right. Okay. That won't be for another ten to fifteen years, though."

"Perfect! I want to make sure I have time to enjoy my family. Weston's son has become quite dear to me." Just the thought made me eager to get back on a plane and cross the ocean to see Sebastian and Weston again as soon as possible, despite being as jet-lagged as I was.

I owed them both a thousand apologies.

Darrell and I spoke a few minutes longer, most of the conversation focused on the explicit agreement that he wouldn't contest my inheritance and that I'd leave him at the head of Dyson Media where he'd teach me the ropes. We decided the details of our arrangement would be settled after the holidays, and I said a hurried goodbye, anxiously excited, already planning what I'd say to Weston when I arrived back in New York. Man, I was looking forward to that surprise.

Except, when I walked out of the office, I was the one who was surprised.

Weston was waiting there. And he wasn't alone. Sebastian was in his arms and Callie and Dana were standing behind him.

"What...? What's going on?" I asked, my heart pounding at the sight of him. "Why are you here? How did you find me?"

"Your mother said you had a meeting with your cousin today. This nice lady," he nodded at Darrell's secretary, "said we could wait out here. As for why...well..." He looked at the women behind him. "We're moving here. All of us."

"What." I was too flabbergasted for it to even be a question. "You are?" I couldn't breathe, fearing it was all a dream.

Callie and Dana nodded, both wearing ridiculous grins.

"Dana's going to work for me," Weston explained. "She's in PR."

"Public Relations! Oh my God!" I'd thought she was a bureaucrat with the State.

"I know, right?" Weston's dimple appeared. "And they really want to move here. It was their idea actually. We haven't packed or arranged the actual moving part, but we all wanted to be together when we told you. So we sort of borrowed a plane and here we are."

"Here you are." I was breathing now, but tears were rolling down my cheeks. *Here he was.* Five feet away, which was still too far, but so much closer than he'd been. "I can't believe you're here." I took a step toward him, needing his arms around me.

"Hold on," he said, suddenly.

I stopped mid-step as he whispered something in Sebastian's ear. Then he knelt to set his child down on the ground, put something in his hand, and gently pushed Sebastian in my direction.

"Give Izzie!" Sebastian toddled excitedly over to me, waving his hand.

I bent to take what was in his tightly clenched fist. He didn't want to let it go at first, and it took a bit of encouragement, but when I pried his fingers open, there was my engagement ring.

I looked back at Weston and found him on one knee. "Elizabeth Dyson King, you're already my wife, whatever the law says. But I'll do it again to make it legal. I'll do it a thousand times over if that's what it takes to make you mine for real. Lizzie, my love. My home. Will you marry..." He looked around at everyone he'd brought with him. "Us?"

I wrapped an arm around Sebastian and lifted him as I stood up, then we crossed over to my husband and the two of us fell into his embrace.

"Yes, Weston, my king," I said between salty kisses. "I will marry all of you."

Weston took the ring from my hand and slipped it on my finger. "I love you," he said softly. "I can't live without you. You're a silly fool for thinking I could even try."

"I know. I was wrong. Thank you for showing me I need you too." We kissed, longer and slower, forgetting for a moment we had an audience until I heard one of the women sniffling behind us.

I pulled away, my cheeks heating, and beamed at Dana and Callie, who was sniffling and red-eyed. "Thank you," I told them. "I'm so grateful. You can't even know."

"What's family for?" Dana asked with a shrug.

I looked back at Weston, a face I could never get tired of looking at. "You better be paying her well."

One eye narrowed. "We haven't really discussed that. This was kind of impromptu."

"Uh..." I bit my lip, trying not to laugh.

"Oh, he'll pay me well," Dana winked.

"He will. I know he will." He was the most generous man I'd ever met, after all.

And it didn't matter that I'd already worked out another plan to get us back together. This one was better. There'd be no flying back and forth, no frequent separations. We'd all be together. Reach would take over Dyson's advertising subsidiary and Weston would manage it. I'd still work less, train with Darrell. Maybe not renew my birth control.

The sound of a phone ringing reminded me we were still in an office. "We should get out of here. Have you checked in to a hotel anywhere? There's more than enough room at my place for all of us."

"We came straight here," Callie said. "Our luggage is downstairs at security."

I laughed. "Let's take care of that."

We stood up together, Weston moving Sebastian to his hip. He looked good as a dad. Grown-up. Sexy.

With his free hand, he took mine and tugged me close so he could whisper in my ear. "Those are dirty thoughts in your eyes, Lizzie. Are you going to share them or keep them all to yourself?"

"I was just wondering how you'd look with a little girl in your arms," I said coyly.

"Not as good as you'd look." He seemed to remember himself. Remembered my former plan to wait. "We'll find out in ten years," he said, a slight hint of disappointment in his tone. "When you're ready to take a break from being the leader of Europe's media empire."

"About that..." Maybe that surprise could wait until we were alone.

"Elligator!" Sebastian said as we squeezed into the small European-style elevator. Weston helped his tiny finger push the button for the ground floor, and my chest blossomed with warmth that exploded and reached throughout my limbs. We were together. All of us. My new family. I'd been a girl who could never want for anything and this ending was beyond any I could have ever imagined for myself.

"Where should we go?" I asked the group. "The apartment or the house in Neuilly?"

Weston peered over at Callie and Dana, who shrugged. "Which do you like better?" he asked me.

"It doesn't matter." I looked around at all of them and settled on Weston. "You're here," I said. "Wherever we go, we'll be home."

EPILOGUE
WESTON

ELIZABETH PEERED over the top of the stroller at Sebastian's pajama-clad body. "Is he asleep?" she whispered tentatively.

I hadn't taken my eyes off him the entire last seventeen trips down the long hallway. His breathing was steady, his cheeks flushed rosy red. His grip on his baby doll had loosened and the toy had slipped from against his face and was now wedged between his torso and the carriage.

"Yeah," I answered just as silently. "I'm pretty sure he's been out for at least ten minutes. Let's hurry and get him to his room before we jinx it."

It was a Saturday evening in early April. The dark, cold months were over, and all of us had settled into France the way spring was settling into the countryside. Dana had given only three weeks' notice at her government job in New York and, as part of her compensation package from Reach, she, Callie, and Sebastian had moved into Elizabeth's Paris apartment before February was over. *Our* Paris apartment—I was still getting used to the whole *what's hers is mine* bit.

Elizabeth had been right in assuming that establishing the

merger and the official new Reach firm in France would be more work than I'd estimated. I spent more hours at the office than I would have liked, more hours than would have been possible were I traveling back and forth to the States. Donovan was a good boy and left me alone, mostly. Dana turned out to be a great right-hand man, though, and Dylan Locke came over from the London office almost bi-weekly to help out. It wasn't a routine I meant to keep up, but it was doable for the short-term.

Elizabeth and I had chosen to live in the Neuilly house. It was definitely too big for either of our liking, but we'd already begun renovations to turn part of the mansion into offices. While neither of us intended to work full-time forever, we did intend to have careers. We also wanted to focus on Sebastian.

And Elizabeth was past due for her next birth control shot. On purpose. Which meant we were officially "trying."

Tonight, though, was for a different kind of trying—it was the first time we had Sebastian for an entire weekend without Callie and Dana. Like any new parents, we were nervous.

And excited.

Nervously excited.

The day had gone well, for the most part. Sebastian had refused to eat the first two meals we'd put in front of him so he ended up having a lunch of animal crackers and chocolate milk, and dinner was corndog bites, but we considered anything in his tummy a win. We'd both played with him all day and packed his nursery with enough toys to entertain him for hours.

Bedtime had been the first real challenge, when he'd refused to fall asleep. After two hours of trying everything we could think of, I'd dragged the stroller in from the garage. We'd buckled him in and used the spacious estate to walk the kid to sleep.

Finally, it had worked.

Elizabeth wheeled the stroller into his room and put the brake into place with her foot. Then she walked around to stand next to me so we could admire our achievement.

"Damn," she said, snuggling into my arms. "That was a pretty great trick, King. Where did you learn this wizardry?"

"The moms."

We stood quietly for another long moment, gazing down on him.

"Now what do we do? Do we try to move him to his bed?"

Last time I'd done this with Callie and Dana, it had been for a nap. And we'd decided to start packing for Paris right after. "Uh... I'm not sure." If we moved him, he'd definitely wake up. "I think we can leave him?"

"Okay." She didn't seem so sure, but she tucked his blanket around him and said it again. "Okay."

I turned on his nightlight and made sure the monitor was on while she pulled the string for the lamp to turn it off. Then I grabbed her hand and tugged her out of the room and shut the door silently behind us.

"Phew," she sighed. "That was..."

"A turn-on," I finished for her. Seriously, she was hot doing the whole mom thing. I couldn't wait to put a baby in her tummy. I especially couldn't wait for all the "trying."

"I was going to say stressful and exhausting," she said, but she was staring at my lips.

So I kissed her.

Her mouth opened easily, her tongue darting out to greet mine as I wrapped my arms around her body.

"Not *too* stressful or exhausting, I hope?" I tested, my lips hovering above hers.

"Definitely not. But we need to go to bed now."

"I'm not going to argue, Mrs. King."

Lacing my hand through hers, I led her to our bedroom, my finger stroking against the ring that said she was mine forever. We hadn't needed to repeat our ceremony, it had turned out. Because of the holidays, the annulment paperwork still had yet to be processed. A simple phone call to her lawyer had been enough to end that near-disaster.

Or, not disaster. I would have married her again. And again. As many times as she'd let me. In fact, we were talking about having a repeat ceremony for our anniversary, just so we could do all the things we'd missed the first time. So we could declare in front of everyone how much we loved each other for real.

Right now, though, the only one I wanted to declare my Elizabeth love to was Elizabeth.

And we needed to be naked for what I had in mind.

In our bedroom, I made sure the baby monitor was turned on, then immediately got to the business of undressing. I was down to my underwear when I realized she was still fully clothed, her attention on a white Priority Mail bubble envelope and its contents.

I came up behind her and moved her red hair to one side so I could kiss the delicate white skin of her collarbone. "Elizabeth, whatever you are doing, that was not what I thought you meant when you said let's go to bed."

"I know, I know," she said, half moaning as I traced my tongue up her neck. "Just...Donovan sent this, and I'd forgotten about it until now."

"Donovan?" God, what a boner killer. "What is it?"

"I don't know. A disc. And a note that says 'To set the record straight.'"

I reached around her and took the note from her hands. There was nothing else written on it. "He sent this to both of us?"

She looked at the envelope. "It was addressed to only you, I guess."

I shook my head, chuckling. Good thing I had no secrets from the woman. She had zero boundaries. "We can watch it tomorrow."

"Come on. Aren't you curious?" she pleaded, her lips turning down into an irresistible pout.

"Not really." I mean, yeah, but Donovan was a mood killer. Whatever he'd sent was certainly not going to lead to getting laid.

Apparently my opinion didn't matter because she was already dragging out her laptop and settling in on the bed.

Fine. But if we were watching it, she was going to have her clothes off while we did.

I climbed up on the mattress beside her and wrestled her shirt over her head while she popped in the disc and opened the only file on the directory. My hand was tucked into her bra cup, massaging her nipple into a tight bud when the screen began playing a silent black and white movie.

No, not a movie.

Security footage. Of my old office.

Starring Donovan and Sabrina.

"What the heck?" Elizabeth asked, straightening her legs to balance the computer on her lap.

Fuck if I knew.

My fingers slowed their assault as I watched the two onscreen, trying to figure out what was going on and, more importantly, what it was Donovan wanted me to see. My gut said it wasn't good.

It became obvious as soon as Sabrina removed her panties and handed them to D who promptly sniffed them before putting them in his suit pocket.

"Oh, no," I said, reaching for the laptop.

Elizabeth bent away from me, taking the computer with her. "No, I want to see! Oh my God, he's going to fuck her in your office!"

"Oh, hell no!" I grabbed again for the computer, outraged both that Donovan would send me this and that he would make it in the first place.

Again, my wife maneuvered the computer away, "Weston, wait, let's watch!"

"You want to watch my best friend—" I reconsidered. "*Ex* best friend, considering the circumstances, fuck my *ex-lover* on *my* desk?"

"Yeah. I do. It's hot." She was turned with her back to me now, her feet hanging off the bed, but I could hear the excitement in her tone. Could hear the rapid rise and fall of her breathing, now that I paid attention.

I crawled up beside her so I could watch her, not the computer, and saw her eyes were dark and dilated as they remained pinned on the screen.

"Mmm," she hummed, biting her lip. "He just spanked her. That's...whoa..."

I peeked at the footage. Sabrina was bent over the desk now, her skirt gathered around her waist. From the camera angle, only the side of her bare ass was visible, but the one cheek was clearly red as Donovan rubbed it. Then he spanked her again.

"You like the spanking? Or the watching? Or..." *I* liked watching Elizabeth this turned on. I was quickly getting hard from her reactions.

"All of it. I like all of it." She was breathy and flushed and God, I was going to fuck her so hard.

I pulled her bra strap down her shoulder. "Is this what it's like watching porn with someone?"

"Yes! Isn't it awesome?" She glanced at me, her lips quirked in a naughty smile. "Donovan's so thoughtful. Making us homemade porn."

I laughed. "I don't think that's why he sent it."

I pulled the cup of her bra down and palmed her tit. She leaned into my hand, moaning. She was so fucking turned on. I had to have more of her. Had to have my mouth on her.

I bent forward intending to bring her nipple into my mouth, and she gasped.

Which was cool, except the gasp came before I'd done anything.

"Wow, Donovan is hung," she exclaimed. "Not King hung, but no wonder he's so confident."

I turned my attention back to the screen late enough to miss his dick (thank God) but in time to watch him thrust into Sabrina who seemed to cry out in pleasure.

It *was* kind of hot, actually. If I didn't look at Donovan. And if I stopped thinking about how weird it was.

"It's really not fair that they got to have sex in your office, and we didn't, though. Oh, shit. Donovan sent this to you so that you'd know that Sabrina was *his*, didn't he?"

That *was* what he was doing. How fucking annoying. "All he had to do was say he was interested. Was I supposed to read his mind?" Oh. That was why he'd stolen my Walking Dead issue. He'd hoped I'd watch this.

Clever. Sort of.

Elizabeth shook her head. "He's such an asshole. But that's kind of hot too. Claiming her like that. Lucky Sabrina."

"Okay, okay, that's enough." I grabbed the laptop and shut the lid before setting it on the nightstand. Then I wrestled Elizabeth's body around so she was underneath me, her hands pinned above her head.

"So I guess Donovan and Sabrina had their happy ending," she said, giggling.

"We're about to have ours too, if you'll cooperate."

"Do we? Have a happy ending?" She was serious all of a sudden, and I could tell she wasn't talking about the same kind of happy ending my cock was aching to pursue.

"Do you really want an ending?" I asked. "That sounds so boring. And over. How about a happy beginning instead?" I rocked my pelvis against hers, though, so she wouldn't forget about the hard steel between us in all this flowery romantic talk.

"I like that. A happy beginning." Then, she was grinning again. "Let's play a game!"

I groaned. I didn't want to play around anymore. I just wanted to be inside her.

"This is a good game," she promised. "You'll like it. You be Donovan, and I'll be Sabrina, and you can spank me for being such a dick-tease." Somehow she managed to roll out from under me before I could agree.

But I was totally going to agree.

Dirty, sexy role play with my gorgeous wife? That was the kind of game I'd always say yes to playing.

This Dirty Universe continues in Dirty Sweet Duet.

British ad exec Dylan Locke isn't looking for love. He isn't looking for fate. He's definitely not looking for Audrey Lind. She's pretty, far too young, and overly romantic--in short, exhausting.

But when the girl, young enough to be his daughter, literally lands in his lap and asks for his expertise, he'd be lying if he said he wasn't interested. In her body, in her innocence, in her philosophy.

In the kind of kismet that starts with kisses.

But Audrey isn't looking for love either--she's looking for lessons, and she's certain Dylan knows everything she needs to learn.

If he agrees to play the teacher can he keep his heart?

Of course he can.

Then again, he might be lying.

Turn the page to start reading chapter one now.

Want to read a free bonus prologue to the Dirty Games Duet? Sign up for my newsletter, and get it delivered straight to your inbox. If you're already a subscriber, you must sign up again to get the bonus.

THE DIRTY UNIVERSE CONTINUES...
DIRTY UNIVERSE READING ORDER

Meet all my Dirty Men.

The Dirty Duet - Donovan Kincaid

Dirty Games Duet - Weston King

Dirty Filthy Fix - Nate Sinclair

Dirty Sweet Duet - Dylan Locke

Dirty Wild Trilogy - Cade Warren

Dirty Sweet Valentine & Other Filthy Tales of Love

Ten Dirty Demands - Donovan Kincaid

Kincaid - Donovan Kincaid

THE DIRTY UNIVERSE CONTINUES...

Visit my www.laurelinpaige.com for content warnings and a more detailed reading order.

ALSO BY LAURELIN PAIGE
WONDERING WHAT TO READ NEXT? I CAN HELP!

Visit www.laurelinpaige.com for content warnings and a more detailed reading order.

Brutal Billionaires

Brutal Billionaire - a standalone (Holt Sebastian)

Dirty Filthy Billionaire - a novella (Steele Sebastian)

Brutal Secret - a standalone (Reid Sebastian)

Brutal Arrangement - a standalone (Alex Sebastian)

Brutal Bargain - a standalone (Axle Morgan)

Brutal Bastard - a standalone (Hunter Sebastian)

The Dirty Universe
Dirty Duet (Donovan Kincaid)

Dirty Filthy Rich Men | Dirty Filthy Rich Love

Kincaid

Dirty Games Duet (Weston King)

Dirty Sexy Player | Dirty Sexy Games

Dirty Sweet Duet (Dylan Locke)

Sweet Liar | Sweet Fate

(Nate Sinclair) Dirty Filthy Fix (a spinoff novella)

Dirty Wild Trilogy (Cade Warren)

Wild Rebel | Wild War | Wild Heart

Men in Charge
Man in Charge
Man for Me (a spinoff novella)

The Fixed Universe
Fixed Series (Hudson & Alayna)
Fixed on You | Found in You | Forever with You | Hudson | Fixed Forever
Found Duet (Gwen & JC) Free Me | Find Me
(Chandler & Genevieve) Chandler (a spinoff novel)
(Norma & Boyd) Falling Under You (a spinoff novella)
(Nate & Trish) Dirty Filthy Fix (a spinoff novella)
Slay Series (Celia & Edward)
Rivalry | Ruin | Revenge | Rising
(Gwen & JC) The Open Door (a spinoff novella)
(Camilla & Hendrix) Slash (a spinoff novella)

First and Last
First Touch | Last Kiss

Hollywood Standalones
One More Time

Close

Sex Symbol

Star Struck

Dating Season
Spring Fling | Summer Rebound | Fall Hard

Winter Bloom | Spring Fever | Summer Lovin

Also written with Kayti McGee under the name Laurelin McGee

Miss Match | Love Struck | MisTaken | Holiday for Hire

Written with Sierra Simone
Porn Star | Hot Cop

ACKNOWLEDGMENTS AND AUTHOR'S NOTE

Sometimes a book journey surprises you.

Dirty Sexy Player and Dirty Sexy Games were supposed to be my easy books. The previous duet, Dirty Filthy Rich Men and Dirty Filthy Rich Love, were edgier and darker and the journey to get those out was not that smooth. So I was looking forward to writing Weston and Elizabeth, thinking their story was more straight forward and therefore easier to write.

Then I got to the actual writing and realized something - I'd set up both characters to have father issues. And *I* have father issues. And thus this "simple" story turned into an exploration through memories of my own past. I had to face things with my parents that I hadn't yet faced. It was tough and therapeutic and I shed a lot of tears. So much of myself is written in Elizabeth and her relationship with her father. So many of her memories are variations on my own wounds. Her grandmother and that house in Utah is directly captured from my own Mormon family that I love very much. In the end, it was a very important story for me to write, and I hope you found as much value in the telling as I did in the writing.

Much thanks is required for books like these, but I'll make it quick.

Rose Hilliard who had enough faith in my concept to offer to publish these in audio first.

Rebecca Friedman who makes every publishing deal a reality.

Candi Kane and Melissa Gaston who run the entire show.

Kayti McGee who knows what I'm trying to say better than I do.

Nancy and Erica and Michele for making sure the words were the right words.

Christine Borgford for making sure the words looked pretty.

My LARCs who give me more support than I deserve.

The Sky Launchers who make my day more than they know.

My readers everywhere who continue to let me write my silly stories and give me a job that I look forward to every day.

My besties in the biz who guide me through every decision I have to make - Melanie Harlow, Kayti McGee, Sierra Simone, CD Reiss, and Lauren Blakely.

My mother, husband, and daughters who show up in more of my books than I should admit.

My God who sticks by me, even when I invite the trauma in.

ABOUT LAURELIN PAIGE

With millions of books sold, Laurelin Paige is the NY Times, Wall Street Journal, and USA Today Bestselling Author of the Fixed Trilogy. She's a sucker for a good romance and gets giddy anytime there's kissing, much to the embarrassment of her three daughters. Her husband doesn't seem to complain, however. When she isn't reading or writing sexy stories, she's probably singing, watching shows like Billions and Peaky Blinders or dreaming of Michael Fassbender. She's also a proud member of Mensa International though she doesn't do anything with the organization except use it as material for her bio.

www.laurelinpaige.com
laurelinpaigeauthor@gmail.com

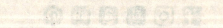